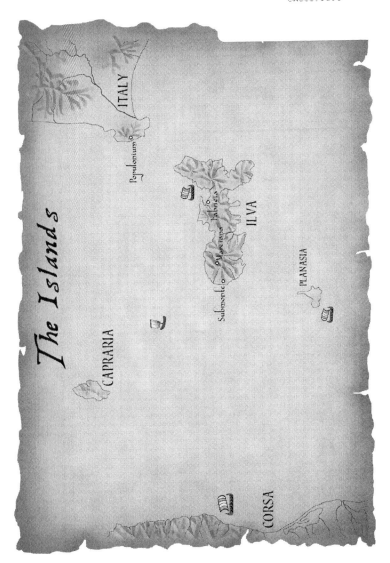

The Islands

ITALY

Populonium

ILVA

Fabricia

Marciana

Submonte

PLANASIA

CAPRARIA

CORSA

AQUILA

CAN SILVANUS
ESCAPE THAT GOD?

VINCE
ROCKSTON

This is a work of fiction. Real people, places,
and events are identified in the appendices.

AQUILA – CAN SILVANUS ESCAPE THAT GOD?
First edition. February 14, 2018.
Copyright © 2018 Vince Rockston.

ISBN: 978-3-9524937-2-4

Written by Vince Rockston.

CHAPTERS

CHAPTER ONE

The Trek

"IT'S NOT FAIR!" My shout causes Hercules to buck, and his hooves scrape on the rocky path. I tap his rump with my stave. "Wasn't talking to you."

My bag thumps against my side as I raise my fist toward the rocky eagle glowering down from the mountain and scream, "It's not fair! Why do you torment me, Aquila?"

Another jerk on the halter. "What's got into you? We'll get nowhere at this rate!" The second mule also hangs back. "You, too, Crispus, come on with you!" We labour up the steep hillside, avoiding treacherous roots and overhanging branches. All three of us are dripping with sweat.

There it is! My heart thumps as I pass the ugly stone that fell from the terrace and caused all my woes. All our woes.

I rip my thoughts back to the present. I'm alone now. What if I twist an ankle? Or get lost. Or robbed. Why didn't I bring Caesar? If he raised his hackles, the boldest villain would cringe.

That fallen willow – I remember it from earlier trips with Father. I used to hide behind it, then pounce on him. He fell for it every time – or pretended to. We were happy then.

It must have been four years ago when he'd announced, "You're a big lad now, Silvanus," which wasn't true. I was only ten and I've always been short for my age. "You can come with me this year. A second pair of hands will be a great help."

Nothing could hold me back. I ran ahead, up and down the hillside, scrambling through the prickly macchia, scratching my knees as I explored gullies and towering rocks, discovering new things at every turn. Father was my hero in those days. He looked after me, whatever happened. And Fabricia was everything he'd promised: the bustling market full of excitement, street musicians, performing monkeys, huge ships cluttering the port down below. No end of surprises.

This time it's different. I know these hills as well as the wild goats. But now I'm responsible for trading these meagre goods for things we need, and doomed to be the man of the family, with all the heavy work falling to me.

My breathing is heavy and my limbs tremble. I should have begged bold Rufus to come with me. Or quick-witted Pontus. But even they would have been no protection against Aquila the Avenger, the ever watching God determined to foil my every venture. I can't escape him.

What's that? A frantic rustle in the undergrowth. Crispus jerks back. I freeze. My knuckles turn white as I clasp my stave.

A huge beast emerges from the undergrowth – matted pelt, vicious tusks curling up under beady eyes. My breathing halts. For a moment it hesitates – attack or flee? It turns tail and stampedes off, hooves drumming on the rock.

I breathe again and on we plod, the sun climbing higher, harrowing us whenever we emerge from the shade of the trees. We pass our waterfall, where the other lads and I spent many a summer afternoon, swinging from creepers and daring one another to drop into the crystal water. I slip off my shoulder bag, crouch to bathe my face in the pool, gulping long draughts. Crispus's bulky load makes it difficult for him to stoop but he manages. I fill my skin bottle and stuff it into my bag. Then off we go again, climbing, climbing. Each step higher than the one before. My breathing is laboured.

"Watch out, Hercules!" Thank Aquila, he didn't lose his balance. My fingers grope for the eagle talisman Aunt Ceres gave me. If he'd fallen… shattered the amphorae… hurt himself…! But he's sure-footed and used to this kind of terrain. Crispus isn't so strong, but his load isn't as heavy.

How stupid to expect Aquila to help. Most likely it was he who made Hercules slip. He must be angry with me. Always spoiling my fun. We sacrifice our best animals – so Ceres insists – and yet he never seems to answer her prayers. She insists I perform all those gruesome rituals, but they don't help. Why are we so poor? Why doesn't he heal Father's leg? Now it's me who has to mend the terraces, tend the vines, take the produce to market. It's not fair!

It's only bushes now, the typical pungent brush of the macchia. The only shade now is from the occasional strawberry tree. At least I can see farther than a few paces. I gaze at the craggy, grey-green hilltops, dropping on three sides to dense woods, to little rocky bays. I make out the one where we found the wreckage of the ship the pirates attacked – I shudder – Can it be that they have discovered the best way to make a living?

A fishing village comes into sight from behind a headland. So near and yet we have no contact. Submonte is so isolated. Yet we're not the only people in this world. Not even the only ones at this end of our island. The vast expanse of sea shimmers in the falling sun, its haze masking the dark blue outline of Corsa.

Ecce! Another merchant ship. Phoenician, from the sails. Where are those traders from and what are they transporting? How fast it glides, driven by the rising sirocco. What magic power Auster has. How does he do it? And why? I want to learn to harness the wind. Someday I'll get a boat of my own – the big, wide world beckons me.

What a foolish dream.

Kili – King of the heavens – soars overhead. He's a real eagle; I don't have to be afraid of him. Round and round he goes, catching the uplift from the evening sea breeze, swooping as something moves in the undergrowth. No luck this time.

"Patience, old boy," I mutter. "You'll find a hare or a pigeon before long." Who taught him to fly with such majesty? Can it be, as Aunt Ceres says, that all eagles are Jupiter in disguise?

We press on, wearier with every step. The land flattens out. Colourful, aromatic heather, gorse and rockrose vie for space among bizarre boulders. My breathing is heavy, my legs are trembling and I'm dripping with sweat. I drop my bag. "Whoa, Hercules, Crispus! I can't go any farther. Let's stop here."

Hercules's amphorae are heavy. "*Festina lente!*" I loosen the rope, reach up to heave the jar of olive oil out of the frame and gently lower it to the ground. "Good, that's one safe." I move around to the other side. "You'll be pleased to be rid of these, I'm sure."

Each one seems heavier than the last. Oh, Rufus, I wish you were here to help me now!

Aquila's in a good mood, it seems. I've managed to unload without breaking any of them.

"All right, off with the frame – so – now you're free! There's water for you here and you can find food for yourselves. Don't run away! Tomorrow is another long day. Not so much climbing, but still hard work."

We don't always take the same path, but I did come this way once with Father. Didn't we discover a shepherd's hut around here? I investigate the surroundings: freakish rocks, gaping potholes, narrow crannies where rich grass and tiny flowers hide from the merciless sun. Sand-coloured lizards bask on the warm stones, peering at me sideways before scuttling off down some hardly visible crevice.

Ecce! A viper glides across the smooth rock, then slithers through the low vegetation. I marvel how it moves so fast and without effort.

Sure enough, there's the stone hut. It'll shelter me for the night now that the wind is rising.

A handful of dry gorse spines, bits of brush, fallen pine branches. I light some tinder with my new flint. I nurse the first embers to a flame, then set a pot of water with some sprigs of rosemary and thyme on a stone to boil.

As I wait, I glance first at one hand, then the other – broken nails, ugly wounds that don't want to heal. I pick up a stick and scratch in the gravel: towering Monte Capanne overshadowing Monte Giove, where Aquila the Avenger lives; a pebble on the coast for miserable Submonte, sullied by Father's sourness and fearsome Aunt Ceres. A spasm runs through me. A stone to the other side of the mountains marks Fabricia, with twig ships weaving in and out of the port. Beyond that? Randomly placed rocks for Rome, Carthage, Troia – the alluring places Vergilius writes about. And, of course, the magnificent city of Constantinople, wherever that may be. No chance of ever seeing those exciting places. Has Aquila condemned me to this miserable life?

The warm drink, a bite to eat and a good fire restores my spirits somewhat.

Should I hobble the mules? They'll be all right. I bank up the embers and wince as I curl up between two goat-skins on the floor of the ancient hut. Searing backache has been my companion these last months. Is Aquila punishing me?

"Don't worry, there's nothing dangerous here."

Did I say that aloud?

Sudden sounds I'm never aware of in the daylight bring the night to life. The rising wind breaks a branch off a tree not far away. A little crack – one of the mules stepping on a dry stick? Agonised shrieks – a small creature falling prey to a marten, perhaps. Rustling behind the hut; something large barges through the macchia. Another boar?

I try to relax. There can't be anything dangerous here.

Now, very near, the mournful hoot of a long-eared owl. And, sure enough, an answering call from farther away. Familiar noises, but tonight they alarm me. I force myself to breathe slowly but my limbs continue to tremble. There's nothing to fear, nothing dangerous here.

Weariness. Uneasy slumber.

I leap up, my heart hammering. What brushed against my cheek? I force myself to lie still, until my pulse slows to normal. A bat. One of many, most likely. I'm intruding in their bedroom. Calm down! There's nothing dangerous around here.

I can't sleep. Should I have made an offering to Aquila, so he won't harm me? If there is such a God, does he take any notice of my acts of piety? He didn't help Father. Does it matter to anyone what I do or don't do? Would anyone care if I never came home? Father's bitter. And so nasty to Mother.

Little Eli would miss me. She does tease me, especially about my mane of red hair. "I thought Silver wasn't supposed to rust!" Silvanus – silver. Very funny. But I love her for it.

Life has been so hard these last months. Pointless. I slave away at repairing the never-ending damage done to the terraces and fences by storms and wild boar. And now I'm here, trudging for days through the hills to sell the miserable items we produce, under the merciless eye of Aquila. Have I brought this on myself? We barely scrape enough food together to keep ourselves alive. And then we die – like so many beetles – never to be thought of again. Doesn't life have more meaning? How can I escape this never-ending cycle?

I shake my fist in the air. "Jupiter, Aquila – or whoever you are out there – speak to me! What's it all about? I want to be free! I want to live!"

Hercle! Is it already morning? I must have slept after all. New noises reach my ears, friendlier sounds of birdsong and the scuttling of day creatures. But the wind is raging even more than yesterday. And far below, the waves pound the rocks, driving white walls of spray high up. A moment later their crash echoes from the cliff face. I stretch my sore back and shift my tender hips. Refreshed I'm not, but it's time to get up and get moving.

Ominous thunderheads form among the clouds to the west. I fan last night's embers, make another drink, take a bite of bread and a handful of raisins.

I can barely lift the amphorae and have no hand free to get the pointed foot through the ring.

'If your arms aren't strong enough, use your head!' Father used to say, back in the days when he was still good-tempered. All right. My head says Hercules is stronger than me. He'll have to be the one to lift them.

"Here, Hercules!" I strap the carrying frame onto his back. "Down, now! Lie down! Yes, I'm serious. Lie down! Here. Between the amphorae." After some resistance, he complies. "Good lad." I repeat yesterday's trick in reverse, lifting the feet of the jars into the rings one by one and making sure they're upright. Luckily, they're all about the same weight, so they balance.

"Come on now, stand up!"

We go back to the hut, so I can load Crispus with the rest of the wares. Goatskins across the top – two for Hercules, two for Crispus – since a storm is threatening. Oh, there's still this bundle of cork. It can hang loose.

"*Pol!* You do look overloaded, Crispus. But Hercules has more weight."

We take the southern route, although it may be wilder. I try to convince myself it's for no other reason than the challenge of novelty. Traces of an ancient path remain, in places swept away by landslides or overgrown with bushes. We head towards the sun, over to where the clouds are less ominous. Thank Aquila, the wind is behind us.

One headland follows another. Never the last. Protruding roots of towering Monte Capanne, preventing him from toppling. They grope for the sea, as if desperate for water. It's impossible to keep level as we negotiate the rough, unstable slopes. I try to stay above the impassable gullies and ravines.

It's well past midday, and the clouds behind us are heavy and dark, ever nearer. Aquila's trying to frighten me, although he lives on the other side of the mountain. The going is getting rougher, too. Wild goats' tracks suggest a way between thorny gorse bushes and large rocks. I fasten the clasps of my cloak at my neck and finger my amulet. The rain starts with a vengeance, beating down, such that I can hardly see where I place my feet.

Crispus bucks and stumbles as a blinding flash forks out, accompanied by a simultaneous deafening thunder-clap. The Gods are warring, throwing their full fury at us. I'm wet through.

"What have you got against me, Mighty Eagle? Did I offend you? Does it give you pleasure to pick on a weak lad like me? How can I appease you?"

There's nothing else for it but to press on. The mules are rearing and side-stepping at the lightning and ear-splitting thunder. Loosened by the torrential rain, surges of sodden rubble smother what's left of the path. Stream beds, dry for months, are flash flooding, sweeping rocks and broken branches down like toy boats. Branches? Then we can't be above the tree line.

We blunder on, stumbling over protruding rocks, slipping on the rain-loose scree. Dark shadows envelop us. Why so early?

All of a sudden, the hillside plunges downwards. Through the driving downpour, I make out the trunks of mighty oaks, rough pines and slender alders. We're stumbling into one of those perilous ravines I'd hoped to avoid. It's steep and slippery, but at least the canopy of trees offers some shelter from the wind and whipping rain. I take the lead, hoping to prevent the overloaded beasts from making a sudden movement that might be disastrous.

Flashes of lightning illuminate sinister chasms among the fierce black clouds. Rumbling thunder echoes into the distance like an incomprehensible challenge from the Gods. Is that a rockface on the other side of the ravine? It might offer protection if we can cross the raging torrent.

That comforting wish is shattered by a terrifying roar and crash from above and ahead of us. Louder. Nearer. Will it never stop? I tremble in my sodden boots. Aquila's hurling great rocks on us from on high. Maybe the start of many actual blows, not satisfied with threatening signs. At last the rumbling settles. I wait, tense, expecting the worst. But there's no repetition.

Down – no other choice – and dusk is falling. But now it's clear: we have no chance of crossing the ravine with its furious torrent. We're stuck!

CHAPTER TWO

Godsend

"WAIT HERE, BOYS!"

Ignoring the mules' plaintive hee-haws, I slither down the slope using my stave as a third leg. The dim light shows a river raging between cliffs. A black patch answers with a strange echo. "*Io!*" A cave. And dry! Has Aquila relented after his game with the thunderbolts and rockfalls?

Caked in mud, my limbs trembling, I clamber back up to fetch the mules one at a time.

The resounding clatter of their hooves suggests the cave must be large. We're safe at last, and out of that vicious weather. I collapse onto the floor, my breath coming in gasps.

But I've still got work to do. I unload the mules, light a fire in the entrance and cook a pot of spelt, enriched with chunks of dried goat meat and a few herbs. The mules are content with a dose of barley. With their front legs hobbled, they soon settle. I lay out my clothes to dry and curl up for the night between the dank, steaming beasts, with the driest of the goatskins to keep me warm.

Sweaty men trudge past in single file, each laden with a strange basket. Down, down they go, their heavy boots thumping on the bare rock. Others almost trip over my feet as they labour back up to the cave, their baskets empty. No one notices me. The taskmaster rhythmically beats his club on a board.

A different pounding starts – vibrant, louder. Someone must be striking the rockface with a pick. Mining something? It's getting louder, coming nearer, threatening…

The regular thudding wakes me. Hercules's hooves stamp on the bare rock floor. Something is upsetting him. Is it that he's cooped up in a dark cave when it's light outside?

Light? Then it must be morning!

I jump up and untie the hobbles. Both mules make their way to a flooded glade next to the raging creek and help themselves to a drink.

The storm has blown over, but it's still overcast. I finger my amulet. "Are you in a better mood today, Aquila?"

I can't risk a broken leg or worse by scrambling back up the muddy slope in search of another crossing, so we're trapped here until the river subsides. Father will be mad at me for not taking the easier path. The path that would have passed Aquila.

I stoke the fire. Warm gruel with raisins cheers me and I investigate my surroundings. The flickering light reveals the cave to be man-made. A mine, perhaps, long since abandoned. Father often told how our island was once famous not only for its iron and copper ores, but also for its magnificent granite. This must have been something else. Something that justified excavating a cave.

The huge boulder that fell last night is lodged high overhead, spanning the ravine. Incredible! Any moment it could crash onto us – with a little help from Aquila.

The cliff is wet and slippery, almost vertical in places, but here and there my fingers and toes find helpful ledges and cracks. I grab a young pine growing in a fissure of the rock. As I pull myself up, it gives way, and I slide down, scraping arms and knees.

"Curses on you, Aquila!"

My wounds sting but don't look deep. I try a different route, but it proves impassable. I'm back where I started. On my third attempt I reach the boulder. My heart thumps as I creep out, peering at the raging stream far below. Inch by inch, I shuffle across, then clamber up, up the crumbling slope on the other side. Scratched and jittery, I reach the gaping hollow which had been the boulder's home for many a long year.

A gasp escapes my lips and I freeze.

The back wall of the crater is covered with sparkling gems! My eyes scan the spectacle – some colourless, milky-white, various shades of pink, smoky brown, one or two greenish. On an earlier trip, Father had to drag me away from a jeweller fashioning similar stones into magnificent rings, necklaces, brooches. These are larger and more glorious. Is Aquila suddenly in a good mood?

I'd need proper tools to prize them all out without breaking them. And how would I bring them down?

With my fingers, I pry a small cluster of pink crystals away from the rock. Must discover what they're worth in Fabricia. Would be risky to have too many at a time.

I need to be sure of the right valley when I return. Behind me is the towering wall of Monte Capanne. Far below a little fishing village nestles at the point where this stream, swelled by many others from the surrounding hills, snakes towards the sea. In the distance, the grey outline of Corsa. To the right, the hill we came over yesterday in the storm. High on my left is another ridge, which we'll have to cross if we ever get over the torrent. Behind that? Who knows.

I scramble down with the cluster of crystals in my mouth, needing both hands for climbing. The river is still too wild to cross. I wash my scratches and return to the cave to admire my treasure.

They're gorgeous. I tuck them away in my little leather pouch. I'll sell them for a fortune. My necklace will thrill some noble princess and I'll be rich…

My heart beats wildly as I pose on a protruding rock, my arms stretched out over my imaginary estate, and slaves unload crates of gold from my ship…

But my family depends on me. I'm needed at home, now that Father can't do the heavy work. Can I abandon them in search of adventure?

"Why don't you help us, Aquila?" I clench my fists and punch the air. "Can't you tell me what I should do?"

Evening comes. I check the mules, cook myself a meal and hope for a peaceful night.

Four scarlet-clad pages with golden scimitars in their belts and each carrying a different banner, escort me into a royal banqueting room and usher me to a throne-like seat next to the king.

Dark-skinned minstrels with golden harps and silver flutes conjure up visions of heroic bravery and gentle romance. Bluish vapours of sweet-smelling incense enhance the magical atmosphere.

Course after course of lavish food is served – roast boar, its tusks decorated with gold ribbons; pheasant stuffed with chestnuts and dates, smothered with a spicy sauce; soft bread rolls; rich, aromatic wines. The climax is a bowl of sweet-smelling red and yellow fruit in a flaming sauce.

I enthral the glamorous princess on my right with tales of storms, pirates and fights with lions. She leans closer. Her perfume tantalises me, and I feel the warmth of her scantily-clad body…

The colours blur and the marble pillars turn into grimy cave walls. I struggle to stay in the enchanted new world in vain. The first rays of sunlight tickle my eyelids and force me to waken. It's back to reality – sore knees and decisions to be made. But first, breakfast.

For the first time since the storm, blue sky appears between the overhanging branches. The air is fresh and bright. Where yesterday a wild torrent raged through the gorge, now a well-behaved brook meanders between boulders. Hercules and Crispus are at ease, grazing on the bank.

Further down, an obvious path comes up the valley, crossing the stream at a washed-out fording place and continuing up the ridge we need to cross. Too bad we missed the way the other night. Or did some unseen power guide me to those crystals?

I load the mules, shoulder my bag, grab my stave, and off we go. We're well rested and I'm eager to sell my crystals in Fabricia. We make good progress across the ford and up the well-used path over the ridge. Planasia appears to the south-west – not much more than a dark blue line in the sea – and, in the distance the hazy tower of Mons Jovis. But over to the east, where we are heading, I make out the far end of Ilva beyond the next ridge. How small our island is. Right on the horizon, that grey band must be the mainland.

I pick up a rock and fling it as far as I can toward that distant goal. A shout of joy escapes my throat.

Somewhere over there is Rome. The first place I'll visit when I have a boat. Rich, powerful people with purple togas; endless straight roads leading to unknown lands; marvellous aqueducts; the huge Colosseum and other magnificent buildings from the days before Rome fell...

Stupid dreams. My head falls as I sigh.

Hour after hour, the path leads us round innumerable headlands. It is downhill most of the time. The setting sun douses the plain ahead in a fantastic orange hue. A tangy pine aroma greets us as we drop through a grove of massive trees into more inhabited regions.

Until now, Father always did the talking, finding us shelter and food, bartering with our goods. Now I must handle all this myself.

The first peasants are friendly enough. But what a strange accent. As we pass through a little village, the dogs protest that we're not welcome. The houses are bigger than in our hamlet, with well-kept vegetable gardens and fruit trees. Grape vines cover every hillside.

The mules are showing signs of tiredness, not to mention myself.

A plump little lady, her weather-beaten face partially hidden by a headscarf, is throwing handfuls of grain to some chickens.

"Er… Ex–excuse me."

She jumps. "Oh, good Lord! I didn't notice you. My ears."

"Do you know someone who could put us up for the night?"

She peers at me and looks around. "Just you and the mules?" Again that funny dialect, but the tone is friendly. "What's a young lad like you doing all alone in the mountains? Where are you from?"

"My name's Silvanus. I'm from Submonte, opposite Corsa."

"With your red hair, I thought you might be a foreigner." She leans on the fence post. "But, even so, that's quite a distance you've come."

"Well, yes. Every autumn we go to market in Fabricia. Father…"

"Our youngsters are away, so there'd be plenty of room for you with us. For one night?"

"Yes, I need to press on. The storm the other day delayed me."

She shows me where I can bed the mules, helping myself to hay.

"Those scratches look nasty. What happened to you?"

"Oh, it's nothing, really."

"Let me put some salve on them. They look inflamed. Come on in."

She seats me on a bench against the kitchen wall and takes a little jar off a high shelf, then pulls up a rickety stool and sits opposite me. My muscles tense as this woman I don't know gently rubs the ointment on my forearms and palms. It has a pungent smell and stings. Her voice is soothing, and her thick woollen tunic reminds me of Mother. I uncover my knees, and let her treat them too.

"Take this little phial and put some on every day until it heals."

"Thank you so much." I drop the jar into my bag.

"I'm sure you wouldn't mind joining us for soup and bread."

"I have food with me," I protest.

She insists and chops vegetables into a large pot on the stove.

"What would you want for putting us up for the night?" I ask, biting my little finger.

"Oh, that's all right." She turns to me. "One thing, perhaps. Didn't I smell labdanum in your baggage? You could give me a lump or two, if you can spare them. I use it in my cough physic. And in the salve I put on your wounds."

Dashing out to the stable, I fetch a handful of the dark resin.

She fingers a lump. "This is excellent. Does your mother make it? I used to prepare it myself from rockrose leaves, but it's such a tiresome task. I'd be most grateful to get some ready-made."

She embarrasses me with profuse thanks.

Her husband arrives. He mutters a prayer of thanks and we enjoy her potage and *focaccia*. They show me to their son's couch. I need little persuasion. And, if I dream, I can't remember any of it.

After breakfast – barley porridge flavoured with honey – the husband helps me ready the mules. He advises me on the best route to take: two or three *stadia* on this level, skirting the headlands; then, at the next village, the steep path down to the plain. From there on, the road is flat and easy. I should arrive in Fabricia by nightfall. I express my thanks for their kindness and set off.

Whistling a tune of my own, I realise I've been through here once with Father. But I'm seeing things with different eyes now. Real people live here, people with families, people who work hard, share things, whose children who go off to the mainland, who get old and frail.

When I stop for a drink, I discover the little lady stuffed the rest of the *focaccia* and a huge bunch of grapes into one of Crispus's panniers. I shake my head. Does their God inspire them to be generous to strangers? Is he friendlier than Aquila?

I long for a God who can show me the meaning of life, who can give me a reason to live. Something to hope for. I want to be free. The wide world is beckoning. I can't see myself getting married and raising a family where we live. Who would there be to choose from? Lucilla? I suppose she'll grow up someday and have other interests than making bead bracelets and giggling with Little Eli over nothing in particular. But my wife, bearing my children? I shake my head.

There are more houses here and more people on the road, some with mules, others riding, one driving a herd of goats. The road takes us right to the north coast, past a little fishing village very different from ours, with a sandy beach instead of rocky cliffs. Everything looks more prosperous – larger houses, well-kept boats, large nets hanging out to dry.

A little girl with a basket of fish gives me one. Do I look so miserable? Or so poor?

We stop for a drink near a brook. I make a fire to roast the fish and eat it with some of the good lady's bread. The mules find their own food. People glance at me as they pass. Can't they see we're headed for market?

At long last, as we reach the top of a wooded hill, Fabricia appears, reigning above its spectacular bay. A large merchant vessel is manoeuvring into the harbour. How wonderful it must be to sail the high seas. A thrill runs through me. I'll buy a boat! I'd almost forgotten my treasure.

Father's friend Albanus runs a *caupona* on the outskirts of town. He'll want payment but I have no money yet.

Ah, that little rise looks familiar. His place should be right behind it. The road is full of people heading into town this evening. Is there a *feria* these days? I hope Albanus has room.

I recognise the wrought iron gate. It's locked. I rattle it until a slave pokes his head through the doorway: "No room! Go away!"

"I'm a friend of Albanus," I shout across the courtyard. "Is he at home?"

"Name?"

"Silvanus, son of Cornelius from Submonte. We always stay here when we come to town." He disappears, returning after a short time.

"Two mules? Bring them around the back." He grabs Hercules's harness and strides ahead. On the way to the stables, he points out a long low building. "Find a space to sleep in there. The boss says he'll take an amphora of wine. He remembers Cornelius always has good stuff. And you can stay a couple of days while you do your business. Help yourself to potage in the *caupona*."

I unload and feed the beasts from my own supplies, wondering if our wares will be safe. The crystals stay with me. What a contrast to last night's reception! But I don't object. I'll have a roof over my head and a straw mattress to sleep on. Thank Aquila, we made it!

The *caupona* is full of raucous travellers, some playing *tabula*, others boasting of their feats. The rancid smell of cheap wine greets me. I venture in, glancing around for a free seat but wary of making eye contact with these strangers.

A large man heads in my direction.

"You must be Cornelius's son! What's your name again, lad?"

"Silvanus, sir."

"Albanus." He nods. "How you've grown! Make yourself at home. There's food in that pot over the fire." He moves on, chatting to one after another of his customers. I keep my eyes down, help myself to a bowl of bean and oatmeal soup and a goblet of watered wine, then make my way to the dormitory, where I curl up between my goatskins, clasping the shoulder bag with my most treasured wares, and fall into a troubled sleep.

CHAPTER THREE

Fabricia

WHERE AM I? I sit up and gaze around, instinctively toying with my amulet. Was it Aquila who helped me to get as far as Fabricia? At least he didn't stop me. Probably had nothing to do with the success of my journey. My legs scream in pain when I stand.

"Well, the first thing is to check on the mules," I mumble, trying to work the crick out of my neck.

Other travellers tend their beasts from the bales of hay and sacks of oats in the stable. Seems to be included in the price of the lodgings. Hercules and Crispus greet me with snorts of recognition. I feed and water them, then make my way to the *caupona* for a bowl of porridge and a goblet of wine.

Back in the stable, I start loading Hercules. A huge man gives me a hand lifting two amphorae into the frame. His soiled tunic, tangled hair and the ugly scar across his left cheek contrast with his friendliness; there's something wrong with one of his arms.

"On yer lonesome 'ere, lad? Where you from?"

I hesitate before answering. "Well, yes. Father... couldn't come this time. I'm from Submonte. Behind Monte Capanne. Father's a friend of Albanus."

21

"Wantin' to sell that there wine?"

I nod, wrinkling my nose at the pungent smell coming from the panniers on his mule. "Is that seafood you have there?"

"Right. Crabs 'n oysters for t'market. Join me?"

I glance at him again and take the risk. "Thanks. I just need to strap on these other panniers. I'll leave Crispus and the rest of the stuff till tomorrow. Do you think it'll be safe here?"

"Stablehand Gaius'll keep an eye on wha' you leave."

"Thanks. I'll keep the valuable things with me." I return to the stable and show Gaius what I'll be leaving: an amphora of wine and a variety of pots and baskets. My pink gems will stay in my bag, whatever happens.

And so we're off: Drusus, he calls himself, with his mule, and me with Hercules. The streets soon fill up with other traders and shoppers. Stray dogs slink between the legs and cartwheels, searching for scraps. Children, large and small, enjoying the festive atmosphere, beg for a piece of sweetmeat from one of the traders, or watch, enthralled, as jugglers perform, and musicians lead a group of young, masked dancers. It's soon the *ides* of October; I'd forgotten the feast of Meditrinalia. There'll be riotous celebration to thank the Gods for the new wine.

Drusus leads, and we drag the nervous mules behind us, squeezing our way through the milling crowds between rickety stalls.

While I keep an eye on Hercules's baskets, the unfamiliar sights catch my attention. A gush and sudden blaze reveal an ironmonger pumping his bellows. His furnace roars and the horseshoe in his tongs glows a brilliant orange as he hammers it into shape. A powerful scent greets us as we pass an apothecary decanting an extract of herbs and roots, a variety of phials and jars arranged on her table. I catch a pungent earthy odour from another stall stocking a tantalising range of leather bags and items of footwear.

And here's a glassblower, rotating a bulbous form with precision and shaping it into a tall, sleek jar. His stand displays a dazzling array of vessels and hanging ornaments – vermillion, emerald green, indigo and every intermediate shade. I stand agog, forgetting I'm with Drusus.

Rushing to catch up, I follow him into a large covered hall full of merchants with their horses and carts. It looks familiar. Yes, Father always came here to sell our goods, but I never paid much attention to how he set about doing it.

We tether the mules and Drusus takes a basket of shellfish on his shoulder, giving me one with huge starry-eyed crabs. I shudder as a gruesome scene from years ago comes to mind. We weave past more substantial booths, specialising in a variety of hardware products, then pass through a doorway to find ourselves in a food market. The confused aromas of meat, fruit and spices are almost overpowering.

Drusus makes his way to the seafood corner, to bargain with the fishmongers. "Fresh as a virgin! Caught las' nigh'," he shouts at a stallholder. "T'crabs are scrabblin', see? And see these here fat 'n juicy oysters!"

"Five *folles* for the crabs."

He almost chokes. "What a joke! Think that's all they're worf when I've been slavin' away all nigh'? Fifteen per libra, I'm askin'." He moves over to the scales on the counter. "Is them weights fair? Lets have a look." He sneaks a stone under one of the crabs. Two 'n a half libra. You can have 'em for forty *folles*. A fair price."

"No way!"

"Thirty-five, then. That's a deal." With a nimble gesture he whisks the stone away while accepting the money with his good hand. Is it as easy as that? "An' wha' abou' them lovely oysters? A righ' delicacy for a nobleman when t'cooks come lookin' for summat special! What'll you offer?"

"Twenty."

"Ri-di-cu-lous! I'll give you half o' them for tha' price. No? Then I'll find summun who knows to appreeshy-ate fresh shellfish."

While this haggling is going on, I glimpse another hall leading off to the right. Goldsmiths and jewellers. Would someone there be interested in my gems? I'll wait for a good opportunity, then have a look. But not while Drusus is watching.

He notices my interest. "Said y'ad summat valuable," he remarks. "You got jewlry you wanna sell?"

"Er… something like that," I reply. "But I'll deal with that later. First I need to sell the meats and wine."

Rhythmic beating resounds from the street outside, getting louder all the time. Drusus notices it and looks up. People rush around, shouting. Boys drag each other out into the street as the sounds of drumming and heavy boots increase. Several young men sidle off through a side archway. To my consternation, Drusus is nowhere to be seen. What's going on?

Venturing out into the bright sunshine, I watch the drama. A tall, proud man in full military regalia is leading a shabby troop of around fifty sweaty soldiers. They march by, accompanied by second-rate drummers and four hesitant pipers. Behind them, a crowd has formed – for the most part children and young women, with a few men – and I join it. Without thinking, we all fall in step with the rhythmic drumming as the procession advances towards the main square.

In the forum, the troops line up in front of a wooden dais. Several important-looking men mount the stage.

There's to be a public address. By now a large crowd has gathered, and I withdraw to the colonnades of the stoa, which offer me welcome shade from the burning sun. From here I can watch and listen without getting involved in something I might regret.

The crowd is restless. A tall, grey-haired man with a cane struggles onto the stage. The murmurings increase.

Next to me, a chubby, middle-aged lady with a string of onions and two ducks over her shoulder is watching the proceedings, wide-eyed. I turn to her. "Who is that man? What's going on?"

Startled, she glares at me. "Are you the only one who doesn't know our venerable Duumvir Maxillus? Where are you from, lad?"

"Sorry. I'm from Submonte and we don't hear much about life in town. You seem worried about what he's going to say…"

"I should say so." She touches my arm in a motherly way. "But let's listen."

Short of breath and leaning on his cane, Maxillus addresses the assembled crowd: "Honourable nobles, respected councillors, worthy citizens, faithful servants, young and old, I welcome you to this gathering on this rather salutary occasion.

"We have much to be thankful for. But I believe it behoves us to look back over the tumultuous years our Republic has been through recently. The older ones among you – like me – will remember, for instance, that divine portent of the sun going dark for more than a year…"

"How well I remember that," my companion exclaims. "Unbelievable. Had no idea what was happening. Could hardly see a thing even at midday. Snow in summer and all the crops failed! A portent indeed!"

"…to warn us of bitter times ahead," Maxillus continues. "Wars and rumours of wars, times of pestilence, affliction and deprivation…"

"Couldn't buy grain for love nor money. Let alone wool or new pots. Tools and weapons nowhere to be had."

A long discourse follows, in which we feel the bitter suffering and tragedy the speaker experienced during the relentless battles with the Goths, Franks and *Alamanni*. He was recovering from his injuries in Rome when that glorious city was brought to its knees under Totila's siege and pillage. It seems the Holy Father Pelagius – he wasn't yet Pope at that time – poured out his own fortune to feed the famine-stricken populace and appealed for mercy. As it was, more than half the citizens starved to death and the city was left little more than a ruin.

"When was that?" I ask my neighbour. My hand wanders to my eagle pendant.

"When our Urbanus was a lad. Must have been… twenty-five years ago or so. Long before you were born! It was about that time that Totila arrested Cerbonius for hiding imperial soldiers…"

"Who?" I glance up at my companion.

She looks at me with disbelief in her eyes. "How is it you don't know our good Bishop? He lives over your end of the island, in a cave on Monte Capanne. Didn't you say you were from there?"

"Well, yes. But I don't know of anyone living in a cave. Why that?"

"I'll tell you later, if you're interested. Let's listen…"

A pompous officer mounts the stage and is introduced as Centurion Didymus from Corsa. "Thank you, good people, for coming here today," he bellows.

"Does everyone in Corsa have such a strange accent?"

"I guess they do," the woman replies.

"Some of you will not appreciate the message I'm bringing, I'm afraid," he continues, flinging his cape over his shoulder to reveal the medals glinting from his leather doublet. "I'll keep it short. Three years ago, a new tribe invaded Italy from the north, the *Langobardi*…"

"Longbeards? Funny name!" I chuckle.

"It doesn't sound like a laughing matter to me," she chides. "Jupiter help us, if there's another war brewing! Haven't we had enough young men's lives wasted?"

He summons all able-bodied men between sixteen and thirty-five to sign up for active service. They are to be trained on Corsa before joining Longinus's troops to repel the aggressors.

"How old are you, lad?" the woman asks. "And what's your name?"

"My name's Silvanus. I'm fourteen."

"Good fortune," she mumbles, her expression halfway between relief for my sake and bitter sorrow, as her next remark explains. "Otherwise it would be goodbye Mother, goodbye Father. See you in a couple of years' time, if the Gods are kind!" Tears well up in her eyes. "Our Urbanus never came back…"

Even as I contemplate her passionate remarks and reach for my talisman, I notice a surging movement in the crowds. Two different streams, in fact. Many of the mature men are stealing away between the market stalls and tabernae, while some of the younger ones push their way in the opposite direction, towards the recruitment desk.

In my puzzlement over what I've heard and watched, I suddenly realise I've forgotten Hercules. He's been tied up for at least four hours, with neither food nor water. And I haven't sold a thing yet. As I weave through the restless crowd, it's clear the whole town is worried by the Duumvir's speech and especially by Centurion Didymus's call to arms. Some people make haste to pack up their stalls and return home. Others rush about, lost in troubled thoughts. A few men huddle together in little groups, their voices rising as they discuss the implications of this new development.

I hurry back to the market hall, threading my way through the agitated throng.

"Hi, Hercules!" I slap his rump. "Everything fine, old boy?" He stamps his back hoof. *Ecce!* What's this? I stagger forward, looking left and right, unwilling to believe my eyes. The baskets are gone!

CHAPTER FOUR

Meditrinalia

HOW LONG HAVE I hung here on Hercules's neck, sobbing, fingering my amulet? I raise my head and wipe my eyes with my sleeve. I still have both amphorae, a sack of nuts and the meats. Whoever stole the rest was in a hurry and only had two hands. And my precious crystals are still safe in my bag.

"New around here, lad?" a deep voice says, startling me. "Something wrong?"

Oh, no, did someone see me weeping?

"Half of my stuff has been stolen!" My blurred vision prevents me from getting a clear view of the speaker. "I left old Hercules here for a short time and now it's gone."

"Wait. I was here all morning. Saw you come." He turns as if he's looking for someone. "That other man. Big one with the bad arm. Reeked of fish. He came back and took those two panniers."

"Drusus? He ran off with my stuff?"

"Don't know his name."

"The beast!" My breath still comes in bursts.

"So sorry. Had no idea. I'd have stopped him. Thought he was a friend of yours."

I look up, my eyes recovered enough to see a grey-haired man wearing a well-worn woollen tunic and heavy boots.

"Can't one trust anyone in this place?" Good thing I never told him about the crystals. Or did I? "Wait till I get my own back!"

"Afraid there are a lot of scoundrels around. 'Specially on market days." He nods and looks me in the eye. His gaze is warm and sympathetic. "Don't try to avenge yourself, lad. Only does more harm. He'll regret it when he faces his maker."

"I should have been more careful. Father will never forgive me!"

"You've still got other things to sell there, haven't you?" He points at Hercules. "Let me give you a hand."

"Oh, please." Still trembling, I'm in no state to consider whether this stranger is likely to be more trustworthy. "Yes, I have this red wine – very good, they say. Oh, and two pots of fine honey and liquamen. And some dried meat and cheese here. Do you know where I can sell these things?"

"Grab a sack or two. I'll carry the jars. Come with me." He ambles with a decided limp. I follow him through a different archway into another hall and between the stalls to a stand with a range of farm produce.

"Antonius!" he calls. "Antonius! You there?"

A small man pokes his bald head from behind trays of onions, cabbages and leeks. "Oh, it's you, Franciscus." He arranges a stack of beans as he comes out. "Bless you. How are you keeping? And how's the lady?" He doesn't seem to expect an answer. "I didn't know you had a grandson. What's your name, lad?"

"I'm Silvanus, sir." My eyes switch from one to the other. "But… I'm not his grandson. I'm from Submonte, over behind Monte Capanne. My Father, Cornelius, comes…"

"Cornelius? I know him," Antonius bellows, stroking his large belly. "You're his son? Well, I never! Where is he?"

"He… He couldn't make it this year. I… I came alone."

Have I put my foot in it? I lower my eyes. "This trip… It's proving a bit much for me. I got caught in a raging storm on the way here."

"You were out in that gale? That can't have been fun."

"No, it terrified me. I thought I'd die. Or that something would happen to the mules. We sheltered in a cave for two nights, thank Aquila."

"Thank the Good Lord, I'd say." Antonius chuckles. "Glad to see you made it all right."

"Well, yes, I got here in the end." I should be grateful for that. "But now someone has stolen my baskets of fruit. And I thought he was my friend!"

"But he's still got these things here," Franciscus remarks. "And the wine. He's…"

"You have some of Cornelius's excellent wine?" Antonius claps his hands. "Never tasted anything better. I'll give you a good price for it. How much have you got?"

"Two amphorae on the mule out there. And one of olive oil back at Albanus's place where I'm staying."

"Show Antonius what you've got." Franciscus nods towards the entrance. "He'll take it."

I leave the jars and sacks for Antonius to examine, while I go back to Hercules. He shifts his weight from one foot to the other before backing out of the stall. I lead him as near as possible.

Franciscus helps me unload the amphorae and carry them to Antonius's stall. He uncorks one and takes a whiff, then raises his eyebrows and his face brightens.

"Wonderful. Superb." He sighs. "Barnus over there could use the liquamen, meat, cheese and eggs. But I'd be delighted to take the wine, honey and nuts, for… let me see, one… one-fifty,… a hundred and eighty *folles* all together. How's that?"

My mouth drops open. I've never seen so much money. I glance at Franciscus, hoping for confirmation that the price is fair.

"Give him two hundred," he suggests. "You'll sell it, no problem. Lad's had a rough time. Storm. Then his fruit stolen."

Antonius counts out the coins and drops them into my empty leather purse. I struggle to pull the strings closed.

"Th–thank you," I stutter, nodding from one elderly man to the other. "Thanks ever so much for your help. And your generosity. I'd never have coped alone."

"My pleasure," says Franciscus.

"No thanks needed," Antonius adds. "I reckon we've made a fair deal, what with Cornelius's wine, the fine honey and these other goods. Can I give you some empty amphorae to take back with you? I have several lying around back here. I'm sure you can find a use for them."

"Oh, I hadn't even thought of bringing any home. Are you sure you don't need them?"

"Of course not. They're in the way here. How many could you use?"

"Well, Hercules here can take four. But I don't have a frame for my other mule. Can I bring the olive oil around tomorrow? Would you be interested in that?"

"If it's as good as the wine, I would indeed. Bring it over."

He carries the empties out and I strap them onto Hercules's frame.

"So that's that. Now, you look weary, young man," he remarks. "Better get back to your *caupona*. I'm sure we'll be able to make a deal tomorrow. *Vale!*"

"*Valete!* And thanks, again!"

What a day! The crowds, the talk of war, the theft of my wares. And now the relief of meeting kind folk who don't try to cheat me. I could do with a good night's rest.

But not yet.

Another blacksmith, this time beating ploughshares, catches my attention with his display of swords and agricultural tools. Father could use a good pick for working the rocky soil. Or should I get him a spade or a hoe? I feel the weight of the coins in my purse.

My hand trembles as I point to a robust looking tool. "How much is that little hatchet?" How will I know if his price is fair?

"This fine piece of craftsmanship? It's not a hatchet. In fact, it's two tools in one: a sharp adze on this side and a sturdy hammer-head on the other, see?"

I run my finger over the sharp blade. It does look well-made.

"And notice the shaped oak handle." He makes a wave motion with his hand. "That will last a lifetime. I can let you have it for forty *folles*." Turning round, he selects another item. "Or, if it's a hatchet you want, I have this one here for thirty. Also with a strong oak handle. Is it for carpentry or for chopping wood?"

"It's my father who needs it. For clearing shrubs."

"So a hatchet it should be." He reaches out to unhook a larger one. "I have this bigger one here for thirty-five. Which will you have?"

"Could… Could you give me the smaller one for twenty-five?"

"Twenty-eight, since it's for your father."

"I… I don't have too much money. And I need to buy other things. What about that pickaxe; how much would that be?"

"This one without a handle?" He picks it up and holds it out for me to see. "Fifteen *folles* for the head. Or I can give you a complete one, also with a strong oak handle, for twenty-five."

He turns his back. My chance to try Drusus's methods? I grab a knife and am about to whisk it into my bag when the blacksmith looks round. "Interested in knives, too?" His frown reveals his suspicion.

"Er… just looking." My hands tremble as I put it back where it was. "I… I think I'll leave it for today. Maybe I'll come back tomorrow."

"Twenty-two for this one."

Whom can I trust? "I want to look around before deciding. *Vale.*"

"It's up to you." As I move off, I hear him shout, "But you won't get a better price for this quality workmanship."

I collect Hercules, cursing him over the theft of my most valuable items, although he could hardly have prevented it. Together we fight our way between the stalls cluttering the huge hall. Fascinating things catch my eye: elaborate wooden boxes, colourful silks, sundry pots and pans, pretty toys, a stall selling writing materials, scrolls and impressive-looking codices, splendid gold and silver jewellery, studded with magnificent gemstones. A goldsmith like this might be interested in my crystals. I must return tomorrow.

As I leave the town centre, a new commotion catches my attention. This time it's not marching – more like a noisy crowd aroused by loud pipe and drum music. The exciting atmosphere lures me in.

Everyone is moving towards a makeshift circus to the west of the town. I can't drag Hercules through this agitated throng and there's nothing left in his panniers, so I tether him among several other mules near the gate and approach the festivities. Jostled by screaming spectators, I push my way into the arena. Of course, it's the *ludi*. They're always on during religious festivals.

Ilva is too small for chariots or even horse races. A group of young men, stripped to their loin cloths, are running around the ring, sweat pouring over their rippling muscles. How many laps will they do? I strain my neck between the screaming, cheering spectators to catch glimpses of the action. As the leaders jostle each other, they're not averse to barging or tripping their rivals. The winning three are welcomed onto the podium to receive their laurel wreaths. Rufus would enjoy this.

Next come wrestling bouts. The ring is raised but it's too far away for me to see much. The yelling from the crowd is deafening. Some illicit betting is being conducted on the sidelines, which adds to the passion. My hand grabs hold of my purse.

I move toward the stands selling food and drink. Much to my amazement, dignified landlords mingle with slaves, many wearing strange little hats. Most are the worse for overindulging in the old and new wine. Frequently, beakers are raised and a toast in honour of the Goddess collectively intoned: "*Novum vetus vinum bibo, novo veteri morbo medeor.*"

I'm glad I'm suffering from neither old nor new ailments at the moment, and am in no need of a cure from that Goddess.

I buy a goblet of new wine, more to identify with the crowd than out of thirst. And here the atmosphere is livening up. A group of musicians on a wooden stage strike up a slow dance tune. And, sure enough, a team of female dancers appear, their glittering semi-transparent robes revealing tantalising glimpses of their athletic bodies as they swing to the mournful rhythm of the music. I can't take my eyes off them.

Now the lead characters appear, wearing symbolic masks representing good and evil powers. A bitter struggle is being enacted. First one side then the other gains the upper hand. The tension builds as the hero surrenders to buy another character's release. The drummers quicken the tempo. The chorus ladies prance and leap, their robes floating high, in ever more dramatic figures until they crumble into a gently pulsating pile. We are supposed to be moved by the melodramatic climax and the crowds around me cheer and clap. But the meaning of the tragic saga is lost on me; instead, the spectacle of those titillating figures causes my whole body to tingle, and I shudder.

The audience becomes more and more bawdy as the cheap wine takes effect. Loud caterwauling and angry disputes all but drown out the musicians. The stage performance loses its fascination, as the crowds themselves dance and sing.

A scruffy boy, younger than me, slinks between the legs of the distracted country folk. I gape as he snatches a pouch from a burly peasant, flings it to one of his allies and dodges away through the crowd. As I watch, it becomes obvious that a whole team – girls as well as boys – is passing booty from one to another, finally to the ringleader in the shadows alongside the stage. Perhaps I could try my hand at that sometime. I clasp my bag tight.

A raucous-looking artisan, impatient to get his wine, pulls at the tunic of a serving maid, causing her to tip the tray she's carrying over several other spectators. She giggles and pulls his beard in response. As his friends goad him on, he grabs her around the waist. I stand to get a better view. Instead of escaping, she lets him drag her onto his lap. He fondles her breasts, dropping a coin down her inviting cleavage, which provokes wild screams from his companions.

She slams her tray on his head and kicks her legs up in mock self-defence, only to have them grabbed by the next man on the bench. Her shoes fly off and she is passed from one lewd fellow to another, who pinch her thighs and pull at her clothes until she is half naked. To my amazement, she seems to enjoy the proceedings as much as they do.

The wine affects my judgement and my muscles tremble as I imagine myself joining in. Contrasting emotions tear at my conscience. I've never witnessed such ribaldry before.

Beyond the tables is a group of temporary structures. Mystical lyre music and incense fumes waft toward me. The curtains of the central tent are open. Inside, on a lavishly decorated pedestal, stands Meditrina herself, in one hand a golden staff, in the other a mixed bunch of herbs.

Humble petitioners, many with obvious ailments, wait in line to approach a priest wearing elaborate robes. He receives their votive offerings: a handful of grain, some pomegranates or grapes, a little stuffed puppet, brass or silver coins. Mumbling some incantation, he deposits them at the feet of the Goddess. Some of these devotees then proceed into one of the adjoining shelters, each of which has a scantily-dressed priestess in attendance.

Is this my chance to satisfy my growing lust? When my turn comes, I drop a handful of *folles* into the silver platter and the priest dismisses me with a splash of strong-smelling potion.

A pretty young woman smiles at me, raising her eyebrows. "Come on in!" She takes my hand and ushers me behind the flap of her enclosure. A hypnotic fragrance hits my lungs. I've hardly caught my breath before she shakes off her flimsy robe and fingers my belt.

Those breasts! That gleaming bronze flesh! That tantalising belly!

My arms hang limp as she undresses me. I shudder as she pulls me close, flesh against flesh. Vaguely, I'm aware of her laying me on the couch, sitting astride me and massaging my body. Then all goes blank.

When I wake from my stupor, I struggle to my feet – my tingling body covered with aromatic oil – and reach for my loincloth and tunic.

"Another small offering for the Goddess?" Still naked, the priestess coaxes me with a sweet smile, while clasping my bag. "Meditrina will grant you health for the whole year."

I fumble in my purse and hand her another five or six *folles*, still too baffled to speak, and tear myself away.

Back at the *caupona*, I toy with my amulet and try to settle. Perplexing thoughts lull me into dreamland: What fiendish distractions Aquila set up for me today! Tempting trinkets. Dishonest Drusus. Arousing artistes. A seductive siren. Confusion. Are the warring nations controlled by the Gods? What about the weather? Is there a purpose to all that happens? If not, why does a poor woman grieve the loss of her son? Who trains boys to steal and persuades old men to carouse with loose women? What overcame me, that I gave in to my craving? And how is it that some people are above all such depravity – kind, honest, generous?

CHAPTER FIVE

Secret Sale

THE PIPES AND *drums hammer a wild rhythm; it wearies my brain. A seductive serving wench steals my baskets of grapes and gives them to the naked dancers on the stage. She laughs at me as she passes, but escapes before I grab her. I call out to her, but no sound escapes from my lips. Drusus chases a herd of donkeys round the race track and I try to run after him, but something holds me back …*

A passing cart wakes me. Bother these dreams. It's a new day and I have work to do. Not only work; I have money now – soon even more – and can pamper myself with some goodies and find presents for Little Eli and the lads. Perhaps I'll get something for Lucilla, too. What might she like?

After a quick wash in the courtyard fountain and a bite to eat, I strap the frame onto Crispus this time. The remaining goods aren't heavy. His agitated hoof scatters his bedding hay and scrapes the bare earth. He's keen for some exercise.

I load the amphora of olive oil without any help, tie on the remaining baskets of berries and herbs alongside the bundle of cork, and we're off. As I join the crowd of market-goers, Crispus's legs twitch and he lurches – no doubt troubled by the unfamiliar noise and bustle. We head through the tempting trinkets and hawkers' banter for Antonius's stall. The hall isn't crowded yet.

I see no one. "*Salve!* Anyone there?"

A bald head emerges and its wrinkled face lights up. "*Salve*, Silvanus. Had a good night's rest, lad?"

"Well, a short one." I lower my eyes. "After I left, I went over to the circus to watch the *ludi* and the dancing. It… got rather late."

"No place for a young lad like you." He shakes his head. "Not at night, anyway. A lot of dirty business there. I keep clear of those events whenever I can. Too much temptation for my poor old soul!"

"Why do people go wild like that?" Let's keep it neutral. "Is it the Gods who drive them to such crude behaviour?"

Antonius sniffs and glances at Crispus's load. "Do I smell olive oil?" He smiles. "Worth a *follis* or two. Let me help you take it down."

Together, we lift the amphora out of its frame and lay it down. "Thanks."

"I wouldn't blame the Gods for all that bad behaviour," Antonius says. "We're all inclined to do wrong. At least, I am. The question is: Do we give in to those temptations?"

"I… I get these wild fantasies sometimes. I can't seem to control my thoughts. I've asked Aquila for help, but it does no good."

Some noisy traders interrupt us, shouting at people to get out of their way as they push and drag a vegetable cart through the growing throng. By the time Antonius has sorted things out and picked up the stack of cabbages they knocked over, our previous conversation is forgotten.

I show him the rest of my goods. He is again glad to buy them for another hundred *folles*. My face flushes and my voice trembles as I thank him. Why is this man so kind and fair, and others so dishonest?

I glance left and right and lower my voice. "You've been very helpful. I wonder if I might still ask you something in private?"

"Of course. Step back in here and we can talk in peace."

At the back of his stall a robust woman is preparing food and drink. "This is my dear wife, Anna." He stands back for us to face one another. "My young friend Silvanus. I told you about him yesterday."

"Yes, I remember," she says. "*Salve*, Silvanus."

I nod my head. "Pleased to meet you." I'm amazed how much room there is back here.

"Please join us for a simple meal." He moves a tray of beans off a stool and I sit.

"Really? That's kind of you. Are you sure that's all right?"

"Talking's easier with a full mouth." He chuckles. "You don't mind if Anna hears what you have to say, do you?"

"I'm sure I can trust you two. But out in the market it's not the same."

"So, what's on your heart?"

I open my bag. "Look, I have other things in here. Perhaps you can suggest where I might be able to sell them." Checking no one else is looking, I take out the pink crystals. Again, both Antonius's and Anna's faces light up in amazement.

"Where on earth did you get those?" asks Antonius, enthralled. "They are stunning, and so big! Flawless as far as I can see!"

"I can't explain where it was," I say, stuffing them back in my bag. "Perhaps it's better that way. I want to go back and get more before anyone else finds them."

"Careful how you talk, then."

I glance up. "Thanks." I nod my head. "Do you know someone who would be interested in buying these for a fair price? I saw a jeweller somewhere over there yesterday.

He had earrings and bracelets, some with precious stones."

Antonius nods. "I guess you mean Sartorius. He might take them. But I know someone I trust more than him. Old Jeremias. What do you think, Anna?"

"Good idea. He's an expert on gems. And he is honest. You could take the lad down. I'll manage here."

I leave Crispus tied up in the stalls and follow Antonius out of the market hall and through narrow, twisting passageways. My heart is thumping.

A large ship with a square, red and white striped sail is approaching the port. Judging by how broad it is, it must be a merchant vessel. What exciting lands has it visited and what exotic cargo is it carrying? As we get nearer, my attention is drawn to a bustling crowd of dockers unloading another moored ship: barrels of oil, sacks of grain, and big wooden chests, perhaps containing glassware or other fragile articles. They stack everything in a large warehouse, which is guarded by two muscular men carrying nasty-looking clubs. A narrow galley with two banks of oars is also tied to the pier – a faster, fighting ship, I guess. Seagulls scream and swoop, hoping to steal some edible morsel.

I follow Antonius through winding cobbled paths. Someone seems to be watching us. He ducks behind a boulder.

We take a side alley, which follows the city wall, go up some steps, through a low archway, then along another narrow cobbled street with overhanging oriel windows. Antonius knocks at a massive oak door. As we wait for an answer, I notice an unusual ornament, decorated with symbolic lettering, on the frame. Another knock and a shout, "Jeremias! It's me, Antonius, from the market. I need to talk to you." We wait.

After some moments, a shuffling behind the door is followed by the sound of massive bolts sliding open. The door opens a crack and a deep, trembling voice greets us: "Oh, it's you is it, Antonius? The Lord bless you. My ears aren't so good anymore."

The door swings back to reveal an aged man with a long white beard in a full-length, grey robe, tied at the waist with a blue cord. He squints as the bright sun bursts into his dark hallway, revealing glittering particles of swirling dust.

"Peace to you, Jeremias," Antonius shouts.

"We use the side entrance. I don't expect visitors at the front door."

"Sorry. You're looking sprightly. Is the family well?"

"Thank you, we are doing fine. Come on in, come on in; we can't talk here."

I stand alongside Antonius in the dim passageway. Jeremias slides the obstinate bolts home, then hobbles ahead of us, mumbling: "Come on in, come on in; we can't talk here." He leads us through a colonnaded walkway, its marble pillars capped with fantastic clusters of fruit. Glamorous odours of herbs and spices tickle my nose. As we advance, we pass a well-kept garden in an inner courtyard, containing a fountain and a huge fig tree, weighed down with a plentiful late crop.

A dimly-lit room with a low ceiling draws us in. Beyond a massive oven, a middle-aged lady is preparing vegetables. Jeremias seats us on a low wooden bench – or perhaps it's a bed – which is decorated with carved ivory branches, gold-plated vine leaves and bunches of inlaid gemstones made to look like grapes. Beautiful. Must be valuable. None of the usual statues of Gods are visible, nor is there any sign of an altar. Instead, a large, many-armed golden lampstand of a kind I have never seen before catches my eye.

The wine we are offered produces a moment of silence. Then Jeremias asks, "How about you? And your lady wife?"

"We are well, too, thank you." Antonius has to shout to be heard. "Look, I've brought a young friend with me. He has something to show you."

"Indeed? So, what is it, my good lad?"

With a glance at my guide, I open my bag. The loose coins jingle but Jeremias doesn't notice. Doesn't even hear. I hold out the pink crystals for him to see. He takes them off me using a soft cloth.

A melodious hum resounds from deep within his throat in time with a rhythmic nod of his head. "Well, I never. Just look at this." He examines the cluster from all angles. "Praise the Lord, my eyes are still bright." He moves towards the window. "Amazing. Amazing. You found it over west, I presume. Monte Capanne? Yes, yes. Granite. These crystals live deep in the granite rocks. Quite rare since the mining has all but stopped. Beautiful. Beautiful. You know what this is, lad? See the long, straight form and the six-sided point? Like the star of David."

I come across and look at where he's pointing.

"You know what this is? Beryl family. Yes. Very special. Beautiful. Aren't they beautiful! Beryls are often blue or blue-green. The bright green ones are emeralds. But these are pink. Pink, partly colourless. Very special. I need more light, Esther!"

His wife shuffles in carrying another lamp.

"See how it shines through the varying shades," he continues. "And the sheen! The lustre! The brilliance! Beautiful. Beautiful… Just imagine what they've been through over the ages… Formed deep down in the heat and pressure under the sea, then squeezed up, waiting for you to find them. Amazing. Amazing, don't you think?"

We nod in silent agreement.

"Did you dig for them? Or were they in a cave? I'm surprised nobody found them a long time ago."

I glance at Antonius. "Well… I did find a cave. It must have been excavated long ago. Maybe for crystals like these. But these weren't in the cave." My hand flies up, then falls. "A boulder came crashing down in a storm. I found them in the hollow where it had been. I could hardly believe my eyes. The back wall was full of crystals like these."

"You mean there were more where these came from?" He claps his hands. "This is fantastic. Worth a fortune! Can you get more? I'll give you a good price."

"I think I can find the place again."

"Be careful, my friend," Antonius interjects. "If someone else hears about this, you'll have rivals trying to steal them."

I nod.

"No danger from a wizened old man like me." Jeremias chuckles. "But he's right. There are villains all around these days."

"You say these are valuable," I venture. "How much would they be worth?"

"Well, let me see. They are indeed beautiful. Hardly a fault. Only the Good Lord is perfect. I'd say they weigh about half a libra, maybe a bit more. When I cut them into separate stones, I can make several fine necklaces. Or fancy brooches. Or rings. Set in gold. There's a good market for quality jewellery on the mainland… I'll give you… let me see… four hundred and twenty *folles* for this lot. How's that? Or two *solidi*, if you prefer it that way."

My mouth drops and I find myself trembling. This is too much for me. Is Aquila showing me favour? Suddenly, my dreams come alive. How much would a boat cost? The wide world is beckoning…

"What's the matter, lad?" In my shock, I must have seemed disappointed. "Did you expect more? Perhaps four hundred and fifty. Would that satisfy you?"

"No, no! The price is fine. I can't take it in that I have stumbled onto something so valuable. It frightens me.

And confuses me, that's all. I'm happy to sell them to you. And I'll go back for more."

We finalise our transaction over another goblet of wine, and I place the two shiny gold *solidi* in my purse. Antonius needs to get back to his stall. Old Jeremias ushers us out through the side door. I thank him again and again as we take our leave.

When we emerge from the narrow street, squinting at the bright sunlight, a figure slinks into an alleyway farther down. Is someone following our every move?

Breathless, I run through twisting streets, stuffing my new purse with the hundred and twenty folles I received from Anna for the labdanum. The coins keep falling from my hand. Every time I bend down to pick one up, a hooded figure disappears into a doorway twenty paces behind me. Where did I leave Crispus? I can't find the spelt and millet. My pursuer is near and I have no idea where I am. A dead end! I turn to face my stalker and swing the only weapon I have – my purse – at his head.

The impact of my bag against the wall wakes me. My fellow travellers chortle as I collect the spilt coins from between the mattresses.

I make my way down to the harbour. Sailors on the deck of a large merchant ship bark at each other as they toss tackle, coil ropes and furl the sails. Casual labourers unload crates, then return with food baskets and large amphorae filled with water and wine for the next journey.

Some way off to the side, men are at work inside a large wooden frame. A strong smell of tar fills the air as I approach. The craftsmen are busy sawing and planing planks, which are then assembled into the graceful hull of a small boat. An older man – tall, stout and almost bald, wearing a dusty tunic and with a bag of tools at his belt – inspects their work, making an occasional remark and holding a beam in place while a worker hammers in a wooden nail.

He notices me watching and raises his eyebrows. I take this as an invitation to speak. "Is that going to be a fishing boat?"

"I'm sure they will use it for fishing," he replies, his eyes lighting up and a broad smile spreading across his face. "But they ordered it for trading local produce around the coast. That's why it has both sails and oars, see?" He points at the rowlocks and mast. "Some places are hard to reach by land, you know."

"Oh, yes, I know. I come from the far end of the island. It took several days to get here, what with the storm."

"That's a long way for a young man like you. Did you come alone?"

I nod. "With two mules."

"I see." He checks a plank one of his men has positioned and says to him, "A bit more off here, Balbus." He marks the place with a stick of charcoal from behind his ear. "And make sure you get the curve right."

He turns to me again. "Why do you ask about the boat?"

"I love boats." I reach out and stroke the elegant structure. "I hope to have one myself one day. I want to explore the world."

"Just place your order, young man." He chuckles. "What's your name, by the way?"

"Silvanus, son of Cornelius from Submonte."

"Cornelius? That name sounds familiar. I think I met him some years ago," he adds. "Oh, and I'm known here as Boatwright Laurus."

"Do you mind if I watch you building? I won't bother you."

"Feel free." He sizes me up with a curious eye. "I'm always happy to find someone who's interested in my craft."

I'm reminded of the times I watched Pontus's father in his carpenter's shop, as the men saw and trim the joists, fitting the tenons into the mortises with precision. The man called Balbus forms the rough curves using a two-handled drawknife, smoothing them off afterwards with a plane.

As the shadows lengthen, I'm shocked to realise I've spent half the day here. And my tasks are far from finished. Before I leave, I pluck up courage to voice what's on my mind. "What would a little boat with a sail and oars cost?"

"Do I have a customer?" Laurus raises his eyebrows. "Think of it this way. I have twelve men working for me. I train them, I feed them, I put a roof over their heads." He points to a long low hut some way off. "And I have a family to keep. I reckon each worker costs me two hundred folles per month. Then there's the material – about ten *solidi* for a small boat."

"So what would that be in total?"

"See that little skiff over there? That took us – what? – about eight months to build. It's ready to be collected now." He places his hand on my shoulder. "How's your arithmetic, lad? Twelve men working for eight months to a year plus material. And a bit of profit for me. How much does that make?"

I close my eyes. "That would be… about a hundred and ten *solidi*. Perhaps a hundred and thirty." I examine his face. "Am I right?"

"Very good. I see you've got brains as well as an interest in boats."

My heart races. What a foolish dream. I'm needed at home. Who else would provide for Mother and Little Eli? "Thank you. I must be off now."

"*Vale.*"

I hurry back up to the town, glancing back now and then.

CHAPTER SIX

Travelling Companion

TWO COPPER COOKING pots and another couple of sacks of spelt and barley. Four pairs of strong leather boots – not elegant but suitable for our rough, rocky hillside.

It's embarrassing to have to fumble in my bag for loose coins to pay for these things, so I buy a larger leather purse. In a secluded corner behind a colonnade, I count out two hundred and ten *folles* and place them, together with the two *solidi*, into the new pouch, which I hang around my neck under my tunic, keeping only a small amount at my belt.

The rhythmic bursts of the blacksmith's bellows on the glowing embers conjure bright orange flames and surging waves of heat. He sells me the hatchet and the pickaxe with the oak handle I admired earlier. I also buy a small hand pick for my special use. For the lads, I find some handsome-looking knives with carved bone handles and leather sheaths.

I'm rich! For Mother I choose two bolts of robust cotton cloth, one white, one blue and white striped, a length of fine Greek linen, some needles and strong thread. She always makes our clothes. A blue bead necklace for Little Eli, and a dragon brooch for Lucilla complete today's purchases.

It's a week since I left. A lot has happened in these few days. It's worked out rather well. Aquila must be smiling on me. I even have the exciting prospect of real riches when I collect the remaining crystals.

On my way back to Hercules, the glassblower again catches my eye. I find myself rooted to the floor as he pumps a bellows to heat a mixture of sand and natron till it's white hot. "What is that you added?" I ask during a pause between the blasts of the furnace.

"Craft secret!" He winks. "No, I add lime to make the glass stronger." He shows me jars of fine powder. "And these different ores – cobalt, copper, lead – give the bright colours." He softens previously made lumps and shapes them into the various vessels he sells. I buy four green beakers and a large bowl – the first glassware we've ever had.

"Careful how you carry them! They break easily," he warns. I wrap them among the folds of linen and pack them in one of Hercules's panniers, along with the knives and other items.

A stall selling ancient scrolls catches my eye, and I wander over to look at their wares. Many are in Greek and other tongues I don't recognise. I pick up a small Latin text by Cicero. I've heard of him, but never seen any of his writings. After glancing through it, I buy it and stow it in my bag. I'll need a peaceful moment to work my way through that mystical language.

Back at the *caupona*, I sort out my purchases, packing the smaller items into the empty amphorae. A generous portion of the ever-present potage satisfies my hunger. I'll set off for home early in the morning before anyone notices.

That good wine I gave Albanus is enough payment for my stay, but Gaius is grateful when I slip him another *follis* for having looked after the mules. And now I'm off, heading west.

My path takes me through brushland with the penetrating smell of the macchia, then into a dense area of tall pines, evergreen oaks and acacia trees. We plod over rolling hills on a minor path, avoiding the main road, and make good progress until well past noon before I think of taking a break for some food.

The agitated alarm call of a disturbed blackbird brings me to a sudden halt, and a scurry between the trees over to my right catches my attention. A wild animal in the middle of the day? But something did slink behind that clump of bushes.

Or was it some*one*? My heart thumps. Am I being followed despite my caution?

Clasping my stave, I dart forward. A slight figure dashes deeper into the forest, with me close behind. A little boy, much younger than me! Nothing to fear from him. But I wonder what he's up to. Did some crook send him to track me down?

"Come back!"

He runs through the undergrowth, whimpering, "Don't hurt me! I haven't done you any harm."

I grab his arm, causing him to wince. "Not yet," I snap. "And I'll see you don't."

Only then do I get a chance to look at him. He's trembling, a thin wisp of a boy – maybe ten years old – with dark skin, a fresh oval face and large black eyes, pleading for mercy. If it weren't for his ragged jet-black hair, he might be handsome. His rough tunic is stained and worn to almost nothing. His legs are bare, and he has neither shoes nor cloak. A leather bag hangs from his belt.

I adopt a gentler tone: "I'd like to know why you are following me? Who sent you after me?"

"I-I'm n-n-not following you! I j-j-just escaped to the woods… And when you came p-p-past I t-t-tried to hide. I was af-f-fraid *you* were after *me*. B-b-believe me, I have n-n-no intention of harming you."

He sounds sincere enough, and I loosen my grip on his stick-like arm.

"All right, I believe you," I say. "Until I find out you're lying. So, why are you hiding in the woods?"

"I'm a slave. Or I was."

"You ran away?"

He nods, then breaks down in sobs. "My master… was horrid." He breathes a spasmed gasp. "I couldn't stand it any longer. I had to flee. Now I'm at my wits' end."

"How long have you been on the run?"

"Two days. Or three. Two nights I've endured here in the woods. It gets so cold." A shudder runs through him. "And there are all those creepy noises. Are there lions around here? I'm so scared." I suppress a laugh when I see he's serious. "I have nowhere to go and only the fruit and nuts I chance upon to eat. What should I do? I can't go back."

"Stop sobbing, to start with. And let's think." I make him face me. "In a way, I'm fleeing too. Only I don't know from whom. I was about to stop for a bite of food. I've enough for two."

"Do you mean that?" His stomach grumbles.

"You know these woods? We could stick together, if you like. What's your name, anyway?"

"V-Valerius. Would you really let me accompany you? I'd feel much safer. There's a towering cliff a bit farther on; it offers some shelter from the wind. That's where I slept last night." He points downhill. "I was creeping back towards town when you saw me, hoping I might find something to eat. I hate to steal, but what options do I have?"

"All right, all right," I say, letting him free. "My name's Silvanus. Let's fetch the mules and you can take me to your hideout. We'll get a fire going and have something to eat."

At first Valerius is afraid of the mules but I give him Crispus's halter and we lead them through the undergrowth and down a slope to his clearing. It's secluded and sheltered, overlooking a cascading brook, with the deep blue sea in the distance. Valerius helps me unload the mules; how much easier it is with two extra hands, even if they are a child's.

I'm again glad for my flint and tinder, and the fire is soon roaring. We boil some water from the stream in a pot hanging from a little trestle frame made of stout branches. It's still warm in the sunshine, and while the barley is cooking, I strip off and go for a dip in a pool below a little waterfall. I haven't had a proper wash for more than a week. While I'm there, I manage to catch two fish with my bare hands.

Valerius has added spices to the potage and produced some unfamiliar plaited bread from his bag. I pass him my knife and he guts and cleans the fish like an expert, roasting them on the hot stones.

I raise my eyebrows. "You know how to cook."

"Thanks."

We enjoy a fine meal while I'm drying in the setting sun. Then I dress and lie on the soft heather, relaxing for the first time since I left home. I relate my recent adventures: the fearful storm and the boulders Aquila hurled down on me; the welcome cave; Drusus's villainous theft of my fruit and nuts; my visit to the Meditrinalia *ludi* and my conflicting emotions; my encounter with kind Antonius. I'm careful not to mention the crystals or the episode with Old Jeremias.

Valerius sits next to me and I show him some of the things I bought: knives for my friends, silks for the girls.

"Did you also purchase that pendant?" he asks, pointing at my eagle amulet.

Only then do I realise I've often been fingering it. "This? No. It's Aquila. My aunt gave it to me. It protects me from the God's anger. I'm not sure it does any good, though. Do you like it?"

"No, no. It's not that. I don't believe in all those ludicrous Gods. There's only one real God."

"You think so? What about Jupiter and Mars and all the others? Aren't you afraid of them?" I stare at him. "Do you pray to your God?"

"Certainly. Although I don't know much about Him." I notice tears forming in his eyes and his voice trembles. "Mother taught me about Him… before…"

"Before what?"

"Before they… killed her."

I flinch as his words sink in. "Killed her? Who did?"

"The *goyim*, Barbarians, I presume. They landed near our city in huge ships. I had no idea what was happening. I was a mere child, playing on the steps near the Church. But… they began to slaughter people with their ghastly swords and axes, and set our houses on fire." He buries his face in his hands and mumbles, "I tried to go home, but they were everywhere. My father and older brother attempted to protect my mother and sister… They were down on their knees…" He breaks down, sobbing.

I move nearer and put my arm round his shoulder. "I'm sorry. Must have been terrible."

He can't speak for a while. Then, "It was horrible. Gruesome. They slashed them down. Left them strewn there, twitching in pools of blood… my whole family. All the servants, too. Everyone. They grabbed me and Salome and some other… children." His hand covers his mouth. "They bound us and dragged us to their ships. I screamed and bit and clawed their faces, but it didn't help." He pauses, shaking his head, the tears now pouring down his cheeks.

I glance round as Hercules comes behind and nudges me. "Who's Salome?"

"My playmate. She lived next door. She had a brother, Marcus. I liked him. We had such mirth together… I never saw him again."

"Where did they take you?"

"How should I know? They caged us in the murky hold of their loathsome ship, along with many other children. It seems they had killed all the grownups who crossed their path." He shudders. "We must have sailed for several days. It was stormy and most of us were sick. They didn't give us any food, only amphorae of water once a day. It was miserable. Everything stank of vomit and piss." He screws up his face. "No one knew what they intended to do with us. We'd lost everything – our parents, our families, our homes, our dignity, everything…"

He buries his face on my breast and I hold him close. War, piracy, murder, abduction – why do people behave like that?

He turns back the collar of his tunic and shows me a carved ivory brooch in the shape of a dove, pinned to the inside. "Mother gave me this. I don't recall what it represents, but it's something to do with God. She used to sing when she put me to sleep. So tenderly. A soothing song about a shepherd. I still remember it." Again, he sobs bitterly. "Oh, how I miss her embrace! We had such a blessed life. It's all gone."

I stroke his jet-black hair. "They brought you here to Ilva?"

"No, not here at first. We landed somewhere else. A bustling port in Italy, I presume, where the people spoke a peculiar way." He looks at the back of his hand. "There were almost no dark-skinned people like us."

"What did they do with you?"

"They dragged us to the market, and… made us stand there… stark naked." He covers his face with his hands. "People came up… peered into my mouth, yanked my ears, pinched my bottom. I was only a… child. Maybe five years old." He looks up to the sky as if trying to picture the scene. "An ominous man in a lavish gown and gold jewellery strutted up… like a peacock. He bought me. Then his *vilicus* grabbed me. It was no use trying to escape. Where would I have gone?"

"Of course, you knew nobody there."

"They took me into another vessel. Not in the hold, this time. They fed me and supplied me with clothes, since mine were filthy and flimsy." He looks down at his shabby tunic. "Then they brought me here, to their imposing villa – you must have seen it – on the hill above the town. They lodged me with their other slaves."

"You've been a slave till now?"

"Yes. It must have been about five years. At first it was tolerable." He nods. "I was taught to wash clothes and such things. I wasn't allowed to assist with the cooking, because they had strange rules about how the food had to be prepared and served. But at least I had somewhere to live and food to eat."

He stands and rinses the dishes. "My master, Elazar they called him, was harsh with his slaves, shouting at us and always complaining we hadn't done our cleaning well enough, or whatever. Sometimes he beat us with a cane." He shudders. "Slaves have no right to complain. But it seemed hypocritical that he behaved like that and yet made the family perform religious rites – especially on Saturday, which they said was a day of rest." He settles on a log behind the remains of the fire. "Although, of course, we still had to work. They put on special clothes and lit a strange lamp with many arms. Then they recited sing-song prayers in a language I didn't understand."

"Some sacred ritual?"

"It must have been." He gazes into the distance. "There was a daughter in the family, Sabina. She's only a year or two older than me. My only friend." He shakes his head. "And now I've lost her, too. Sometimes they took me into the family's quarters – the other slaves weren't allowed there – to keep Sabina company." He tosses pebbles towards the stream. "We dressed up her dolls and played together. She taught me to read her scrolls. She sang lovely songs about the one true God. But when I asked her about the Christ, she didn't know what I was talking about. I loved to dance while she played her harp, and that made her laugh. Those were pleasant moments."

"That doesn't sound bad." I throw two figs to the mules to get them away. "Why did you want to escape?"

"Things changed… But I don't want to talk about that."

I shrug. Valerius shivers. The stars are appearing, so I suggest we stay here for the night. I get the mules to lie down near each other and spread one goatskin on the ground between them.

Before he lies down, Valerius faces the sky and chants a strange-sounding song: "*Adonay roei lo echsar. Binot desheh yarbitzaini, al mei menuchot yenahaleini…*"

He goes on and on in a beguiling lilt. When he stops, I ask, "What's all that about? I didn't understand a word."

"It's the language of my people. I don't understand it myself, but my Mother always used to sing to us in the old tongue. I think it's a prayer for safety at night."

He's shy about us sharing a bed and has difficulty lying down. Something is hurting him. He insists on being behind me, so I face towards Hercules and pull my cloak and the other goatskin over us. It's good to have each other to keep warm in the chilly night, and we sleep soundly.

I wake to a bright day and admire the spectacular view of a pretty little bay between wooded hills. In the distance, a merchant ship sails north, and I think I can make out the hazy outline of an island. Could that be Capraria? It looks fascinating.

The mules are feeding nearby.

Only then do I notice that Valerius is no longer next to me. My heart thumps and I jump up. A glance at the bags and panniers shows everything to be as it was last night. His bag is lying where he left it. He wouldn't have gone off without that. Perhaps he's relieving himself behind some bush. I light the fire.

As I make my way down to the brook to fetch water, I'm arrested in my tracks. Valerius is bathing, and hasn't noticed me. Two details make me stop in my tracks.

CHAPTER SEVEN

Stolen Bread

I BLINK MY eyes once, then again. Valerius is still splashing his naked body in the pool.

But... Two red welts line his back, the flesh torn by vicious blows. And... Valerius isn't a boy at all!

For a moment I stand there, gaping. When I get my breath back, I force out some words: "Valerius…"

She screams, curls up and tries to hide in the bushes; then screams again as they prick her.

"Or whoever you are… You need help with those wounds!"

"Oh, I didn't want you to know." She sobs. "Now all is lost. Again. You won't want a girl, especially an injured one for company! Oh, God, have mercy on me!"

"Come on. Don't be silly." I take a step nearer. "All right, you're a girl. So what? Those gashes worry me. They seem inflamed. You need to let me look at them." She cringes. "I have some salve that works wonders." Though my scratches weren't anything like as bad as her welts.

She refuses to leave the pool.

"I'll find the phial. You can wrap yourself up if you're embarrassed." I try to sound comforting. "But you must let me tend to those wounds." I make my way back to our camp and take out the labdanum.

After some time, she appears, wearing a loincloth and holding her tunic in front of her. Her sodden hair draws my attention to her sad eyes and cute face.

"I'm so sorry," she says, biting her lip. "It hurts. I was trying to cleanse the lesions myself, but I can't reach my back."

She lies face-down on the goatskin. I'm struck by how thin her body is, with no flesh covering her ribs. Doing my best not to hurt her, I examine the festering welts. One place, below her left shoulder blade, is oozing pus and worries me. She winces and stifles a scream as I dab it with a wet strip of cotton from the bolt.

"I'm going to put some salve on now. It'll sting at first." She flinches again but doesn't call out.

I cut off a longer strip of cotton and wrap it around her chest – over her tiny breasts – to protect the wounds.

"All right, you were brave." I help her up and put the phial in my bag. "But I'll need to take a look again in the evening."

Whilst she dresses, I cook up some oats and a hot brew of thyme and mint. It's good I bought those beakers. Warm food calms her and does me good, too. After washing the pots and clearing up, I get her to sit opposite me. "So now, my little Valerius, it's time to tell me the truth, starting with your name. And who gave you those lashes."

Her head droops. "Very well." She pulls up her legs into a squatting position. "It's no use concealing things. I'm at your mercy."

"I'm no monster."

"I know. I appreciate your treating my wounds. And not ranting when you saw I wasn't honest." She screws up her face. "God abhors liars. I reckoned I was more likely to escape as a boy." She fingers the back of her neck. "That's why I cut my hair." Her head drops. "I had lovely black locks almost down to my waist."

She falters, tears welling up in her eyes.

I reach out and put a hand on her knee. "Your hair will grow again. I can tidy it up later. But go on."

"My name's Virna."

"Virna. Lovely name."

She nods. "Everything else I said was true." She breathes deeply and turns her head aside. "They murdered my family. And captured and enslaved me when I was five."

"Cruel." I fling a stone towards our pool. "And those wounds, how did you come by them? Was that why you ran away?"

"Well, yes…" She peers at me for a moment with a questioning gaze. "Can it really only have been a few days ago? My mistress took Sabina and the boys over to the mainland for a relative's wedding, I think." She picks up a twig and scribbles in the hard soil. "I had my chores in the kitchen but I was lonely with my friend away."

"Didn't you get on with the other slaves?"

"They weren't unkind, just grownups." She stretches her arm up as far as she can. "We were baking *challah*, so it must have been *dies Veneris*. They need that special bread for their Sabbath celebrations. I don't understand what it's all about. I loved plaiting the dough, although it's not easy.

"Then Laban said the master wanted to see me. That surprised me. I never went into their rooms except with Sabina. I washed my hands, changed from my baking clothes and made my way up to the *oecus*. He was lying on the couch. He smiled at me.

"'You called for me, sir?' I said.

"'Come over here, my dear,' he said in a soft voice. He'd never spoken tenderly to me before. I had to obey. 'Don't be shy!' He grabbed my arm…" She grips hers. "…and pulled me closer, stroking my hair. 'You're a pretty girl, Virna. Soon a beautiful woman. I like your wavy black hair.' I couldn't understand what was happening.

"He offered me wine. I dared not look at him. He wanted me to drink from his goblet. What could I do? I took a sip." She rubs her mouth with the back of her hand. "It was so strong! Not like the watery wine we slaves were given. I nearly choked, and he laughed. He told me to drink more. It made me dizzy. I still had no idea what he had in mind." She sinks her head in her hands.

I move to sit next to her and put my hand on her shoulder. "Take your time. Talking about it will help. It's over now."

"Yes, I suppose so." She's breathing in spasms now. "It's no good pretending it didn't happen." A loud sob shakes her whole body. "I haven't explained the lashes."

"Tell it as it happened."

"Well, I'm only a girl. I don't understand the ways of men with women. He got up, still holding my arm, and took me into his bedroom…"

I wait for her to control her jitters. "Go on."

"I'd only been in there once when their maid was sick. I had to empty the chamber pot and help the mistress with her hair. She's away now, as I said. He… He pulled me to the side of the bed and lay down, muttering silly things about my beautiful eyes and hair." She shakes her head. "He was only wearing a loose bath robe and it was half open. I saw his hairy chest, and… oh!" She screws up her eyes and sobs. "He seemed to be wriggling on purpose so that the robe opened up more and more. I'd never seen a man naked before. Not even my father or my brothers. I tried to turn away, but he still held my arm.

"Then he said: 'It's warm in here.' A good fire was roaring in the grate. 'Wouldn't you like to take off your tunic?' I was so shocked. 'You could snuggle up with me in bed. I'd like that.' I wanted to scream. He grabbed me round the waist and covered my mouth with his free hand. What could I do? A slave daren't disobey her master.

"When he pulled up my tunic, I couldn't stand it anymore. I tore at his face with all my strength and sank my teeth into the hand covering my mouth."

Without thinking, I wince, then say, "Well done!"

"That made him pull back, so I yelled at the top of my voice. He was still holding my tunic with his other hand and he got angry, shouting what an ungrateful, vicious little slut I was. Everyone must have heard, but I guess they were as afraid of him as I was.

"He was so furious, he got up – his robe was just hanging over his shoulders – and grabbed a strigil from the bedside chest. He pressed my face onto the bed with one hand and hit me with his full force across my back. After two blows – my screams were too muffled to be noticed – he must have felt ashamed. I was in agony, shaking and sobbing into the bed linen. I couldn't move. But at least he had stopped tormenting me.

"He said he'd kill me if I told anyone, and sent me out, forbidding me ever to return to their quarters. I could hardly get up, my back ached so much. But somehow I ran down to the slaves' dormitory…"

She needs time before she can go on. "I hid in the corner and wept. It must have been hours. I couldn't bring myself to undress in front of him. It's not proper, is it?"

"Certainly not. Sounds disgusting."

"My back hurt frightfully. But what was I to do?" She holds out her hands, palms up, and looks at them. "What could I do? My only friend was away in Italy. And, in any case, he said I was never to go back to their rooms." She turns to look at me. "I had to escape."

Her big, dark eyes plead for sympathy. "It was the first time I stole anything. I sneaked into the kitchen, took a *challah* fresh from the oven and a knife, and grabbed a bag from near the door. I ran and ran, not knowing where I was going. Out of town and into the woods, hoping no one would find me." She pauses. "I cut off my hair so I wouldn't be recognised." She sniffs. "The rest you know."

I chuckle. "So, it was stolen bread you provided for our first meal together."

Her head hangs. "It was still in the bag. The first day I couldn't eat. I only drank from the stream. My back hurts… especially when I lie down. I tried to make a bed of heather and dry leaves. But it gets so cold at night! I thought I would die." Her gaze is engaging. "You've been so kind."

I bite my lip and drop my gaze, then lift my head and look her in the eye. "I'm so sorry. Really, I am. I didn't want to be cold. I shouldn't have teased you about the bread. What can I say? You've lost your family. You've been harmed by a lewd man. And you've also lost your only friend."

She moves to a kneeling position in front of me. "But now I've found a new one. Is it all right if I call you my friend, Silvanus?"

I place my hands on her shoulders. "Of course. I feel we know each other quite well already. I like you. I admire your courage. Yes, let's be friends."

"Thank you." A spark of joy glints in her tear-swamped eyes. She wipes them and her face brightens. "You never told me what you are up to, here in the woods. Where are you going?"

"Didn't I?" I gaze at my shoes. "Well… Father sent me to Fabricia to sell our wares and to buy new supplies. And now I'm on my way home. We live over west, behind Monte Capanne."

"I see. On your way home…" Her eyes water.

"I'm in no real hurry. They expected me to be away for some time. Let's stay here and talk. Then we can go on together tomorrow. That is, if you want to come with me."

"Oh, may I? I have nowhere else to go."

We leave the mules to graze while we explore our surroundings. Climbing to the top of a rocky crag, we have a good view of Fabricia on the hill to the east.

I point to the port. "See that ship leaving the harbour? I'm sure they had to use the oars to manoeuvre round the point but now they're hoisting the sails. Favonius is showing them favour; they're already filling! Fantastic! I often wonder how he makes the wind blow and how great ships can glide without any effort across the water."

"It's not Favonius, silly. It's God," she says. "But why try to understand how things work? I can't take my eyes off that villa on the hill. Do you see it?" She shudders. "That's where I lived as a slave for five years."

"Oh, really? I noticed it when I was walking up from the harbour one day. It looks fine."

"It is. But I don't miss it. Here I'm free to enjoy the smells, the flowers, the beautiful view. I've never been out like this before. I wouldn't mind staying here with you forever. It's lovely." She jumps up onto a big boulder, raising her slender arms in the air. "Oh, thank you, God Almighty. Thank you for delivering me! And thank you for letting me meet Silvanus. I praise you for this wonderful world you made for us."

"Do you really think your God had something to do with us meeting?" I turn and gaze around. "Perhaps you're right. It's not the sort of thing I expect from Aquila."

Over to the west are higher hills, leading up to majestic Monte Capanne. Its peak is in the clouds. One or two other villages are visible and in the distance another little harbour.

"I've decided to go back a different way." What reason should I give? "Coming here was rather difficult." I'll have to go for the remaining crystals another time. I point over to the right. "We'll take the north path. There's a good mule track Father used last time."

"That's fine. I have no idea about the rest of the island. Everything is exciting for me, if I don't have to be afraid of that tyrant with his evil desires. But will you take me back to your home? Do you think your parents will agree?"

"Well, I'm not sure how Father will take to the idea. I… I'm not on good terms with him these days. But we'll find somewhere for you to live, don't you worry."

In spite of her wounds, Virna is nimble, running and jumping over the boulders and daring me to catch her. I call her over to show her a snake sunning itself on a rock.

When she sees what I'm pointing at, she screams. "I hate snakes. They're creepy."

"They're not at all when you get to know them. Some people think they're evil spirits. Others claim they have healing powers. I love them."

"Aren't they dangerous?"

"Well, yes, this one's a viper and is poisonous. But you don't have to be afraid if you know what you're doing." I pick up a twig and tickle it.

"Hey!" She jumps back as it slithers across the bare rock. "I never thought it could move so fast. How does it do it?"

"I thought you weren't interested in the hows? Don't you believe your God made them like that?"

"Of course He did."

"I've watched snakes a lot and I know how it does it." I place my right fist on my left hand. "When it stretches, its scales stick out." I uncurl my fingers a bit. "When it contracts, they hook onto any rough place or lump, and so it pushes itself farther." Closing my fist again, my hand moves forwards. "It can also wiggle sideways, sort of throwing itself forwards." I wave my arm back and forth. "Once I tempted one with a mouse."

"Yuck! A live mouse? That's cruel!"

"It's not cruel! It's nature. We all have to eat." I snap

the twig and throw it away. "Did you know vipers don't lay eggs like other snakes? Their babies are born alive in the autumn."

She shudders. "Does their mother feed them?"

"Of course not." I laugh. "They have to fend for themselves. They don't eat anything for a few days, until they lose their first skin. Then they sniff around and find what they can – little insects and tiny worms. Later, they stalk up on mice and birds. They snap at them so fast you can't see them move, and then inject their poison. The victim soon goes limp and the little wriggler gobbles it up head first."

"I'm more interested in all these fascinating plants." It hurts her to bend, but she plucks some sage leaves and smells them. "We can collect some and make a nice soup."

"You can. I have a different idea. Let's see who gets the tastier ingredients."

Leaving her to her proposition, I run back to our camp for a knife and a length of twine. Rabbit droppings litter the brush and I soon find a path they frequent, leading to a burrow. An upside down gorse bush rigged across the track makes a suitable snare, and I fit a noose made from the twine.

As the warm afternoon advances, rabbits appear on all sides, scuttling around among the heather, broom and rockrose, nibbling grasses and herbs. A pair of eagles – probably some of Kili and Kwee's offspring – notice them, too, circling overhead, awaiting their chance. I watch from behind a boulder. Each time an eagle swoops low, the rabbits scurry off into their burrows, following their well-used paths. A short time later, forgetting the danger, they come out again to feed.

When I've almost lost hope of snaring one – afraid Virna will win the cooking competition – both the male eagle and I are in luck. He catches a large buck and soars off, his mate following him. Terrified, a young rabbit flees straight into my trap and gets caught in the noose. I grab it as it kicks and squeals, slit its throat and drain out the blood.

Back at our site, I'm met by a delicious aroma from Virna's soup. She found acorns, chicory root, garlic and asparagus, flavouring it with sage and thyme. I skin, clean, and cut up the rabbit, adding it to the stew. We enjoy a tasty meal and a hot rosemary drink.

Before the light fails, I insist on changing Virna's dressing. She submits without resistance. Her wounds hurt more in the evening. They are still red and sore, and she winces as I apply the salve and bandage her up again.

Again, she chants her goodnight prayer. My whole body tingles as she snuggles up behind me between the goatskins with her arm around me.

CHAPTER EIGHT

Almost Part of the Family

I WAKE EARLY, troubled by dreams of dancing girls in flimsy robes. Did the rosemary not agree with me? Or is it that I've never shared a bed with a girl before? Virna is fast asleep, her arm still on my chest. She's only a child, like Little Eli. What has come over me?

She wakes as I rise and smiles at me. "Is it morning already? I could have lain here for ages."

I run to the pool to wash out the foul-smelling discharge from my loincloth.

She's still between the goatskins when I return. "Get up!" I clap my hands. "I can't wait around for you all morning." To calm my irritation, I stir up the fire and cook some oats. "Come on! We've got a long road ahead of us." My voice is croaky. "And I still have to tend your back."

Consternation shows in her eyes but she lets me examine her wounds, flinching when I touch them. Perhaps my mood makes me callous. She doesn't complain.

As soon as we've eaten, we load the mules and retrace our steps through the thick undergrowth and massive pines to the path we left two days earlier. On we go, over wooded hills, which hide the view of the coast most of the time. Only the ever-rising sun at our backs assures us we are heading in a westward direction. The occasional wayfarer, hastening on his own business, passes us with a murmured greeting. No one is surprised by what looks like two lads leading overladen mules away from town.

"I've come this way before," I remark. "Did I tell you that?"

"You did. But tell me about your family." Her voice trembles. "I miss my people."

"It… it must be so hard with no one who cares about you."

"Oh, don't *you*?"

"Well yes, of course I do." My disturbing dreams still cramp me, but I try to be kind. "You're so full of life and fun. I like that. But we've only just met. It's not the same as a family… people who have known you all your life…"

She wipes her eyes and turns away.

"I'm sorry, I didn't want to upset you."

"It's… it's not your fault." Another sniff. "I feel so lonely."

No words of comfort come to me.

It's an uphill path and Hercules often needs encouragement, which I provide with my stave across his rump. He's got used to a lazy life these last few days. Crispus follows with Virna at his side.

The weather is fair with an occasional puffy cloud. Here and there the trees open up and we glimpse the deep blue sea. I point out Capraria in the distance. "Someday, I want to go there."

"I'm happy enough staying here." Virna rests her arm on Crispus's back. "Now I'm free and no one's trying to hurt me." An idea seems to come to her mind. "Do you have brothers and sisters?"

"Only Eliana – Little Eli I call her. She's about your age. A silly girl with nonsense in her head, but I love her a lot."

"Do you play with her? Or what do you do when you're at home?"

70

"Well, I have a lot of work with our crops. Especially these days. When I'm finished I like to go exploring with my friends Rufus and Pontus."

"What about Eliana then? Do you leave her all alone?"

"She often plays with Lucilla. That's Pontus's little sister. She's a lot of fun, too. Sometimes the girls join us when we go to the waterfall or collect nuts or whatever. Caesar comes, too. He loves to chase rabbits and play in the pool."

"Who's Caesar?"

"Our dog. He's almost part of the family. He's meant to be a watchdog – chasing the wild boar and goats off our vegetables – but he's not as good as Cori."

"Cori?" She chuckles. "Who's that?"

"My tame raven. Although by now he's adopted the whole family. I found him when he was a chick and had pity on him because he seemed to have been abandoned." I reach up to pick some ripe fruit from an overhanging strawberry tree and offer one to Virna. "He eats almost anything, but grapes are his favourite. Now he doesn't want to leave."

"But a grown-up raven is huge. Aren't you afraid of him?"

"No. He's not dangerous. But he's cheeky, jumping out on Mother when she isn't expecting it and stealing Little Eli's jewellery."

"Oh, I'd love to meet Eliana."

"Well, you will in a day or two. Cori often perches in our oak tree, then warns us when there's anything unusual around. He's even learned to talk a bit! He shouts: 'Silé! Dinner time!'"

"Silé. I like that. Can I call you Silé?"

"If you like. That's what my friends call me."

She breaks off a sprig of some sweet-smelling herb I don't recognise and, later, a branch of an elderberry bush still bearing a dried-up bunch of black berries. "You talk a lot about animals. Do they mean more to you than people?"

"I'm not sure. I find it fascinating to watch their antics – where they live, what they eat, how they mate and raise their young. With mice and rabbits and things like that, the mothers feed their babies with their milk, you know."

She flicks my neck with the leafy branch in her hand. "I'm not that stupid!"

I turn around, surprised at her nerve, and wave my stave at her. "Watch out! I have a bigger stick than you."

She only laughs.

"What was I saying? But perhaps you don't know that eagles – all birds, in fact – also take care of their young for weeks. Not with milk, of course."

"How, then?"

"They catch a dormouse or a frog and chew it, then throw it up into the chicks' mouths, when they're small."

She turns up her nose in an amusing grimace. "Sounds disgusting!"

"Lizards and things like that don't bother with their babies at all. When they hatch, they have to survive as best they can without any help. Most of them starve or get eaten."

"I wonder if that's how God meant it to be? Struggling to survive, killing and eating, abandoning babies to fend for themselves." She pops another strawberry fruit into her mouth and chews it slowly. "At least with people it's different. Parents care for their children until they can manage by themselves." She says nothing for a moment, then murmurs, "Except in my case."

"Yes, you see, people aren't that much better than animals." Too late, I realise I've again been unkind. "In some ways people are worse. Animals kill to eat, but they don't make war on one another like we do. And what for? To be able to say this bit of land belongs to me now? It's stupid, if you ask me."

"Animals don't murder each other and take little girls as slaves, either."

I don't know what to say.

Here the trees are thinner. Far below us is a tiny fishing harbour, a few scattered houses and cultivated fields.

"You haven't said much about your parents," she says after a while.

"No…" Painful recollections trouble me. "Well, Mother is always busy cooking our food, spinning wool from the goat hair, weaving cloth for blankets or clothes."

"Did she make that cloak of yours?"

I glance at it, slung across Crispus's load, as we sweat and pant our way up the steep path. "Yes. Who else?"

"I… I had nothing at all when I was taken captive. Until the master provided decent clothes for us." She tries to rub dirt from her tunic. "But, now I've only got these rags. Does Eliana have chores to do, too?"

"Of course. We all need to help feed the hens, weed and water the vegetables, pick the grapes and things like that. Mother can't do everything by herself."

"Does she love you?"

"What sort of question is that? Of course she loves us." I frown. "She mends our clothes, comforts us when we're upset. She even gives us her own food when there isn't enough to go around. Says she's not hungry, but I don't believe her."

"We always had plenty of food."

"Most of the time we do too. But when the winter is long, we sometimes run out of grain. And the vegetables in the field wither. Maybe we still have some dried goat meat. Or we collect late fruit and nuts and roots and things in the woods." My gaze scans the vista before us. "Some people go fishing or collect shellfish. But that's not so easy in winter, either."

"Are there many other families where you live, then?"

"Not many. Two, no, three, with little children. And some older couples whose children have left home. We don't have much to do with them. Then there's Pontus and Lucilla. Their father, Brutus, is the village carpenter and their mother mills the cereals. And Rufus – he lives with his father. His older brothers and sister have moved away. His mother got sick and died a few years ago."

"That must have been tough for him." Her big dark eyes reflect her sympathy.

"He's got over it." I never gave it much thought. "We all help each other as best we can and share what we have."

"Is that the whole village, then?"

"There's also Uncle Aelius. He does all sorts of odd jobs. And, of course, Aunt Ceres. She has no family." I frown. "She's the priestess of Jupiter – or Aquila, as she calls him. She's also our teacher. A bit of a monster. I don't like her."

"Your teacher? What sort of things do you learn?"

"We read Vergilius's dreary old poetry. That's all she has. And learn to write, of course."

"So you can read those philosophers?"

"I can make out the words, but I can't always get the meaning." I shrug. "I think she doesn't understand them herself. Pontus makes some sense of them. He's bright."

"What's the point of reading then?" She shakes her head. "At least the verses Sabina taught me to read were encouraging. They turned my heart to God."

"Ceres tries to make us believe in her Gods. Aquila's her favourite. She makes us bring him offerings to per-suade him to give us a good harvest, and not to harm us." I take out my pendant. "This amulet is supposed to protect me when he's angry."

"That's nonsense!"

"Well, I don't want to risk offending him." I finger the talisman. "He glares down at us all the time from the mountains. I wouldn't be surprised if he sees everything I do. Perhaps he knows all I think and say. I think he has favourites and pet hates."

"I'm not afraid of those silly Gods." She kicks a stone away. "How old are you, anyway? Your voice seems to be going funny sometimes."

"I can't help that. I'm fourteen."

"And you trade your goods alone at that age? That's great." She peers at me. "What about your father?"

"Yes, Father." I sigh. "I used to love him so much."

She stops and peers at me. "Don't you love him anymore?"

"I… I'm not sure. He used to be my hero. I thought he knew everything and could do anything. I was so excited when he told me he would take me with him to Fabricia a few years ago. We had such a good time then."

"And now?"

We rest a moment in the shade of a lone pine tree. "I wish I knew. He's changed so much in the last year. Now he always seems to be angry, shouting at us for no reason. I'm worried he might hurt Mother or Little Eli one of these days."

"Did something happen to make him change?"

"Well, yes." How much dare I say? "We… We live on a steep, rocky hillside." I point at a hill to our left. "For generations, I guess, our people have built little terraces all the way up the slopes to make patches of flat soil for vines. They get damaged by the rain and the wild boar, so we have to keep repairing them."

"That must be tedious."

"It's tiring." I rub my back as I struggle to my feet and urge the mules on, realising they'll soon need a drink. "Well, earlier this year he… fell and broke his leg." I look away. "He… he had to drag himself down."

"Didn't anyone see? Surely he shouted?"

"After a while, Mother heard him and went out to help. His leg was all twisted. She bandaged it as best she could with splints. Ceres sacrificed two chickens and our last oats at Aquila's shrine; she said Father must have done something to offend him and this was his punishment."

"I'm glad I don't have to believe in such a cruel God," Virna says. "Did the ritual do any good?"

"I doubt it. At any rate, Father stayed in bed for several months. Ever since then he's been getting more and more bitter. Now I have to tend the vines by myself. It's not fair. Working with those big stones all day. I want to be with my friends."

She nods.

"Since he's stuck in the house, he tells Mother off about everything. Like how she treats us children. He keeps screaming at Little Eli when she comes in to play; he wants her to be out working in the vegetable patch or feeding the animals all the time."

"Poor Little Eli. So you're not happy at home?"

"Our life has become so miserable that I go off into the hills whenever I can. I love to watch the eagles… the snakes… and the ships sailing past. And I dream…"

The sun is high overhead as we pass a gurgling brook. The mules need a drink. We sit on a rock under the shade of a great cork oak and share the last nuts and figs. I fill up my water skin and pass it to Virna before taking a long drink myself. It's good to have a break from the hot climb.

Virna prances around collecting twigs from different shrubs, all the while humming a tune and sometimes adding words I can't make out. She sings on as she weaves a wreath, decorating it with bright berries and cones. I take out my knife and cut a straight stick from a young willow sapling. Intrigued by what Virna is doing, I make a few cuts in the twig and soften the bark in my mouth. Gentle tapping loosens it and I soon fashion a whistle. I try to play the tune of Virna's song.

76

She rushes up, laughing, her colourful wreath adorning her black hair. "How did you make that?"

"It's easy. Father taught me when I was little."

She reaches out to take it. "Let me try."

"Careful. It's not very strong."

She takes it from me and soon can produce simple tunes. "That's wonderful. You can play for me and I'll sing."

All of a sudden, her face darkens and she seems far away. "Mother used to sing so beautifully at bedtime. I still remember her songs. About God's love." She's fighting tears. "Sabina taught me some songs like that, too. Did I tell you she plays the harp? It makes such a beautiful sound. I couldn't help dancing. Those songs gave me such joy and hope."

"Hope? Although you were a slave and had lost your family?"

"Yes. They helped me believe there's a better world somewhere. That I'd see Mother and Father again. And all our worries would be over." Her raven eyes seem to penetrate my breast. "What do you dream of, Silé?"

I turn away. "Different things." I don't admit what I dreamt last night. "Of leaving home, sailing to far-off lands where I can be free from Father's bickering. I think a lot about why I'm here at all, and what's the purpose of life. And what will become of me when I'm older."

"I've never thought of tomorrow. All I wanted was to stay alive. Never imagined I'd be free one day."

"I can't talk with my friends about such things, they're not interested. Rufus is strong and practical – he's almost a man now, afraid of nothing and useful when there's hard work to be done. Pontus is always trying to understand how things work. Like why the sun gets higher in summer than in the winter or how to build some contraption for diverting the stream to water our fields."

"Boy talk!"

"I suppose. All I know is, I don't want to spend my whole life in our miserable little village, nursing an injured father and doing heavy work all day. I want to be free, to travel, to have adventures and enjoy life. The wide world is beckoning me."

"The raiders' ship cured me of wanting to travel. I'd love to have a simple home where I'm safe. No cruel men or silly Gods to worry about."

"You don't believe in our Gods, then? Mercury, Mars, Venus, and Jupiter, or Aquila the Avenger as he's known around here? And all the others."

"Certainly not. There's only one God. And He loves us."

"One God. How can you be so sure?" I jerk my arm out in derision. "And if he loves us, why is life so cruel, so miserable?"

"I can't explain it. I was so small when they took me away." She shrugs her shoulders. "But He watches over me. He helps me. That's why you cared for me."

"That's stupid. I just saw you were frightened and hungry, so I helped. Neither your God nor my Aquila had anything to do with it."

Her head drops. "I'm not clever enough to argue with you."

Her ideas and her assurance baffle me. They're so different from what I've been taught. I remain silent.

Setting off again, we come to a fork. We take the higher route up to the left, although it's rather steep and rugged. The other branch leads down to a village and the small harbour we had seen earlier.

The evening sun dazzles us when it penetrates the shrubs, strawberry trees and massive oaks around us. The path is washed away here and there by angry streams. We walk in single file, me leading Hercules, Virna with Crispus, with only the occasional remark about the vegetation or the mules. The day wanes and, as we continue to rise, the vegetation thins and the path flattens out. A grove of tall pines has shut out the sunlight over the centuries, and what little there is in the way of undergrowth has barely managed to raise its head. Secluded behind a huge fallen tree, we unload the mules and kindle a fire for a much-needed meal of lentils. Virna says her wounds are still painful, and I do my best in the poor light to tend to them. Then we settle down for another night's rest between the goatskins. This time, I'm not troubled by carnal dreams; I'm too tired. Virna never seems to have trouble sleeping.

I wake, refreshed, much more relaxed than yesterday. Virna opens her eyes and smiles as soon as I stir. She lets me dress her wounds, then prepares a warm breakfast spiced with herbs she collected on the way.

Apart from the occasional spot with a partial view to the coast, we are shrouded by high trees and thick bushes. Soon we notice signs that the path is more frequented. Another track joins ours as we struggle up a muddy ravine littered with large boulders and fallen trees.

"Footprints," I shout. "Several people. Came up this valley and joined our path."

All four of us come to a sudden halt as a loud honking bursts forth from somewhere ahead. I've never heard anything like it. It must be an alarm call of some animal. We huddle together and try to stop the mules from bolting. The uncanny clamour is repeated.

CHAPTER NINE

Sage and Time

WE TREMBLE, PARALYSED by the mysterious hornlike call.

"Wait here." I grip my sturdy stave. "I'll–I'll go and see." As I scout around, scrambling over boulders and between spiny shrubs, the scary cry recurs. It comes from higher up the hillside to my left. My heart is pounding, but I press on.

A moment later I jump, biting my lip, startled by a totally different sound... loud, deep-throated laughter. My head snaps round in the direction it came from, expecting to see a madman. But there's nothing insane about this guffaw. On the contrary, it's warm and welcoming.

This is confirmed by the cheery words in an old man's voice. "*Salve!* Did my watchmen alarm you?" A chortle interrupts whoever it is addressing me. "So, have you decided to come at last, my son?"

"*Salve!*" I peer around. "Who are you? I... I can't see you..."

"I was led to believe there would be two of you."

"How...?" The rocky hillside reveals no human figure. "Well, yes, my friend is waiting below."

"My limbs are no longer as nimble as they used to be. Please join me here in my humble villa, and ask your friend to come too. Don't be afraid. We'll have time for explanations."

"Thank you," I call back. "But we can't leave the mules alone."

"Indeed, indeed." Still no one visible. "In my advanced years, I overlook such worldly matters. Indeed, you should unload them."

"Er… We're just passing through. I'm on my way home." I look back to where Virna is waiting. "There's no need to unload the mules. We–we'll be moving on."

"After venturing so far to meet me? Unthinkable!" Again, that jolly chortle. "Out of the question. Quite out of the question. Do please accept my invitation so that we may talk at ease. Your beasts will come to no harm *in situ* until we find a better solution."

It makes no sense. Yet the self-assurance and the warmth of this voice are compelling. I go back for Virna.

"I heard you talking to someone."

"Some old man up there thinks we should visit him."

"Who is he? What does he want with us?" She frowns. "Can we trust him?"

"I really don't know." I shake my head. "But something about him makes me feel we should."

We tie the mules to an overhanging tree and climb up the steep slope to meet this mysterious host.

A stooped man in a full-length grey robe waits outside a simple cave. His flowing hair and dishevelled beard contrast with his warm smile and twinkling – somehow penetrating – eyes. He spreads his arms wide. "At last, at last! Welcome to my abode."

Virna holds back. "What do you want with us?"

His warm gaze disarms her. With a sweep of his arm he indicates a rough boulder, barely sheltered by a rickety aw-ning of unhewn branches, pine twigs and dry ferns. "Please be seated. A throne for you, sir, and one for the lady."

We glance around, then sit on the rock, staring at this strange but charming figure. How does he know Virna is a girl?

She pulls her knees up to her chest as two large white birds of a kind I've never seen before snap at our legs. From their deep clucking sounds, I realise it was they that startled us with that alarming honking.

"Don't be afraid; my guards won't hurt you," our host assures us. "Allow me to introduce ourselves. This is Dela and over there is Runel. My guardian geese." He reaches out as Dela waddles up to have her neck scratched. "Ah, and no doubt you are wondering who I am…" He suppresses a chuckle. "I am known as Cerbonius. And this is my mansion!" His arm sweeps round, pointing to the cave.

"Cerbonius? That sounds familiar." I screw up my face, then snap my fingers. "The farmer's wife… in the market square in Fabricia. She spoke of a Bishop Cerbonius who lived in a cave."

I glance around at his meagre habitation, at a loss for words. "I didn't imagine anything like this." I pull myself together. "And, please excuse my rudeness, sir. My name is Silvanus. And this is my friend Virna."

"My pleasure to meet you at last, Silvanus. And your charming companion, Virna. My pleasure."

"You speak as if you expected us, sir. How can that be?" I lay my stave on the rock and gaze at our host.

He laughs. "All in good time, all in good time. My Friend let me know you two would be coming."

"But… no one can have known that," I argue. "We didn't even decide to come this way until a short time ago. We could just as easily have taken the lower path down to the coast."

"So you may imagine! When you see the light, my lad, you'll discover causes are often not evident. Oh no, very often not. Powers exist of which many people are ignorant." Twirling his beard, he continues, "Or of which they prefer to remain ignorant." He hobbles around, looking for something. "Yes, primal powers. Later you will understand. I fear false guides have misled you in the past. Dark lights. It's no doubt for this very reason you were led to me. To discover the true light."

"I have no idea what you are talking about, sir. In fact, I fear you may be mistaken. Nobody guided us to you." I stand. "We really should be moving on. I'm concerned about leaving the mules alone for too long."

"*Festina lente!* No haste, my lad, no haste! I'll not force you to stay. But it would be in your best interest. A heavy burden is troubling you, I believe."

I cock my head. "What sort of burden? And how can you help?"

"Trust me, my son. Since my Friend informed me you were coming, I assume He intends this encounter to bring you relief. But before we weary ourselves with chatter, let us take some refreshment."

"We have grain and spices with us." Virna's voice takes me by surprise. Has the old man won her heart? She smiles at me before continuing. "I would be happy to prepare a meal. I see you have a hearth."

His eyes twinkle. "Your young companion may well be more advanced than you on that path of enlightenment. But you will reach the goal in time. Yes, one day you will reach the goal."

Then, to Virna, "Yes, my dear, please go ahead."

She clambers down to fetch the ingredients, her awkward movements reminding me she is still in pain.

"But what did you imply before, sir?" I ask, when she is out of earshot. "Is she better than me because she likes to cook?"

He is so overcome with amusement he clutches his belly and has trouble speaking. "No, no! No, no! It's nothing to do with her culinary skills! Nothing at all. But you will come to understand in time. In time." He leans closer and speaks in a hushed tone. "I see your merry companion is hurt."

"Yes. She was struck by her master and her wounds are festering."

"I fear she needs treatment."

"I have been dressing her lashes with labdanum salve," I say. I light the fire in the hearth and gather fallen branches from the surrounding woods as Virna sets about cooking. Cerbonius observes us in silence.

When the potage is ready, Virna pours watered wine into three goblets and we sit around the steaming pot. She brings out the remains of the stolen loaf.

"*Challah!*" Cerbonius raises his eyebrows. "Did you make this yourself?"

Virna nods. "Well, yes and no! I formed the dough. And when it was baked, I… I snatched it from my master's kitchen… and ran away."

Another chuckle. "A runaway slave serving us stolen goods! I seem to have the honour of entertaining remarkable guests."

Cerbonius raises his hands, faces the sky and shouts out, "All praise and honour to you, almighty Lord, Creator, Redeemer, Paraclete. You, who search the hearts of men and graciously draw us to yourself, I thank you for leading these your chosen son and worthy daughter to my humble home. You see their plight. Grant them the grace of your forgiveness, I pray, and favour them with your many blessings. For this, your generously provided food, whether honestly or fraudulently obtained…" Virna gapes wide-eyed, while I struggle to suppress a laugh. "We offer thanks from grateful hearts in the name of your Son, my Friend, Jesus Christ. Amen."

Turning back to us, he adds, "Please help yourselves from this grand meal our young guest has prepared."

I dip pieces of bread in the pot. "It's very tasty."

Cerbonius's amiable tone has put me at ease and loosened my tongue. "When I was sent to bring our wares to market, I took the southern flank of Monte Capanne. As it turned out, this wasn't the best idea. But it took me past Kili and Kwee's hunting grounds."

"Kili and Kwee?" Cerbonius interrupts. "Strange names indeed."

"They're my eagles. Real eagles, not like Aquila. I think of them as mine, since I know them so well," I say. "And sure enough, I saw Kili soaring and swooping for prey." I glide my arm through the air. "I could watch him for hours – how he can master the sky like that always baffles me."

Cerbonius nods, giving me his full attention.

"But then the storm came." I cringe as I recollect that moment. "Aquila threw boulders down on us. I was terrified. Another of the Gods – I doubt it was Aquila – led us to a cave where we sheltered for two days until the waters had abated."

"You were there for two days? What did you do there?"

"Well, a day and two nights." I don't want to exaggerate. "I… explored the area around the cave. It used to be a mine, I think, a long time ago."

"And then?"

"As soon as we could cross the gorge, we set off east, over a series of hills." I avoid going into any more detail. "I had fantastic views over the rest of the island. And Corsa, Planasia and Mons Jovis."

"You know those islands?"

"Only by name. I've never left Ilva. A couple of merchant ships sailed past. Oh, how I wish to have a boat of my own and learn to harness the wind." I shake my head, then gaze towards the horizon, now lost in mist. "The wide world is out there waiting, and I'm stuck in a faraway corner of a little island, looking after goats and repairing terraces."

"But you did go as far as Fabricia, I believe."

How does he know? My brows furrow. "That's right, I sold my wares and bought what we needed. Then, on the way home, I met Virna, here."

"Silvanus was very kind to me," she remarks. "He shared his food and tended to my back."

"I noticed you were in pain."

"Yes. But… that's another story." She shudders and pauses before continuing. "We enjoyed our time together. And he taught me a lot about snakes and things."

"Snakes? Is that another interest of yours, lad?"

"Yes. They intrigue me," I say. "How they glide across the rocks with so little effort."

He claps his hands. "Eagles, snakes, and ships. You are in good company, my boy. As the wise man said, *tria sunt difficilia mihi – viam aquilae in caelo, viam colubri super petram, viam navis in medio mari…* Three things are beyond me – the way of an eagle in the sky, the way of a snake on a rock, the way of a ship at sea." His eyes twinkle. "And I dare say the fourth matter will preoccupy you in due course!"

"I don't know what you're talking about."

"Of course not. The time will come. Did you conduct that trade yourself? How old are you, lad?"

"Fourteen, sir."

"You were indeed entrusted with a demanding mission. How were you able to master it?"

"I've gone with my father every autumn for the last few years, so I have some experience." I lower my eyes. "This time he… couldn't come."

Cerbonius's eyes penetrate my soul. "And what were your feelings on being sent to do this task alone?"

"I… I was anxious. I didn't know if I could cope for days, sleeping rough and providing for myself."

"Nevertheless, you did survive. What else?"

"I was angry." My fists clench. "It wasn't fair for a boy of my age…"

"And…?"

"And afraid… of Aquila."

Cerbonius points at my pendant. "I see you wear his motif."

My hand moves involuntarily to the talisman. "Ceres – my aunt – gave me it. I have to wear it until I am of age."

"The priestess Ceres is your aunt?" His bushy eyebrows rise and he nods. "I see… I begin to see…"

"Is she a friend of yours?"

"Only inasmuch as every man is my brother and every woman my sister. No, I don't know her except on hearsay." He continues to nod. "Tell me, why do you fear Aquila?"

I frown. "Well… he never leaves me in peace. He watches everything I do. And… he tries to make my life miserable. I think he hates me."

Virna suppresses a giggle.

I glare at her. "And you can stop mocking me!"

"Moderate your tone, dear friends. I would like to understand the matter deeper. Do you present offerings or petitions to Aquila, Silvanus? Have you evidence he wishes you ill?"

"We have to bring gifts to his shrine on feast days. And whenever something is threatening us like bad weather or sickness, for instance. And…" My eyes pan from the pendant to meet his. "Well, when I was alone in the storm, I did ask him to help me."

"You prayed to that lifeless idol?" Virna glares at me with her dark eyes. "You never told me!"

"Why should I? I don't tell you everything I do. You're too little to understand. And only a girl, anyway. What's it to you?"

"Come now, my dears. Let's lay down our swords and enjoy our meal in peace. Then I see there is need for action on my part." He raises his goblet. "Oh Lord God, bless and consecrate this cup that it may bring peace to all who share it. And as we call on your Holy Name, grant that we who drink it may experience health of soul and body. Through Christ my Friend. Amen."

Virna also mumbles, "Amen."

We finish our meal in subdued silence. Suddenly, Cerbonius claps his hands. "The mules! I almost forgot. Silvanus, doubtless you can handle them yourself. Lead them some three or four stadia farther along the same path you were on." He points west. "It's flat and safe. When you arrive at a clearing, you will see a cottage, partly concealed among trees. Announce yourself as a friend of Cerbonius and ask the good people to tend to the beasts. Marcus will be pleased to oblige and will help you unload them. As a brother in Faith, he is fully trustworthy. Then return here with whatever you need for the night."

My head jerks back and I stare at him. "I don't understand. You expect us to stay with you here overnight?"

"No, son, only you." He pats my shoulder. "Virna will be leaving us."

"What?" I cry out, as Virna's hands shoot up to cover a gasp.

"Don't be alarmed. The little lady has urgent need of help, and, as I observe, you don't see eye to eye about certain important matters."

"But… you can't separate us at your whim," I protest.

"It wouldn't be right for her to spend the night here with two men."

"She was coming home with me."

"Nor can you journey on together in your present state of discord."

Virna grabs my hand. "We're still friends. I have no other friend than Silvanus."

With a firm but gentle movement, Cerbonius releases her grip, then places both his hands on her shoulders, fixing her eyes with his gaze. "My assistant, Titus, is about to arrive. He'll take you to Mother Martha's House of Healing. She'll care for you, body and soul. But I still have certain matters to discuss with you while Silvanus stables the mules. You'll leave before he returns. Would you like to say goodbye now?"

I'm at a loss for words. Virna bursts into tears. After a moment, she turns to Cerbonius, sobbing. "Would you have a *menafa*?"

He reaches into a wooden chest, takes out a small flannel and offers it to her, then places his arm around her shoulders and nods his head. "I thought so, I thought so."

I'm baffled by this exchange but let it go.

"It's best for both of you," Cerbonius adds.

When she recovers from her sobs, she gazes at me, her dark eyes pleading. "Oh Silé!" She shakes her head. "I've been a brute. I mocked you for fearing that God of yours, Aquila, or whatever he's called. Please forgive me. I'm most grateful to you. You saved my life. You did." Another sob rocks her. "But the good Father is right when he says we must part. Go home with your purchases. I don't know what will become of me, but I trust our host. Farewell, dear Silé. Who knows, we may meet again sometime."

"Virna, I… I like you. I… thought we were friends. It was fun with you for those few days. I… I don't understand how meeting this man has made us fall out. But I'm afraid you are right. Our ways must part." I take her hands in mine. "*Vale*, Virna. I hope you get better soon and enjoy a healthy life."

And so, I leave to deal with the mules. I glance back once. Virna catches my eye and we each raise a hand in parting. Is this the last I'll see of her? How is it I accept Cerbonius's proposition without further question?

I find the hut without difficulty, and Marcus and his wife, Maria, welcome me. We unload the animals and tether them in an outhouse, a stable for Marcus's goats when the weather is severe. Hercules and Crispus guzzle the oats and water Marcus offers them. I take my cloak and the goatskins, and make my way back to the cave.

Virna is nowhere to be seen.

CHAPTER TEN

Recollections

MY HEAD HANGS as I approach the dying fire.

Cerbonius raises his eyes. "My dear Silvanus, the events of this day have troubled you. Trust that I wish the very best for you. Come, sit here next to me."

I sit in silence and gaze across the treetops to the vanishing sea.

"You were fond of little Virna."

"Why did you send her away?" I clench my fists. "We were friends."

"She is indeed a little jewel. She told me of her tragic life. And of her master's ill-treatment." After some moments, he adds, "And now I know. *Menafa*. How strange."

"What's that supposed to mean?"

"That is precisely the point." He chuckles. "You don't know the meaning. It's an ancient Carthaginian word for a napkin or small piece of cloth. So her dialect told me she comes from the same great city as I – Carthago, that most majestic port of Africa." He nods, communing with his own thoughts. "Though our Byzantine forces recaptured the city from the Vandals thirty years ago, the *Mauri* have continued to raid." He seems hardly aware of my presence as he continues, "It was her dark skin that first led me to suspect it. The brooch she has from her mother – she cried as she showed it to me – it depicts the Holy Spirit as a dove."

"So she's from Africa? I'm sorry she left. I did like her. And I'm worried for her."

"She is in good hands."

I remain locked in reflection. Then Cerbonius's earlier remarks come to mind. "You are right, sir, I do bear a burden. More than one."

"I'm listening."

"I'm angry and troubled about some of the things that happened in Fabricia."

"But that's not what's bothering you most."

I gaze at him, perplexed. How does he know my thoughts? "You're right. What bothers me most is having to face Father."

"I thought as much," he says, to my consternation. Does he know of our quarrel? "Is your father the brother of Ceres?"

"He is. But that has nothing to do with it."

"Are you certain?" A penetrating glare. "I think I first owe you some explanation as to how I was expecting you both."

"Yes, I was going to ask you."

"From childhood you have been brought up to fear the Gods. Especially Aquila. Is that not so?"

I nod.

"As such, you are familiar with transcendent powers."

I frown at his difficult words.

He sweeps his arm from sky to earth and rests it on his chest. "Powers in the heavens. Powers, perhaps, in in- animate objects. Powers that rage in our hearts. Powerful spirit beings, whom we cannot normally see."

Captivated, I stare at him.

"I'll not persuade you to renounce the beliefs you have been taught." He clasps his hands together, his elbows on his knees. "But I know another power at work in this world. Much more than a power. A Friend." He looks up and catches my gaze. "We don't see Him, but He sees us. He watches us with kindness and generosity. I talk with Him often and try to heed His Word. I tell Him my joy at the beauty of the many creatures He has made. Such as your snakes and eagles. He is indeed the Great Creator." He stretches his arm out over the magnificent vista.

"Without fail, He provides for my needs," he continues. "And even for some of my desires." He chuckles. "One morning, after I had expressed my wish to be alerted of approaching visitors, He sent me my faithful Dela and Runel." The geese look up as he mentions their names and come waddling over. He nods at them. "You provide me every day with an egg or two. Thank you."

He turns to me. "And surely it was my Friend who moved Virna to supply this day's potage – from your reserves, no doubt." His head nods as he chuckles. "I had nothing to offer you."

"I'm glad we could be of service."

"It was my Friend made me understand some days ago that I was to receive a visitor – a young lad in need of advice, who was troubled by a great burden." He nods. "This morning, before daybreak, as I was praising Him for granting me a new day, He let me know there would be a second visitor – a girl. Whether He caused you to come or merely forewarned me by His eternal providence, I cannot tell. Yet come you did!"

I screw up my face. "You talk with this unseen power, and it answers you?"

"Dear child, He desires you to meet Him. You are at the threshold of His path of enlightenment." He places his hand on my shoulder. "One Word I leave with you, before we sleep, for the day is waning. Tomorrow you will proceed on your homeward journey, with this Word in your heart, until we meet again. 'To all who received him, who believed in his name, he gave the right to become sons of God; they are born not of blood, nor of the will of the flesh, nor of the will of man but of God.'" He recites it again. "Can you remember that?"

I frown as I puzzle over the meaning, then try to quote what he said. "To all who received him, he gave the right to become sons of God…" I hesitate. "…Who are not born of man, but of God. It's not quite right, I know."

Patiently, he repeats it, prompting me where I'm uncertain.

"I've got it now." An idea springs to mind. "May I also write it down?"

"You know how to write?" He claps his hands and adopts a pensive stance. "Wonderful!"

"Ceres has taught me to read and write. But she has no such inspiring texts as this." I see before me those hateful scrolls of hers. "I left my tablet with the mules. Perhaps I can do it tomorrow. For now, I'll think about those words in my heart."

"Very good, my son. Do you have what you need for the night? Make yourself comfortable over there." He indicates a flat area under the awning, then unrolls his own mattress and spreads it out in his corner. "I'll close the day with the prayer my Friend taught us. Afterwards, let us remain silent."

Raising his arms towards the heavens, he again adopts a kind of chanting. "Our Father in heaven, may your name be kept Holy. May your Kingdom come soon. May your will be done on earth, as it is in heaven. Give us today the food we need, and forgive us our sins, as we forgive those who sin against us. And don't let us yield to temptation, but rescue us from the evil one. Amen."

As my host takes to his bed, I settle between my goatskins, wondering what will become of Virna. I reflect on those words of promise Cerbonius gave me – sons of God – but also on that last, powerful prayer addressed to a Father in heaven.

The words still dance around my mind *Sons of God... Our Father in heaven... we forgive those who sin against us...*

I'm woken by a strange chanting coming from some way off. I blink, adjusting to the dim, pre-dawn light. Cerbonius's bed is rolled in the corner. He must have risen early.

The flickering light of a lantern reveals Cerbonius kneeling on top of a rock, obviously praying to his God. For a moment he's silent. Then he rises, stretches his arms high in the air and shouts with a tremor of elation.

I shake my head. What is he up to? My stomach grumbles and I'm keen to leave. I light the fire.

When he finally comes down with a tatty-edged scroll under his lantern arm and a sturdy staff in the other, his face expresses an uncanny radiance.

He greets me: "*Mane bonum!* Did you sleep well?"

"Thank you, yes. I dreamt about your words last night."

He claps his hands. "Nothing better to feed your soul than words from our Lord."

Does he live in a different world from me? "And you? You seem to have woken early."

"No earlier than usual. I have an appointment with the angels every morning before the sun rises. Their songs of praise thrill me."

"You hear angels singing? I only heard you chanting."

"Not all are able to hear them. Many years ago, the Holy Father Vigilius summoned me to Rome after complaints reached his ears that I celebrated the Eucharist too early for the parishioners to attend. It was quite an adventure,

I can tell you." He chuckles to himself. "His Holiness was sceptical when I spoke of the angelic choir. So I woke him in his chamber one morning before dawn." He chuckles. "He couldn't deny hearing something supernatural."

Making his way to the back wall of his cave, he places his scroll in a chest. "I do so love to meet with my Friend each morning, to read from His Word, tell Him my cares and listen to His bidding."

My eyebrows rise. "And what did he say today?"

"He assures me sweet Virna is safe and well, and exhorts you to hurry to your father's house, where you will find a distressing scene. I don't know what exactly. But he urges you to foster peace."

"You mean, your unseen friend talked to you about me? Why?"

"He loves you dearly and desires your well-being."

"And he wants me to go home right away?"

"We'll have breakfast and then you must leave. Proceed along the path you were on yesterday and you may reach your village before nightfall."

In haste we prepare oatcakes, enriched with a goose egg. Before he lets me go, he lifts a solemn finger. "Heed those words I quoted last night. Do you remember them? I suggest you write them on your tablet as soon as you reach the mules."

They have been taking root in my mind during the night and I am able to repeat them with only minor hesitation.

"Very good, my lad. May these holy words be as first food for your soul, to set your feet on the path of enlightenment. Take them to heart!"

"I will. But you say 'first'. How shall I hear more, after I return home?"

"My friend has finds ways and means of speaking to us. However, I believe we'll meet again." He taps the rock with his staff. "Yes, we'll meet again. Then I will be delighted to further feed your soul, as you may have need."

"I'm not sure I'll be coming this way again." I shrug my shoulders and look around. "But thank you for your hospitality and your kind words. I'll try to remember them."

"The Lord knows your going out and your coming in. But for now: Farewell. *Festina! Et sit Dominus tecum!*"

"Farewell."

I collect the goatskins and make my way to Marcus's hut, where I make a point of writing that promise and what I can remember of Cerbonius's prayer on my tablet. Marcus helps me load the mules and I offer him five *folles*. He refuses. Instead, he insists on me accepting a loaf of fresh bread. "I'm only too happy to serve you for the Lord's sake and in honour of our worthy Bishop."

All this unexpected kindness overwhelms me. Especially after also experiencing Drusus's dishonesty. Marcus sends me on my way with another word of blessing.

As we set off, childhood memories spill through my mind.

One day in particular is still so real to me. I had barely turned ten when Father announced he'd take me to Fabricia to trade our produce. He could do with my help. I think he also wanted to introduce me to the realities of the world. I'd never been anywhere other than the hills above our village. In my excitement, I behaved in such a silly way – pestering Little Eli for no reason, dropping a pot of cabbage soup Mother passed to me, and forgetting to feed the hens.

I could never have slept. What was I to take in my little backpack? My catapult, of course, in case a wild animal attacked. And some suitable stones. Tossing to and fro, I tried to imagine what it would be like. Alone with dear

Father for several days, trekking through the hills, sleeping I knew not where, perhaps seeing new animals. And then, at last, the view from the other side of the great mountain. Perhaps I would even see Italy if the air was clear.

Father was never talkative, but he'd told me a bit about his previous trips, so I had some idea of what it was going to be like. Majestic villas with high walls and wrought iron gates; many-sailed ships from around the world; people of all races and languages; noise; music; the bustling market with everything conceivable on sale – spices, sweetmeats, exotic fruits, books, parrots, monkeys, toys, jewellery, glass, colourful material, tools, fishing gear – whatever I might desire.

While we were away, Little Eli was to take on some of my chores – feeding the hens, fetching wood, making sure the fire didn't go out. She could keep those duties when I got back, as far as I was concerned. "You're big now. You'll be a great help for Mother," Father had reassured her. It was true. At eight, she wasn't small any more. And she was thrilled to be given new responsibilities.

"When do we go?" I jumped up and down. "And where will we sleep? Won't it be cold? I'll take the new cloak Mother made me. Isn't it dangerous in the mountains? Should I take my bow and arrows, in case? Will you buy me new shoes when we get there? And a better knife? And something pretty for Little Eli?"

"Go get some sleep," was all the answer I got. "We're leaving early."

A shady silhouette of Corsa appears through the trees. We're getting nearer to home. And Father.

We did the trip together every autumn for the next few years. That first time seems like ages ago. But now things are so different. My childish expectations were so mistaken. Mistaken? No, one sided. I didn't expect the crooks, the dirt, the unsuccessful sales, the price of everything.

This time I was on my own. Or only Aquila was with me, bent on ensnaring me. The storm. My injury. Drusus the thieving cheat. Temptations. Drunkenness. Lechery. Was it he who made me fall for it all? He wants to make my life miserable. Am I not my own master?

How easy life was as a child. Of course, I had work to do every day, repairing the fences for keeping the wild boar out of our vegetable patch; feeding the hens and collecting the eggs, until Little Eli was old enough to take over. Then chopping wood, repairing paths damaged by the overflowing stream, collecting herbs or mushrooms.

Father often complained I spent too much time with the other boys – hare-brained and lazy, he called them – instead of tending the goats or helping him repair the terraces. The goats managed quite nicely by themselves, I thought. And repairing the terraces is a never-ending task; it can wait another day. But roaming the hills with my friends, exploring the caves and old mines, climbing trees, and swinging on creepers across the waterfall – such things couldn't wait.

"How d'you like the view, Hercules?" We catch glimpses of the coast as we trample fallen leaves on a well-used path between stunted pines, strawberry trees and bizarre boulders. He increases his pace. Does he realise we're getting near home? The tantalising scent of the macchia stimulates further reminiscences.

As a child, I'd spent many hours alone in the hills, climbing towering cliffs, exploring crags and potholes, and thinking about life. What is the meaning of it all? Why do grownups have to work so hard to survive? Why does Father give me so much work to do? Why do people get sick? Why do we all die sooner or later?

Yet I also experienced friendship, a more pleasant mystery. I do truly love my parents and Little Eli – even Rufus, Pontus and his little sister, Lucilla, in a way. Do I love Hercules? Ceres doesn't approve of his name; it's disrespectful to the Gods, she says. Caesar has always been a faithful companion, though I do get mad at him when he doesn't obey. What's the difference between loving an animal and loving a person? Am I going to marry someday? Would I love my wife? Impossible ideas.

On my ramblings, I was always wary of going too near stone-faced Aquila the Avenger. Stupid. If he was as jealous and powerful as Ceres made us believe, he was able to see me and bug me wherever I went. And whatever I did. But what if he is no more than some kind of religious fantasy? Till now, I've never been able to consider such a possibility.

We're getting near now. He must be right around the corner. What did Cerbonius say about him? I can't remember. Now I'm about to face him. I understand my real reason for choosing the southern route on my way to Fabricia. But I can't avoid him today.

Hercules bucks, as a real eagle – Kili himself! – swoops down and catches a young hare. Why do some animals have to die to keep others alive?

CHAPTER ELEVEN

Returning Home

"COME ON, HERCULES, it's not far."

He nods his head, as if he understands.

Screaming seagulls glide overhead. A whiff of salt breeze. The faint rhythmic whoosh of waves sucking at pebbles. In the distance, the colourful sails of a trader. Oh, to be free from this tedious yearly routine… free to explore the big wide world! How is it possible for a set of square sails to harness the power of the wind and drive such a large ship from one land to another? And how can it be controlled by a small rudder?

I have no idea what lies beyond the horizon. I see Corsa more clearly now and Capraria looming dark to the right. I often wonder where those ships come from, where they are headed, and what sort of merchandise they carry.

Why are there so many people in the world? Are they all like us, or quite different? Virna's skin is darker than mine. I wish I knew how she is and what she's up to. Do all people have such a hard life as the grownups here seem to have? What makes people want to travel and trade things? Here on Ilva, we provide what we need for ourselves. I can't think what people want from other parts of the world. Or what others might want from us.

Perhaps those ships aren't carrying peaceful traders at all. Perhaps they're pirates. Or even barbarian invaders. Would I be able to tell from this distance?

Someday I'll learn to sail, to harness the wind. I'll have a boat of my own with a red sail, a rudder and oars, and I can explore other worlds. Someday.

But first, the big challenge. We have to pass Aquila. I finger my amulet.

Hercules has slowed down again. And now Crispus's shoulder has begun to twitch. Even the mules are nervous!

Fearful stone monsters rear up around every corner. An irate giant, brooding revenge as he glares across the endless sea; a distorted beast, ready to pounce on me as I sidle past. Who can protect me from their powerful malice? And, worst of all, what is Aquila himself intending to do when I'm right within his reach? This was why I chose the southern route.

What was it Cerbonius said? "*Festina!*" I should hurry home. Is Mother ill? Have pirates attacked our village? Why would I be needed so urgently?

"*Et sit Dominus tecum!*" he added. I have no idea who his lord might be and what good he would do if he were with me. I'm not aware of any good-natured influence accompanying me at the moment.

I purse my lips and frown. Instead of trying to escape from Aquila, I might try to appease him. Make him a gift, promise him my loyalty. Why didn't I think of that before? Perhaps he would let me pass in peace. He might even decide to be kind to me.

Where do these thoughts come from? I have all this money. I'd quite forgotten about it whilst I was with Cerbonius. Other things had carried so much more weight. But I need to do something about it. I can't show Father such riches. I'd have to explain how I got them. I'd have to tell him of the crystals. Who knows how he would react? I'd certainly never be able to buy a boat and sail the seas.

Could I leave it in the care of Aquila? Or most of it. I need to bring a fair amount home to prove I'm not a total failure.

I round another bend and there he is – huge, vigilant, ready to pounce. Quite as terrifying as I remember. But my new resolution is taking hold in me. "I'll entrust the profits of my sales to you, Aquila," I shout out.

I hope he'll let me collect them later.

A blinding flash tears the sky apart and a simultaneous deafening thunderclap causes Crispus to rear and bray like I've never heard before.

I shake as I grab his halter, struggling to pacify him. He cut his leg on a jagged rock and now he's limping. He needs a rest. But why does it have to be under the shadow of fearsome Aquila?

I shudder, then start to recite, "Our Father in heaven…"

Another blinding flash startles me and the mules pull at their lines. This time, instead of a deafening clap, a long rumble follows, which comes over as an angry rebuke. As it echoes from the hillside, I hear him threaten, "How dare you call on your Father in heaven? You belong to me, Aquila, lord of the heavens. Do you not bear my image?"

I grab my amulet. Is Aquila jealous of this new God Cerbonius has talked of?

"Of course I belong to you, O Aquila. Since birth I have been devoted to you." My voice trembles and my thoughts are in turmoil. "I don't wish to offend you. What do you want of me?" I remember what I was about to do. "I'll offer you my profits, Aquila." Immediately, another flash lights up the sky and a crack like the first thunderclap resounds.

I can't risk the mules bolting if a storm breaks, so I tie them to the thick strands of ivy enveloping a large oak. I won't be away long.

Have I understood right? Aquila is demanding me to surrender my gains to him? To give up my dream of freedom? I pull my purse from the bottom of the pannier and again count my winnings: two hundred and ten brass *folles* and two shiny gold *solidi*. How they sparkle in the bright sunshine!

Sunshine? I scan the sky. Thunder and lightning but no clouds. Strange.

I take my time to return the coins to the purse and tie the leather thongs with a double knot. I still have enough in my belt pouch to show Father my trip was worthwhile.

I force my eyes toward the daunting rock formation. They drop again to the little pick, which fell from the pannier. Grabbing it, I strike it three times against my left hand, then stride forward between large boulders. Prickly gorse bushes yield to my hacking and I avoid facing the ever-watchful giant eagle. As I approach, my whole body quivers. The ground seems to vibrate under my feet.

I steal a glance at him. Up close, he doesn't look like an eagle at all. Can this haphazard stack of boulders really be a mighty God? The suspicion allays my fear to some extent, and I clamber among the rocks we all think of as Aquila, seeking a safe hideout for my purse.

Oblivious to the awesome presence, sunbathing grey-brown lizards scuttle off and vanish into a cleft between stones. Perhaps they are showing me a suitable cache. Clearing away some loose pebbles with the pick, I push my hand into the crack. Sure enough, the space becomes wider farther in. By shifting the coins around in the purse, I flatten it enough to squeeze it through into the inner chamber. I jam a few stones back into the opening, making sure the lizards can still pass. As an afterthought, I wedge the little pick under a large rock. It would be hard to explain my reason for buying it to Father.

"Please take care of my riches until I come back." Am I addressing Aquila or Cerbonius's God? Hardly the reptiles. I snort at the thought. Have I done the right thing? Will I find the hole again, or will someone else find it first?

A strange calmness settles over me. For the first time, I notice the magnificent view from this vantage point. Hill after hill and bay after bay extend into the distance. That must be Italy in the haze. If I hadn't been told to hurry home, I might stay here for hours and admire the scenery. Which God made this beautiful world?

I head back to the mules, now lying in the shade of the overhanging oak. How is it that we had no rain after those blinding flashes and violent thunderclaps? That was no natural storm. Could it have been the rantings of Aquila the Avenger? Then why did he not challenge me when I drew near with my offering?

Crispus's wound has dried up and doesn't seem too bad. I apply some labdanum, which makes him twitch, and bandage his leg before getting him to stand. The rest has done the mules good. I give them oats and water. We set off as the sun begins to dip, dazzling me and preventing me from seeing how many headlands we still have to cross.

It was up near the crag I called The Chariot, I recall. I was still a child, watching Kili and Kwee enjoying the blustering wind, when I noticed a large merchant ship sailing northwards close to shore. Suddenly, a small rowing boat appeared round the headland and advanced on the trade vessel. I watched in amazement, then horror. The little boat was attacking the large one.

"Look out! Pirates!" I shouted, though of course no one could hear. The raiding ship, which was built for ramming, struck the side of the two-masted trader. The terrifying crash reached my ears moments later. In less than no time, nimble assailants had climbed on board and were grappling with the few crew members. The defenders fought back with scimitars and the battle was gruesome. Some of the combatants lost limbs, others were cut down and thrown overboard.

Screwing up my face and clenching my fists, I forced myself to watch. "No!" The merchant sailors had no chance. Outnumbered. Unprepared.

I guess those ruthless pirates knew what they were after – gold or jewellery, perhaps. Their sleek little galley wasn't damaged by the collision and they retreated as fast as they came, leaving the wrecked ship at the mercy of the roaring wind and raging waves.

"Save them, Aquila!" I cried. But it was no good. The stricken vessel crashed against the jagged rocks. Plank by plank, the cracked hull broke apart and sank! Any sailor who hadn't been slashed to death by a pirate's gladius surely drowned.

Tears streamed down my cheeks as I ran home, stumbling several times and scraping my knees. Mother saw me coming and swept me into her arms. I sobbed so much I was unable to talk. By the time Father arrived, I had calmed down enough to describe what I'd seen.

Mother gave me a hot drink, then put her arm around me and ushered me to bed. I didn't sleep much the next few nights.

My horror had somewhat abated when, days later, I was fishing for shrimps for supper. I spotted a pile of planks, then ropes and bits of torn sail, several wooden crates and many broken amphorae – cargo and flotsam from the sunken trader. I raced from one treasure to another. The wood would come in handy for enlarging our shed. And many of the other articles would be useful, too.

Some of the crates were still intact. One box contained metal items, many of which I didn't recognise – tools of some sort. Among them were some handsome knives. I chose one for myself. For Father I found a hoe, which I was sure he'd appreciate. Another one was full of colourful material. I dragged it home and Mother said it must be silk, it was so fine and smooth. She thought she could wash the salt out and make beautiful clothes. Little Eli jumped for joy, ran up and hugged me.

Rufus and Pontus joined me scavenging among the rocks and coves to see what else there was. Broken bits of this and that turned up, but many things like the foodstuffs were ruined by the sea water. Some sacks of flour and cereals were still dry inside, so we brought them home, as well as a whole crate of fruit which Father said were oranges. Rufus tried biting through the skin, then nearly threw them away. Father showed us how to peel them and then we nearly made ourselves sick by eating too many.

Next day I returned, climbing over rocks from one little inlet to the next, still searching for treasure.

I shudder at the recollection.

A scuttling movement caught my eye and I went to investigate. Several large crabs were crawling over a dark shape, partly covered by sand and seaweed. A foul stench made me stop in my tracks. One hand sprang to my mouth and I supported myself against a rock with the other. Again, I rushed home. "There's a dead man on the beach." I struggled to bring out the words between my sobs. "And the crabs are eating him!"

It was too dark to do anything about it that day, but I told Father where I'd seen the body. Early next morning, he took the pickaxe, collected Rufus's father and went to see what they could do. I think Ceres went with them; she would have known what rites were needed to protect us from the anger of the Gods.

I never did hear exactly what they did – I didn't want to think about it. For a long time, I couldn't bring myself to go anywhere near that cove. I vowed to never again eat crab.

I scan the view before me as Hercules, Crispus and I plod on. Boulders burst out between bright clumps of gorse, heather and rockrose, with the occasional small tree standing guard. Far below, gentle waves never cease to lap the rocky shore. How beautiful and tranquil the world now seems.

My thoughts return to earlier days.

As a child, my life was easy – carefree. Except for that one aspect – Ceres. Father's sister lived alone in a shack next to the Jupiter shrine. She was the village school-teacher, teaching us the basics of reading and writing. And although she had precious little for me to read, I quite enjoyed the lessons.

It wasn't her role as teacher that made Ceres the bane of my life. She was Jupiter's priestess. As such, she dominated our tiny community under the mountain. Some of her powers were harmless. She was the one who divined all the babies' names. Silvanus – God of animals and the woods; I didn't object to that. Eliana – our little sunshine. Ceres also consulted the Gods when decisions had to be made about when to plant the crops or slaughter the goats.

She was never content, and her cold, harsh demeanour scared me. She terrified us with her unfathomable Jupiter, who demanded burnt offerings on feast days and whenever a tragedy occurred, like an outbreak of sickness or a death. He overlooks our hamlet in the guise of Aquila – this pile of boulders I had just approached, which looks like an eagle from some angles. Sometimes, she says, he soars silently, lurking, ready to pounce and frustrate any plan he doesn't approve of. It was she who gave me my eagle pendant and insisted I wear it day and night to protect me against evil spirits. I never dared to disobey, although I can't say it has ever given me any comfort.

Was Kili Aquila in disguise? I couldn't believe that.

I remember asking her to tell me about her Gods – who they were and why they always needed to be appeased. That made her furious. "Don't talk about things you don't understand!" was all she said. From then on, she had something against me. Somehow this one person spoilt the atmosphere of the whole community.

The worst times were the Vinalia festivals, when Ceres summoned all the men over twelve from our end of the island for three days in Marciana. It can't be true, but it looked to me like thousands of people. That scared me, coming from such a tiny hamlet. After some ritual involving pouring wine on the altar and sacrificing a goat kid, wild music began and a great feast ensued. I can't imagine where all that food came from.

Many of the men got drunk – even Father and Uncle Aelius. They went into one of the tents next to the temple with Ceres or one of the other priestesses, taking offerings of fruit and money, or even the blood of a pigeon or a goat, as a sacrifice to the great God Aquila. When they came out, their faces glowed and they looked strangely happy. It always brought me out in a cold sweat. Now I knew why.

I could feel something evil about the whole event, as if the sky were bearing down on me, or as if invisible beings – I had no name for them – lurked behind every tree and boulder, watching, waiting, wanting to harm me.

Sometimes these sprites tried to creep into me, which made me want to scream. They seemed to be servants of that fearsome God Aquila, who demanded gifts from us but was never satisfied, never helped us, never gave us anything in return for our devotion.

"So, Hercules, we're nearly there."

My first time away from home alone has been more than two weeks. I long to see Mother and tell her of my adventures. How has Little Eli has got on with tending the fire? Will they like the things I've brought for them?

I'll face Father. I wonder what he'll find to complain about – that I've been away far too long, haven't brought back enough grain, sold the goods too cheaply, whatever?

What trouble has Rufus got himself into this time? And what new inventions has Pontus come up with? Have giggly Lucilla's breasts begun to grow, like Little Eli's?

It's beginning to get dark, as we scramble down the familiar slope under the mournful trees. We follow the gurgling stream, past our favourite pool with the waterfall. The path has been washed away in places, and large stones from the terraces are lying about. Hercules and Crispus increase their pace.

Cori raises the alarm, of course, and Little Eli is the first to run out to meet us. Oh, how good it is to be back. And welcomed. I drop my stave and hug her tight.

She winces, stifling a scream.

CHAPTER TWELVE

Discord

CAESAR BOUNDS UP, yapping wildly. I pull back from Little Eli, staring at her. "What's the matter? Did I hurt you?"

"Sorry. It's my back." She shivers and straightens her tunic.

"What happened to you?"

She reaches up, beaming, and throws her arms round my neck. "Oh, I'm all right. You must have touched a sore spot. But it's wonderful to have you here again, Silé. We've missed you. How did the trip go? You're looking well. Come in and tell us all about it."

"Well, a lot has happened. On the whole, it's gone quite well." With my arm on her shoulder, we move towards the door. "But tell me why you're hurting."

"It's… it's a long story." She stops and takes me aside. With hands shielding her mouth, she whispers, "I was collecting nuts with the others a few days ago. Pontus and Lucilla took their baskets home and I stayed out with Rufus a while."

I clench my fists. "Did he do something to you?"

"No, no. Not at all. We were chatting."

"So what's that got to do with your back. Did you fall over?"

"No, silly. We were just having fun together. But it got a bit late. And when I came home, Father was mad at me."

I'm ready to fight. "Don't tell me he hit you."

"He didn't like me being out alone with Rufus." She blushes and looks away. "But the real problem was: I'd let the fire go out."

"Tell me straight. Did he hit you?"

"You know how he's been since he broke his leg. He's sour with everyone. Any little thing can make him furious." Her head drops. "He shouted and screamed and dragged me to the hearth. I was terrified. He poked around in the embers. They were still warm but not glowing. He was so wild with rage, I had no idea what he was going to do…"

I snatch up my stave. "Wait till I see him. What *did* he do?"

"He… he pushed me outside. I thought he wanted me to collect wood and start a new fire." Her voice trails off and she begins to sob. "But he struck me with the poker. It was still hot."

"What? I hate him! Let me see."

She hesitates, then pulls up her tunic and, although the light is failing, I see a dark welt on her ribs, seeping pus.

I can't believe it. My thoughts flash back to Virna – sweet, lonely Virna. Why are men so cruel? Even to helpless girls? I'll never be like that.

"You heard him give me the job of making sure the fire doesn't go out." She winces again as I examine her wound, and she whimpers between sobs. "I thought I managed pretty well."

"I'm sure you did." I'm so glad not to have that tiresome job anymore.

"I stoke it up every night right before bed and get up as soon as Cori starts crowing, and put more wood on." She shakes her head. "I get so tired because I don't get enough sleep." She's crying without restraint now.

I pull her into my arms, careful not to touch her injury. "What's so terrible about the fire going out once in a while? We can always light it again." I take deep breaths in an attempt to control my trembling limbs. "He must be out of his mind, hitting you with a hot poker. Just wait till I see him!"

"Please, Silé, don't be angry with him." She lets her tunic fall. "Mother's been tending the wound. It's getting better. It's not Father's fault he fell down the terraces that day." She doesn't notice my gaze drop. "He can't do what he used to anymore. That's why he gets so short-tempered. Now you're back, you can help again."

For a moment my eyes wander to the distant hills, then I shake my head and turn back to Eli. "It's no excuse for hitting his little daughter with a hot poker."

"I'm not so little any more, Silé. I'm growing up, too." She pulls her shoulders back and tries to look tall. Even that movement makes her face screw up. "Don't make things worse by confronting him, please. We've been so anxious for you. We've been making offerings to Aquila to bring you back safe. I was so thrilled when Cori called out your name! Please don't spoil our happiness."

So, even before I see him, I'm furious with Father. I'm not afraid of him anymore. I'm ready for a fight. So much for Cerbonius's advice to foster peace.

He comes out with Mother. The air is tense. I'm still seething.

Mother rushes up and hugs me. "Oh, Silé, I'm so glad you're home again. Why did you take so long? Is everything all right?"

"What's wrong with Crispus?" Father snaps, pointing his cane at the bandage on the beast's leg. "Can't you even look after the mules?"

I press my lips together, then snarl, "It's nothing serious."

Mother steps between us and touches my elbow. "Come in, Silé. Let's all have a hot drink. You must be weary. Then you can tell us how things went in Fabricia."

"I'll unload the mules first."

I stack the panniers and sacks next to the house. Father offers token help lifting down the amphorae, although they are nowhere near as heavy as they were when full of wine and oil. We avoid facing each other.

Now free of their burdens, Hercules and Crispus find their way to the stable, where there's plenty of hay and water.

In the house, Little Eli is bustling around collecting ingredients for a herbal beverage. We sit on the bench near the hearth.

How should I begin? "There was a bad storm the day after I left."

"Yes, we worried for you," Mother passes round a dish of her delicious oatcakes. "Did you find shelter?"

"In the end, yes. But it was frightening to be out as the lightning flashed. We even had boulders crashing down around us."

"Aquila was angry," Father remarks.

"I don't know what he has against us." My thoughts go back to that massive rocky structure where I've buried my treasure. What makes us think of it as a God? "Anyway, we survived." I don't go into details. "We reached Albanus's place on the evening of the – let me see – it must have been the fifth day…"

"Five days to go to Fabricia?" Father curls his lips in a sneer. "I used to take two. When I was fit."

I glower at him.

"Please calm down, Cornelius." Mother stretches out her hand towards him. "He doesn't have your experience. And it was a terrible storm. Don't you remember how the stream broke its banks? That hasn't happened for years."

"Anyway, I bought all the things we needed." I decide not to mention the theft of my fruit. "And some little gifts for each of you."

"Really?" Little Eli jumps up and down. "What did you get for me? Let me see."

Collecting the pannier from outside the door, I first take out the copper cooking pots, the glass bowl and beakers. Mother appreciates them. Then I find the girls' presents. "I thought this necklace would suit you, Eli. And I got this brooch for Lucilla. But you can swap them if you prefer."

"Oo! It's beautiful. Just my colour. Thank you so much." She gives me a big hug, then slips it over her head. "And I'm sure Lucy will love the dragon."

"I have some knives for the lads," I add. The boots, linen and dress material aren't so exciting at this stage.

"And here's the money I made, Father." I empty my pouch onto the table and count a hundred and seventy-five *folles*. I chuckle when Little Eli's eyes almost pop out of her head.

Father sweeps the coins off the table and into his own purse.

"The sacks of cereals and things are outside. And I brought some tools, too – a pick and a hatchet."

"You know I can't work any more."

I struggle to control my breathing. That's all the thanks I get.

It's back to the daily grind. Father has a string of jobs for me to do. What's most urgent? I make a temporary fix to the fence around the vegetable patch and then set about carrying the stones back up to repair the terraces, one by one.

I shudder as I stumble on the stone that started this misery. One can't change the past.

It's wearisome, backbreaking work, especially as we're having a hot spell, and my hands are soon scratched and swollen. The work is never finished – Father makes that clear to me.

A week has passed, and I need to escape the strained home atmosphere. I set off for the hills, slapping my forehead when I realise I've forgotten to take my trusty stave. With my knife, I cut a strong shoot from a young hazelnut shrub, then trim off most of the side branches, leaving a short stub to form a crook. Shortening my new cane to be slightly taller than myself, I keep another stout section, about as long as my arm.

I wander through the dark, damp woods. Father resents my having fun with Rufus and Pontus, although some of our enterprises have benefited the community. How is it that he gets so mad at Little Eli for no good reason, even injuring her? My sister. His daughter.

I kick a large stone and watch it tumble down the hillside.

What does it matter if the fire goes out now and then? She said he was also angry with her for staying out with Rufus. Aren't we allowed to have friends?

Life is so hard. Just getting along with one another. I long to share my thoughts and plans with someone. But Pontus is only interested in material things and Rufus laughs at my questions. People are so demanding, so easily offended, so resentful, so selfish. Perhaps I am, too.

Father is devoted to serving Aquila. I don't understand why. In my opinion, all the offerings and rituals at his shrine are nothing but a burden to us all. Worshiping him never seems to have benefited us. It's all because of Ceres. She has us totally under her thumb. Especially Father. He does whatever his big sister says.

But now I've seen Aquila up close. I've heard him mock Cerbonius's God and claim me as his own. But I'm not so afraid of him now. Someday, I'll collect my treasure from him and get myself a new life. The wide world is beckoning.

Is my life controlled by the Gods? Which one? Does any God listen when I cry out for help? Is some spirit capable of calming my churned-up thoughts and longings? Or even of delivering me from this pitiful drudgery? I wish someone would give me a reason to live.

Cerbonius's God is different. I determined to meditate on those moving words of his and his prayer, but I've failed. My anger at Father distracted me. Wasn't there something about forgiving others? When I get home, I'll have to read those wise words again.

Thoughts of Cerbonius remind me of Virna. I hope she's well. I wonder what she's up to.

A prominent outcrop lends itself as a seat, and I start chipping away at the cut-off length of wood I had kept. I'm glad my knife is sharp. As I remember Virna's jolly way of singing, I'm inspired to try making a flute. Not a simple whistle from a tender twig but a proper instrument with holes for the different notes. I'll have to find a way to hollow it out.

From up here I can scan the towering rocky cliffs, and am relieved Aquila isn't in sight. Before me is a hazy suggestion of Corsa and proud Capraria rises farther north. To my left, the dark line of Planasia contrasts with the shimmering lighter blue sea, broken here and there by tiny white bursts of spray. Fresh dreams awaken of far-off shores, free from the toil of life in Submonte.

It's calm at the moment, the sky a rich azure. But ominous clouds are rising in the distance and spreading out like Uncle Aelius's anvil. There may well be rain later.

Below me in the village, most people shelter from the high, fierce sun. Mother fills the water trough for the hens. The girls play with Caesar, throwing two sticks in different directions and laughing at his confusion as he tries to fetch them both. They have no cares. The boys join them and tease them about something. Rufus grabs Little Eli and lifts her over his head, making her scream. Caesar barks madly at him. Their cries waft up to me, but I can't make out their words.

I shout to them and wave, but they don't seem to notice.

Now Pontus has grabbed Lucilla's arm and is dragging her off towards their house. Why doesn't he let her do what she wants?

There's a slight struggle. She breaks free and runs off into the shrubbery, leaving him to go on alone. Good for you, Lucilla. She's got pluck, that little one. She's growing, too. There's something attractive about her carefree laugh and the way she brushes her wild hair out from her lively brown eyes. And her lithe body is taking shape; even the many scratches and bruises from her climbs and tumbles give her character.

Rufus stays chatting with Little Eli. Although he's really big and strong, she doesn't look as small as I thought when she stands close to him. She turns to face him, and he puts his hands on her shoulders. What's going on? After some moments, they sit on a stone in the shade of the apricot tree. Caesar settles there, too, no longer aggressive towards Rufus. My view is hampered by the shadows, but they seem to be very close together. Can it be that Rufus is attracted to Little Eli? She's only – how old? – twelve. And he must be nineteen at least.

Licking my lips, I make my way to a little stream for a drink and help myself to some juicy figs and nuts.

Up at the old quarry, I look out for Vipi or one of the other snakes. Crouching on all fours, I creep across the hewn rock to their usual haunt, then lie down on my belly, propping myself on my elbows, and wait.

So, Rufus is interested in Little Eli.

An incident from a couple of years back springs to mind. We three lads were enjoying a swim in our pool – as we often did in the hot afternoons – when we heard girlish giggles. They didn't often come up to the waterfall. Lucilla has been afraid of running water ever since she fell in and nearly drowned when she was little.

As the girls approached, Rufus suddenly clambered out and ran off between the trees. I'd thought that odd.

They said Father was angry that I'd been out all day. I should have been helping him with the terraces. I had to go back right away.

While drying off in the sun, Pontus and I enjoyed the honey cakes the girls had brought. Rufus only came out of hiding when they left to say I was on my way.

"They're just little girls," I said, "What's got into you?"

He was obviously embarrassed to be seen naked. He'd never been like that before, as far as I could remember. We teased him that he looked like a monkey, but he seemed rather proud of his muscles, his body hair, his deep voice. He told us he sometimes dreamed about naked girls – even Little Eli, which made me mad – and woke up with his *cauda* big and hard; then it erupted, and a creamy humour came out before he could stop it. Afterwards he felt happy and relaxed.

It wasn't big and hard then; shrivelled up from the cold, rather. What was he on about? We got dressed and I hurried down to face Father's wrath.

Now I understand Rufus's embarrassment back then at that pool. And his dreams. I close my eyes and breathe deeply as my night with Virna replays itself in my

119

imagination. That, also, seems such a long time ago. Will I ever see her again?

In the meantime, Rufus's interest in Little Eli seems to have grown. It's no longer only dreams. How can he be attracted to such a little girl? Perhaps she's not a child any more.

Intense heat radiates from the roughly hewn granite. A sweet aroma from the broom, rockrose and lavender wafts over me. Grasshoppers and other busy insects incessantly chirp, buzz and hum.

CHAPTER THIRTEEN

Enough

A TICKLING SENSATION on my bare arm startles me, and I open my eyes. A sand-coloured lizard cocks its head, then scuttles off into the scant vegetation. How long have I lain here, my head resting on my crossed arms? Shaking off sleep and flexing my stiff limbs, I revert to my observation. The sun is high when a slithering movement under a broom bush catches my eye. Vipi emerges. As always, I'm captivated by his incredible agility as he glides over the smooth rock, then wiggles rapidly across a sandy patch, leaving a peculiar zig-zag pattern. I admire his sleek body with its characteristic markings, his cold unblinking eyes, his arrogant upturned nose. All the while, his forked tongue flicks in and out, probing the air for the scent of anything edible.

Something heavy lands on my back. Instinctively, I roll to my side, tipping my assailant into a clump of heather.

The resulting giggle reveals it's only Lucilla.

Once my fighting stance relaxes, I laugh too. "What was that supposed to be? You shocked me. I almost attacked you. And I've got a knife." I help her get up. "How did you know I was here, anyway?"

She can't answer for a while, trying to suppress her laughter. "I saw you. Up on that rock when you shouted."

She still needs to catch her breath. "When Pontus tried to drag me home, I escaped. Eli's so caught up with Rufus these days, she forgets about me. So I sneaked up on you." She giggles again.

"So you've been trailing me for hours? I didn't notice a thing." I nod my respect. "Well done."

"I found you by the stream and followed you over here. I tickled your feet while you were sleeping." She giggles. "Didn't you notice anything?"

"I wasn't asleep. Only dozing."

"Oh, but you were. Look how far the sun has moved since you came here." Her arm sweeps halfway across the western sky. What an elegant motion. "I took this bit of wood from your belt. I saw you working on it earlier. What's it meant to be?"

I'd forgotten all about it. "Give it back. I'm making a flute."

"Come and get it!" She holds it out of my reach. "How do you know how to make a flute?"

"I don't. But I want to try." I lunge for it but miss. "I'd like to learn to make music. It would help me when I'm thinking about life."

She chuckles. "What's there to think about? We have all we need. Let's have fun together up here. There's no one watching."

"Don't you ever wonder what will become of you when you're older? Don't you wish there was more to life than scratching in the earth to produce enough food to survive?"

"Not really. I'm happy as things are. Up here with you." She runs around, hopping from boulder to boulder. I chase after her and grab her tunic when she hesitates to jump from a high rock. She turns to face me, giggling, holding the flute in the air. With one arm round her waist, I prise the stick from her hand. Tottering near the edge of the boulder, she clasps me tight. We stay a moment locked in each other's arms, breathing heavily. My body tingles as I enjoy the warmth of her hug.

She rests her head against my chest. "I can hear your heart beating. Thump, thump."

Get a grip on yourself, lad! "I expect yours is, too." I ease myself out of her arms. "Come on. I'll help you down."

I jump to the heather, then guide her back to safety. She keeps hold of my hand, turns and gazes at me with those intense hazel eyes of hers. "I don't think I've ever been here before. It's lovely. Especially with you. Why did you come here, Silé?"

"I love roaming these hills by myself." Her eyes cloud as I free my hand from hers. "I came here to see my friend Vipi."

"Vipi? You have a friend living up here?" She glances around the overgrown rubble of the quarry. "I saw no one all afternoon."

"Not a person, silly. Vipi's a viper. Didn't you see him a moment ago?"

"Whaaat? A viper?" She jumps back, her mouth gaping. "And you call it your friend? You must be crazy."

"I'm not crazy at all. Animals fascinate me. I could watch them all day. They're often more interesting than some people I know." I raise my eyebrows. Lucilla frowns. "For one thing, they don't shout at me and complain that I haven't done my work well enough."

"I know what you mean." She points at my flute. "You must show me when you've finished making it. We can come here and you can play tunes to me. I might even be able to dance for you." She lifts her arms and skips around, her tunic swinging out as she leaps and twirls. Then she comes close and grabs my hands, her fluttering eyelids inviting me to join in the romp.

I shake her off. "It's time to go." Glancing around to make sure I haven't forgotten anything, I stick the flute in my belt and pick up my new stave.

Her eyes plead. "Oh, you're not going home already? Can't we stay here a bit longer? We could lie down in the shade and chat." Then, with a teasing look, she adds, "Or would you prefer to spend the night with your friend?"

I can't let this silliness continue and we set off, although I'm in no real hurry to get home.

A sudden cool breeze surprises us, as a dark cloud covers the sun. Without further warning, a terrific thunder clap resounds and the cloud bursts. A typical summer downpour. No chance to take shelter. But summer rain doesn't kill, as they say, and the storm is soon over.

"Hee-hee! Drowned rat!" Lucilla laughs, pointing at my dripping hair and soaked clothes, then brushing her hair from her eyes.

"You're no better off. Just look at you," I reply, shaking my tunic loose from my legs. "But we'll soon be dry."

Before we reach our village, we need to cross the unpredictable stream. It's gushing wildly and already overflowing its banks. Lucilla's eyes grow wide and she trembles.

"When I came up here, it was hardly a trickle," I remark, looking for a place to cross. "How are we going to get over?"

Lucilla presses on downstream, searching for a narrower spot or some stepping stones. I follow her, scrambling through the dense undergrowth.

A thorny branch springs back as she passes, and hits me in the face. "Ow! That hurt."

"Sorry, Silé. I didn't realise you were so close. Let me see. It's bleeding."

"It's nothing serious."

She grabs my head and pulls me to a spot where the sun is penetrating between the overhanging boughs. She licks her finger and wipes off the trickles of blood. "You've got two nasty scratches across your cheek. I'm so sorry."

"It'll heal soon enough. I've had worse injuries."

"It's good it wasn't higher." From barely a handbreadth away, her beautiful hazel eyes peer deeply into mine. The scent of her breath is tantalising. I shake myself free from her grasp and take the lead.

We press on, still trying to find a suitable crossing place. An overhanging bank on our side provides the opportunity I need, and I leap over. "Made it. Now your turn. I'll catch you."

Lucilla holds back. "I'm frightened, Silé!" She stands, paralysed, staring at the rushing water. "I can't do it."

Her horror of running water comes to mind. But I can't jump back up to that outcrop. "All right. Let's find a better place for you to cross."

"I can't hear you," she screams above the roar of the raging water.

I shout. "We must find a better place!" I point to my left. "Take your time!"

As we clamber through tangled creepers and over ancient fallen trees, slowly making our way downstream, we often lose sight of each other. Round each bend, I search for a crossing. Nowhere does she dare to wade through or jump.

We come to an area of taller trees. Standing on a boulder in the stream, I call across to her. "There's an overhanging branch. Grab it and swing towards me. Don't look at the water."

She trembles. "I'll try. Will you catch me?"

In spite of her anxiety, her strength and agility impress me, as she reaches up and makes her way, hand over hand, along the branch. At last she's near enough for me to reach up and grasp her around her waist and thighs. The rapid lub-dub of her heart and her soft little breasts pressing against my cheek cause my whole body to tingle again.

She clasps me around my neck.

Careful not to lose my balance, something resists my movement as I try to carry her towards the bank. "What's the problem?"

"My tunic's caught on something."

"Where? Can you free it?"

"Oh Silé, I can't let go." She shudders.

My foot slips off the boulder and I stumble. Her tunic gives way with a tearing sound. Hugging her close, my feet grope for solid ground.

"This time it's your heart that's racing." I suppress a chuckle at the sight of her torn clothes. "It was thumping in my ears. If you turn around, I might be able to see it."

"That's not funny. This is my new tunic." Lucilla bursts into tears, trying to pull the torn halves together.

"I'm sorry." I put my arm on her shoulder. "I'm sure you'll be able to mend it."

Her sobbing calms as we make our way side by side out of the woods and across the flatter land towards the village.

All of a sudden, Pontus appears, an anxious expression on his face. "There you are, Lucy. Where on earth have you been all afternoon?"

His mouth drops open. "What have you done to my sister? You brute!"

I can't believe my ears. "Hey, hold on there. I didn't…"

"Leave her alone. Come here, Lucy." He snatches her from my arm. "What did he do to you?"

"I…"

"You monster! You fiend! I thought we were all friends. And you go and molest my sister!"

"But, Pontus, you don't…"

"Shut up! I don't need any excuses. I can see for myself." He clenches his fist, but then backs off. "Don't you dare go near Lucy again!" Then to Lucilla, "What happened?"

A lowering glare in Lucilla's piercing eyes shocks me.

She clings to Pontus and starts to weep. "He… he grabbed me. Up by the quarry. He tore my beautiful new tunic."

For days, now, I've been aware of sidelong glances from the villagers I pass. Even Mother sizes me up with suspicion. Not a word is spoken but the reproach is tangible.

I'm about to join my only remaining friend Rufus at the beach, when a shout from Father halts me. I've avoided talking to him since that last row. He's limping up the slope as fast as he can. "Silé!" His voice is scathing. "The goats are in the field. You didn't fix the fence!"

Cori warns us whenever wild boar come for our vegetables after dusk. But goats are also partial to cabbage if they get a chance.

As I run up to the top of the cultivated area, Father is uttering unintelligible screams and brandishing his walking stick. It's not clear if his outburst is aimed at me or the old billy, which flees back through the gap in the fence.

Biting my lip, I start repositioning the displaced posts and making sure they are properly interlocked, expecting a tirade of reproof at any moment.

Instead, I jump as a hand reaches under my outstretched arm to support the stake I'm about to hammer into the rocky soil.

Father is helping me!

The silence between each blow is oppressive, as he holds one post after another, allowing me to swing my mallet and drive it in.

I wipe the sweat from my brow as I complete the task, neither of us having the courage to face the other.

And then he speaks, his voice slow and morose. "I'm good for nothing with this gammy leg."

I turn towards him, still not making eye contact.

"I should be providing for the family. Keeping the

127

fields and terraces in order." He's almost weeping. "But I can't. Walking uphill is too painful. Climbing the terraces is impossible. Mother, Eliana, you, Ali – even Rufus, now – have to do what should be my work."

I have no words. After a final check that the fence is stable, we trudge together in silence towards the house.

And then he blurts out, "Perhaps I could make a living for the family as a fisherman. If I had a little boat."

Father's lament stuns me, and I falter. I turn towards him and he stands still. Straggly hair merges with an irregular beard covering much of his sun-ravaged face. Though his eyes don't meet mine, they radiate deep despair.

For the first time, I'm conscious of looking down on him. "How on earth do you imagine – with those miserable vines and a few goats – you could ever afford to buy a boat?"

"Of course we can't." He rocks his head in silence. "I've entreated Aquila. Sacrificed our best goat. Didn't do any good. It's no use dreaming."

"So, Aquila has let you down," I spit out. "That's no reason to make everyone else's life miserable. Why don't you at least…?"

"Mind how you talk to your father, boy!" His face turns dark red and his voice trembles.

"It's true." My pulse is throbbing in my temples and I have great difficulty keeping my voice calm. "You sit brooding in the corner of the kitchen gazing at that sickle on the wall. Are you jealous that everyone else has a life to live?"

"Listen here!"

"Whenever Mother comes in, you shout at her, criticising whatever she does…"

"Don't you tell me how to manage my own house!"

"And then you attack Little Eli with a hot poker. For nothing! Nothing! You're destroying our family."

"You insolent brat! How dare you?"

"How dare *you*?"

"For that, you can dig the top patch this afternoon and plant onions. I don't care how hot it is. No gadding about with those lazybones today."

I press my lips together, holding my breath to suppress the rage boiling within me. He knew I'd promised to help Rufus shift boulders this afternoon. We're making a sheltered swimming area in a cove a bit farther along the coast. Under my breath I mumble, "I can't bear this – being pushed around by a miserable old man who treats me as his slave."

He may not be able to beat me anymore but still I have to obey. I rush off to fetch the spade and pickaxe – leaving him to hobble home – then return to the enclosed field to carry out my penalty.

My mind is made up.

CHAPTER FOURTEEN

Fathers and Sons

KNIFE. SKIN OF wine. Oat cakes and smoked sausage. Flint. Cloak. Goatskin and stave. And my half-finished flute. Not even Cori raises the alarm when I leave.

Here I am again in the bats' bedroom. This time with no mules to worry about.

But I've left home. Childhood is over. I'll have to look after myself from now on.

I won't miss Father. Nor double-crossing Lucilla and gullible Pontus. Although we used to have fun together.

Tears well up in my eyes.

But Mother. And Little Eli. Will I never see them again? Sorrow prevents me from settling and I go outside for a stroll.

Winking stars vie for my attention. *Ursa Major. Ursa Minor.* And, of course, the Pole Star. That bright one to the north-west might be *Vega*. And that constellation must be *Hercules*, if I remember what Pontus taught me. None of the stars Scipio's grandfather mentioned in that scroll I bought.

If only I could have a life down here – Rome, Carthago, Constantinople – before I end up in one of those spheres. Some hope. It makes no sense. Cerbonius will help me with these riddles.

Tomorrow.

Although I was half expecting the ruckus, Dela and Runel's loud cries still startle me as I approach the sage's lair.

"At last!" Cerbonius's hearty chuckle greets me, as I climb towards his cave. "So, Master Silvanus hasn't forgotten his old mentor!"

He stands before me, wearing the same long grey robe as before, his arms spread wide. The familiar warm smile and lively eyes welcome me. Has he been expecting me?

I fall to my knees before him. "*Salve*, domine."

He reaches out, takes my hand, pulls me to my feet.

"Forget the formality, my lad. Aren't we all children of the King and brothers to His Son? But it's wonderful you have returned."

"I felt a yearning, drawing me back to you. I couldn't resist. What can that be?"

"You are in need of further guidance, which I am more than willing to give, as far as I am able. But do sit down and let's first take some refreshment." He indicates my wineskin and I pour a tot into each of two goblets, adding water from his urn.

As before, he incants a prayer of thanks for the drink and we sit alongside each other on the rocks before his cave.

"And now, my lad, tell me what's bothering you."

"What makes you think I'm troubled?"

"Come, come. There's no need for such reticence. You were drawn to my home by my Friend for me to offer you the consolation for which you yearn."

"I don't understand. Who is this friend of yours? And what does he want of me?"

"In time, lad, in time. But first, please recount the matters that burden your heart."

Why does he keep harking on about that? He possesses some mysterious insight into my disposition, which I cannot deny. I take a deep breath. Skipping over everyday incidents, I tell of the bitterness I feel for Father, Rufus's intrusion into our family life, my broken friendship with Pontus and Lucilla.

He nods and takes time before responding. "To what extent were you to blame for these disagreements?"

I jump up to face him, my fists clenched. "Why do you blame me?" Can he see my darkest secrets? "Father treats me like dirt. Not only me, Mother and Little Eli too. We can't do anything right. He even beat his daughter with a hot poker. For nothing!" I'm sobbing now. "And Lucilla told a damned lie about me!"

"Take care, my son. Your accusations can only cause further harm – both to their hearts and yours." He leans forward, his gnarled hands grasping mine, his eyes penetrating me. "And how did you seek to heal those injuries – your father's, your former playmate, Lucilla's?"

I break down, shuddering violently. "H… how could I h-heal those w… wounds? Th… that's unfair!" My tears flow freely.

"No, no, lad." He offers me a little flannel. Is it the same one he lent to Virna? What was that strange word she used for it? I can't remember. He continues. "The last thing I want is to distress you. I'm sorry I caused you anguish. Believe me, it was necessary."

"W-what do you m… mean? Nec… ess… essary?"

"You are strong, my lad. Far too strong."

I try to control my heaving chest. It takes a moment before I can answer. "I have no idea what you mean."

"My Lord says: 'My power works best in weakness.' Your strength, young lad, needs to be defeated. Only then will you be able to receive His strength." Cerbonius pulls me to sit next to him and places his arm around my shoulders. "Perhaps it's too high a notion for you to grasp at this stage. In time, you will understand these truths. Come now, we have a task to perform."

He ushers me under the awning in front of his cave to a flat wooden board, balanced on rocks. I don't remember seeing this last time. Rolled-up parchments and two inkpots, each equipped with a magnificent goose quill – a workplace for two scribes. He indicates I am to take a seat on the thick drape covering another rock, then sits and turns to me. "You said you know how to read, is that correct? I am in need of an assistant."

Relieved for the change of subject, I warm to the suggestion I can help him. "Well, I'm not sure how accomplished I am. I can read Latin texts. In Fabricia I bought a work of Cicero – it quite confused me."

"Indeed?" He nods, as if that truly interests him. "We'll talk of that later. How skilled are you at calligraphy?"

"Ceres tells me my writing is neat, if rather slow." I examine the writing implements. "I've only had wax tablets. I've never used a quill and ink."

"You'll soon learn. These here," he says, indicating the stack on the left, "are precious scrolls in urgent need of being preserved. You may have heard of the heretical *Langobardi* who even now are plundering our homeland, God grant them mercy."

"Yes, the Duumvir in Fabricia was recruiting young men to fight them off."

"Truth and love are stronger than the sword, my lad. But those misguided souls take pleasure in destroying such literary treasure. So, faithful men devote themselves to transcribing documents like these and distributing them far and wide, before all is lost. As you see…" Cerbonius chuckles. "I'm old and frail, and ready to pass over to more pleasant shores as soon as my great Friend summons me. And it's my conviction that you, young Silvanus, are to play a major role in the continuation of this noble task after I am gone."

"You trouble me again. I came here for advice. Yet your first remarks had quite the opposite effect, driving me to tears and baffling me."

"I regret the need."

"I was glad at the thought I could help you. But now you suggest your life may be drawing to a close."

"Not to a close." Cerbonius seems amused. "I'll soon be released from this earthen vessel. It has served me well for many a long year and granted me many a pleasure. But it's nearing the end of its service. I'm now looking forward to a far more glorious body, free of these aches and frailties, and fit to enjoy eternity with my Friend and Lord on His new earth." As he speaks, it's as if he is unable to remain seated. His arms rise above his head; his face adopts a mysterious radiance. "But who knows when that will be? Till then I may still be granted many years of service. Would you assist me?"

I nod. He both enjoys this life and is eager to die. But his challenge motivates me. "I'll be happy to do what I can."

He spreads a virgin parchment before me and unrolls a scroll. "Can you copy this text?"

"Er… Would you have an old parchment for me to practice first?"

He fetches a damaged sheet and under his guidance I make my first attempts. My letters are deformed and interspersed with many ink blots. Twice he has to sharpen the quill after I damage the point, but soon my skill improves, and I start on a clean parchment.

Hour after hour I copy the scroll before me, letter by letter and word for word. As such, I pay little attention to the meaning of the text. I'm thrilled to be doing something useful for my host, and take pains to form and align each character. I'm slow, but Cerbonius is pleased with my work.

As I get near the bottom of the page, the letters form themselves into words and the words into a wonderful invitation, even a familiar one.

Quotquot autem receperunt eum dedit eis potestatem filios Dei fieri his qui credunt in nomine eius qui non ex sanguinibus neque ex voluntate carnis neque ex voluntate viri sed ex Deo nati sunt.

I run my fingers over the words once more.

'But to all who received him, he gave the right to become sons of God, those who believed in his name, who neither of blood, nor of the will of the flesh, nor of the will of man but of God are born.'

I jump up, shouting, "This is what you recited as I was leaving! I had nearly forgotten it. What a coincidence that it's on this scroll today."

Cerbonius bursts out laughing. "I'm impressed that you remember. But I hope you don't think it's pure chance. You underestimate the wisdom and ingenuity of your heavenly Father. And His desire to comfort you."

"I know no heavenly father," I reply. "I know only Aquila. And he is no comfort at all."

"Please clean your quill and put the parchment aside to dry. You can continue later."

"Oh, I can do more." I turn to face him in dismay. "I've hardly started."

"It's enough for now." He rolls up the original and adds it to the stack, then comes to sit next to me. "You say you know only Aquila. Tell me: How has that knowledge benefited you?"

"Benefited me?" My cheeks get hot at the suggestion. "Why, in no way at all!" I rinse the quill in a pot of waste water and replace it next to the ink jar. "How could knowing Aquila be of benefit to me?"

"I'm convinced there is some profit in everything that happens to us, Silvanus, if we look for it in faith," Cerbonius replies. "Didn't he hold you back from a variety of evils?"

"Evils? What do you mean?"

"Envy, greed, spite, malice and such like."

I'm taken aback. "Are you suggesting such feelings are bad?"

"What do you say?"

"Surely not. One can't control one's thoughts. They just come."

"'Out of the heart come evil thoughts which defile a man,' the Scripture says." He gazes at me, nodding. "And perhaps fear of that lifeless God also restrained you from wicked deeds – lying, theft… or sexual immorality." Do I detect a smirk on his face? He elaborates. "You are young, but old enough to succumb to lust."

"I think that is no concern of yours." My cheeks grow hot at the recollection of my encounter with the shrine harlot.

"True, lad. And I'm not pressurising you to confess your sins to me." He pauses. "Rather, I suggest even misplaced devotion may guard you from doing wrong. Wouldn't you agree?"

"Misplaced devotion?" My eyes follow the struggles of a large, blue beetle as it attempts to climb a rock, falling back frequently but never giving up. "Perhaps… perhaps fear of his wrath did stop me from doing some things that weren't right." With my finger I gently help the beetle up the steepest section. "But not always. Sometimes the temptation was too great, and I did what I knew I shouldn't."

"Such is our human weakness." Cerbonius pulls at his beard. "And it's not always others who are to blame, is it?"

I nod.

"But do you therefore agree, even Aquila helped you to some extent, in a negative sense?"

"Somehow, yes." My eyes drift to the deep blue sea far below. "But I hate the feeling he's watching me all the time."

For a long moment, Cerbonius taps the table with his finger, nodding his head in time with the beat. "Tell me about your father." He looks up at me. "Are you afraid of him?"

"Of course I am." My hands rise, palms upward. "He's so strict and demanding." I drop my hands to the board.

"What pleasant memories do you have of him?"

I breathe deeply, trying to stay calm. "He was always busy tilling the vegetable patch, tending the vines, repairing the terraces."

"Was he a good father?" Cerbonius persists. "Did he care for you?"

"Why do you ask me such questions?" I snap, then let my head hang. "I suppose he did. But he didn't show much affection. None at all these days. So, no. He wasn't a good father." The cheerful melody of a thrush makes me lift my gaze. "Although, of course, when we were small he did provide for our needs and teach us things."

"What did he teach you?"

"Practical things. To understand the weather; to milk the goats; to dig the soil and grow vegetables; to build fences." I draw figures in the dust with my finger. "I suppose it was also he who taught me to lever out rocks for the terraces with a stave. And to sharpen our tools and prune the vines."

"Many a useful skill. Did he take time with you and your sister, telling you stories or playing with you?"

"I don't remember him doing anything like that. When he wasn't working, he was performing religious rituals – making an offering to Aquila or attending the festivals."

"And how did he behave toward your mother?"

"Earlier, he was civil towards her. But not affectionate. Now things are different."

"In what way? You have often referred to a change in his behaviour. What caused it?"

"About a year ago, it must have been…" – How can I say this? – "he was working on the terraces. After a storm he often had to replace fallen boulders and make sure the water channels were free. I… I wasn't with him that day… So I… I don't know exactly what happened. But he fell. He broke his leg badly."

"So who helped him?"

"That's the thing. No one was around. He bled a lot and had to drag himself down the path until Little Eli heard his cries. Mother rushed out. She got him home somehow and did what she could for his leg. It never healed properly. He couldn't even stand. For months." I lower my eyes. "Now he limps and walks with a stick. He's angry all the time. Shouts at us for little things. Even threatens to beat me when I don't do exactly what he wants." I clench my fists and mutter through my teeth, "Never again. I'm bigger than him now."

"I'm afraid I have riled you with this relentless interrogation." Cerbonius scans my face. "However, I do have a reason for asking. One more: Since you judge your father not to have been one, what qualities would a good father have, in your opinion?"

"Another strange question." I bite my lip as I rest my chin on my fist, my elbow on the board and gaze at the treetops. "Well, he should be strong and wise." I glance at Cerbonius. "But not harsh." My finger traces the grain of the board. "He would provide for his family – food, clothes, shelter. Father did that as long as he could." I nod. "He would guide and support the children as they develop, teach them new skills, let them try things out for themselves." My finger circles a knot in the wood. "If one of them hurt themselves… or fell – when they fell – he would help them up. And encourage them to do better next time."

"Anything else?"

"If they got into real trouble – a bad fight or a serious accident – he would go out of his way to save them, whatever it might cost him."

"Where would you find such a father?"

"What a question! A father isn't something one can choose."

"Let me ask an even more absurd question. Consider well before you answer. How does a child acquire a father?" He fixes his gaze on me as he waits for the idea to sink in. "Whose choice is it? And why do some children not have the father they would desire?"

At first, I'm speechless; the question does seem ridiculous. "It's the man – and, I suppose, also the woman – who choose to have a child. At least, it is their responsibility." I shake my head. "The child certainly can't decide by whom he is conceived. He doesn't even exist."

"And what if he could?"

"Could what? Choose his parents?"

"Yes, suppose a child were able to choose his father. Wouldn't he choose one such as you described – caring, guiding, ready to rescue in a crisis?"

"Well, of course he would. But he can't. He's already born as a result of his father's action."

"Isn't it possible to change one's father? To choose a better one?"

I take a moment to consider what sounds like another stupid question. "Well… sometimes a child is adopted. If his real parents die, for instance. Or if they neglect him. There again, it's not for the child to choose his adoptive parents."

CHAPTER FIFTEEN

Sons and Fathers

CERBONIUS TURNS TO the workbench and reaches for a parchment. Has he so quickly lost interest in this weird exchange? He picks up the sheet I was working with. "Do you remember that promise I quoted? The one you copied."

Why is he changing the subject? I scan the page to remind myself.

'To all who received him he gave the right to become sons of God…' And then it hits me. A different father, God himself! '…Not born of the will of man.' That's incredible! Hearing it made me feel good, but I didn't understand what it really meant.

I nod and take time to respond. "Now I see what you are suggesting." I take the page from him and tap the words I wrote. "I still can't grasp it. Who is this talking about?"

"It speaks of my Friend. In time, lad… In time you will get to know Him." His eyes twinkle as mine meet his.

I wish he'd explain what he means. My lips move as I read the text again, then roll up the parchment.

Cerbonius stares at me as if deciding whether or not to speak. "I had a father once."

I peer at him. "I think everyone has a father, whether he knows him or not."

"My father was a severe man. Righteous. Diligent. Pious. A merchant at heart. For me he remained distant." He covers his face with his hands. "I believe he did love me. Yet he – like yours – also failed to show his affection. Never were my achievements good enough for him. He always insisted I should study more, work harder, sleep less." His fingers tap the table. "He never respected my heart's desire. I was supposed to take over his trade. But I had no interest in worldly riches. I wanted to serve God."

"That must have been hard for you."

"I neither bowed to his wishes nor appreciated his care. When I was twenty, and the Vandals were attacking Carthago again, I fled to Italy with some friends and Bishop Regulus, who later trained me for the priesthood." He raises his head, but his eyes focus on nothing. "I never saw my family again."

The silence becomes uncomfortable.

He drags his gaze back to me and his voice trembles. "Later, I also had… a son. Raguel." His head swings back and forth. "I knew no better than to raise him as my father had reared me."

I stare at him in silence.

He turns and scans the distant horizon. "I failed you, Raguel." His voice cracks. "My dear Raguel, I'm sorry."

I hold my peace.

"He was a dreamer, a poet… I taught him the fear of God… I drove him ruthlessly to work in the fields. I persuaded a friend to train him to use a sword, to toughen him up." He rubs his brow and his breath comes in gasps. "His mother pleaded with me to relent, but I persisted. I quashed his talents and forced him to be what he was not. God vouch for me, I loved him… but I fear he never knew my love."

He pauses, then looks up. "When Raguel was twenty, he left for Rome to join Belisarius's troops battling the

141

Goths. He took the sword I had taught him to wield."
He buries his face in his hands. I hear sobs. "He never
returned."

Touched by his remorse and sorrow, I reach out and
place my hand on his arm. Here's a father who loved his
son, yet failed him.

Glancing up at the sky, Cerbonius shakes himself from
his morose reflections. "No fear of the weather turning.
We can leave these here for now and you can continue
with the copying later. I want to show you something."

He makes no suggestion of eating, although it's well
past midday. Instead, he picks up a basket and hands me a
spade and a hoe. "Follow me."

With his staff in his left hand and the basket hanging
over his shoulder, he makes his way up the rough hillside.
There's barely a suggestion of a path. The geese waddle
after us, as if Cerbonius's invitation was addressed to
them. We pass the rock where I saw him performing his
morning devotions. His pace slows as his breathing grows
heavier.

At last we reach a flatter area that has been cleared
of trees and – judging by the pile of rocks at the back –
prepared for cultivation. Tidy rows of thriving vegetables
greet my eye – cabbages, leeks, onions, turnips, beans. The
patch is bordered on one side by a row of vines, a fig tree
and an apricot tree. On the other side is another field that
looks as if it had borne a cereal crop – emmer, perhaps, or
oats. But it has long since been harvested.

Cerbonius gives me the task of hoeing between the
rows to remove the fresh weeds, while he potters around,
mumbling to himself, as he lovingly examines one plant
after another. On his instruction, I dig up four fat leeks
and pick some beans, then join him.

He takes me over to the vines and checks that each
bunch is hanging free and not in danger of breaking the

shoot under its weight. He picks two large clusters, tossing a few fat grapes to the honking geese. "Grapes need as much sunlight as possible to ripen. These leaves have done their job and now they're in the way." He gently breaks off the yellow and brown ones.

"I remember, Father used to do that." I nod. "I never thought why. I was more interested in the wild animals."

He takes them to a pile of rotting vegetation in the corner. "When this decomposes, it makes excellent food for next year's crops. I spread it over the field and dig it in after the harvest is over." He chuckles. "The geese contribute with their droppings, too."

Then he points at the thriving fig tree. "Have you ever seen ripe figs in October? This tree here is *sui generis*, a special bounty of the Lord." He selects a few of the choice fruit to take back with us.

"You've left a cabbage over there," I remark. "And what is that? An overgrown turnip? They seem to be past their best. Why haven't you picked them earlier?"

"Consider, lad. How would I manage next year if I didn't let some of each kind grow to seed?"

"Of course. Father must have done that, too. It didn't occur to me that that's where he got the seeds from."

"I've stored the emmer, barley and oats with Marcus." He moves to another bed. "I'll take some of these beans and dry them. And the seeds of those," he says, pointing at the plants I mentioned, "I'll plant next spring near the cave. I nurse the seedlings there until they are strong enough."

"And then you'll transfer them up here?"

"They will go over there where the cereals were. It's always a good idea to move things around from year to year." His arm swings from one side of his patch to the other. "And I try to leave one area fallow so it can rest."

"Perhaps we should have done that, too."

"Indeed, the Lord has entrusted Mother Earth to our care. She deserves our respect. As we tend them, each seed produces fruit after its own kind. Like father, like son."

"Yes…" I nod in reflection. "Although the seeds are tiny, and many look rather similar, they seem to know how to produce the same crop as the parent plant."

"Have you noticed that certain plants…? Let me see… I'm sure you're familiar with the mastic shrub." He glances up and I nod. "It grows in two forms – male and female. One alone can't bear fruit – as it is with animals and indeed mankind." He winks. "We inherit features from both our father and our mother – our stature, the colour of our eyes and, usually," he says, chuckling at my wild locks, "that of our hair. But also our character. And that's why it's crucial who your father is."

We return in silence to our baskets.

"Oh, I almost forgot. I wanted to show you something special." He leads me over to the apricot tree.

"That's strange," I observe, peering at it from all sides. "Are those two trees intertwined? No, I see only one trunk. But those are almonds. How can that be?"

He chuckles. "Very observant. The apricots are over by now. I'm drying them for the winter. But, as you see, this is an almond branch growing on the same tree."

"But…"

"It's grafted. A young almond tree was growing among the rocks there. It didn't really stand a chance. I cut a twig from it, inserted it into a side branch of this faithful apricot tree and bound it up until it had accepted its new parent, so to speak."

On close examination, I see the join. "Two different things from one tree. I wouldn't have thought that possible."

"And now both branches produce good fruit. Because the stem is healthy, and the soil is rich and moist. Of

144

course, it only works with similar fruit. I couldn't graft almonds onto a fig tree."

My eyes sweep over his tidy patch. "You have so much in this small plot of land."

"Shouldn't a kind father be generous to the child He loves? Doesn't He promise to send sunshine and rain in due season, so that the land bears fruit? Where my Lord is pleased to bless, my plants are happy to produce in plenty."

Shaking my head at his straightforward faith, I turn to collect the tools. Together we carry the basket with the produce we picked and make our way to his cave.

Returning to the writing board, I unroll the parchments and reflect again on Cerbonius's puzzling ideas. I pick up the quill and proceed to copy the next page. The day wanes while I persist at writing out those strange sayings.

I shake my head as I roll up the original and spread out my copy to dry. I'm pleased with its tidy appearance, even if the content baffles me.

"Why did he change his name?" I blurt out.

"Who do you mean?"

"John's son is given a new name."

"The Baptiser? He had no children."

"No, not *that* John. Simon's father. What's wrong with being called Simon? And what is that new name, Cephas, supposed to mean?"

"Simon the Rock!" He laughs. "He behaved more like an impetuous donkey, I'd say. Only much later was he worthy of that new name."

"Was he supposed to become a rock, then?" My eyebrows rise. "What would that be like, I wonder?"

"He inherits his new father's character. Isn't that the true meaning of sonship?" He smiles, then pierces me again with his gaze. "Were you a good son to your father – heeding his advice, loyal to him?"

Further uncomfortable interrogation. I change the

subject. "Are you saying this Simon is going to be adopted by someone else?"

Cerbonius's eyes twinkle. "What could be better, if his new father is strong and loving and just? Indeed, he was adopted. In time – as he recognised his own failures and weaknesses and my Friend's kindness – he came to inherit a character worthy of his new father."

"I don't know what you mean. Did Simon's father die? Why did he need an adoptive father?"

"In time, lad, you will understand. And then your true purpose will be revealed to you."

Over the next months, I get to know Cerbonius much better. He is a diligent worker with a fervent will to complete his treatise. But he also takes time to counsel the many peasants who come seeking his advice on all sorts of practical as well as spiritual matters. His seedlings thrive under his tender care; he studies the role of insects in the development of the flowers and berries on wild shrubs; the song of the migrant thrushes enthrals him. Wherever I can, I give him a hand and take every opportunity to probe his knowledge of natural phenomena and his wisdom about life and spiritual matters.

His simple lifestyle and inspiring advice make me reflect on life back home. If anyone ever mentioned the Gods, it was only to instil fear in us children. We never talked about why we are here or how we should relate to one another. Life just happened, and we either suffered or enjoyed it without giving a thought to what it was all about.

I do miss my family – at least Mother and Little Eli – but also the lads. And Lucilla, even though she was so horrid to me. But I need to start a new life, a life of my own, and seek my fortune.

As I persevere with copying the scrolls, they often confuse me. Sometimes I dare to ask my mentor for an explanation.

"'*Spiritus ubi vult spirat, et vocem ejus audis, sed nescis unde veniat, aut quo vadat,*'" I quote. "This sounds beautiful, but is it true? Of course, we hear the wind, but does no one know where it comes from? I thought Favonius brought the west wind and Auster the violent storms from the south."

"We hear the wind, for sure. We feel it, too. Powerful and often frightening and destructive. But where it comes from and where it goes, that is surely not for us to fathom." Cerbonius scans the sky from west to east. "Those Gods you mentioned are a fanciful attempt at explaining something that is beyond our comprehension. But the point of that saying follows." He comes over and searches for the line he is looking for. "As astonishing and powerful as the wind is, so strangely active are all who are born by the Spirit of God."

Strange ideas, which again baffle me.

I press on with my copying. "What's this? A snake! Someone lifted it up on a pole. Why did he do that?" I point at the place on the parchment. "I've watched snakes a lot, wondered how they slide without effort even on sand or smooth rocks." My hand makes a wriggling movement. "I've fed them grasshoppers and mice. But I never tried lifting them up. That could be dangerous. Once, I was bitten by a viper and it was very painful." I peer at the middle finger of my right hand. "I sucked the poison out as fast as I could, but my whole hand swelled up. I vomited till nothing more came."

"How did you treat it?"

"Mother gave me mastic to chew. It was weeks before I was well again."

"Thank God you survived. But it was a bronze serpent that Moses hung up on a pole. If someone looked at it after they had been bitten by a venomous snake, they recovered."

I shake my head.

A discussion arises as to where God should be worshipped. We have our shrines and temples, with all their attendant practices – sacrifices, incantations, harlots. Cerbonius doesn't approve of all that. He talks of a different God. According to this script I'm copying, that God doesn't mind where one worships him. So long as it's *in spiritu et veritate* – whatever that means.

This hero I'm writing about has other miraculous tricks up his sleeve. Healing a dying child and a crippled man with a mere word, feeding thousands of people with a boy's lunch. But what strikes me most is when he walks over the sea to his friends in a boat. How could he do that? And was it a rowing boat or did it have a sail?

Will those crystals be worth enough to buy a boat? One day, I must set off to collect them. But I'm not ready to venture off on my own yet. And, anyway, Cerbonius needs my help.

CHAPTER SIXTEEN

Wives and Gems

AGAIN, THE SOUND of chanting wakes me. I rise, stiff, and splash my face with water from the urn. A bright, clear sky promises another pleasant autumn day.

Will I ever see Mother and Little Eli again? Shaking myself, I gather wood and start a fire. Soon a gruel is simmering, to which I add berries from a nearby bush. I'm not sure if Cerbonius takes an egg for breakfast.

Cheerful chatter makes me start. Has he a visitor? No, my host is mumbling to himself – or to his God.

"Wonderful!" he proclaims. "Faithful Sol has risen again, banishing the terrors of the night. And the birds wake to praise their Maker. Thank you, Lord, for my health, that I may still serve others." He claps me on the shoulder. "Are you well rested?"

"My bones ache a bit, but I slept well, thank you." I point at the steaming pot. "I made some porridge, if that suits you."

"Thank you." He prays, we eat, and I clear up. Cerbonius takes the second quill and labours at a work of his own. I'll have to read it when I get a chance.

Inspired by my text, I inadvertently break the silence. "Did you have enough wine?"

He looks up, a puzzled expression on his face. "On what occasion, lad?"

"You mentioned your wife yesterday. Did you have enough wine at your wedding?"

He chuckles. "Did you think I asked my Lord to make wine from water?" His merriness turns to a frown. "I didn't know Him as my Friend at that time." He nods for some moments. "If I had, I might have saved Raguel."

His frown draws my attention. "Your son?"

"Oh, those barren years." He's near to tears.

"Did you choose your wife yourself?"

He lays down his quill. "As I said, we travelled to Italy. We landed near Pisa and stayed with a Godly man of means. Bishop Regulus was a strict mentor and I none too diligent as his disciple. To memorise the texts I was supposed to learn by heart, I used to recite them aloud while walking through the maze-like gardens.

"One day I was trying to learn a Psalm and couldn't recall it fully. So I kept repeating the great promise, 'I will instruct you and teach you in the way you should go: I will counsel you with my eye on you.' in the hope it would remind me of the next line. To my amazement, I heard a woman's voice from behind a hedgerow reciting: '*nolite fieri sicut mulus quibus non est intellectus.*' It was the line I had forgotten." He chuckles.

"I can laugh about it now, but it was humiliating to be corrected by a woman, especially as she quoted that scathing line, 'Don't be like a senseless mule!' It peeved me, and I tried to find the speaker. I discovered a beautiful girl on a bench, also meditating on Holy Scripture. When she saw how annoyed I was, she burst out laughing. In the end I saw the funny side."

"Did you find out who she was?"

"It turned out she was the daughter of our good host, about fifteen years old… and not married." He smiles. "To our wonder and joy, that encounter led before long to our marriage."

"So easy!" My attention is caught by the melodious song of a thrush at the top of a pine tree, as the incident with Lucilla at the old quarry clouds my thoughts. "It must be wonderful if you truly love each other."

"Naturally, we discussed things with her parents and my mentor, but I'm sure it was our heavenly Father who brought us together."

"But you said you disagreed about how to bring up your son."

Cerbonius nods and taps the board before him. "Ah, Julia. What a wonderful woman you were. So gentle, so sensitive, so selfless." His eyes close and his rhythmic tapping continues. "How unworthy I was of your affection. You loved Raguel so dearly. You tried to compensate my harsh discipline by comforting him." A pause. "And how you praised your Lord! Many of your Psalms still enliven my dawn devotions with the angels."

"Were there other children?"

He turns, as if surprised by my presence. "Alas, no. My Julia was never strong and after the birth of our son her health declined. We couldn't consider having further children." He lowers his eyes, unable to speak for some moments. Then, "When Raguel went to war – full of fear and qualms – she lost all desire to live."

Does he see her there, in his mind's eye?

"O, Julia, and yet you never failed to love me. Through your faith and devotion I came to know our Saviour not merely as Lord but also as my Friend. How grateful I am that He cares for me – indeed for all people, all His creatures. How can I thank you, dearest Julia?"

I respect his moment of reverie, then say, "Thank you, sir, for being so honest. If I ever marry – which I don't plan to – I wish my wife might be like your Julia."

"Indeed, such a wife is worth far more than gems." He nods again. "But, as Julia taught me, even more wonderful than finding a devoted wife is coming to know and trust my loving Friend."

"You keep making such remarks. But I don't know who you are speaking of."

"In time, lad. In time you will become acquainted with Him, of that I am sure. But we have talked enough for the moment. I have an errand I would like you to perform."

He sends me to his attendant Marcus to place the freshly written scrolls in safe storage. My eyes almost pop out at the sight of shelf upon shelf of further documents, all labelled. Marcus points out the Scriptural texts and mentions the names of several other authors. I return to my mentor, laden with new parchments, a pot of soot and pine resin ink, a skin of wine, and a fresh loaf of bread.

To my consternation, Cerbonius raises his arms and shouts, "I bless your glorious name, most gracious Provider!" He's addressing his invisible Friend.

We press on with our scribal duties. An incident in the text reminds me of something I had intended to discuss with Cerbonius. "This magician who changed water into wine – he didn't like traders, it seems."

He bursts out laughing. "Magician! No, no. He is far greater than a mere wonder-worker. But what makes you think He doesn't approve of trade?"

"It says here he tipped out all their money. That was rather mean. Was it wrong in his eyes, to buy and sell things?"

"You haven't grasped the meaning of that incident, I fear. Those money-changers were more concerned for their profit than to serve the Lord. Greed is a grave sin. Comparable to serving idols." His eyes study my frown. "But I suspect there was an ulterior motive for your observation."

"Well, yes." Can he read my thoughts? "It's a long story."

"Tell me what's on your heart."

I boil some water, adding a selection of herbs from the dry bunches hanging on the walls of the cave. A drink and some figs refresh us.

I study the old Bishop's wrinkled face. Clasping my hands together, I grope for words. "Last year I was on my way to market…" I pause, wondering if this is a good idea. "If you remember, I was caught in a storm. Aquila wanted to destroy me." Cerbonius snorts. "But I found shelter in a cave."

"And you hid some details from me, I believe."

I gape. This is uncanny. "What do you mean? Must I tell you everything?"

"Of course not. But if you are seeking guidance, it's best to be open."

I nod. How do I start? "For two days we were stuck at the cave. The stream was so wild, there was no way we could cross."

"You say 'we'. Who was with you, if I may ask?"

It's my turn to laugh. "Just me and the mules." It would have been good to have someone like Rufus with me. "I began to explore the gorge. A huge boulder had crashed down from higher up the mountain and got stuck bridging the ravine."

He nods. "You climbed up and crossed over?"

His perceptiveness unnerves me. "Well, yes. And no. I couldn't possibly take the mules that way, so I had to come back. But that's not the point. The fact is, I found where the boulder had been. There was a trail of crushed shrubs and shattered stones leading from a huge hole in the side of the hill. I clambered up and…" My fingers wiggle as my hands swing wide, indicating the size of the hollow. "It–it was full from top to bottom with the most amazing crystals!" I'm at a loss for words. "Huge colourful gems. All along the back wall."

Cerbonius's eyebrows rise. "No doubt that wakened your commercial inclination."

"It did. Is that wrong?" Do I perceive a twinkle in the merry old man's eye? "My first thought was how I might be able to buy a boat. I could set off on my travels at last. The wide world was beckoning me."

"And were you able to sell them for a good price?"

"I only took a few with me. But yes, a gem trader in Fabricia bought them for much more than I even hoped for."

"I see. So what did you do with the profit?"

"I… I kept it hidden." No time for reflection. "And one of these days, I want to go back to fetch more crystals. Would you agree?"

He chuckles. "You aren't answerable to me, lad. I truly appreciate your help with copying those manuscripts. And I have tried to offer relief for your troubled soul. But you are free to leave whenever you want." He peers at me. "And to return if and when you wish to."

My fists clench and I find myself shouting, "I can't go back home." I break down. "Everyone hates me. What have I done to deserve that?" Even as I speak, my conscience pricks me. "Have I no right to enjoy my life?"

A pause. "And who should give you such a right?"

"You know what I mean. Those gems will let me seek my fortune." In my mind's eye, I'm sailing to far-off lands.

"Beware. Things may turn out different from what you expect. I, too, once sought a new life overseas." He laughs. "And look where I've ended up."

A smile breaks out. "You've been very kind to me. And taught me a lot." I pull myself out of my dreams. "But do you know Aquila – the rock, I mean – a league or two from here?" My hand has risen to my pendant.

"I have never been there. But they say it does, indeed, resemble an eagle, when seen from this side."

"I don't believe it's Aquila himself. I've been right up. It's only a pile of boulders." My arms trace their form.

"That's where I hid my coins. I retrieved them again on the way here." I point to my bag in the cave. "That grotto full of crystals." My eyes pan to the distant horizon. "A boat… The Colosseum and the aqueducts of Rome. The great fortresses and palaces of Constantinople. Perhaps I'll discover new lands no one has ever seen."

Cerbonius chuckles. "Ambitious you are, I must say. Yet I believe your calling may be far higher than such worldly feats." He sidles over to his larder. "Aren't you hungry?"

"Oh, yes." I light a fire under the pot, while Cerbonius chops in some leeks and mixes it with oats and beans.

During the meal he recounts some of his adventures in Africa and Italy and I enjoy the more relaxed conversation.

I can't sleep. The experiences and exchanges of the last few days scurry around my mind.

As a child I was content. We had what we needed. Father taught us to survive in our remote corner of the island. Mother worked hard and looked after us. And I learned to read and write.

Pontus pointed out how the planets move across the sky in their spheres and he was the one who designed our water wheel for grinding grain. We had fun with the girls and Caesar. And I often sneaked off when I should have been working, to watch my eagles, study the snakes. The passing ships always captured my attention.

What about all Ceres's Gods? Are they friendly or hostile?

I toss about on the hard floor of the cave, trying to find a comfortable position.

That happy world is now a thing of the past.

Cerbonius is different. He doesn't take our Gods seriously. His God is a friend who talks to him and who desires us all to live in harmony.

Peace and conflict. Fun and work. Riches and poverty. What is life all about?

Our days repeat themselves – transcribing texts and performing a variety of practical tasks – and shorten as they run into weeks and months. The alders and many shrubs lose their leaves. Often a howling wind disturbs my slumber.

CHAPTER SEVENTEEN

Mediation

IT'S EVENING, AND a visitor arrives – an imposing, fatherly figure, a close friend of my host, who has apparently been travelling for the last year. When Cerbonius introduces me to him – his name is Titus – he peers at me, then asks if it was I who came with Virna last year.

My heart beats faster. "That's right," I say. "Why do you ask?"

"I brought her down to the House of Healing."

I remember the name. But I was taking the mules to Marcus's place, so I never saw him. Memories flash through my mind. "How is she now?"

"Mother Martha cares well for her patients." As an afterthought, he adds, "I believe someone was asking about you a couple of days ago."

"What?" My heart races. Has Father sent someone to look for me? "Who was he?"

"I don't know his name. Wasn't a local. Had something wrong with his arm. Said he was looking for a lad with a strange accent and red hair who brought his wares to market by mule. Didn't say why."

Titus tells of a serious dispute in the village. Would Cerbonius agree to arbitrate?

It seems the slave of a rich and influential landowner

named Romerius was attacked by pirates and sold to another wealthy man from a neighbouring village, one Ignatius. Now these two are contending over the ownership.

They discuss the convoluted matter. At length, Cerbonius agrees to try to resolve the strife. Since both families are embroiled in the feud, he consents to go down to the village tomorrow to hear the case.

Before Titus departs, Cerbonius prays.

"Gracious Lord, assist us with this complex case. You see the hearts and true motives of Romerius and Ignatius. Grant us wisdom to perceive the issues behind the present dispute, that we may arrive at a peaceful and just verdict. We bring the injured young man before you. In your love, show him mercy. We pray in the name of our Lord and Friend, Jesus Christ, who brings down princes from their thrones and exalts the humble."

Titus responds with, "Amen."

What God is this, who takes an interest in such worldly squabbles, and may be willing or even able to help resolve them?

Titus departs, and we retire for the night.

In the morning, Cerbonius selects a particular scroll and packs it in his *scrippum*. Dense cloud envelops us, producing a mysterious murky light, as he grabs what looks like a shepherd's crook and steps with caution down the steep, rocky path. The visibility is even worse under the overhanging trees. The balmy scents of the macchia are almost hypnotic. This would be no journey for the old man alone. How will he make his way up at the end of a demanding day?

We approach the village, which I have only ever seen from a distance on my trips to and from Fabricia. I keep my eyes skinned in case Drusus is around.

Dogs announce our approach as we reach the first walled plots. The path becomes wider and consists of large, regularly placed stones. The occasional step lessens the slope, and a wide gutter hints of abundant water in the rainy season.

The first people we meet hurry off without a word. A skinny boy with tousled hair, some years younger than me, leading three brown goats, greets Cerbonius as a friend and stares at me through wide black eyes.

"*Mane bonum*," I venture, to break the tension. "I'm Silvanus. Nice goats."

"*Salve*." He looks at his charges as if for the first time, tapping one with his stick when it tries to jump onto a wall. "Thanks. They're not bad."

"What's your name?"

"Catalus. Never seen you before. Where're you from? You speak funny."

I grin. "I was going to say the same about you. I'm from over behind the mountain. You're right, I've never been here before. I stayed with Cerbonius for the last year."

"I hear he's going to judge the quarrel over Gallus. That'll be a riot."

I grab his shoulder. "Gallus? Is he the slave who was caught by the pirates? Will he be there?"

"I'm sure he will. Romerius and Ignatius will both be trying to grab him." He laughs. "But really, their fight is much older."

Cerbonius had been half listening, amused at our casual exchanges, but now he shows keen interest. "You say their animosity has other causes. What may they be?"

"Oh, many things. Don't you know? Those clans have been at each other's throats as long as I can remember. Ignatius says Romerius's son got his niece pregnant." He winks. "And refused to marry her." He calls to the goats. "Then one stormy day some boundary stones disappeared.

Romerius accused Ignatius's men of removing them. One thing blows over and another crops up." The goats are getting impatient. "They argue about who owns which part of the mine. And the workers are always wrangling about the channels for watering the vineyards. It never ends. I think it's because of Ignatius's God, Mercurius."

"Very interesting," Cerbonius mumbles, rocking his crook to and fro. "Very interesting." He looks up. "Run off with your goats, lad. Silvanus will reserve a good corner for you to watch the proceedings."

We emerge from the thick clouds and make our way through the village. The path gets steeper and narrows to an alley between tall granite houses with arched doorways. The air is still damp and the sun barely penetrates the clouds. Side roads cross ours at various angles and more people are pottering about, most of them also heading down towards the square. Everyone recognises Cerbonius and many greet him warmly.

Stately houses form one side of a flat, paved area. Opposite, a low wall offers a dramatic view of a little harbour far below. A reed-roofed platform with four sturdy chairs awaits the trial. Jostling villagers gather in noisy groups. When Cerbonius is whisked off by an official, I choose a spot on the wall near the stage and survey the milling crowds. No sign of Drusus.

Catalus's shaggy head appears and I wave. He joins me and points out Ignatius's clan from the neighbouring village. They stick close together as if they're afraid.

The magistrate calls Cerbonius onto the stage, along with white-haired Ignatius and seriously overweight Romerius. Cerbonius tries to keep a semblance of order, posing an occasional question to clarify some detail, as they air their disputes over land, livestock, mining and water rights, as well as malicious accusations of a personal nature, dishonest trade dealings and physical injuries.

Time and again, shouts and jeers burst from one side of the square or the other.

The hearing has been going on for hours. I can't follow the arguments about various intrigues going back over generations. Catalus and I invent a game. One of us picks a person in the crowd, mentioning some particular feature – a red scarf or a bag on their shoulder; the other then has to locate him or her. I study the ruddy faces and imagine their different characters.

We lean closer when Cerbonius calls out, "Is the lad, Gallus, present?" A handsome young man of about eighteen stands up. Cerbonius continues, "Please come here where everyone can see you." He mounts the stage. "How long have you served Romerius?"

Gallus stands erect and looks him in the eye. "I was born in Romerius's household, Your Honour. My parents are freedmen who have worked for him for many years. When my schooling was over, he gave me certain administrative duties."

"What sort of duties?"

"Bookkeeping. I recorded the revenue from selling our produce, charges for transporting goods, payment of the servants. Things like that."

"So, you are good with numbers. And did you do this work willingly?"

"Oh, yes. It was exciting to see how the family business thrived and I enjoyed working for my master."

"Romerius, did Gallus prove trustworthy in your service?"

"Most certainly. He was bright, diligent and reliable. That's why I chose him to carry out my errand."

"I see. And may I ask what that errand was?"

Romerius glances round. "I had certain gold reserves

with which I wished to support the efforts of the Emperor to repel the barbarian invaders. Gallus was to deliver my *solidi* to Centurion Didymus in Populonium, who would pass them on to Exarch Longinus in Ravenna. Gallus was then to collect a necklace I had commissioned for my granddaughter's wedding."

"Was it not somewhat risky to entrust such tasks to a young man? Did you send an escort with him? Or arm him?"

"I thought a young man with a small pouch, mingling with other passengers on a merchant vessel would be safe. He was armed with a *pugio*."

Cerbonius again addresses Gallus. "And did you fulfil your mission?"

"It wasn't difficult to find Centurion Didymus and I entrusted the five hundred and seventy-five *solidi* to his care." I gape at the amount. "He was most grateful and gave me a receipt. He wanted me to join his troops, but I persuaded him I had other business to conduct. I collected the necklace from the goldsmith. A splendid piece of work. It would have suited Paulina wonderfully."

"Would have?"

"Well, that's the tragic part." He lowers his eyes and clutches his right shoulder. "I found a place on a fishing boat returning to Ilva. It was stormy, and we sailed under the lee of the island. My attention was drawn to the red cliffs we were passing when, all of a sudden, a rowing boat appeared round the headland and attacked us. I had heard tales of pirates but didn't expect…"

"Oh, but there are pirates around here," I whisper to Catalus. "I've seen them attack!"

Gallus is still talking. "…the four of us – three fishermen and me. We didn't stand a chance." He buries his head in his hands for a moment, before continuing. "They killed the owner right away. Slit his throat. His son jumped out and swam ashore. I tried to fight but they stabbed me in the shoulder and I dropped my *pugio*. They took me and the other hand captive and stole the boat. And that beautiful necklace. And the receipt for the gold. Everything. They sold us as slaves in Fabricia. Ignatius's *vilicus* bought me, although at that stage I had no idea who my new master was."

"Romerius, do you believe this story? Might Gallus be deceiving you?"

Gallus blurts out, "I would never do that. You know that, master…"

"I addressed Romerius," Cerbonius says.

He answers without hesitation. "Indeed, I believe him. Gallus is an honest lad. And there's no doubt he was wounded."

Cerbonius now looks at Ignatius. "So, please tell me how you came to acquire Gallus."

He fidgets with his hands. "As he said, I had sent my *vilicus* to Fabricia to look for an intelligent young slave. And he returned with Gallus. He didn't know where he came from. He paid a handsome price for him."

"Although he was injured?"

"It didn't look too serious. And we needed him for light work, to replace our old bookkeeper."

"How long ago was that?"

"I would say about six months." He glances towards Gallus but makes it clear with his glare that he is not to speak.

"And has he proved useful?"

"I have had no direct dealings with him. He works under the oversight of my *vilicus* and lives in the barracks."

"Gallus," Cerbonius addresses the slave and observes his reaction. "How was your service with Ignatius?"

"When I first arrived, my wound was festering. I was feverish and couldn't work at all for some weeks."

"Who looked after you? Were you given medication?"

"No. I lay on my couch in the barracks. In terrible pain, drenched with sweat. One of the women brought me wine and some dry bread and fruit."

"Is that how your slaves are generally treated, Ignatius?"

"Certainly not. I knew nothing of this. I shall speak with my *vilicus*."

Turning back to Gallus. "But you recovered. What then were your duties?"

"Yes, I recovered after a time. It was only then I realised where I was – quite near to my rightful master. They gave me humble tasks around the *atrium* and herb garden. Cleaning. Feeding the dogs and parrots. Attending to the household shrine…"

Ignatius mutters, "Is there any harm in that?"

The exchanges continue at length, but I can't follow. Not wanting to lose our convenient place, we take turns running off to relieve ourselves in the fuller's tub. On the way back, we help ourselves from the honey-sweetened beverage, which someone has placed at the disposal of the crowds. I share the dried figs I brought with my friend.

The proceedings are paused. A servant mounts the stage and serves refreshments. Cerbonius consults the notes he has taken on a wax tablet, then discusses something with the magistrate.

The Bishop rises to make a pronouncement. "Magister Procius, Sextus Ignatius Alba, Aulus Romerius Avitus…"

"That's the first time I've heard their full names," Catalus remarks.

"…And citizens of Marciana and Podium, I have listened carefully to the lengthy pleas of the heads of these two noble families, and have given them due consideration. Before I state my conclusion, however, I wish to stress a matter of principle. I was of the understanding that you both acknowledged the supremacy and authority of our Lord and Saviour, Christ Jesus."

He pauses, glancing first at Romerius, who responds, "Certainly, your Honour." Ignatius gives an evasive nod.

Cerbonius removes the scroll from his bag and finds a particular place. "You are therefore familiar with our Lord's teaching, where He says: 'Beware! Guard against every kind of greed. Life is not measured by how much you own.'"

He scans the entire crowd, which is now silent and attentive, then refers to the scroll. "He spoke of a rich man whose ground produced fine crops, and who said to himself, 'What should I do? I don't have room for all my crops.' Then he said, 'I know! I'll tear down my barns and build bigger ones. Then I'll have room enough to store all my wheat and other goods. And I'll sit back and say to myself, 'My friend, you have enough stored away for years to come. Now take it easy! Eat, drink, and be merry!'" He pauses for the point to come home. "But God said to him, 'You fool! You will die this very night. Then who will get everything you worked for?' Yes, a person is a fool to store up earthly wealth but not have a rich relationship with God."

Many in the audience nod in agreement, but the story makes me think. What's coming now? Cerbonius turns to the men.

"Both of you are successful and wealthy landowners. To you, as elders of your clans, I repeat the Lord's admonition: Beware of greed! It might lead you astray."

They lower their gaze.

"Two further matters, Ignatius. You have in your home a shrine, to Mercurius, I believe."

The hoary-headed patriarch jerks back, as if struck in the face. "How do you know that? Anyway, it has nothing to do with this case."

"I implore you, in the name of our Lord: Stop compromising with the ancient Gods which are no Gods! I urge you and your household to serve the one true God and Him alone." He allows Ignatius a moment to collect himself. "And in future, make sure your slaves are treated with kindness, knowing that you also have a Master in heaven."

Ignatius glowers.

Cerbonius now addresses the hushed crowds. "I am old and cannot tolerate deceit and unnecessary delays. I will therefore be brief about pronouncing my judgements. With regards to the slave boy, Gallus, he belongs rightly to Romerius…"

Ignatius jumps up. "But I paid a handsome price for him. Who will repay that?"

Cerbonius ignores the objection and looks to the burly gentleman on his right, whose face breaks into a smile. "He was reared in your house and was harshly treated by those crooks, whom we cannot today bring to justice. Consider the well-being of your slave as more important than the jewellery that was stolen. Your granddaughter may have to wait for another wedding present."

Laughter arises from the crowd.

He turns to the slumped old man on his left. "Indeed, Ignatius, you lost the price you paid in good faith for a handsome slave." He raises both arms and faces the crowd. "So both parties have suffered undeserved financial loss. The sums in question don't concern me. I hope this hearing will be a valuable warning against greed to all here. Gallus will return to the household of Romerius." He again turns to the man on his right, who nods his thanks. "Let him be restored to his former position."

Cerbonius refers to his tablet. "Now to the other disputes. Water and mining rights, road maintenance." How will he handle that? "Ignatius, have you within your household a man with mechanical skills, who knows how to construct things of stone and iron?"

Ignatius's face reflects relief at the apparent reprieve. "Certainly. My son Tercius has proved excellent at designing mechanical devices – pumps and lifts and such like."

I am reminded of the dam and water wheel we built with Pontus's advice.

"Very well," Cerbonius responds, "assign him two of your able-bodied slaves."

He turns to his right. "And you, likewise, Romerius. Choose a skilful craftsman from your household and two strong slaves. These six men will be answerable to Magister Procius, here."

The magistrate sits up straight.

"You shall supervise these workers and ensure they provide a fair and just solution concerning water distribution, access to the mines and road repair. The costs of any construction work shall be borne equally by both parties.

"And now, I'm weary. I understand there are other private matters of discord between the two families. I have neither the strength nor the inclination to pronounce on such issues. You surely have, between you, enough wisdom to seek resolutions which are gracious even towards guilty parties, and also both just and appropriate." He picks up his cloak, replaces his tablet and scroll in his *scrippum*, and makes to leave the stage. "I thank you all for your attention and future compliance with my judgements. May the Lord be with you."

Magistrate Procius makes some closing remarks and the crowd begins to disperse.

Catalus has to run off home. "*Vale*. I hope we meet again."

CHAPTER EIGHTEEN

Farewell!

TITUS INVITES CERBONIUS and me to his home
for a meal. His wife, Septima, welcomes me warmly, as if
she had been hoping to meet me. What do these people
know about me? We are no sooner seated than several
young children rush in, gathering around Cerbonius,
competing for a seat on his lap and all talking at the same
time. He welcomes each by name, commenting on their
hair, their clothes or how much they've grown.

"Whoa! Have mercy on the old man." Titus laughs.
"He's weary after listening to the people's squabbles."

A moment later another boy, about six years old, hobbles in on crutches. His right leg is badly deformed, and
his dark skin shows he's not a natural child of Titus and
Septima. He stands back but Cerbonius draws him to his
side. "There's always room for you, Kanmi."

The sun has long disappeared behind Monte Capanne
by the time we finish eating. Cerbonius is exhausted and
we have a long climb ahead of us. I'm struck by how old
and frail he looks. How much longer will he be able to
live by himself in those primitive conditions, writing his
discourses and resolving disputes in the community?

"Come," Titus exclaims. "I see you are not in a fit state
to return to your cave. You two shall stay here tonight. I'll
see about getting you home in the morning."

Septima smiles and Cerbonius accepts the offer without objecting. We are shown to a guest room. One of the children prepares a hot bath, offering to scrape us down with a wooden strigil. I decline but Cerbonius welcomes the refreshing treatment.

We have to laugh when Titus arrives early next morning with a rough wooden contraption carried by four young men – two young tree trunks strapped to the sides of an old chair. We finish our breakfast and say goodbye to Septima.

At first, Cerbonius refuses to be carried, but the children insist he should sit on the makeshift litter. They hang from the beams when the men lift it, each trying to outdo the other with their antics. Kanmi watches, amused by his adoptive siblings' pranks but unable to join in.

Cerbonius tells them to come down from the poles. "You've had your fun, now. Think of the poor slaves who have to carry such a load."

The men laugh and lower the seat to the ground. Cerbonius has a brief word with one of them. "All right, children. No swinging from the poles, but you can run along with us as far as the top of the village. Kanmi will ride with me in the chair. You others can help him get home afterwards."

And so we set off, a jolly troop. It's not easy for the porters to navigate through the steep, narrow passageways. The last wall of the village is the signal for Cerbonius to be set down. He thanks the children for accompanying him – quite a crowd has gathered by now – and sings a little ditty with them. Then Titus sends them off home. A tall young man lifts Kanmi onto his back and one of the boys takes his crutches. We continue up the steep, tree-lined path.

I come alongside the litter. "I liked the way you handled that dispute yesterday."

"Thank you. It did prove somewhat tedious. At the end of the day I was quite worn out."

"How did you know about the extent of their grievances?"

"A divine fluke!" He glances at one of the porters who stifles a laugh, then back to me. "Your friend... What was his name?"

"Do you mean Catalus?"

"Yes, Catalus. Without realising, he gave me vital clues as to the roots of their quarrels."

"I see. But do you think Romerius and Ignatius will accept your decisions?"

"Romerius, for all his self-indulgent tendencies, will take the Lord's warning to heart. He has understood that the welfare of a soul – even that of a slave – is far more important than any amount of gold..."

Titus interrupts. "Would that were more generally recognised."

"As for Ignatius," Cerbonius continues, "he persists in worshipping Mercurius, no doubt hoping for more wealth, and we heard how his slaves are treated. Despicable. As if they weren't human. I worry for his soul."

"Indeed. If only he saw the light," Titus says. "It would be wonderful if the two clans would learn to cooperate in place of their constant rivalry."

No one speaks.

"Catalus mentioned something else," I say after some moments. "About Ignatius's pregnant niece. Did you not think that mattered?"

"On the contrary, my lad," Cerbonius answers, "it's so important that the families must resolve the issue themselves. After all, it concerns the life of one of God's children. What could be more important on this wonderful earth?"

I had never thought along these lines. "So what do you think should happen?"

"Clearly, the young man – Romerius's son, I believe, or

was it his grandson? – must take responsibility for both the girl and the baby. If possible, they should marry and then care for this and any future children. If that isn't possible, he must nevertheless provide a home and a living for them. At least until she marries another, or the child comes of age."

"That is a big commitment for a young man to make. You seem to consider it a very serious matter."

"Indeed. A wife should be loved and provided for. And children need the discipline and instruction of both father and mother if they are to grow into wise and mature people with an upright heart. Be careful not to make the same error I made."

I smile. "Thank you for your advice, but I have no intention to marry. I want to get a boat and explore the world."

We reach the cave and Cerbonius climbs out of the litter. The porters are hot and tired. I bring them a flagon of wine and prepare a meal for everyone. Cerbonius suggests the litter be taken to Marcus's place so it is available for another occasion. The porters bid farewell and leave.

Cerbonius and Titus deliberate some matter of faith or politics.

As I go back to the scrolls, a robin's rich melody comes over as a plea for the days to lengthen. My attempt to whistle the same tune sets me in a pensive mood.

Through seeds, a parent plant passes its characteristics to its offspring. It's the same with people. Except we also learn a lot from our parents and depend on them for years. The riddle becomes more complicated when an almond branch is grafted onto an apricot tree. It's as if it has a new parent. Simon was given a different name – as if he now belonged to a new family – when he started following that wandering preacher. He even said, if someone believed in Him, he could become a son of God…

And Cerbonius… He failed to truly love his son. Ignored his gifts. Forced him to be what he was not. Can a father's mistakes be put right?

Several times my mentor has spoken of greed. The traders in the temple. The disputing elders Romerius and Ignatius. Am I, too, at risk? Could those crystals become my downfall instead of a blessing?

Is it right that a girl like Virna can be taken captive, sold as a slave and molested? Shouldn't she have the same rights as freemen?

Pirates. I've seen their brutal deeds. What drives them to deny all honour and live as outlaws? Gallus was a victim, too. How could such attacks be stopped?

And now, war is again looming. Will I have to join the army to fight off the invaders? What if we don't succeed? Will we all be enslaved? Or killed? Or starve to death? Why can't conflicts between tribes be resolved peaceably?

Titus leaves at last, and I take my chance to question Cerbonius.

"While you were talking, I've been thinking about the texts." I point at the stack of scrolls. "I have some questions…" I drum my fingers on the writing board. That's not what I wanted to say.

"I'll be glad to offer you some explanation if I can. But I think you have another matter on your heart."

"Well…" I'm convinced he can see through me. "It's been over a year since I came back to you. I've been thinking a lot. And as I said the other day, I'd like to go for the remaining crystals. Try my luck at selling them in Fabricia."

"Feel free to follow your desires." He nods, gazing up to the hills. "I'll miss you. And will welcome you if you decide to come back."

We eat supper and I'm no further with my understanding of those troubling questions. Cerbonius performs his usual bedtime ritual and we retire for the night.

Flaming arrows tear across the bows of my boat and crash onto the towering trireme that emerges through the spray from my left. Its sail blazes and lights the dusk. One after another, frantic sailors try to douse the flames, while others load large boulders into catapults and launch them back at the aggressor. A noxious cloud from burning tar engulfs me, obscuring my view of the action, but failing to smother the resounding crashes of rams, accompanied by terrifying cracks of splintering timbers. Intrepid cries from the attackers and agonised screams of victims pound me from all sides. What are they fighting about? And how is it that my little vessel is caught in the midst of this battle? Tossed about by the churning waves, I pull in my sail and try to manoeuvre my skiff away from the heart of the fray.

A harsh cry resounds. "There he is! He's got them. Get him!"

A grappling hook lands on my bow and is pulled taut by a chain. My little boat is being drawn to the side of a huge galley. Horror. It's me *the warring parties are seeking to capture! Help!*

My scream wakes me. I shake my head in an attempt to rid myself of the fearful scene.

Why were they after me? The crystals! Are they to be my doom?

The trees loom dark and threatening against the paling sky. Cerbonius is up. Singing with the angels, no doubt.

The developing storm will make travelling difficult, especially if I can't see far enough to get my bearings. I'll be approaching the valley from a different direction. I doubt I'll be able to collect the crystals and return in one day. Perhaps I should go straight to Fabricia, make my fortune and set off for the East. But then I might never see my mentor again.

Breakfast is unusually quiet. Cerbonius observes me with his hawk eyes but waits for me to speak.

"I've packed my things and taken the liberty of stealing some of your bread and a skin of wine." My attempt at humour falls flat. How to say goodbye?

I glance around at the cave, the swaying trees, the prayer rock, the distant sea, whose roar reaches me even up here as it throws up whitecaps. I pick up my bag, my cloak and my stave, then put them down again. Bowing on one knee, I grasp Cerbonius's right hand with both of mine. I'm not the only one with tears in my eyes.

"I'm… very grateful for your hospitality." What a stupid thing to say. "Your concern… your advice… your…" My head drops to our clutched hands. My breath comes in gasps. I force myself to raise my gaze and look into his eyes. "…Your love."

"My son, I do love you. I wish you Godspeed on your venture. And I look forward to your return. Farewell."

The geese cackle wildly as I make my way down to the main path and head east, intending to pass around the massive range of Monte Capanne.

The first part of my trek is familiar but then, instead of dropping down to the plain, I take the higher southward branch, crossing through lonely, bleak woods. The path has disappeared in places, but I press on, lured by the occasional glimpse of grey between the trunks of the massive pines, which have largely replaced the oaks. The crest of the ridge is near but I still have a steep and rough climb to overcome. I decide to rest as soon as I get to the top.

Sure enough, I'm now on the brow of a mountain range. The vegetation is totally different here – almost no trees, only small shrubs and scattered boulders. Now and then a stretch of coast peeps through the low cloud. Out there, other islands are hiding. And the big, wide world.

I take the promised break for refreshment and scan the nearer slopes.

Yes, far below, I'm sure I see the path I took last year after having found the crystal grotto. Behind the spur to my left must be the village where that couple put me up for the night. I wonder what they are doing in this harsh weather.

I run down the steep hillside, cloak and bag flapping behind me, stave held high. Loose stones cause me to slip. I lose my balance, stumble and roll into a gorse bush. My injuries are nothing more serious than a scraped knee and a few painful spines in my arm and neck.

A small bird flees for safety as I hasten across familiar headlands and dales, between bizarre boulders and aromatic clumps of macchia, on towards where the setting sun should be. There's no one in sight.

The clouds close in, dark and ominous, and the wind rises, attacking me in gusts. I finger my amulet. Has Aquila again decided to torment me? Does he not approve of me claiming those crystals? He unleashes a new weapon against me. Tiny white flakes swirl around me. More and more fall – bigger, thicker, faster. I feel coldness touching my face and hands where they settle, only to melt to droplets of water a moment later. Snow. My first encounter.

Spiky bushes and sharp rocks adopt a soft white mantle. I stoop, scoop up a handful of this new substance and squeeze it into a ball. It shatters when I throw it at a rock face, leaving a white mound like a young woman's breast. If it weren't so cold, it could be fun.

Billowing flakes penetrate my loose-fitting clothes and make me shiver. I unroll my goatskin, throw it over my head and shoulders, and clasp it together with the *fibula* from my cloak. Walking becomes difficult as I slip on the new carpet underfoot.

Now my surroundings have all but disappeared in a pale shroud. Boulders and bushes startle me as they burst out in front of me, then vanish again as I pass. I hope I'm maintaining my bearings.

On I plod. I whistle to revive my spirits. I'm about to collect the crystals. Why didn't I think of taking another bag or basket?

Each step is now hesitant. The hillside is becoming steeper, curving down to the right. I have no chance of identifying any features of the landscape in this swirling snow.

I become aware of large pine trees ahead, their boughs sagging under their icy load and forming a tunnel, under which the ground looks wet but still dark. As I push the branches aside, they spring up, dislodging a heavy load of snow over me. I stumble and fall onto my grazed knee, then slide down a muddy slope.

"I hate you, Aquila!"

CHAPTER NINETEEN

Daylight Robbery

PICKING MYSELF UP and scraping the worst of the mud off my breeches, I find myself in a narrow, wooded valley, somewhat protected from the snowstorm. I scramble down to the stream, then make my way up along its treacherous course, leaping from boulder to boulder and clambering over fallen tree trunks.

On and on I struggle, weary now, as the dusk dims the meagre light filtering through the overhanging branches.

Io! I'm at the ford I crossed with the mules! From here, I have no difficulty finding the cave. The embers from my last visit are still visible. Untouched. Why didn't I bring a pot to brew up something warm to drink?

A fire, a bite of Cerbonius's bread, and a swig of wine is all I allow myself before settling for the night, wrapped as best I can in my single goatskin.

I wake, confused by strange dreams. Hungry. Aching. Cold. It has continued to snow through the night.

I kindle the fire, eat the rest of my bread and take a sip of wine. Now for the grotto.

The little pick is a great help as I scale the steep rocks of the canyon. I smile as I pass the place where I slipped and grazed myself more than a year ago.

Yes, the huge boulder is still wedged in place, spanning the ravine. Dare I cross? I hadn't bargained for it to be covered with a layer of snow. With a twig from a nearby ash, I scrape the worst of it off, then venture out on all fours. The muscles in my arms and legs twitch as I crawl forward, inch by inch.

When I reach the other side, I breathe again. Of course, the slope up to the grotto is also covered with that icy peril. Again my pick comes in handy, and I clamber to the lair.

A whoop escapes my lips. My treasure appears even more glorious than I remembered. I take a moment to gaze at the exquisite shapes and fabulous shades of pink and brown gems. Jeremias will cut them into magnificent forms and mount them on gold to make exclusive necklaces, brooches and rings.

I squeeze my upper body into the cramped space and set to work levering the massed crystals from the rock. Some clusters come away without difficulty, but soon I regret not having brought a hammer and chisel. I pry them out with my pick and cringe as one handsome group after another splits apart, leaving several fine specimens cracked and marred.

Now a new problem arises. How can I carry all these crystals down? When my bag is full, it's almost too heavy to manage. If I had a helper, I might lower it on a rope. But I can't let anyone else in on my secret. There's nothing for it but to make several descents.

Edging my way back across the boulder with the bulky bag over my shoulder, I squirm as the sharp contents jab into my flesh every time it bounces, threatening my balance. With this lopsided burden, the cliff face also proves precarious. But I make it to the cave, empty the bag and set off for another load.

All day I'm at it, before the entire hoard is safe in my lair. My knuckles are bleeding and my legs ache. But as

I arrange my treasure in a semicircle around me – first sorting them from largest to smallest, then according to the varying shades from almost colourless through amber and brown to bright pink – my excitement knows no bounds. One cluster strikes me as particularly beautiful. It's a tall, smoky-beige central figure conjuring up an image of a proud, confident king, protected on either side by his shorter but equally splendid attendants. I hold the constellation up towards the mouth of the cave to let the failing light shine through, and imagine the Emperor – I don't remember who succeeded Justinian – radiant on his throne in Constantinople. What wars or what scandals is he brooding over at this moment?

Back to reality. How am I to transport this entire load to Jeremias's place in Fabricia? Why didn't I plan this task better? Though my stomach rumbles, I have no choice but to sleep with the problem unresolved.

Still hungry but somewhat rested, my basket-making skills come to my aid. Flexible willow and hazel shoots are available among the pines and alders, and I experiment with different solutions – a larger knapsack, two hanging baskets balanced on my stave. In the end, I fashion a container with two long poles, which I'm able to drag behind me without too much effort.

The snowy carpet enveloping the earth proves helpful and today the sky is bright and cloudless. Has Aquila forgotten to torment me? With my stave to steady me, I struggle to keep the basket flat as I drag it down the rocks, along the bank of the stream, across the ford and up the steep hillside. Twice it tips, and I scrabble in the snow to gather the scattered crystals. I strap the goatskin over the top.

The path should be familiar from last time, but the white blanket makes everything so different. And difficult. Here and there I see yesterday's tracks. Or was it two days ago that I came through here? My shoes are far from adequate for these conditions, but I persevere.

One more hill, one more vale. On and on it goes. The cool, clear air is refreshing, and though I'm dazzled by the low sun reflecting off the snow, I recognise the distant headlands and inlets.

Hunger and weariness overcomes me; my scratched fingers are sore, and a searing ache develops in my back, twisted from pulling my precious load. A lone pine, contorted by years of extreme weather, has preserved a dry nook among large boulders. I pull the basket to safety, drop my stave next to it and settle on a patch of heather. The shade and the chance to rest are most welcome. I chew my last raisins and try to quench my thirst with handfuls of snow.

All around me, droplets of water fall from the heavily-laden branches, as the sun reveals its power. A lone robin flies to the top of my tree and celebrates the start of the thaw in song. I whistle in imitation of its melody.

I've succeeded! I throw my hands in the air for joy. "Thank you, Aquila." Jeremias will be delighted by these gems. I'll order a boat from that boatwright – what was his name? – Laurus. And I'll have enough money left to enjoy life, relaxing in a *caupona* – not Albinus's – whilst it's being built.

Or I could help that couple who showed me kindness – Antonius and Anna – perhaps even stay with them. Then Rome, Constantinople, Alexandria await me.

"Need a hand with tha' there load?"

I jump. My heart thumps. The mocking voice from behind the rocks makes me cringe. Don't I recognise it? Trembling, I turn to look. Sure enough: it's Drusus. I struggle to my feet, too shocked to respond.

His raucous laugh frightens me. That was no offer of help. "Thanks for draggin' them precious cryssals so far." His one good hand points a *pugio* at my basket. I can't ignore the implication. "Gettin' a bit too much for the li'l lad?"

"W-what are you doing here?" I glance around. Perhaps I could outrun him. But then I'd lose my crystals. I eye my stave. "H-how did you find me?"

Another spiteful cackle. "Let's say Chione was doin' me a favour. Sent t'snow jus' as I was about to lose yer tracks. Afterward 'twas simple."

"You mean you've been following me for days?" My jaw drops. "To the cave and back?"

"I was about a day behin' you. So I only had th'one night in them charmin' woods by t'stream." He smirks. "While you was doin' the hard work for me."

"For you? What on earth do you mean?"

"Is tha' so hard t'unnerstan'?" He snorts and waves his *pugio* in my face. "You chiselled 'em out 'n dragged 'em here. I'd never have managed tha' alone. So thanks." He advances, moving between the basket and me. "Them's mine now."

"My crystals? My boat?" I stare at him, my mouth agape. "You're robbing me. Again. Stealing everything I've worked for. My whole life."

"Let's not be so dramatic." He leans against the boulder. "Wha' makes you feel you have a special righ' to them gems? If Fortuna had chosen diffren', I might have been th'one to find 'em. Jus' happened to be you. You dug 'em out. And now yer givin' 'em to me." He sweeps his arm across the bare hillside.

Feigning despair, I fall back against the gnarled tree trunk, then slide down to the hard earth. In an attempt to distract him, I move one hand towards the basket while with the other I grab my stave and leap up. "I'm not afraid of you, Drusus."

He grins. "Oughta be, lad."

I raise my stave with both hands as he steps nearer. "Don't come closer!"

"Or what?"

I swing the staff towards his face with all my strength.

He ducks faster than I would have thought possible, then lashes out with a vicious kick at my right knee. I scream and collapse in a world of pain.

As I fall, he knocks my stave away and kneels on top of me, his pugio at my throat. My breathing stops and vivid images flash through my consciousness. Little Eli rushing out to welcome me home; Lucilla flirting at the quarry; Virna curling up behind me between the goatskins; Cerbonius chuckling at my inability to understand his God.

"Yer no match for me, lad." A maniac chortle emerges from his throat. "I've dealt with dozens like you afore now." He moves the weapon away and stands up.

I breathe again.

"But you got spirit, an' I like tha'. So, here's the deal. You help me get this here booty to t'next village, an' maybe I'll take pity on you. But make another move agains' me and I'll end you. Han' me yer knife!"

How dare that robin continue to rejoice, though my world has fallen apart?

Booty, he calls it. Horrible visions spring to mind as I imagine what that dagger of his has wrought in the past. Rage boils within me but I dare not show it. Perhaps if I appear to comply I'll have a chance to outwit him later. My fingers tremble as I loosen the sheath from my belt, then hold out my knife to Drusus. His eyes glint with spite.

"Get up! We'll pull t'load together. I see yer strength is failin'," he snarls. "But I warn you: Don't think o' tryin' any funny business!"

I drag myself to my feet. Drusus sticks his pugio and mine into his belt and grabs one pole with his good hand. I have to take the other. The wretched load continues its journey between us.

Red and brown feathers flash in the sunlight as the robin takes to the air and flies on ahead of us. At least I still have my bag with the coins and pick.

I was so sure my hopes were coming to fruition. At last I would be able to escape this island.

The hours go by. I scowl and shake my head. So, Aquila has succeeded in tripping me up again. My back aches from the twisted effort of pulling the load. I glance at Drusus, yearning to get revenge. He ignores me, a contented smirk on his face. He's not planning to take a break any time soon. We plod on.

Far below on our right a village appears and, later, an abandoned harbour, likely built in former days for transporting granite. The sun is now overhead and the snow is melting. It becomes more difficult to drag the crate over the rocky hillside between the wiry shrubs.

A crack and a jerk alert us that something has broken. We stop and examine the damage. My basketwork has succumbed to the harsh treatment. Without a word, I untie the goatskin and empty the crystals onto it.

Drusus gathers the spilt ones, letting out a whistle as he examines their clean form and exotic colouring. It's the first time he's seen the gems. He insists I mend the basket. Should I refuse and leave him stranded? I'm not willing to abandon my treasure.

On this barren hillside, with no fresh shoots to replace the worn-out ones, my repair is far from satisfactory. It won't last long. We reload the basket and press on as best we can.

Our trudge continues in silence and our shadows lengthen ahead of us. Signs of human presence appear – a fence, a path, cultivated vines and soon the first houses, accompanied by the aggressive barking of dogs. I remember coming through here. Can it be little more than a year ago? Elderly farmers raise their heads at the unfamiliar sound of our burden dragging along, suspicion in their eyes.

Glib-tongued, as when I first met him, Drusus purchases a replacement basket from an old man for a single *follis* and negotiates a ride into Fabricia on a bullock cart. I make a move to climb in, but he pushes me off.

I gape at the disappearing cart, unwilling to believe what's happening. He's running off with all my crystals and abandoning me! I'm too shocked to react.

At the last moment he flings me my knife and shouts, "Highwayman's honour!"

The sun is setting and I stand alone, unmoving, gazing at my shadow stretching far along the empty road. My world has collapsed.

"I thought that wily fellow was a friend of yours." The words of the old man who sold Drusus the basket pull me back to reality. "Did he leave you here?"

"That bastard!" I shake my fist in the air. "He ran off with my treasure."

I tender a half-*follis* in the hope of some food, but he's happy to share his bread and soup with me without payment. He even offers me a bed for the night. I accept without a second thought.

Troubled thoughts swirl through my mind, keeping sleep at bay.

Did Cerbonius have a premonition that something like this would happen? That disaster was looming because I'd set my heart on wealth and a chance to escape from Submonte? He sensed my broken relationship with Father was the root of my unhappiness. That was near to his own heart, since his father hadn't understood him, and he'd admitted he hadn't done any better with his own son – what was his name? – Raguel.

Yet he seemed to think he knew a remedy for my bitterness. Something to do with his friend as he called him. In some way he claims it's possible to become a child of that God of his – to be adopted by him, so to speak. Simon was given a new name – Peter, the rock – to show he had a new father. A new father? What new name would I be given?

Should I have fought for my treasure? Drusus only had one good arm. If I'd reacted faster, I might have overpowered him with my stave. But he was armed. I still had a knife… and the pick. He seems to have no scruples. He would have stabbed me, maybe even killed me on that desolate slope. Except, of course, that he needed my help to drag the basket.

If I'd been satisfied with only a portion of the crystals, I could have gone back for the rest. That option is out now. At least I have the coins I retrieved from Aquila's care: two golden *solidi* and a couple of hundred *folles*.

Will the Gods show me favour yet?

A crow wakes me. After a plentiful breakfast, I thank my host and prepare to leave. He insists I accept a loaf of bread, a large bunch of grapes and a skin of wine. Some people really are kind and generous.

Where am I to go?

I take the higher path northwards. Like last time. Perhaps to avoid following treacherous Drusus and my lost treasure. Soon more dwellings appear, and I recognise the path to the left which I took such a long time ago with poor Virna. Pretty, forlorn Virna. It will take me back over the mountain towards Cerbonius. What will he think, if I confess what has happened?

Smatterings of snow remain on the ground as I trudge through the woods. Night is falling, my feet are frozen and my heart heavy, but there's still a long way to go. All of a sudden, a bouncing glimmer of light flickers between the dark tree trunks. Soon I hear the cheery tones of a song I recognise.

The old Bishop – wrapped in a rough woollen shawl – lumbers toward me with the aid of his staff, then stretches out his arms in greeting. Can he have known I was return-ing and come out to meet me? I left him only three days ago, but so much has happened.

Without a word, he transfers the lamp to the hand holding his staff, puts his free arm over my shoulder and draws me close. We plod on in silence.

After some moments, I pluck up courage. "Well… I got them."

He sees through me, I'm sure.

In my mind I replay the events of the last few days. The tedious hike across the mountain range, the bitter wind and snow, the difficult scramble to the grotto, the painful effort of chipping away in the cramped space, trying not to damage my precious gems more than necessary… How many times did I climb up and down? Five? Two freezing nights with hardly any food.

I shake my head. "And I lost them."

My head drops into my hands and I break down, unable to suppress my tears. My chest heaves in time with my sniffs, my mouth remaining locked shut. We plod on.

He waits.

I continue to stare at the suggestion of a path ahead. "I don't think I mentioned I was robbed a year ago."

"Indeed, I don't remember you saying anything about that."

"I was so foolish. I trusted this fellow, Drusus. He offered to help me sell my goods." I slap my forehead again and again with the palm of my hand. "So young and so foolish." I pick up a fallen branch and slash at the nearby bushes. "When I left Hercules for a short time, Drusus stole my baskets of fruit and nuts." My hacking becomes more viscious, then stops. "I felt such a failure. I couldn't tell anyone. Least of all Father."

Cerbonius pulls me to a halt and turns to face me. "Another obstacle to your relationship, I fear."

I nod. "After I left you, that villain followed my footprints in the snow." I point at the tracks Cerbonius made when coming to meet me. "It must have been he who was asking about me in Marciana."

I fling the stick away and shout, "He robbed me again and ran off with my precious gems!" Again, I slap my forehead. "All of them!"

In the wavering glow from the lantern, Cerbonius's gaze seems to penetrate my soul, but it's sympathetic, warm. For a long time he says nothing. Then, "Yes, it's the price of wisdom."

I glance at him askance. "What is that supposed to mean?"

"You have to make a choice. Seek wealth or wisdom. Many a worthy man has stumbled through yearning for riches."

"Are you saying I should not have gone for the crystals at all?" I feel the heat rising in my cheeks. "Is it wrong to want to buy a boat and sail the seas?"

He smiles. "Perhaps you aren't yet ready for such a venture."

The lantern flickers once more and dies.

CHAPTER TWENTY

Apprentice

I TURN TO Cerbonius but make no comment. We plod on.

Uncanny shadows of the surrounding trees paint fantastic moving shapes on the ground around us as the full moon rises in the east. It draws my attention to the myriad stars, and I look up to regard them. Vega over on our left is the brightest tonight and, further west, just above the horizon, Cerbonius points out Altair in the constellation Aquila. It was he who carried Jupiter's thunderbolts when he waged war, he says.

Aquila. Is that God haunting me?

"Those are the ever-spinning stars. I see none of the nearer celestial orbs." I scan the firmament. "Is it true that everything here on this central sphere is perishing, whereas above the moon all things are eternal?"

"An idea from Cicero's Somnium, I believe," Cerbonius counters. "Was that the work you wanted to discuss with me? As I recall, that wise man claimed the souls of worthy men are taken up to the highest celestial sphere."

"That's right. In his dream, Scipio peers down from the heaven of heavens. The Earth looks so small to him. He's ashamed of our empire, a mere point on its surface."

It's too dark to see his facial expression but I hear a chuckle. "Indeed, what are the achievements of men?"

I reflect on Cerbonius's words. "Africanus says our lives are controlled, or, at least influenced, by the heavenly spheres circling the Earth."

"Do you remember them?" Cerbonius seems to be familiar with the treatise I bought.

"All of them?" Pontus spoke of them, but that was a long time ago. "Well, the first is Luna, the moon… then Mercurius, I guess, and the sun…"

"What about the charming Goddess of Love?" He chuckles. "Is she of no interest to you?"

"All right, Venus. Then Sol, Mars, Jupiter, Saturnus. Is that right?"

"Correct. And then?"

I wave my arm across the sky. "All these stars, of course." Is he expecting more? "Beyond them, the place where Africanus was with the supreme God, I guess."

"And how did he come to live there?"

"He said eternal happiness was the reward for souls who faithfully served their country."

"You remember it well, my lad. Do you agree?"

What a question! "Ceres taught me Aquila the Avenger is an incarnation of Jupiter. Is that true?"

"A counter-question! Very clever!" There's a rustle as Cerbonius brushes a branch away with his staff. "I'm not concerned about the influence of the spheres. Nor do I fear the pagan Gods. My Friend offers me a far more wonderful prospect."

His assurance ruffles me. "When he saw how content his grandfather was up there, Scipio came to despise all earthly matters. He wanted to die and join his happy forefathers in the celestial realm." I pull my mantle tighter around me. "But I want to seek my fortune down here while I'm young."

A sigh. "Which man deserves eternal bliss?" He lets me ponder that a moment. "What then is your purpose here on earth?"

I turn towards him. "Apart from exploring the world? How should I know. What are you suggesting?"

"Africanus asserts that man is responsible for preserving this world, and at the same time promoting justice."

"As I recall, it was Scipio's father – Paulus, I believe – who said that."

"Perhaps you're right. But what do you say to those two obligations – to care for this earth that is entrusted to us and to try to be just in all our affairs?"

"In my experience, most people have other aims." My mood darkens as I remember Drusus. "They exploit the earth's riches and take advantage of weak people." A new thought crosses my mind. "But surely we all have to look after ourselves?"

"Not I." He pauses. "Another cares for me."

Marcus, who brings him food and other items? Or Titus?

Cerbonius continues. "Paulus also claims we each have a specific duty, an agreeable and profitable task to fulfil while here on earth." He waits for this thought to sink in. "For Scipio it was to conquer and rule my home city, Carthago. But yours and mine are doubtless quite different."

"You think I have an agreeable and profitable task to fulfil here on Earth?" That's a new idea. "For me, life has been a rather unpleasant struggle – under constant threat from that hostile God."

"Just now you recalled his view that man is trapped in his body and condemned to linger, wretched, on a doomed and decaying earth."

He doesn't accept my silence. "I ask you, do you agree with Paulus's proposition?"

"How so?"

"Well, are you in truth trapped in a repulsive body?" He waits for me to consider. "And is this earth completely corrupt? Is no part of your life agreeable?"

My stomach tightens. "I no longer have a home. And now all my prospects of riches are dashed." My passion rises. "What does life hold for me? And when I die, well… I have no reason to hope that my soul will rise to the highest heaven."

"My Friend doesn't want to wait until you die. He desires to meet with you here and now." We have reached his cave at last. "But it seems you are tired, lad, and can't think clearly. Let us postpone further discussion."

Cerbonius's chanting makes me shudder. What reason does he have for such happiness so early in the day? By the time he comes down, breakfast is ready.

Before we eat, he again thanks his friend for the new day, the chirping birds, the glittering sea and the food in front of us. But he also prays for wisdom and guidance for me. This puzzles me more than it comforts.

"What makes you think your friend has some influence on my life?"

My mentor takes his time to finish his mouthful of porridge. "He cares for all His children."

My hand stops halfway to my mouth and I stare at Cerbonius.

He has another shock for me. "You must leave. A new prospect awaits you in Fabricia."

I start. "I had the same idea. Do you think I can get back my crystals from that bastard, Drusus?"

"It would be most unwise to try. No, another opportunity will open for you, which may bring you greater fortune."

"Greater than all those gems? What are you saying?"

"A far worthier fortune – healing for your soul. At this time I can't say more. My Friend will guide you."

"Your friend! Your friend! Where is he? I can't see him, I can't hear him. How can he guide me?"

"Too many questions, my lad. Have faith! One day you will meet Him."

It was still cold when I left Cerbonius, equipped with fresh bread, dried apricots and a skin of wine. Now the sun is high, the air clear. Beyond the rolling ridges and rocky bays, the mainland beckons.

From the top of the last hill, I look down over Fabricia. I can't stay with Albanus. News of my whereabouts would get back to Father. Anyway, I have no amphora of wine as payment.

I buy a slice of *focaccia* and a bowl of soup at a different *caupona* and sit while I eat. Three old men linger at a corner table, drinking and chatting. Others are playing *tabula*. A group of children drop a coin on the counter and present their pots to be filled.

That mass of black hair! Those intense dark eyes! No, what would she be doing here? In any case, she must be bigger by now. They run off with their purchases.

A young man with dishevelled hair and dusty clothes pauses and peers at me as he enters. He buys a bowl of soup, then approaches me. His powerful but deformed hands draw my attention. "M-may I j-join you?"

I frown, trying to assess his motives, but wave towards the bench opposite me.

"H-haven't I seen you b-before, lad?"

I gaze sideways at him. "I don't think I know you. Who are you?"

"Th-they c-call me B-Balbus. Think I st-stammer f-for fun." His face contorts into such a ridiculous smile I have to laugh. "I w-work for B-Boatwright Laurus. I s-saw you t-talking to him once. You were v-very interested in b-boats."

"Oh, now I remember. Were you the one who was planing a beam on that little coastal skiff?"

Before I know what's happening, he grabs my hand and, uttering a masterful imitation of a plane scraping wood, waves it to and fro across the table.

I pull my hand free.

"Wh-what b-brings you to t-town ttoday? P-pretty g-girls?"

Avoiding his question, I introduce myself.

Balbus comes straight to the point: Would I be looking for employment? It turns out business is doing well and Laurus is keen to find a replacement for an injured worker.

"What happened?"

He shows me his left hand. Two fingers are missing. "The m-master t-takes one f-for every m-mistake you m-make."

My jaw drops, but Balbus grins. He tells me the master is exacting but fair, insisting on hard work and precision. On the whole, the atmosphere among the workers is amicable. I tell him I have next to no experience with wood, but he suggests Laurus might take me on as an apprentice. Not quite what I had expected while I was rich, but I'm willing to look into it. When we've both finished eating we head down to his place of work.

Can this be the new vista that Cerbonius foresaw for me in Fabricia?

Boatwright Laurus matches the picture in my memory – tall, perhaps a bit stouter and balder. He remembers me well, saying my intelligent questions impressed him at the time. He doesn't probe deeper when I say I've left home, and agrees to take me on as a labourer right away. "You can live with the other workers in the barracks."

Sweaty, snoring bodies on all sides don't prevent me from sleeping soundly.

After a communal breakfast, Laurus calls me into his workshop. I ask if he could keep my bag safe. He peers at me with puzzled eyes but takes it and locks it in a cabinet behind him. Then he spreads out the plans of the ship they're currently building – a small trade vessel for transporting merchandise between the island and Italy. He points out the main features of the structure: the critical joints holding and fir beams of the keel, which take the most strain from wind and waves. His ships are designed to be fast and manoeuvrable. Opening the tool cabinet, he emphasises each worker's responsibility for keeping his tools clean, sharp and tidy.

I'm assigned to Balbus's supervision. He wastes no words when showing me how to clamp a rough beam in a vice, shape it into a round pole using an adze, then finish it off with a plane. I'm introduced to the other tools – saws, a bow drill, chisels, hammers – and given the task of making a mortice and tenon joint for practice.

Day by day, I follow my teacher around, doing whatever odd jobs he gives me. He shows me the improvised kiln for making tar to waterproof the hull, and I detect a twinkle in his eye as he watches me cover the dry pine roots with soil and inexpertly stack the firewood around it. He bursts out laughing when after some time the furnace explodes, spattering burning drops of tar and glowing embers over myself and all around.

Some of the other men tease me about my youth, calling me Semimodius and asking why I still wear my bulla. Balbus then comes to my defence, stopping things from getting unruly with a wave of his hand.

The bustle of keen workers, rhythmical hammering and sawing, the pungent smells of linseed oil and tar, sawdust everywhere – the boatyard soon comes to feel like home. I'm thrilled to be mastering the craft and seeing real results.

The work isn't easy, and the days are long. Although it's only spring, I'm hot and weary at the end of each day. Whenever I can, I take a quick dip in the sea beyond the headland. As often as not, I collapse onto my couch right after our evening meal.

As I dose, Cerbonius's words come to mind. 'My Friend will guide you... One day you will meet Him.' My head shakes. I have so many questions I'd like to ask him about this friend of his.

After several weeks, Laurus calls me into his workshop. He sits behind a desk, looking down at some documents. "How are you getting on here?"

I study his face. "Er... I enjoy the work." I come a bit nearer and put a hand on the desk. "Of course, I'm not very good at the tricky bits yet. But Balbus is a patient teacher. He certainly knows his craft and I've already learnt a lot."

"I should think he does. I trained him." He chuckles. "I've been watching you both. You seem to be a good learner, and always ready to help your tutor."

"I do my best. By the end of the day, I'm exhausted."

He smiles. "It's not child's play, but you'll get used to it." His middle finger taps a beat on the desk. "I would like to keep you on as an apprentice." He looks up at me. "What do you say?"

My cheeks get hot. "That's what I've been hoping for. I want to master your trade." Dare I say what's uppermost on my mind? "And I really want a boat of my own one day. Working for you seems like the best way to set about getting it."

"I see. Then that's why you were so keen to know how much it would cost, back then?" His eyes twinkle. "And can you afford the hundred and thirty *solidi*?"

"No, of course not. But I could do most of the work myself. And perhaps you will pay me something. In time, I could refund the costs."

"Not so fast, lad, not so fast. I have drafted a contract

for your apprenticeship." He picks up a parchment. "You do read?"

I nod.

"Very good. Since, as I understand it, you are no longer under the authority of your father, for whatever reason, you need to see if you agree with it."

I read through the document Laurus has written: "*In this the eighth year of Imperator Flavius Iustinus Iunior Augustus, on the Ides of Martius, in Fabricia of Ilva, Silvanus, son of Cornelius, being sixteen years of age* – He's done his homework! – *is apprenticed to Laurus, son of Flavius, Master Boatwright, for a period of two years, who shall teach him fully the whole craft of boat-building as he himself knows, maintaining and clothing him and remunerating his labour to the amount of three folles per day, subject to his performance being satisfactory…*"

After studying it a second time, I look up at Laurus. "I'd be very happy to accept that arrangement." I sign the contract. "I'm so excited to learn your trade. And I'd like to start working on a boat for myself, in my free time, of course."

"Indeed, you are ambitious, lad." Laurus's eyes twinkle. "Let's see about that in a couple of months' time when we're not so busy and you have acquired the skills."

"But… I already know quite a bit. If you show me where I could build a frame and let me have some timber I'd like to start as soon as possible. I could make a down-payment for the materials now."

He smiles. "And where would you find the money, my boy?"

"I do have some money. From some goods I sold two years ago." I ask him for the bag I entrusted to him and offer him the coins. "I don't really need that, since you provide my food and accommodation. I don't have any other expenses."

Laurus's eyes stare at the gold coins. "All right." He breathes heavily. "I'll accept that and keep a record of what else you use."

So now, every evening after our meal and on most feast days, I'm busy constructing my own boat. Balbus helps me erect the frame and often comes by with a word of advice and a helping hand. He insists I adopt Laurus's special design for the keel beam – protruding about a whole *pes* below the actual hull and weighted with lead. He claims it improves the boat's stability and manoeuvrability. I work till it's too dark to see what I'm doing, then crash onto my couch. Who would have thought a little skiff would take so much hard work?

The months pass. My skill develops, my muscles grow, and my language gets coarser as I adopt the ways of my fellow-workers. But what pleases me most is that my boat is also growing. It looks magnificent, and every nook and cranny of it is familiar to me.

Now and then something reminds me of the words of wisdom I copied while with the old Bishop. A violent storm causes the nearby brook to overflow, and I remember how that Friend of his once said if someone believed in him, streams of living water would flow from within them. Strange ideas indeed.

During the six days of the *Ludi Florae*, no one is supposed to work. I decide to visit my old mentor and see what new pearls of wisdom he has for me, now that I'm working hard.

Cerbonius isn't surprised to see me and is happy to hear of my progress as an apprentice.

"In a year or two I'll have a boat, my own boat!" – I can hardly contain my excitement. "Made with my own hands!"

"Building a boat for yourself is indeed a magnificent task, my son. But perhaps not in the way you imagine."

Always these cryptic remarks. More important, in his opinion, is that I continue with my transcription of the scrolls. "Do you recall the last text you copied?"

"I remember it well, but it was very baffling." We sit opposite each other at the wooden writing board. "That prophet Jesus – you call him your Friend?"

"He calls me His friend."

"But… never mind." I shake my head. "That friend of yours said, 'Every one who sees the son, and believes in him can have eternal life.' Who is the son? Was he speaking about himself? He also spoke of a spirit, which gives life. And then, 'No one can come to me unless the Father who sent me draws them to me.' I couldn't understand who is who in all of this."

He nods approval. "Keep on with your assignment. I believe my Friend's Spirit is speaking to you."

Two days I've been at it, occasionally discussing a point with my mentor. I clean my quill and pack away the scrolls, then let out a deep sigh. "Let me see if I understand. You say Jesus came from God?" Absent-mindedly, I pick up a twig and point it to the sky. "So as to help ordinary people like me…" – I indicate to my chest – "get to know his father." I point the twig back towards the sky. "Is that correct?"

He nods. "Indeed, you have understood the key truth."

I continue. "He wasn't interested in rituals, rules and religious institutions. His readiness to help, to forgive and to love people led many to follow him and turn from their bad ways. That makes sense." I tap my knuckles with the twig. "And now, since he is no longer here on this earth, you say he gives his spirit, like fresh water, to those who believe in him?" There's a question in my tone. "Such people are adopted as sons and daughters of God, and given the power to serve him?"

"So it is. From our first meeting, I sensed you were receptive for the light." Cerbonius nods. "May this Evangel permeate your whole personality, extending from your mind to your heart."

Again, I'm not sure what he means. But I continue, reflecting on how these ideas might affect my behaviour. "It seems to me, if we all really trusted in this Jesus and let his spirit guide and empower us – if we were true sons and daughters of God – we would have no reason to fight and steal from each other. We could live together in peace, helping one another…" The twig traces figures on the writing board. "And, when someone did something wrong, we could forgive him. Like Jesus forgave that woman they dragged before him."

This exchange has so engrossed us that we hardly noticed the day passing.

As we share a meal, another idea crosses my mind. "If all this about your Jesus is true, I don't see where our Roman Gods like Venus, Mars, Jupiter – or Aquila – and all the others, fit in." My eyes search out his. "Are they all false Gods?" He is listening but gives no sign of his opinion. "And what about Scipio's dream? Was Africanus deceived about who goes to heaven?"

Cerbonius dips his *focaccia* in the potage, takes a bite and chews it slowly. "Those are difficult questions, my lad, and I think now isn't the right time to discuss them. But, as you are well aware, tomorrow is the festival of your Goddess Flora, and I have been asked to bless the newly planted crops. I think it would be a good idea if you were to go with me. Later, we may further discuss the matter you raised. But now I need to prepare tomorrow's address."

Aquila, Jesus, Flora. Who has the truth, Ceres or Cerbonius?

CHAPTER TWENTY ONE

At the Fairground

TITUS ARRIVES WITH some friends to carry the old Bishop down in the litter. I help, sharing the tiring work on this warm May morning.

Cerbonius, having no need to concentrate on where to put his feet, observes our surroundings with keen attention. "Stop a moment, please!" We lower the litter, glad for a brief rest. "Look at those tiny pink cyclamens which have struggled up between the dead leaves and fallen twigs." We bend to admire them as he points with his crook. "Beautiful. Creation also celebrates the *Ludi Florae*. Even Solomon in all his glory was not dressed as beautifully as they are."

Leaving the shade of the forest, we find ourselves among pruned vineyards and patches of sprouting cereals and vegetables, each enclosed by dry-stone walls. In the village, the powerful scent and dramatic colours of lavish flower decorations accost us from every doorway and intersection. Jaunty pipe and *cithara* music and raucous laughter echo between the houses, as children rush around, and older people gather in small groups, all drifting towards the central square.

At the sight of the litter, a little boy and girl rush up, shouting, "Father Bonius! Father Bonius! D'you 'member us? We saw you at Aunt Septima's house. We followed you up the hill. You had Kanmi in the chair with you, 'member?"

Cerbonius chuckles. "It's a pleasure to see you again." He places a finger on the boy's chest. "Now let me see. Your name is Marcus, am I right?" The lad nods, beaming, as the old man continues, "I have a neighbour called Marcus. You're so big already!" Then he strokes the girl's wild hair. "And you must be Lydia – curly-haired Lydia."

She giggles and snuggles up under his arm.

"As soon as these crowds let us, we'll make our way to the common. Are you both taking part in the games?"

"I'm going in for the sprint," Marcus answered. "But Lydia's scared." He makes a face at her and she sticks her tongue out.

"Now, now," Cerbonius scolds, "let's be friends. Jesus loves us all, even if we're not good at running. She may be better at something else."

Some people make way for us and one or two greet the Bishop with hesitant glances.

An area below the main village is set up for races and other entertainment – much smaller than the field used for the Meditrinalia ludi in Fabricia. It also has a stage for musicians and other performances, lots of little stalls, and tables and benches where food and drinks are served. The whole common teems with colourfully clad people, young and old. Mixed smells from the many flowers, honey cakes, baklava, and wine fill the air. Contagious sounds of happy laughter and excited children's cries compete with shouts of encouragement and cheers from around the race track.

Someone brings Cerbonius a drink, then fetches more for us who have been doing the hard work of carrying him. It's most welcome, as the day is already hot. Cerbonius climbs out using his crook as a staff, and we move the litter out of the way. He's uncertain on his feet here where the ground is uneven, and prefers me to stay by his side to support him.

Two handsome young men in loincloths are wrestling, their powerful muscles dripping with sweat. Wild cheers acclaim the winner as he is presented with a laurel wreath. Then there's an obstacle race for the smaller children and sprints for the older ones. Marcus comes second in his race and we all congratulate him.

One little boy stumbles and screams in pain, unable to put his weight on his left foot. Parents and other children gather around, each giving different advice. Someone shouts, "Take him to Mother Martha!"

Mother Martha?

A man picks up the boy and carries him over to a first aid post. The boy's cries bring a young woman to the tent door.

A shudder runs through me at the sight of her dusky face and large black eyes. Could it be? She disappears before I get a second look, taking the boy in for treatment. I feel obliged to stay with Cerbonius.

Together with a horde of children and their parents, I settle on the ground before the main stage. Someone brings a stool for Cerbonius. First comes a juggler; a master with balls, rings and skittles. My mouth drops open as a hand always emerges from nowhere to catch things before they fall. He calls a boy from the audience to help with his magic tricks. Everyone cheers as the artist pulls coins from his ears and produces a dove from his tunic.

My legs follow the rhythm as a musician with a drum and cymbals strapped to his chest, bells on his legs and a sort of flute fixed in front of his face plays a lively tune while dancing a jig.

Every now and then I glance over at the first aid tent, but no young woman is visible.

The next act makes me laugh, as two huge red, yellow

and blue parrots open their own cage and prance around, reciting rude words and stealing things hidden among the handler's clothes. Then four little white dogs with black patches run yapping onto the stage. With perfect timing, they jump through flaming hoops, balance on a see-saw and dance on their hind legs while the man plays a tune. Next is a monkey, which swings from ropes, before leaping onto the trainer's head to snatch a handful of nuts from his bag. The children scream with delight when it jumps into the audience and steals a fat lady's hat.

Bread, potage and wine are available for everyone all day long, as well as cuts of pork from whole pigs roasting over a crackling fire. I can't imagine who pays for all this. As the day advances, a group of musicians mounts the stage and plays jolly tunes, inspiring people to dance.

Still no sign of life from the first aid tent.

Cerbonius stands and shuffles about, observing what is happening. I stay at his side, ready to steady him if he stumbles, and catch no further glimpse of the young woman at the medical tent. From the shade of a stand selling sweetmeats, the Bishop gazes at the shrine in honour of Flora. Sorrow and anger mark his face. A drummer is beating out a solemn rhythm.

A statue of Flora stands on a pedestal, adorned with flowers and fruit. Her priestess, attired in an extravagant scarlet and blue robe and yellow turban, mutters incantations to humour the Goddess. She swings a censer of burning incense back and forth, her movements as in a trance. Devotees approach her in a line, presenting gifts of money or produce, no doubt hoping their crops will thereby thrive. She receives the offerings, placing some at the foot of the statue and burning others on an altar.

She turns in my direction. My eyes widen, and my mouth drops open. I shrink further behind the wooden structure, trembling. It's none other than my aunt Ceres performing the rituals. I'm glad I never got around to shaving my beard, scraggy though it is, and that I'm wearing clothes I received from Laurus; I beg the Gods that no one will recognise me.

In a whisper, I inform Cerbonius and explain why I need to stay hidden. His voice remains unperturbed, but his clenched fists tell another story.

A moment later, Ceres beckons to two young women, little more than girls, wearing gaudy clothes. They emerge from behind the shrine and step onto the platform.

My cheeks burn. Shameful memories cloud my heart. I have never confessed to Cerbonius what happened at the Meditrinalia festival. I stay below the roof of the stand to watch, unseen.

Accompanied by a flautist and drummer, the girls begin a seductive dance, their many-layered diaphanous robes fluttering high as they leap and twirl around. The crowd screams and whistles, bawdy men pushing forward to get a better view. As the beat gets faster, the dancers each unwind a stole from the other and fling it towards their admirers. I wriggle and adjust my loincloth.

One by one they cast off their colourful garments, revealing ever more enticing views of their lithe figures. The spectators goad them on with lewd jeers, until – to a climax of drumbeats – the last article is discarded and the girls leap, naked, into eager arms below. They are passed around by groping hands until they disappear among the frenzied men. My whole body tingling, I bury my head in my hands, as vivid images of what is happening to them now course through me.

After a moment, I remember my responsibility for Cerbonius. He is looking heavenwards, muttering something into his beard – is he praying? – then turns to move on. Nodding at my pleading look, he accepts my wish to stay concealed.

The light is fading and many of the smaller children have disappeared. The main arena is now lit by flaming torches, as are the tables where people are eating and, more importantly, drinking. Cerbonius has been invited to hold a speech and no doubt to pray to his God for good weather and a successful harvest. He mounts the stage, making much use of his crook for support.

To my surprise, the crowd falls silent as he waves for attention before addressing them. His voice is strong and authoritative. Although I am some distance away, still hiding lest Ceres see me, I have no difficulty hearing what he says.

"Citizens of Ilva, I count it a great honour to address you all at this spring festival. You have all worked hard to prepare your fields, removing stones and weeds, ploughing and manuring. And you have carefully sown the seeds you saved from last year's harvest. And yet you are well aware that the success of your crops doesn't lie in your hands. I am pleased to pray for Almighty God's blessing on your behalf."

He falters, and a stool is brought for him to sit. Then he raises both arms, holding his crook high, and continues. "Gracious Father, Creator of all things living, we praise you for the beauty and wonder of all your handiwork. You cause your sun to rise on the evil as well as on the good, and send rain on the just and on the unjust. We appeal to you in your infinite goodness to bless the lands and multiply the harvests of these your people, protecting them from violent storms and scorching drought." In his enthusiasm, he stands again, his crook still high. "Show your loving-kindness, Lord, that our land may give her increase and so fill us with good things that the poor and needy may give thanks to your Name; through Christ my Friend. Amen."

A murmur of gratitude runs through the crowd as Cerbonius again sits. But he has not finished. I am so keen to hear what he has to say that my plan to check the medical tent has to wait.

"I feel constrained to add a further remark. It is indeed appropriate to be happy and take pleasure in the glorious profusion of this spring season. Indeed, I was thrilled at the beauty of all the floral decorations and the joy of young and old at the games and innocent fun." Cheerful mutterings arise from the audience, reverting to shocked silence as his voice takes on an impassioned tone. "But my spirit was enraged at the sight of the disgusting acts of worship performed by many of you at the shrine of that disgraceful effigy called Flora. Such a wooden image in no way deserves your devotion. Indeed, it has no power at all over sun, wind or rain, nor can it grant increase to your crops or…"

"Aiiyeee! Curses on you!" A piercing cry from the side lines interrupts Cerbonius's speech. All eyes turn to discover the source. I cover my mouth in horror. Ceres is rushing up in her full priestly costume, a tangle of bones and sharks teeth clattering around her neck, her golden staff held high. A group of attendants – also wearing strange dress and swinging censors of burning incense – accompanies her. As she approaches the stage, she repeats, "Curses on you, base priest and deceiver! May Trivia haunt you by day and terrify you at night. May your memory be confused and your mind addled, that your speech be no longer coherent."

In slow deliberation, Cerbonius rises, glaring at his adversary but showing no fear. With his eyes towards heaven, he raises his crook high, then thumps it down on the stage, shouting, "Silence!"

My fist flies up and I shout, "Well done!" as Ceres collapses into the arms of her aides. A strange stillness envelops the crowd.

Cerbonius ignores her but trembles as he points his staff at first one, then another man amongst the listeners.

His voice has a power I've never heard before. "You waste your hard-earned money on this woman's worthless idol." Quivers of shame run through the audience. "You add depravity to stupidity, allowing yourselves to be provoked to flagrant obscenity by the seductive behaviour of those fair but wretched maidens. My heart wept at the sight of them – doubtless under the influence of some noxious brew and entirely against their better judgement – driven to a life of promiscuity and vice." Some men jeer while others groan as he continues. "Such behaviour is doubly hateful to the God of all Heaven, whose blessing you requested me to invoke."

He collapses onto the stool, his head bowed. For some moments he remains silent. Then, in a mild and entreating tone, he again addresses the crowd. "Yet God is merciful. Oh, how I know it. Truly, He is merciful. I beg you, burn your worthless idols!" He is pleading now. "Turn from that sinful perversion! Think of your wives and your daughters. Repent! Return to the merciful Saviour who offers forgiveness through his eternal sacrifice, and to His gracious Father, who alone is the source of the abundance of the land! I implore you – for the benefit of body, soul, and those of all your families – repent!"

Titus rushes up onto the stage to catch the Bishop as he almost falls from his stool, then helps him down and out of the bright torchlight.

Several men sidle up to Cerbonius. I rush forward, concerned for his safety. But it's no assault. Challenged by his words, they are seeking his counsel. Frail though he is, he welcomes them, again urging them to destroy their idols and shrines and put their faith in his God alone.

Among them is the goatherd I'd met at the slave's hearing, Catalus. Titus has approached him and they are engaged in intense conversation. I take advantage of the moment to run over to the helper's tent.

Here a commotion of a different nature is developing. An angry male voice resounds from inside the tent. "She's coming with me!"

An older woman counters, "First you must overpower me. I shall not hand her to you. You have no right to take her."

"Stand back before I knock you down! What do you know of rights? Ever thought how a dark girl came to be on Ilva in the first place? She's coming with me. To her rightful owner."

Tent pegs are ripped out and I hear the sound of tearing cloth in the ensuing struggle. The elderly woman cries in pain and a younger one screams. But they are clearly no match for the large, raging man who appears, dragging a slight female form.

The lantern outside the tent sways ominously. Its light reveals little, but enough. I freeze. My heart races. That olive skin and sweet face are unmistakable.

"Virna!"

Her huge dark eyes open wide as she turns in my direction. "Silé!" Her captor wrenches her arm behind her back. She wails. "Oh, help me, Silé!"

I rush at the burly ruffian, halting him in his stride by grabbing his cloak. "Let her go!"

He swings round, wrenching himself free from my grasp.

"Let her go!" I repeat. I knee him in the groin and he doubles over, jerking Virna's arm. She screams. I tug at the hand holding hers, but a massive elbow smashes into my teeth. A thousand stars explode across my eys and I fall to the ground while the abductor drags his victim off into the darkness.

As soon as I recover enough to stand, I stumble over to Cerbonius's litter. "Domine!" The bearers halt. I'm out of breath and speaking is painful. "Domine… Virna has been abducted… And Mother Martha is hurt."

"What are you saying, son?" Cerbonius grasps my arm. "Are you sure?" He addresses Titus. "Run to her tent and see what has happened." He turns back to me. "Did you see who took her and where they went?"

Still panting, I try to recall what I saw. "There wasn't much light. He was big, rough, said he was taking her back to her rightful owner." I cover my mouth with my free hand. When I remove it, it's full of blood. "Martha tried to stop him…" My breathing becomes more normal. "I tried to save her but he hit me in the face and knocked me to the ground."

Cerbonius bows his head and nods slowly. Is he praying? It's a long time before he speaks. As if in response to an inaudible question, he murmurs, "Yes, indeed," then looks up at me. "God wants to show us His greatness."

"What…?" I study his face. He's quoting from the text I copied the previous day, from the encounter between Jesus and the blind man. Is he suggesting his God wanted Virna to be abducted?

He continues. "For sure, she is in the Father's hand."

"She's not! That brute has her."

"Of course, I'm concerned that he might harm her. But we have no idea where she is, so we can't do anything tonight. I repeat, no man can pluck her from the Father's hand. Let's trust Him to care for her."

He's right, we can't help Virna. Why am I seething with rage and so concerned for her safety? What has come over me?

Cerbonius puts an end to the matter. "I'm tired. Tomorrow I will ask my Friend what we should do."

That night, I toss to and fro on my thin matress.

Oh, Virna! It begins to makes sense now. Mother Martha. The House of Healing. At least you weren't one of those poor girls in the clutches of that dreadful aunt of mine. But that brute! Why?

Dear Virna, I had given up hope of ever seeing you again. Yet you had not forgotten me! 'Help me, Silé!' you cried.

Those days together with you – only a child then and now a beautiful young woman – they meant so much to me. You shared your heart – your bitter grief and your simple faith. Oh, Virna, how I miss you. Don't let that cruel man harm you!

But how can she protect herself? I've failed the only person who took me to heart. No, that's not true. Cerbonius also cares for me. He promised to speak with his friend about her – as if he could save her.

It's a new day and I set to work with half a heart copying my texts.

Toward evening, hurried steps resound on the stone path. Panting and sweating, Titus appears. He has no breath for speaking.

Cerbonius rises to meet him and grasps his hands. "Hail, brother! What troubles you?"

"*Salve…*" He takes deep gasps. "You must come to Fabricia right away."

"To Fabricia? Right away? I haven't set foot there for several years. What can be so important and urgent that I would need to make that gruelling journey? And so quickly?"

"It's Virna."

"What happened?" I, too, jump up. "Has that brute harmed her?"

"I think not," Titus says. "But he wanted to sell Virna back to her former master, Elazar. For some reason the deal wasn't carried through and the matter is to be brought before the Duumvir. The court will convene on *dies Veneris*."

My thoughts are in turmoil. When the feriae are over, I need to be back at work. But I can't get her plight – and my failure to help her – off my mind.

Titus still addresses Cerbonius. "I've arranged for a cart to take us there tomorrow…"

CHAPTER TWENTY TWO

Liberta

"HOLD ON, HOLD on! Not so fast." Cerbonius indicates Titus to sit. "Explain yourself. Of course, I also care for dear Virna. And I believe she has an important mission. But I don't see how I can help if she is being returned to her former master."

"The parties have appealed to the Duumvir."

"And I trust that the Duumvir will judge with justice."

"But you should be present, Domine."

"Let me first talk with my Friend."

Next morning, Cerbonius appears in woollen *braccae* and a shabby brown tunic, gathering his flowing hair under a felt cap. He chuckles. "I haven't had reason to wear this costume since I fled from the treacherous *Langobardi*."

The carriers hesitate on arrival. Titus smiles. "And what does this mean? Were you trying to escape?"

Cerbonius's eyes light up. "My Friend has given me permission to accompany you. A local person should accompany me to the tribunal, but I must remain incognito."

I object. "I can take you. Virna's my friend. I can tell Laurus I'm not well or something."

Titus and Cerbonius glance at each other. The Bishop replies, "Some people might associate you with me. You can attend the hearing. But you should keep away from me." He points his finger at me. "And please consider well what reason you give your master."

Titus ignores my suggestion. "My friend Nicolaus lives near the forum. He will offer you a bed and go with you to the trial."

My work at the boatyard – and the chance to continue with my little skiff – distract me from Virna's plight. I can't help her. On Friday I ask Laurus to excuse me and position myself near the front of the forum under a colonnade. Cerbonius is nowhere to be seen. The number of people already gathered suggests Elazar must be well known. Respected or despised?

Stout and wearing a magnificent toga, his complexion dark and his eyebrows menacing, he takes a seat on the right of the podium, flanked by two attendants. On the left sits a huge dishevelled man – doubtless the one who snatched Virna from Mother Martha's tent – with his counsel. It's said he asked five hundred *folles* of Elazar's *vilicus* to get her back. And he wouldn't pay.

Two *lictors* carrying *fasces* march onto the podium and stand erect beside a stately chair, to which the Duumvir Maxillus limps, aided by his cane. He then calls each party's advocate to present their arguments; a scribe in the background records the entire proceedings.

My eyes fix on the serene figure of Virna, as she is brought in by two *vigiles*, her wrist bound to one of them, to stand behind her captor. Tall and slender in her loose grey tunic, her profuse black locks tumble over her shoulders. Even from my distance, I see her kind eyes scan the crowd and darken as she glances at her former master. For a moment she lifts her gaze heavenward, then lets it drop, adopting an attitude of confident humility. That brief glimpse of her olive-coloured face quickens my heart. I struggle to stop myself calling out to her. What senseless words would I utter?

Claims and counter-claims wash over my head, as I marvel at her calmness and poise although her fate is again in peril. Tempers rise and the public jeers – hostile toward both sides, it seems.

A hush envelops the crowd as the Duumvir teeters forward with the aid of his cane to announce his verdict. "I have listened to the cases of both parties. The matter is clear. The slave girl was bought in good faith by the defendant and served in his household…" He consults a scroll. "For five years. For whatever reason, three years ago she ran away from said household and has been…"

Is no one interested why she fled? This is outrageous.

The magistrate continues. "That the plaintiff apprehended her gives him no right of ownership and thus no just cause for demanding reimbursement…"

Is he really giving her back to that monster Elazar with no reservation at all? I can't believe it. He'll kill her.

"I therefore rule that the girl known as Virna be returned at once and with no compensation to the…"

A shout issues from the otherwise dumbfounded audience. "One moment!"

All eyes turn in the direction from which it came. "I wish to challenge the proceedings!" As he pulls off his cap and raises his crook – how did he smuggle that into the forum with no one noticing? – everyone recognises Cerbonius.

Virna's eyes grow larger and brighter, her face radiant.

Her captor grips his chair with both hands and stares. Elazar's self-righteous frown deepens.

The Duumvir gapes and steadies himself with his cane. "Y-y-your Grace…"

"Most honourable Maxillus," Cerbonius shouts. "Please excuse the interruption, but I have something important to say, which may influence the verdict. May I join you on the stage?" The throng parts to let him shuffle through, assisted by a young man.

With great deference, the magistrate welcomes the Bishop to the platform. "Your Grace, I had no idea you were here. Please take a seat. Why didn't you say you were coming?"

Stretching over the seated plaintiff, Cerbonius places a hand on Virna's shoulder. Both *vigiles* reflexively step forward, their free hands moving to the hilts of their clubs. But there is no cause for alarm. Virna smiles – Oh, that lovely face – and exchanges some words with the Bishop.

Cerbonius follows the Duumvir to the centre of the stage, declining to sit. Before speaking, he peers at each person for a long time. "Honourable Maxillus," he begins. "Do I have your permission to question the parties involved in the case?"

"Why certainly," he replies. "We all respect your venerable wisdom."

"Dominula Virna…"

She titters at the unfamiliar title but looks up to face the Bishop.

"Would you please tell us exactly what happened on the evening of the *Ludi Florae*?"

She throws a brief glance at her captor, then raises her chin. Her voice is calm as she declares, "I was helping Mother Martha to minister…"

"Where was that?" Cerbonius interrupts. "It's important that the Duumvir can imagine the scene."

"She had a tent. I was with her in the tent." Her free arm swings around. "If someone was injured or if they felt unwell, they came to the tent for treatment."

"And did any such casualties come?"

"Oh, yes. Many. Several people were stung by wasps, two boys sprained their ankles in the races, another fell and gashed his knee. Then there were those who felt nauseous from eating too many sweetmeats."

"And at the moment in question, were there patients present?"

"Certainly. I was bandaging a boy's leg while an older lady lay on the couch. She had fainted from the heat and was still weak."

"Go on."

"This ruffian," she says, pointing at the plaintiff, "… burst in and started dragging me out of the tent. Mother Martha made every effort to restrain him and they bawled at each other. The boy screamed."

"Do you recall what was said?"

"He said something about taking me back to my rightful owner." She glances over to her former master. "And then he punched Mother Martha in the face and she fell." Her head drops into her hand and she can't continue for a moment. She shakes her head. – Oh, Virna, what a sensitive, caring woman you have become! – "I'm sure she received a black eye."

"I believe she did. But go on. What happened next?"

She again looks at her captor. "He knocked over one of the poles and the tent ripped. Then he tugged me outside. The lantern was swaying. I was afraid it might start a fire. And then I noticed Silé."

"Silé?"

"A friend." – A friend! – "Silvanus is his name. We met a few years ago."

"The lantern was lit. Was is not dark?"

"Getting dark, yes."

"So how did you recognise this Silé?"

"His voice." She giggles. "And his curly red hair."

"I see. And what did he do?"

"He tried to set me free." Again, she glances as the plaintiff. "But my captor twisted my arm – my shoulder still hurts – and overpowered Silé. Then he absconded with me."

"Where did he take you?"

"I was terrified. Away from the fairground it was pitch-black. I could not conceive what he intended to do with me. He forced me to walk for hours. Eastwards. I could tell by the stars. Then he fettered me in a small hut in the woods, guarded by a friend of his."

"That was six days ago. Were you otherwise harmed?"

"No." She stalls, as if the suggestion surprises her. – How innocent she is. And brave. Oh, Virna, how I love you! – "No. In fact, my new custodian, he called himself Sergius, but I don't think that was his real name, was compassionate. As soon as this man left…" She points at her captor. "…he unbound me and offered me victuals. At first he insisted I stay in the house."

"Did you have no thought of running away?"

"He would have caught me. There were no other houses nearby. Where would I have gone?"

It wouldn't have been the first time she escaped to the woods, I recall.

Cerbonius nods. "Please go on."

"I was terrified at the thought of having to go back to my old master – he'd been so horrid to me." Her head drops. "Sergius tried to console me. He recounted his time as a sailor and how he lost his arm."

"Lost his arm?"

"Yes, he has a wooden arm."

"I see. And you stayed there several days? Where did you sleep?"

"There was but one room. We each had a couch."

Someone in the crowd guffaws.

"One day this man came back." Again, she points at the plaintiff. "He said the *vilicus* refused to pay and that the case was to be heard here in Fabricia. I wept." She can't bring herself to face Elazar. "Sergius offered to steal away with me. But I prayed. And God assured me I could trust Him, that He would arrange for me go back to Mother Martha. She's wonderful. She is so loving and has taught me so much about Jesus and how to minister to poorly people."

"Thank you." Cerbonius turns to her captor. "Do you have anything to add?"

He sighs. "I did not intend to hurt Mother Martha. I had no grievance with her. But that lad had no cause to interfere. Serves him right if he got a knock on the head."

Rage rises in my breast.

"And the girl? Has she no rights?"

"She's a slave. She belongs to his lordship. I only wanted to return her to her rightful owner."

"And make a handsome profit by it?"

He shrugs. "Remuneration for my efforts."

A murmur rises from the crowd.

"Thank you." Cerbonius turns to Virna's former master. "Elazar, I believe the name is." The other nods. "I have not yet had the pleasure of meeting you."

"If you wish to discuss the details of the case, please refer to my advocate, sitting…"

Everyone jumps as Cerbonius slams his crook onto the wooden platform and glares at the nobleman, who jerks back in his seat. "The Duumvir has given me permission to speak with you." He points his crook at Elazar. "And with you I wish to speak. I understand you live in that prominent villa overlooking the town…"

"What is the relevance of that?"

"…and therefore need a fair number of servants. How many slaves do you have in your household?"

"Ask my *vilicus* if you want to know the exact number. Probably about fifty, I should say, including the children."

"Fifty, including the children. I see. And from what age do you require a slave child to work?"

"That, again, is a matter for the *vilicus* to decide."

"Perhaps already from the tender age of five?"

Elazar shrugs his shoulders. "Perhaps. But I don't see what this has to do with the case before us."

Cerbonius turns towards the magistrate. "I happen to possess certain facts which may surprise you. May I continue?"

"By all means," Maxillus answers.

"Elazar, did you purchase this slave girl as a child of five in Populonium?"

He shrugs. "That is possible."

"And do you know from where she came?"

"A slave is a slave."

Again, Cerbonius thumps the boards with his crook. "By pagan Roman law that may be true. A slave is nothing more than a piece of property. But I maintain – and so should you – that a slave is also a person. A person who has, or had, parents, brothers and sisters. A person who is a child of God."

"I cannot concern myself with the history of every slave in my household."

"You are a son of Abraham, is that not so?" Elazar starts. "An Israelite indeed, in whom there is no guile? With a name such as yours, I believe you are of a priestly line. As devout Jews, your family sings psalms to the Lord and observes the Torah. Your pagan slaves are required to bake *challah* for the Sabbath. Am I correct?"

Virna blushes. How sweet those flushed cheeks.

Elazar nods. "Ours is a Godly household."

Maxillus gapes and shakes his head. I smile at the different reactions to Cerbonius's in-depth knowledge of the lifestyle of a person he has never met.

"I shall not judge you, a Jew, by the standards of the Christ. But I challenge you with the Law of your people. What does your Law say about the treatment of slaves and about injuries inflicted on slaves?"

"I-I am not sure."

"Is not one of your tribe destined to be a teacher of the Law?"

Elazar lowers his eyes.

Cerbonius produces a scroll and unrolls it. "Let me see… Ah, here it is: 'If a man hits his male or female slave in the eye and the eye is blinded, he must let the slave go free to compensate for the eye. And if a man knocks out the tooth of his male or female slave, he must let the slave go free to compensate for the tooth.'" He peers for a long moment at Elazar. "Might not the same ruling also apply when the injury consists of lacerations to a slave's back?"

Virna freezes, staring at the old Bishop. How well I remember applying that labdanum salve to those wounds. And enjoying her innocent company. She was a starved and frightened little girl then. And now? A poised and attractive young woman. Can she be no more than twelve years old?

Elazar has jumped up and shouts, "What are you suggesting? My slaves are not treated like that."

With calm forcefulness, Cerbonius continues. "My intelligence is to the contrary."

"It's her word against mine. Do you accept the word of a slave girl rather than that of an honourable patrician?"

"Self-esteem is often biased, in my experience." He lets that imputed accusation sink in. "I have witnesses who can testify to having treated those wounds. We shall not go into the circumstances when those injuries occurred."

"What? Who dares to make such a claim?" Elazar stiffens and looks around. "I see no witnesses."

Cerbonius turns to the Duumvir, who has meanwhile sat down, his wounded leg unable to take the stress. "Do you wish me to call a witness? There is one here who can confirm my remarks."

My hand jerks to my mouth, and I gasp.

"I think that won't be necessary under the circumstances," the magistrate replies.

I breathe again.

Cerbonius fumbles through his scroll to find another location and again addresses Elazar. "Let me remind you of another tenet of your Law. 'You shall not give up to his master a slave who has escaped from his master to you. Let him live among you in any town he chooses, and do not oppress him.'" His piercing gaze, so familiar to me, causes the noble patrician to shrink in his seat. "What do you say to that?"

Elazar cannot utter a word.

A hush envelops the forum. Virna's captor looks around as if he's considering fleeing. Elazar, his face pale, peers at the Duumvir, then back at Cerbonius.

Cerbonius breaks the tension. "Honourable Maxillus, before I intervened, you were on the point of pronouncing a judgement – in favour of the illustrious Elazar, if I am not mistaken. Such a verdict would comply with Roman law." He waits for the Duumvir to comment, but no response is forthcoming.

Elazar, however, interjects, "Indeed! Let justice be executed! The girl shall return to my household, for my *vilicus* to chastise as befits a runaway slave."

Virna gasps, her free hand covering her mouth. Many voices jeer. My fists clench and my jaw locks.

Cerbonius, still facing the Duumvir, again thumps the stage with his crook. "Not so! A higher law applies here…"

"What higher law is there than the Law of Rome?" Elazar shouts.

"The Law of my God, and of yours!"

Elazar's mouth remains shut. The Bishop again addresses the magistrate. "It will not have escaped your attention, most honourable Maxillus, that our celebrated Emperor Flavius Constantinus granted Bishops the supreme authority to judge both ecclesiastical and civil matters." The Duumvir nods. "And, as you well know, this edict was recently upheld by none other than the late worthy Emperor Justinian." Another nod. "So today I am exercising my episcopal right to pronounce judgement in the case before us, a judgement founded on Holy Scripture as quoted and in accordance with God's gracious mercy toward the defenceless and oppressed."

He pauses, all eyes now fixed on him. A tremble runs through me, as words from my scribal task spring to mind: 'The law was given by Moses, but grace and truth came by Jesus Christ.'

"Dominula Virna, the former slave girl..." Cerbonius lets this word take effect, as he scans the crowd and the participants on the stage. "The former slave girl Dominula Virna, shall be set at liberty! Free to live wherever she chooses."

I jump in the air, clapping my hands above my head. Gasps and cheers of respect for the old Bishop's application of divine justice rise from all around the audience. The two *vigiles* support Virna to prevent her collapsing. Her captor and his advocate lean towards each other in a hushed consultation. At Elazar's bench, heads are shaking. Cerbonius approaches the drained Duumvir, shakes his hand, then sits alongside him. After a brief exchange, Maxillus turns to his scribe, then with a great effort, rises to address the court.

"I declare the judgement of our worthy Bishop to be legitimate. I deem the claim of the plaintiff for payment to be unjustified; he shall pay one hundred *folles* towards the costs of the trial." Virna's captor half rises from his seat but is dismissed with a wave of the Duumvir's hand. "I will not pursue the matter of injuries inflicted on the former slave, as it appears she has recovered.

"However..." He addresses the defendant, indicating he is to come forward. "Elazar bar Nadab, in the presence of the citizens of Fabricia, you shall release her." He offers him his cane.

The nobleman hesitates, looks around, then snatches it without a word and strides across to Virna. She cringes. The *vigiles* brace themselves. Elazar touches her forehead with the cane, muttering something I can't hear, and brings it back to the Duumvir.

"Everyone here has witnessed her liberation." Shouts of joy issue from all over the forum. Maxillus continues to address Elazar. "You shall duly sign the edict of manumission which my scribe is drafting." With deep sighs and a reluctant gait, the once proud nobleman moves over to the desk, waits for the document to be ready, then complies.

"Dominula Virna," the magistrate continues. She looks up, her eyes wide and mouth open. – Oh, how beautiful she is! – "I hereby declare you *liberta*." Wild cheers burst from the crowd and many hands wave in the air. Virna crumples and is lowered to a seat. I push through the masses in an attempt to get near.

At a sign from the magistrate, the *vigiles* release her bonds. She drops to her knees, both hands raised high in praise to her God. Is it indeed the same God as Cerbonius's? She rises, glances left and right, then runs over to Cerbonius, who stands to welcome her. Again, she falls to her knees and grabs his hand. In an act of blessing, he strokes her bowed head, then pulls her to her feet, resting his palms on her shoulders. Their lips move in a moment of private consultation.

I long to greet her; to gaze into those profound, wistful eyes; to congratulate her on her freedom; to hear her speak my name; to embrace her. But the teeming throng – everyone proclaiming their pleasure and wishing her well – prevent me from approaching.

With a final brief caress, she leaves Cerbonius, rushes to the edge of the stage and jumps into the arms of a waiting man. Is that the fellow Sergius? My pulse quickens. Pushing through the crowd, I struggle not to lose sight of Virna and this friend who is ushering her out of the forum, his arm tightly around her shoulders.

A crash from the stage causes everyone to turn. In spite of the shock, Virna's face is beaming. That of her companion makes me freeze. Drusus!

CHAPTER TWENTY THREE

Tables Turned

TOO LATE.

A hand on my shoulder recalls me to the present. Cerbonius stands next to me, supported by the young man who must be his host, Nicolaus. I wipe my tears away with my sleeve. *Menafa* – Virna's giveaway – springs to mind.

I have no words.

They respect my grief. Cerbonius hobbles along with the help of his crook, his vigour exhausted. Nicolaus ushers us through a narrow alleyway and into his home. When we are seated, he offers us wine. I can't drink.

After a moment the Bishop speaks. "You look dismal."

I raise my head, then shake it and bury it in my hands.

He clasps my hand. "What troubles you?"

I still have trouble to speak. "I was so happy when you set her free. She was magnificent… so poised… so beautiful. I-I wanted to… to congratulate her. To wish her well…" I screw up my face and hit my forehead with my clenched fist. "But now she's lost."

Cerbonius starts. "Why 'lost'?"

"Didn't you see?" I gape. "But, of course, you can't know…"

"What riddle is this? What do I not know? Please speak plainly."

"That man." I shake my fist in the air. "That man who took her off. He is that evil creep Drusus."

For a moment the Bishop is at a loss for words. Then, "Are you sure?"

"Of course I am." I shout. "I know him only too well. That monster. That wheedling liar."

"I see." He nods his head. "So that was Drusus." Our eyes meet. For a long moment his head hangs, his eyes closed. Then he looks up. "Yes, God wants to show us His greatness."

I jump up, screaming. "How can you say that? How can you approve of a vile criminal running off with an innocent girl? He's a brute!"

"I do not say I approve," Cerbonius counters. "But I trust my Friend will use even this incident to reveal His glory."

"You and your friend!" I protest, on the verge of tears again.

"Do you remember the promise He left with His followers?"

I take a moment to reflect. "That he would do whatever you ask for in his name."

"Whatever I ask for…" He chuckles. "Or whatever *you* ask for." His penetrating gaze startles me. "And what did we ask for in His name?"

"I don't remember." I have to turn away. "That Virna would be set free… delivered from harm and set free."

"And to that end we offered ourselves in His service, did we not?"

"Yes. You remember better than I do."

"Well, did He grant those requests?"

I gaze at him, my eyes staring. "I suppose… I suppose he did… to some extent. But it was you and the Duumvir who…"

"Precisely. Often, He answers our prayers through our

own hands or through His other children. Let's thank Him for His gracious mercy."

Cerbonius utters a short prayer of thanks for Virna's release and again prays for her safety. Nicolaus responds with a loud "Amen!"

"And now, if our host would be so kind, I would appreciate some food. Will you join us?"

My heart is still heavy as we enjoy dried figs and goat cheese after a satisfying potage of emmer and beans.

The door bursts open and Titus enters.

"I followed them," he blurts out. "They went…"

The fig remains halfway to my mouth as I interrupt. "Virna and Drusus? You followed them?"

"Indeed. The Bishop said I should watch where she went if she was released. But you speak of Drusus. She called him Sergius. Do you know that man?"

"Do I know him? Far too well, I'm afraid. The villain. Probably has several other names. Couldn't you get her out of his clutches?"

"Hold on, lad. Hold on." Cerbonius puts a hand on my arm. "She was liberated. Set free. To go wherever she wished."

"But he's a crook. Why, oh why did she run off with him of all people? He's not going to protect her."

Titus gazes at Cerbonius, then at me again. "I'm confused. What makes you think he can't be trusted?"

I thump the table with my fist. "He's a thief. A deceitful good-for-nothing. He'll harm her, I'm sure. Or lead her into a life of crime. We've got to save her."

"Silvanus… You need to learn to trust our Father in heaven, whom Virna also knows as her Father." He again looks deep into my soul. "And you must leave the matter with Titus and me. We'll do what we can to find her. You aren't the right person to intervene in this affair." His arm rests on my shoulder. "Besides, don't you have duties at the boatyard?"

Laurus was aware of the hearing and, like everyone else in Fabricia, knew Elazar as the rich and somewhat pretentious nobleman who lived in the grand villa on the hill. Not more than that. He had no interest in the outcome of the case. I tell him Virna is a friend of mine and is now a *liberta*. He shows no objection to my having attended.

It's late. Restless, I relive Virna's smile, her locks, her courage. Why was I not able to reach her before that villain? What will he do to her? I ponder Cerbonius's words: trust the Father in heaven and leave the matter with Titus and him. Did his God indeed answer his prayer?

Back with Balbus, my mind is not on the job of planing beams. "What's b-bothering you, l-lad?"

"Nothing." I look up. "Why?"

"L-look like you swallowed a p-pot of tar."

I lower my eyes. "You heard of the trial in town yesterday? About the escaped slave girl?"

He nods.

"Well, she was a friend of mine. She was liberated."

"I'm s-s-sorry."

I glare at him, before realising he's joking. "She ran off with a good-for-nothing crook. Who robbed me. Twice." The rhythmic scraping of the plane prompts me to ponder. "Virna. She was a little girl when we met. Years ago. Sad but sweet. She isn't safe with that blackguard."

"P-plenty of other p-pretty girls. Time a m-man like you f-found yourself one, S-Silvanus."

A man? I glance at my calloused hands, my tanned arms, my toned muscles. I've learnt a trade – measuring, sawing, drilling, chiselling. I know how to build my own skiff.

I peer at him, feeling my face getting red. "As long as I'm an apprentice here and with nowhere else to live, I can't think of getting married." A few more strokes of the plane. Under my breath, I mumble, "But she would have made a wonderful wife."

"Whats'at?"

"Nothing." I pretend to concentrate on the beam I'm working on. "Do you know the old Bishop, Cerbonius?"

"H-heard of him."

"I lived with him in his cave for over a year. He taught me so much about nature and also about life – what's important, what's right." The shavings fly as I continue to scrape at the joist. "Told me about how harsh his father was and how he'd failed his son."

Balbus looks up and sighs. "S-so was m-mine."

"Your father was stern?"

"B-brutal."

"Mine too," I say, scraping. "Nasty to all of us. Ever since he… fell… and broke his leg." I hack at the beam. "That's why I ran away."

"R-ran away?"

"Yes. Cerbonius was like a new father for me. Or grandfather. He talks a lot about his friend." I scrape on. "Jesus."

"C-careful. You've t-taken enough off there, I'd s-say."

I glance sideways at the profile and put the plane down. "I wish I could believe in his God. He seems so kind." I finger my amulet. "Not like Aquila the Avenger."

Balbus laughs.

"I've been copying his holy scripture. It's fascinating. But much of it I can't understand." I peer at Balbus. "Somewhere it says anyone who believes in him – in Jesus, that is – can become a son of God. It's like getting a new father. And have a rich and satisfying life."

"Sounds too g-good to be t-true."

"Cerbonius says the life he offers is much better than being rich."

"D-don't know about th-that."

"I believe him, though. He's so content. Although he has nothing. He pray to his Friend… and sings." My head nods and I gaze into the distance. "Many people turn to the old Bishop for advice. Or to seek justice. It was wonderful how he stood up for poor Virna."

Balbus chuckles. "Sp-spring is in the air."

The months go by and still I have no news of Virna. Did Cerbonius's God not hear his prayer?

Perhaps I could try praying. Does it need some special ritual to make it work? I go out to my boat – it's slowly taking shape – where I'm sure to be alone. "Jesus… if you can hear me… Please keep Virna safe. And please let me have news about her. I would love to see her again." What is it they say at the end of their prayers? "Amen." No idea what that's supposed to mean, but there it is.

I go to bed.

"*Salve!* How are you keeping?" I call as I pass the vegetable market after buying some items for Laurus.

Antonius comes out and peers at me. We haven't seen each other for years. His face lights up and he grabs me by the shoulders. "Silvanus! How good to see you." Holding me at arm's length, he looks at me. "What a fine young man you are now. You ask how we are. Well, our health is as good as we can expect at our age, thank you." He shouts, "Isn't it, dear?"

An affirmative grunt comes from the back room.

"The winter was tough. We feel it in our bones when it gets cold and damp. When the harvest is over there's not much to sell. But now business is looking better. What about you? What have you been up to?"

I grasp his arms. "I got the chance of my lifetime! An apprenticeship with Boatwright Laurus. A wonderful master. I'm here to buy some things for him. He's even let me build my own boat."

"Your own boat? What do you want a boat for? Isn't there enough for you to do on Ilva?"

"There's no future for me here. I want to see Rome, the aqueducts, the Colosseum, all the other great buildings. And then I'll sail to Constantinople and the East. I want to explore the world."

"Someone is ambitious!" He nods. "I wasn't aware of you being with Laurus. But then I seldom go down to the harbour. My son fetches fruit from the boat and drags it up here for me." He offers me a fig. "How long have you been with him?"

"Over a year now. I started in Januarius last year."

"Then you must have heard of the fuss over Elazar's slave girl. What was her name?"

"You mean Virna? Yes, she's a friend of mine. I was at the trial." I take a bite of the fig and lick my lips. "Cerbonius was wonderful."

"I think most of Fabricia was there; they made such a big thing of it." He pauses in thought. "Tell me, do you know Cerbonius?"

"Oh yes. I've often been at his cave. He's been teaching me things from his holy scriptures."

"Wonderful. A real man of God."

"I was so pleased he managed to stop Virna being sent back to that cruel man."

"Elazar? He is a bit grim, that's true. But cruel? What makes you think that?"

"I met Virna soon after she escaped. I saw the slashes he gave her. He tried to molest her." The recollection of treating her wounds is bitter-sweet. "I wish I knew where she is. She ran off with that crook who stole my wares. Remember?"

"Really? I wonder why."

"He's so slick-tongued, he can fool anyone. But he's a real villain at heart. I should know."

"And she fell for him? Don't worry. The Good Lord will look after her. She said she had faith in Him, didn't she?"

"You're another one who says that." I shake my head. "I don't understand how you can simply trust him and not do anything. That attitude makes me mad."

"I'm not saying we shouldn't do anything. We can pray…"

"I have prayed. Doesn't seem to do any good, though."

"Pray and trust our heavenly Father. And then do what He asks us to."

Anna comes out from the back of the stall with a tray of figs. "Did I hear you talking about that poor slave girl?"

I turn to the little woman, full of anticipation. "Yes. Do you know something about her?"

"Well, I saw her at the trial, of course." She fills one of the displays. "And she was here in town a couple of days ago. With a strange-looking man."

I start. "What was he like?"

"Well, let me see… Untidy hair. An ugly scar on his cheek… And a bad arm."

"Drusus!" I grit my teeth. She is still with him. "What were they doing?"

"Went over to the jeweller… What's his name?" She turns to her husband. "Sartorius. I think he had some gems to sell."

My crystals!

I force myself to chat with these dear friends over a cup of hot mint. They are so kind-hearted. But I can't wait to see Sartorius.

Splendid brooches and rings are on display. A wizened old man, walking with the help of a gnarled olivewood stick, squints as he comes out. "May I help you? Looking for a present? For a lady?"

"Err… Do you make these things yourself?" How does someone with such obviously poor eyesight cut and set gems to such perfection? "What sort of stones are those?"

He shuffles over and peers at the necklace I indicate, made from pink and brown crystals like mine. "All my own work. Beryls. Similar to the emeralds there."

"Where do they come from? Are they local?"

"Of course. Ilva's famous for its gems." He looks at me as if I'm daft. "Fellow came in a few days ago. Shifty looking rogue. Pretty girl with him. Sold me a lovely group. Come."

He takes me through to his workbench. Among the fine tools a round glass object in a frame catches my eye. "What's that for?"

"Never seen one? Have a look through it. At that ring."

I bend over it, then stagger back. "It makes it much bigger! So, that's how you're able to do such precise work."

He ushers me through to the main part of the shop. I catch my breath. In a position of honour is my crystal formation – the Emperor with his attendants! My fists clench and I take deep breaths in an attempt to control my anger.

He doesn't seem to notice. "Beautiful, isn't it? Said he'd bring more. On market day."

"That's in two days' time, isn't it?"

"Let me see… That's right."

"I need to get back to work with these supplies. But I hope to come again when I have more time." On market day. "*Vale.*"

"*Vale.*"

The seats in this *caupona* get hard when you've been warming them since early morning. Across the road, next door to the fuller's workshop, is Sartorius's shop. Other customers drop in and some stop to chat. I've been playing *tabula* with an elderly man. He beats me easily.

We're about to start another game when they appear: Drusus – still looking shabby – followed by Virna in a long, coarse tunic, her glossy black hair hanging loose.

In my rush to get out, the *tabula* board flies off the table and I bump into an old lady who was hobbling past. "Virna!"

She jerks round. Her mouth drops open.

Everything stops. My limbs become rigid. Fury emanates from Drusus's eyes.

She runs up and embraces me. "Silé! Oh, Silé. At last!"

My tears flow as I clasp her to me, her firm breasts pressing against my ribcage. She must feel my heart thumping. Her head drops to my shoulder. No words find their way to my mouth.

Towering over me, Drusus grabs my arm and tears us apart. "Wha's the meanin' o' this, you dirty li'l coward? Leave her alone!"

Virna, tear-stained, glances from Drusus to me and back again.

I break free from his grip and position myself between him and Virna. "Don't you dare talk to me like that, you thieving bastard! First my gems and then this innocent girl – my friend."

"Yer friend? That's a good 'un. Who's been lookin' after her these pas' months?"

People stop and gape.

I stare at Drusus, then at Virna. She holds my gaze. If only I could see into her heart. Looking after her? Or was he taking advantage of a beautiful, naive girl? What does she feel for him?

She screams and a passer-by shouts, "Look out!"

Drusus has thrown his bag at Virna's feet and drawn an ugly-looking *pugio* from his belt. It looks familiar. He raises it to strike. "Keep back, Virna," he hisses. "This is 'tween me an' him."

I observe every movement of his body as he advances. He lashes out. I duck, the blade narrowly missing my shoulder. I wouldn't be his first victim. We dance around, each waiting for the other to make the next move.

Virna's scream has brought Sartorius out from his shop and a shadowy movement in the doorway of the *caupona* distracts me for an instant. Drusus takes advantage of my inattention. I jump back and deflect his blow, but the knife finds its way through my thick woollen tunic and gashes my chest. "Brute!"

Virna sobs and shouts, "Stop it!"

Searing pain rouses my fighting spirit. I rush forward, pushing his good arm out of the way. He retreats. Back and forth we go.

Then reason takes over. He's armed; I'm not. I can't defeat him by sheer force. *If your arms aren't strong enough, use your head, Silvanus!* Tricks I learned from many play fights with Pontus and Rufus come back to me. My eyes follow his arm as he raises it for another strike, but I watch his feet. I let him advance, swinging the blade at arm's length towards my neck. He's a brute-force fighter, no tactician.

In a double parry, I fling my left fist up to meet his falling forearm and jerk my foot out to block his right leg. The impact of our clashing arms causes him to lose hold of his pugio; it glances harmlessly down my tunic and bounces over towards the entrance of the *caupona*. His leg stalled, he loses his balance. He stumbles, knocking his head on the fuller's pot and emptying the stock of urine into the street. Spectators jump back with shouts of protest.

He knees me in the groin as I push him down, causing me to crumple and roll onto the cobbles. A new burst of energy fills me. I jump on his prone body, sit astride his chest and pin his arms to the ground. For the first time I see the rough shape of his wooden arm with its iron hook – vicious but for the moment disabled.

I clutch his throat and my carpenter's hands are about to squeeze the breath out of him when an inner voice shouts '… as we forgive those who sin against us'!

I relent.

Virna sobs and has trouble speaking. "Do you… Do you know each other? Wh-what are you fighting about?"

I dare not turn to her. "Keep back, Virna. He's a creep. He robbed me. Twice." I glance at the red patch growing on my tunic. "I'm sure that's not all he has on his conscience."

A wry cackle issues from Drusus's throat. "If only you knew…" He has difficulty speaking with me on his chest. "Where d'you think I earned this?" He waves his wooden arm. "And this 'ere scar?"

Virna's tone is pleading. "You told me it was an accident – unloading wood or something."

He sneers. "An' you believed me. I'm sorry, my dear. Yer jus' too angelic t'hear 'bout my exploits."

She gasps and covers her mouth. A murmur runs through the knot of observers.

"Over west, where yer friend comes from. Them Phoenicians 'ad the nerve to fight back."

Hideous childhood memories flash through my mind. Was he one of the pirates in that attack I watched? Was that one of his victims I found decaying on the shore?

"Give him what he deserves!" A deep voice from the *caupona* doorway startles us. My *tabula* partner is holding Drusus's pugio in his hand. "That crook needs to be taught a lesson. He's well known around town."

"I spoiled your plan, didn't I?" My face forms a smirk. "Where are my crystals?"

His reflexive glance at the bag next to Virna gives me my answer.

"I'm taking them back. But first we have some matters to deal with."

Drusus makes a sudden upwards thrust of his belly in an attempt to throw me off. He doesn't succeed. "None of that!" I dig my knee into his side as a warning. "You're at my mercy now."

Virna takes a step forward. "Stop fighting, you two! What are you thinking?" She looks down at my captive. "You were kind to me, Sergius. You could have taken advantage of my weakness. But you didn't. I wish to thank you."

"Heh?" I glance at her.

"Yes, Silé." She again turns to Drusus. "Thank you for caring for me when I had nowhere to go. And protecting me when your friend wanted to molest me."

He scowls. "That bastard! I'd never've let 'im touch you." Then his voice becomes gentle. "I was so sorry for you, m'dear. You were so… pure." Another deception? "Somefin' stopped me defilin' you." He shakes his head. "'Ow pretty you looked as you slept." His voice changes a plea. "Don't desert me now Virna!"

My breathing quickens. Jealousy boils in my bowels. He shared a room with her for months. Can it be that he didn't harm her? It doesn't add up.

Drusus mumbles. "P'raps yer God did 'ear yer prayers."

"I wish you'd take to heart what I told you about Him." She truly cares for the wretch. "Especially now I've heard another side of your story." She picks up Drusus's bag. "But I'm giving these crystals back to Silé; he's the rightful owner."

What boldness! Drusus again struggles to free himself in vain, and utters an incomprehensible grunt.

Virna now addresses me. "Silé, I never forgot you. Those were wonderful days. I was thrilled to see you at the fairground and you did your best to rescue me. And now you've convinced me I shouldn't trust Sergius."

"Drusus. Whatever. He's a filthy deceiver and a crook."

"Maybe he's learned a lesson today. I've been praying he would see the light. You, too, as far as that goes."

See the light? What was that Jesus said? 'Children of the light, who no longer stay in the darkness'.

She continues, "But you can't stay there, lying in the street like irresponsible infants. Stand up, both of you!"

The audacity! But she's right. My wound throbs and my breath comes in gasps as I stand. Drusus also gets up. I thrust him against the wall of Sartorius's shop, making it clear I won't let him escape.

"Yer right, Silvanus." Am I hearing right? "Heart or hand, I dunno, but I've been a crook all me life. Ever since me mother died. When I was six. Never 'ad a father. I was nuffin but a robber – an' then a pirate. 'Til this 'appened." He raises his wooden arm, but it's no threat. "Since then, trickery an' pilfering's been th'only way I know to survive. Them crystals helped, o' course. Kept yer sweet Virna alive too, as a matter o' fact. But that income's over now, I guess."

Is this remorse genuine?

His next remark offers some hope. "I've lost them gems. An I've lost tha' wench. I'll seek me fortune on t'mainland. I'm off. You won't have no more trouble from me."

"Good riddance!" It's the elderly man from the *caupona*. He addresses Drusus, waving his pugio in the air. "But let me tell you, young man, if you so much as set your foot on Ilva again, I'll see you get arrested and punished as you deserve. Sartorius here is my witness." The jeweller grunts his assent. "Now get lost!"

Drusus makes no attempt to recover either his bag or his knife. He gazes at me. I take a step backwards.

Virna springs towards him. Without a word she kisses his cheek. He blushes and is off.

I clasp the wound in my chest and gaze at Virna. She faces me, big questions in her bright eyes.

I reach out. "Come with me."

Virna smiles and takes my hand.

My pulse races. "I know someone who will let you stay with them, I'm sure. And patch up my wound."

Sartorius has retreated into his shop and the bystanders have dispersed. I pick up Drusus's bag. How heavy it feels. And how it stinks from the spilt urine.

The elderly tabula-player hands me the pugio. "You handled that very well." He glances at Virna, who is still gazing at me with an enquiring look, then back to me. "I wish you health and much happiness."

CHAPTER TWENTY FOUR

At Last!

ANNA NEEDS NO explanation when she sees the blood on my tunic. Leaving Virna to introduce herself to Antonius, she ushers me into the back of her stall. She applies some salve to my wound, which stings at first, and then a dressing. I rinse the stains from my tunic and Anna darns the slash.

I find Antonius and Virna chatting like old friends. "…I was dumbfounded when the Duumvir pronounced me *liberta*. Sergius was delighted and welcomed me back."

"Sergius?"

"Or Drusus…"

"Drusus? Silvanus doesn't seem to like him."

"No…" She glances at me. "But that's another story. Anyway, Sergius had been amiable to me since his friend captured me at the fairground. And I couldn't find my way home."

"Where did he take you?" The thought still riles me.

"Back to the abandoned house they used as a hideout. Somewhere in the hills south of town, I believe."

"I saw the them near Sartorius's shop this morning," I say. "We had a row…"

"More than a row, it seems," Antonius remarks.

My hand moves to my ribs. "Drusus wasn't happy to discover Virna was my friend." Do I detect a blush on her face? "He was trying to sell my gems. When he attacked me, I overpowered him. He said he would leave the island. There were many witnesses."

"Virna…" I glance at her, questioning. "doesn't trust him anymore."

"I was entirely ignorant of his misdemeanours. You're right. What I heard shocked me."

"Now she has a problem." I hesitate. "I wonder if you might be able to put her up for the time being. Until she has somewhere else to go."

"I wish to return to Mother Martha. I'm sure she pines for me."

"But that's a long way away. You can't go back alone, that…"

Anna interrupts. "Of course she can stay with us. Our boys have long since left home, so if you don't mind simple fare?"

Virna claps her hands, then embraces Anna. "Oh, that would be wonderful. I can sleep anywhere."

"That's very kind of you, Anna." Then another thought crosses my mind. "If you like, Virna, I could ask my master for a couple of days off, and then I could take you back to Mother Martha's."

She looks at me with a twinkle in her eye. "Like three years ago? I'd enjoy that."

A week has passed and Laurus has agreed to my request.

Grabbing my cloak, I leave early for the market. Virna is tidying up Antonius's stall, removing vegetables that no longer look fresh. She's wearing a different linen tunic – no doubt one of Anna's – and her hair is tied back in a ponytail. She runs out to me.

"Today's my rest day and Laurus says I can take another two days off. Are you ready to go?"

"Right away!"

My pulse quickens, and I feel the blood rising to my cheeks.

"Hold on, you two. Not so fast." Antonius comes out and turns to me. "Are you running off with our faithful slave," he says, chuckling, Virna starts, "without even letting her say goodbye?"

"Sorry." In her excitement she has trouble to speak. "I'm so eager to see Mother Martha."

Oh, is that it?

Antonius continues. "She's been wonderful – full of fun and most helpful. A great cook and a hard worker. We'll miss her." He turns to Virna. "Do come and see us if ever you're in town. You're always welcome."

"That's so kind of you. I've really enjoyed these few days. But I do want to get back, now I'm truly free. If I ever come here again, I'll make a point of visiting you."

Anna comes out from the back of the shop. "Are you really leaving us, my dear?" There are tears in her eyes. "At least, this old mother has some sense." She's carrying a cloak for Virna and a bundle. "I don't know how long it will take you, but it may get cool and you'll need some victuals on the way. I've packed a pot in here – vegetables, bread, some fruit, and a skin of wine."

In my excitement I'd given no thought to taking food. "Oh, thank you."

Both are sniffing as they hug Virna and bid us farewell.

As soon as we are out of town and on the path up through the woods, Virna's tongue loosens.

"Do you recall meeting Cerbonius? How his geese frightened us." We both laugh. "He dispatched you with the mules. I had no idea where Titus was taking me. I feared I might never see you again."

"Was it far?"

"Not too far. Somewhat below the hamlet where Titus lives."

"What is the House of Healing?"

"Mother Martha started it many years ago in her home. She's a wonderful woman, so gracious and loving. And always singing. Praising God and expressing thankfulness in all circumstances."

"Like Cerbonius."

"Exactly. I believe it was he who introduced her to Jesus."

"Do many people live there?"

"Sometimes up to thirty. Some only come for a season, to recover from an injury or some traumatic experience. Others would be unable to live anywhere on their own."

"So why did you stay?"

"With Martha's treatment, my wounds healed rapidly. But as I had nowhere to go, I helped her with other patients. I learned so much from her. Not just practical things. To love God and to worship Him… and pray for Jesus to heal people."

"Do you believe he does miracles when you pray?"

"Have you tried?"

"Me? No." A thought comes to mind. "Well, I did pray once. And now I think about it… it did work!"

"Who did you pray for, then?"

"For you."

"For me?" She stops and stares at me. "But I wasn't ill."

"No, I prayed I would get news of you. And the next day I happened to meet Anna – I hadn't been to their stall for ages – and she said she'd seen you at the jeweller's place a few days earlier."

"Really?"

"I also prayed that Jesus would keep you safe…"

"He did! Sergius might have cast me out… or molested

me. Something stopped him. Oh, Silé, Jesus granted your request."

"That's not all." Memories flood back. "I'm not sure if you'd call it a prayer. I also told him I'd love to see you again." My open palms beckon her. "And here you are."

"That's wonderful, Silé." Her big dark eyes pierce into my soul. For a moment she hesitates. Then she lunges forward and hugs me tight.

My heart thumps.

"Do you see how God loves us?" She breaks free and waves her arms high above her head. Her tunic swings as she sings thanks to God for his kindness and love.

I don't know what to make of all this. But it thrills me to see Virna so happy.

We turn round to admire the view over the bay below Fabricia. Vessels of all sizes are manoeuvring outside the harbour, many of them familiar to me. Then, moving on, we soon both recognise the spot under the tall trees where we first met. We stop, look at each other and burst out laughing.

"I thought you were a boy following me."

"And I was sure you were commissioned by Elazar's *vilicus* to capture me and bring me back."

"You were so skinny. And you had cut your hair. It was a real mess."

She grins. "Thanks for the compliment."

"It's lovely now." I reach out and grasp her ponytail, letting my hand slide down the full length. "Beautiful and so silky."

She beams, then suddenly plants a kiss on my cheek.

I feel my face get hot and let go of her hair. "Shall we go down to your clearing and have something to eat?"

"That would be wonderful."

As we descend through the strong-smelling macchia, a loud *ka-chu-chu* startles us. A fat brown partridge darts out and flaps off in a half-hearted attempt at flying. Far below in the little cove, gulls swoop over the restless sea.

Old memories return of her bathing naked in the pool and my discovering she was a girl; I wouldn't behave like that now with this modest young lady – the tragic story of her capture as a child in Carthago, slavery, her master's attempted rape – chasing each other around and then enjoying a delicious rabbit stew – feeling so embarrassed after my first wet dream that I was harsh towards her. Enough of that.

Virna gathers herbs and brews a potage. She lifts her arms in thanks to God for his provision, before we dip in our chunks of bread. It's the tastiest lentil soup I've ever had.

It would be so pleasant to spend the rest of the day, and the night, here, but we must press on. I can't be away from work too long.

Evening falls and we make another fire, eat some bread and fruit and settle for the night in a grove of trees. It's cooler than we expected, so we spread my cloak on the dry leaves and snuggle up together, with the cloak Anna gave over us. My contentment at feeling the warmth of her body behind me and hearing her regular breathing dispels any lustful feelings. We sleep well, and wake refreshed.

At the path's fork, we take the right branch, down towards the villages. I would have loved to go on to see Cerbonius and let him know Virna is free, but we don't have time. In Marciana, we pass Titus's house. He's not at home but Septima is overjoyed to see us both and wants to hear the whole story. We give her a shortened version and she says Titus will pass on the good news to Cerbonius.

Virna leads me to the House of Healing, a magnificent mansion, which must have belonged to a wealthy family.

Virna hides behind me for a moment in the entrance portico and my eyes scan the scene in the inner courtyard. Two small children, one with severely deformed legs, are teasing a small dog, while a huge green parrot squawks in irritation; or is it jealous that it's missing out on the fun? A powerful aroma issues from the garden in the centre, where a woman is breaking off dead flowers. Two girls are busy distributing drinks and grapes to several elderly people reclining on couches under the pillars. A short, burly woman with silver curls hustles out from a side door to wrap a shawl around a grey-haired man. Virna bursts forward. For a moment, Mother Martha seems paralysed. Then she squeals with joy, rushes forwards and hugs Virna so firmly she can't utter a word for a long time.

It's vegetable soup and bread again. But the love and laughter shared by both helpers and patients – some crippled, some blind, some simple-minded – in this haven of song and praise move me to tears. Never before have I experienced such warmth and joy. After the little ones are put to bed and the wounded and disabled cared for, Mother Martha takes time for Virna.

She knew from Titus about the trial and Virna's release but was very anxious when she heard she had gone off with a suspicious-looking character. Even more than her physical well-being, it seems the state of Virna's soul concerns her. Her happiness overflows when she hears Virna has kept her faith in God alive and even tried to persuade her captors to believe.

"Do sit down." She indicates to a couch, then addresses me. "You must be Silé. Virna often spoke of you with gratitude for having helped her. But she worried what had become of you after you returned to your home. She was afraid you didn't get on well with your father."

"I'm surprised she cared. But yes, I had another row with my father and decided to leave home. For the last

246

year and a half, I've been doing an apprenticeship with Boatwright Laurus in Fabricia."

"That's a good thing for a lad like you. How old are you?"

"Seventeen, now. And, yes, it's been a good time – hard work, but it's what I love. I'm building my own boat. I want to get away from Ilva; I feel the wide world beckoning."

"That's interesting." She nods and glances at Virna. "How did you two find each other again after so long?"

"I… often wondered what had happened to Virna. She meant a lot to me although we had only seen each other for a few days and she was only a girl…"

"Only a girl!" Virna repeats.

I ignore her challenge. "I had no idea where she was. And then, it sounds crazy – or maybe not to you – I asked God to let me get news of her. And I did. Someone I knew had seen her. And I was able to track her down. Together with that villain Drusus."

"Drusus?"

"He used a different name – Sergius. He'd been holding her captive in a secret house. I hated him; he robbed me. Twice! He used to be a pirate until he lost an arm."

"Lost an arm?"

Virna chips in. "Yes, but you hardly notice it. He masters so much with the wooden one. It has a hook for grabbing things. He hides it in a glove."

"Sounds like a colourful character," Martha adds. "But I'm so glad you got away from him, my dear. Where is he now?"

"He said he was leaving the island. Going to the mainland." I shake my head. "I only hope that's true."

"And you were so kind as to accompany Virna back here. Praise God, she is well. I've missed her so. She was such good company and always helped me with the little ones."

"I'm so pleased she has somewhere to stay, where she's loved and appreciated. I need to get back to my work, but…" I look at Virna. "I wonder… Could I visit you here sometimes?"

Her eyes seem even larger and more profound than ever and her olive cheeks take on a pinkish colour. "I'd love that." She turns to Mother Martha with an imploring look. "It wouldn't be a problem, would it?"

Wrinkles grace her brow and a broad smile appears as she replies, "Of course not, my dear. You may only be thirteen, but I trust you and you deserve a day off now and then. You work so hard here." She turns back to me. "But do stay here tonight. You can leave in the morning."

Over the months, I've made that journey so many times. I no longer cross over the high ridge; it may be longer to take the coastal path and then the winding road up the hill, but it's quicker. If I leave at dawn, I can be at Mother Martha's before midday.

Sometimes Virna and I walk together hand in hand through the profuse flowers and penetrating smell of the macchia. As the seasons change, she admires the colourful acacia trees contrasting with the evergreen oaks and tall pines, and the strawberry trees' white flowers and yellow berries turning to bright red.

The swifts and other migratory birds leave for warmer climes, storms rage and soon the first bright blossoms of broom and heather appear.

We have a favourite spot on a headland, with little more than snakes for company and eagles soaring overhead – perhaps Kili and Kwee's offspring. We can see much of the north coast and all around from mainland Italy in the distance to Corsa over on the left. Now and then, my attention is drawn to a trade ship plying the waves. What does she carry and where is she bound? In the hazy distance, a rocky island protrudes from the often turbulent sea.

I grasp her hands. "Will you come with me to Capraria, Virna?"

"To that bare rock?"

"It does look bleak, but somehow it attracts me."

"Do you really think you could sail that far? I'd be afraid in those waves."

"Nonsense. I've been out a few times with the ships we've built. I've learned to handle a boat in all weathers. And mine's nearly finished."

"Already? That's wonderful, Silé." She claps her hands. "I'd love to go with you but… I'm not sure I'm brave enough."

Virna often sings when she's preparing a meal or making a flower arrangement. I've been perfecting my flute and sometimes I'm able to accompany her. She says her songs are mostly Psalms from her Holy Scriptures; some she learnt from Elazar's daughter, Sabina. I like the ones she has made up herself. They speak of peace and beauty, of hard work and the joy of sharing.

Best of all is the one based on the first prayer Cerbonius taught me:

> *My Father in heaven, I honour your name!*
> *And long for your will to be done,*
> *That earth would be filled with your fame.*
>
> *I look up to You for all of my needs;*
> *And beg you forgive where I fail,*
> *As I forgive when my heart bleeds.*
>
> *I'm easily tempted and fall into sin.*
> *Please save me from evil and doubt.*
> *O Father, Your kingdom shall win!*

The song runs through my head as I rush home from one of my days with Virna; it keeps me company while I work on my boat and it's the last thing on my my mind before I fall asleep. Oh Virna, I wish I could share your faith.

I've often been thinking of Cerbonius and one day, Virna asks me to take her to see him. Dela and Runel announce our arrival; they seem to remember us. The old Bishop heartily welcomes us as we approach hand in hand.

With a twinkle in his eye he repeats the saying he mentioned on our first visit, when I spoke of my special interests. This time he completes the citation: *tria sunt difficilia mihi et quartum penitus ignoro – viam aquilae in caelo, viam colubri super petram, viam navis in medio mari et viam viri in adulescentula.*

Three things are beyond me and four I can't under-stand – the way of an eagle in the sky, the way of a snake on a rock, the way of a ship at sea, and the way of a man with a young woman.'

I shake my head in bewilderment. Is this some kind of joke? Did he anticipate our romance all those years earlier?

Although he'd heard from Titus that she was back with Mother Martha, he is delighted to see Virna so happy and well. He questions her about her time with Drusus, again showing particular interest when she says she prayed for protection and spoke to her captor about God's love for him.

I don't understand.

"I'm sure the Lord heard your prayers."

"Oh, He did. Wonderfully!" She jumps up and sings thanks and praise to God. "And I believe… I'm sure that one fine day he will turn from his misguided ways and believe in Jesus."

Her regard for the well-being of her captor – my assailant – baffles me. Whether he comes to faith in her God or not is of little interest to me. Let him be damned.

We talk of Virna's time with Antonius and Anna, of Mother Martha and the special people in her House of Healing, of the progress of my boat-building, of our carefree days in the woods and on the headland gazing out to sea and dreaming. Virna brews another of her wonderful potages and we share an enjoyable meal together.

Dusk falls earlier now and it's soon time for me to take my dear friend home.

Before we leave, Cerbonius places an arm on each of our shoulders and prays for our growing love for each other, for protection over our hearts and guidance for our future. He also asks God to open my eyes of faith, whatever that means. Virna responds with a hearty, "Amen". I am thankful for their concern but can't identify with their convictions.

As we are about to leave, I say, "May I speak with you alone next time, Cerbonius?"

"Certainly, lad."

Virna looks at me with a puzzled expression and shrugs.

We set off down the hill in the growing darkness. After seeing her home, I still have a night trek before me. And a burden on my heart. But tomorrow is a working day.

CHAPTER TWENTY FIVE

Ceremony

MOTHER MARTHA SAYS Virna is in the *balneum*. As I raise my eyebrows she adds, "It's all right to go in. She's helping Mater Agathe."

I approach without making my presence known. Virna is singing while she lathers an elderly woman's hair, whose arms and legs, hanging from the coarse drape that envelops her, are disfigured by dark blue and brown patches. A smile of deep gratitude radiates from her sightless eyes, as Virna gently dries and brushes her hair, then massages her calves with aromatic oil. I watch, speechless.

When she notices me in the doorway, Virna's face lights up. She rushes over and flings her arms around my neck. For a moment I'm overwhelmed by her lavender fragrance. I pull her close and for the first time revel in the passionate pressure of her tender lips on mine. Our eyes close. Her firm breasts dig into my chest and I stroke her lustrous, raven hair.

I could stay like this for hours, but my *cauda* grows, struggling for space. She feels the movement against her loins. Embarrassed, I open my eyes. They are met by a twinkle from hers.

What does she know of such matters?

She moves back a step, still clasping my chest. "Not yet, my dear. When the time is right."

"Oh, Virna." My heaving chest makes speaking difficult.

"You came at a good moment, Silé." She kisses my forehead. "Could you help me take dear Mater Agathe to her room?"

She introduces us but, instead of taking one elbow, as she expects, I pick the old lady up in my arms. She utters a weak cry. Is it fear or joy?

"Which way?"

"Oh, Silé, you're so strong!" Her mouth hangs open. "Through here. That's her bed there."

I lower Mater Agathe onto her couch and Virna spreads a blanket over her with tender movements.

After packing some dried apricots and figs into her leather bag, Virna calls to Mother Martha that she'll be out for some hours.

The early spring sun smiles on us as we make our way, hand in hand, through the intoxicating scents of the macchia. From the profuse array of flowers, Virna singles out a picturesque clump of violet cornflowers among brilliant yellow brooms. "How exquisitely beautiful!"

"Not a patch on the beauty of my sweetheart."

She gives me a peck on the cheek.

On reaching our hideaway among the bizarre boulders on the headland, we sit facing each other, knee to knee. A lone rock thrush greets us with its clear, melodious call.

I smile. "You remind me of Jesus, Virna."

Stunned, she asks, "What on earth do you mean?"

"The way you washed Mater Agathe. Like Jesus washed His friends' feet. Such tenderness."

"Don't be silly. That was quite different." She ponders. "But it is Jesus's love that enables me to love her. And the other patients."

I reach forward and place my hands on her shoulders. "Do you have any left over for me?"

Her gaze meets mine. Oh, those gorgeous, fathomless eyes. A teasing twinkle brings them to life. She cocks her head as if to say, "Why do you ask?"

"Because I love you, Virna." Tears form in my eyes. "Oh, how I love you."

Her face unfolds into the warmest of smiles. "Silé, I think I've loved you since we first chased each other among those mysterious rocks in my hidden clearing." She reaches out to cradle my face in her hands. "That was so long ago." Her lips touch mine. "Now I love you so much it hurts. Thank you for coming. I was afraid you wouldn't make it."

"I went to see Cerbonius." I feel my face flush. "I needed to talk with him."

"About the scrolls?"

"About you, my dear."

Now it's her turn to blush.

"I…" How do I say it? "Will you…" I observe every twitch of her face. "Will you marry me, Virna?"

Her head falls onto our interlocked knees, her long black hair reaching the ground. She shudders. Have I said the wrong thing?

The thrush experiments with a variety of melodies. I wait, paralysed, for her to respond.

She raises her head. Tear-stained but joyful. "Oh, yes, Silé. Ever so willingly. I've been longing for you to ask." She leans forward and kisses me.

"I don't know where we'll go but I need to leave this island. And I want to have you with me, dear Virna. I'll care for you as best I can."

"Oh, Silé, I'll make you happy in every way." Another kiss. "I'll follow you wherever you go, even if it means braving the waves in your magnificent boat." She pulls my head to her shoulder and whispers, "I want to bear your children, lots of them." Her eyes twinkle as she feels an involuntary twitch in my legs. "But not yet, Silé. Not just yet."

"Oh, Virna." My face is also wet. "I'm so happy. I understand. I'll wait." I pull back and peer into her eyes. "Cerbonius said he could marry us."

"What? You've already discussed it with him? You rascal. Shouldn't you have first asked the bride?"

"I'm sorry." I hang my head. "I have now."

"So when will it be? I'm ready."

"As you know, he takes things very seriously."

"I should think he does. So do I."

"Yes, of course. He says we must first be baptised…"

"That's no problem. I love Jesus. I've promised to trust and serve Him with all my life. Haven't you?"

"I… It's not that simple, Virna." How can I put it? "Cerbonius's faith, and yours… and your love for God… I don't believe in Aquila and the old Gods any more. But I don't have the same convictions as you do. I'm not sure if it's right to be baptised when my faith is so uncertain."

"Then… in that case… he wouldn't marry us?" Her smile dissolves and her sweet eyes cloud over. "Oh, I can't bear to live without you, my darling Silé."

"Cerbonius said something strange." I pick up a stone and balance it on another. "You know how he often smiles with his eyes as if he's plotting a joke."

"Yes, but this is no joke."

"No, of course not. But he said he was convinced we were meant for each other…" Her smile returns. "And he understood it was rather urgent."

"Urgent?"

"Yes. For two reasons. He's getting old and thinks he may soon die." She gasps. "He didn't say it like that. He's looking forward to seeing Jesus face to face, and having a new body without all the pains and limitations he has now."

Her eyelids drop. "Of course… it has to happen some time. But it'll be such a tremendous loss for all of us." She looks up. "What was the second reason?"

I hold her gaze. "He understands I can't wait much longer."

"Oh, Silé, I understand." She rubs my thighs. "I'm also longing for that intimacy – with nothing at all between us. But I'd enjoy it much more if we were married…"

"So… he said he would be willing, as a Bishop, to bend the rules a bit."

"Bend the rules? What do you mean?"

"He says, he has noticed how my faith has been challenged as I have been copying the Scriptural texts. He feels sure God is working in my heart. And that He will lead me to that conviction which he – and you – enjoy."

"But how long might that be? Oh, Silé, why don't you just accept that God loves you? Then we could both be baptised and marry."

"Cerbonius said he would baptise me, expecting that I will soon put my trust in Jesus. I don't understand these things, but I'd say that's real faith."

"So, he will marry us!" She claps her hands and leans forward to plant a kiss on my forehead. "That's wonderful. Wonderful. I'm so happy, Silé."

"He wants us to think about it – and pray, if we are able – for a month or two. Then he would conduct the ceremonies for us."

"A month or two? I can wait. How about you?"

"I don't know. But I won't force you, my dear."

These last months have been turbulent. Each time I visit Virna it's an indescribable joy but also a struggle as I resist my yearning to go all the way. She's aware of the tension and doesn't wish to torture me, but says she prefers to wait.

We've discussed things with Cerbonius and he has agreed to celebrate both our baptisms and our wedding now, during the feriae of the Ludi Florae. Can it be only one year since Virna was captured? Antonius and Anna have agreed to accompany me as witnesses. It's the first time they've been so far west. I'm wearing a plain new tunic for the occasion. This May weather is warm enough that I see no need for a change of clothes.

Virna entreated Mother Martha to be her escort; she could only be persuaded to leave her patients when Septima offered to look after the House of Healing in her absence. Martha has made a long white tunic for Virna's baptism and she likes it so much she says she'll keep it on for the wedding. She doesn't care that it will be wet through. She has woven a wreath of pink cyclamens from the woods and brilliant purple cornflowers to wear in her hair for the ceremony.

Titus and his friends have carried Cerbonius, who's also dressed in a white robe, down here in the litter. Several of their children have come too. A little waterfall has formed a pool, shaded by overhanging trees, which will serve for our baptism.

So everything is ready. My heart is thumping.

All those present – about sixteen in all – raise their arms as Cerbonius says a prayer and then together they sing a Psalm. Although it's unfamiliar to me, the combined voices of these dear men and women of faith warm my soul.

The Bishop takes his place in the shallow water at the edge of the pool and beckons Virna to enter where it is deeper. Her raven hair hangs loose over her shoulders and her face is radiant.

"Dominula Virna." The expression startles her. Then both chuckle. "Your parents strove to bring you up to know and love the Lord, before they were cruelly taken from you while you were a little girl." He pauses a moment and her head drops, but she looks up when he continues. "You have faced many trials and hardships in recent years. But your heavenly Father has never let you out of His hand and now He has placed you in a pleasant situation. I understand from your mistress, Mother Martha," he says, turning to her, who watches wide-eyed, "that you love the Lord Jesus and seek to serve Him, often with a song of praise on your lips. Is that so?" Both Virna and Martha nod. "And so I ask you: Do you believe in God the Father, Maker of heaven and earth?"

In a clear voice, her eyes shining, Virna answers, "I do. Indeed, I do."

"Have you turned from the ways of darkness, putting your faith in the finished work of Christ, the Son of God, who died on the cross for the sins of the world, and have you accepted His forgiveness?"

"I have. Oh, thank you, Jesus."

"Have you received the fullness of the Holy Spirit, to comfort you and equip you for service?"

"I have." She raises her arms and gazes heavenward.

"Then I now baptise you as a new-born child of God in the name of the Father and of the Son and of the Holy Spirit." He places his hand on Virna's head and gently pushes her under water. Her hair spreads out around her like a wondrous flower. "May His Spirit fill your soul."

As she rises, helped by Cerbonius's proffered hand, a sunbeam penetrates the dense foliage and lights up her glowing face. She jumps in the air, arms held high, and shouts, "Hallelujah! I love you, Jesus!"

Am I the only one who notices how the thin tunic clings to her shapely body?

Cerbonius still has another remark to make. "As is the custom, I now give you a new name, a Christian name." She gapes and covers her mouth. "From now on you will be known as Priscilla."

Another leap of joy. "Priscilla! How wonderful!"

From all around shouts of "Bless you, Priscilla!" and "Praise the Lord!" resound.

Martha wraps a shawl around her shoulders and draws Virna – Priscilla – out of the pool, then proclaims in a loud voice, "A word from the Lord for you, my dear Priscilla: 'Fear not, for I have redeemed you; I have called you by name, you are mine.'"

Priscilla hugs her. "Amen! Thank you, dear Mother Martha."

Others gather around, reaching out their hands to bless her; they pray for her health, her welfare, her future. A little boy adds, "And, God, please don't let her go away." Several people chuckle. What a wonderful, caring family she has.

Now it's my turn. I tremble as I respond to Cerbonius's invitation to enter the water.

"Silvanus – 'lover of the forest'. How appropriate that name has been. You were brought up to fear the Gods of the celestial bodies, and especially the vengeful God Aquila, a sinister embodiment of Jupiter, the so-called king of the Gods."

I nod. Where is this going?

"I have introduced to you a greater God than Aquila, a kind and loving God, the Maker of heaven and earth, who came into this world as the man Jesus, full of grace and truth."

That phrase rings a bell.

"This Jesus is the good shepherd who gave his life for His sheep and who said, 'I have come that they may have life, and have it more abundantly.'"

Another passage I recognise.

"I understand you're not yet ready to put your faith in this God, to accept His forgiveness and to commit yourself to serve Him wholeheartedly."

I lower my eyes and nod.

"That day will come, I have no doubt. So now I ask you: Will you continue to devote yourself to studying and preserving Holy Scripture, and remain open to the voice of Jesus as He speaks to your spirit?"

Is that the way to find the joy and assurance these people share? I look into Cerbonius's eyes and nod. "Indeed, I will."

"In anticipation of the day when you will become His adopted son, I now baptise you in the name of the Father and of the Son and of the Holy Spirit, and entrust you to His eternal care." With gentle pressure, he pushes me under water.

My body trembles as I rise. The onlookers again shout, "Praise the Lord!" But do I detect less enthusiasm than before?

"To you, also, I give a new name." My eyes open wide. "As future husband of Priscilla, I name you Aquila."

I gasp. "Me? Aquila?" I grasp the amulet concealed under my tunic, which I had almost forgotten. "What do you mean by that?"

"I believe the time will come when you and your beloved will show the same loving hospitality and the same wisdom to instruct others in the Way of Jesus, as did your biblical namesakes, Aquila and Priscilla."

What a promise! I must find out more about that couple. But what a challenge! I stagger out and Antonius throws a coverlet around my shoulders. He also has a word from Holy Scripture for me. It's more of a challenge: 'Do your best to present yourself to God as one approved, a worker who does not need to be ashamed and who correctly handles the word of truth.'

As Titus helps Cerbonius out of the pool, others gather around me to pray. One of the hands on my shoulder is that of Virna. How will I learn to call her Priscilla? The overwhelming sensation of love and hope from all these friends prevents me from singling her out for acknowledgment.

"I need a break," Cerbonius announces, smiling, "before we proceed with the marriage ceremony."

We all relax on the rocks and roots surrounding the pool. I sit between Antonius and Anna, Priscilla next to Mother Martha, who places the floral wreath in her hair. Cerbonius is weary, his breathing heavy, but his face is radiant.

Someone starts reciting a Psalm and others join in, in a kind of chant:

I will lift up my eyes to the hills –
From where does my help come?
My help comes from the Lord, Who made heaven and earth.
He will not allow your foot to be moved;
He who keeps you will not slumber.
Behold, He who keeps Israel shall neither slumber nor sleep.

The Lord is your keeper;
the Lord is your shade at your right hand.
The sun shall not strike you by day, nor the moon by night.
The Lord shall preserve you from all evil;
He shall preserve your soul.
The Lord shall preserve your going out and your coming in
from this time forth, and even forevermore.

Do they all know their Scriptures by heart?

Cerbonius stands and everyone else follows his example. "In the presence of God, Father, Son and Holy Spirit, you have come here together to witness the marriage of Aquila and Priscilla, to pray for God's blessing on them, to share their joy and to celebrate their love. For us, who believe in Almighty God, our Heavenly Father, marriage signifies much more than a mere social contract to maintain order and bring children into the world. God's gift of marriage draws husband and wife together in the delight and tenderness of physical union and joyful commitment for the rest of their lives. It's intended to be the foundation of family life in which children may be born and cared for, and in which each member of the family, in good times and in bad, may find strength, companionship and comfort, and grow to maturity in love."

He beckons us to stand next to him and turns first to me. "Aquila, do you take Priscilla to be your wife? Will you love her, comfort her, honour and protect her, and, forsaking all others, be faithful to her as long as you both live?"

"I will, with all my heart."

Then, addressing my sweetheart, "Priscilla, do you take Aquila to be your husband? Will you love him, comfort him, honour and protect him, and, forsaking all others, be faithful to him as long as you both live?"

"Oh, yes. Most certainly. With all my heart."

Cerbonius turns to the group. "Will you, as friends of Aquila and Priscilla, support and uphold them in their marriage now and in the years to come?"

All those standing around say, "We will."

Cerbonius raises his hands in prayer. "God our Father, from the beginning you have blessed creation with abundant life. Pour out your blessings upon Aquila and Priscilla, that they may be joined in mutual love and companionship, in holiness and commitment to each other. We ask this through our Lord Jesus Christ, your Son, who is alive and reigns with you, in the unity of the Holy Spirit, one God, now and forever."

A hearty response comes from the witnesses. "Amen."

"Aquila and Priscilla, I now invite you to join hands and make your vows before God and his people."

I take hold of Priscilla's hand. Cerbonius leads and I repeat his words, phrase by phrase.

"I, Aquila, take you, Priscilla, to be my wife, in good times and bad, in sickness and in health. With God's help, I promise to love you until death separates us."

On her finger, I place a ring I carved from oak and decorated with a fine pattern of interlocked strands. To my joy, it fits. Priscilla's eyes shine.

Cerbonius addresses her and she repeats after him.

"I, Priscilla, take you, Aquila, to be my husband, in good times and bad, in sickness and in health. With God's help, I promise to love you until death separates us."

She also has a ring for me. It looks to be of silver, with a similar pattern of intertwined branches. How did she come by that? And how amazing that it has a similar design to mine.

"In the presence of God and before all who stand here, I proclaim Aquila and Priscilla husband and wife. Those whom God has joined together, let no one separate."

He closes with a prayer, to which all respond, "Amen."

Priscilla and I fall into each other's arms and remain like that for a long time.

Cerbonius then leads another short ceremony, in which we all share bread and wine. Everyone joins in, as if it's familiar to them. In my present state, a mixture of unspeakable joy and emotional exhaustion, I fail to understand the significance.

Mother Martha says she ought to get back to the House of Healing, then surprises us with a question. "Where you will live now you're married?"

CHAPTER TWENTY SIX

Embarkation

WE STARE AT each other, then fall into each other's arms again, laughing.

It seems incredible, but we hadn't given a thought to the question of where we were going to live. Surely, everything would fall into place?

After a moment, we realise it's a serious matter.

To Mother Martha I can only say, "Er… I don't know. My apprenticeship is almost finished, and my boat too. We'll have to find a room somewhere. Or build a house…"

She raises a hand to stop me. "I have an idea." Her warm gaze swings between Priscilla and me. "Mater Agathe is blind, as you know, and depends on our care. Her husband died several years ago and she hasn't heard from her son since he left for the army many years ago. Her house, you know it, Virna – Priscilla, I mean." She smiles at her confusion. "The one in the dip behind the trees. Well, she suggested I could use it as an extension of the House of Healing. But I haven't been able to take her up on the offer, because I had no one to oversee it…"

We look at each other, questions in our eyes. Have we understood what she is proposing?

"Oh, Martha," Priscilla whispers. "Of course I know it. I often used to go there to help dear Mater Agathe, before she came to stay. Are you… are you saying we could live there?"

"Well, it's empty. It might be a solution, at least for the time being."

Priscilla jumps in the air and claps her hands. "That would be wonderful. What do you think, Silé? How can I remember to call you Aquila? The house is old and somewhat dilapidated, but I could make it into a snug little home for us…"

"Thank you so much, Mother Martha," I say, then lower my eyes. I'm again dependent on someone else's kindness.

Cerbonius, tears in his eyes, embraces us before being carried off in the litter. We others make our way down through the steep woods to the House of Healing. Antonius and Anna spend the night there before returning to Fabricia.

Priscilla and I seek out Mater Agathe to thank her for letting us use her house.

"I'm so happy for you, my dears," she says. "You know it's no longer any use to me. May the Good Lord bless you both. And make you a blessing to others."

Mother Martha hands us a bag of food and we take our leave of these dear friends. At last, my darling Priscilla is mine. She skips as we make our way to our new home for our first night with nothing at all between us.

How many days have passed? We haven't left the house. We've only got up now and then for a bite to eat. We sleep. We talk. We laugh. Priscilla sings. Oh, how I love her voice, her songs of praise to her God. And we cuddle up together on the prickly mattress, delighting in each other's bodies, caresses, and sweet words.

A warm spring sunbeam bursts through the window onto Priscilla's peaceful face and wakes her. I gaze at her, enchanted. "My *Nitela*, my dormouse! I love those huge, dark eyes of yours; they seem to suck me into your soul."

"Come in, my sweetheart! Come in and discover who you've married."

She rolls onto me and I stroke her back. My fingers stop and explore some raised skin – the scars inflicted by her former master Elazar. "Does it still hurt, my dear?"

"Not often. Sometimes they itch like mad and I can't reach to scratch."

"That man's a beast."

"I've forgiven him." She kisses my lips. "I no longer have cause to hate him." She sits up and my hands rise to fondle her pretty breasts. She smiles, then reaches over to feel my side. "What about that gash from Drusus?"

"It was only a scratch. There's no sign any more." Bitter thoughts darken my mind. "But I'll never forget that brute's attack."

An earnest expression crosses her face. "Silé – I mean, Aquila – do you remember the prayer Jesus taught us, 'forgive us our sins, as we forgive those who sin against us'?"

I sit up and put my arm around my sweetheart. My eyes wander to the ceiling, as I try to sort out these new ideas.

Meanwhile she sings a soothing Psalm about the Lord, her Shepherd, who satisfies her needs; then another where He's described as a refuge, a fortress, in whom she trusts. She plays with the hair on my chest, then prays, fervently thanking Jesus for giving her a strong, handsome husband, and for the joy she is experiencing. Privately, I wonder what He had to do with it. She asks Him to heal my bitterness over the wrongs I have suffered. And to guide and provide for us in the days ahead.

Another kiss lands on my cheek. "Don't you want to talk to Him, my hairy *Ursus*?"

"I'm not yet very good at praying, you know." Her huge dark eyes are so persuasive. "But I'll try. Do you think it's all right like this?"

"Like what?"

"Well… you know… naked? And after what we've been up to?"

"Oh, my thick-skulled bear. Do you think He's shocked or offended when we make love? It was His idea in the first place, remember? He created us and He led us together."

She giggles, as I free my arm from behind her and clasp my hands together, then try lifting them, palms upward, unsure what the right posture is.

"It doesn't matter what you do with your hands, silly Silé. Nor whether your eyes are open or closed. Do just what feels right when you think of God as your Father."

My father? For a moment I stop breathing.

"All right." I drop my hands and close my eyes. "I am happy, God, very happy that Virna – or Priscilla, if You prefer – is mine now. She's lovely, such fun and so kind. Not only to me. But I suppose You know that already. It's so good not to be alone any more. And I really want to make her happy. Oh, and thanks for letting us use this house, if You had anything to do with it. I'm excited to discover what the next days – and years – hold for us. I hope you'll look after us and show us what You want us to do." I turn to her. "Am I supposed to say 'Amen'?"

"You can if you want. But *I'll* say 'Amen!' That just means I agree with what you prayed. It was a lovely prayer, my darling Aquila."

I get up and dress. "I could stay in bed with you for days, but we must think about what we need to do, my *Nitela*. When I was talking to God just now, a thought came to me…"

"Yes, He often speaks to us when we pray. If we're paying attention. What did He say?"

"I ought to go back to…"

"Oh, my *Ursus*, you're not going to leave me already? I couldn't bear it."

"Just for a day or two, to sort things out at the boat-yard." I stroke her cheek. Then another idea pops up. "If you want, you can come with me."

She stares at me. "I'd be afraid of seeing Drusus again. I'm not sure what he would think about us being married. And anyway, Mother Martha needs my help." She dresses. "No, you go, but come back as soon as you can."

"I want to sell off the rest of the crystals, remember? And then I need to settle up with Laurus. If there's anything left over, I could buy some things in town. What do you think we need?"

"We have most things we need here in the house." She glances round the small room. "But we ought to have a decent pot for cooking… and some plates and cups. And, of course, spelt… and oats… and vegetables. Perhaps some fruit that we can't find around here. And, if you can, some nice fabric for a new tunic."

"I hope I can find something you like. I don't really know what you like yet."

"I'll be happy with whatever you bring. I'll need needles and thread. And a better knife. And shoes, you know, those new sandals that are in fashion these days. *Carbatinae*, I think they call them…"

"Any chance of getting something for myself?"

"Oh, I'm sorry, my dear. I'm so selfish. Forgive me, Jesus! Yes, get whatever you need, too. I hope you'll have enough money from the gems."

"I expect so." A thought crosses my mind, I never looked into that bag of Drusus's. "There should still be quite a lot left."

Her hand goes to her mouth. "Oh, something just

occurred to me. How are you going to bring all those things back? Silly me. You can't carry so much."

"That shouldn't be a problem. I'll come in my boat."

"What? Is it finished?" She gapes. "Do you think you can sail it all the way here, all by yourself?"

"Of course. It's small and easy to handle. I'll tie it up in the harbour down there." I point to a group of houses far below, clustered around a natural bay, where some fishing boats are moored. "Then maybe I'll find someone with a mule to help me bring things up here."

I collect Drusus's bag with the gems, which, like my own, I had deposited with Laurus, and make my way to Old Jeremias's house. This time I knock at the back door. His wife opens it and immediately recognises me.

"Come in, lad, come in." She has her husband's habit of repeating things. Or he hers. "My, haven't you grown?" The same strong scent of herbs greets me, as she ushers me through the colonnaded walkway into the room with the golden lampstand. Only the high central lamp has a flame. Jeremias is reclining on the couch in the semi-darkness, looking much older than last time I saw him.

She turns to me. "I'm sorry, I've forgotten your name. So sorry."

"Silvanus – or now I'm known as Aquila."

She shouts at her husband, "You remember Silvanus?"

"Who?"

"Sil-va-nus. Came with Antonius a couple of years ago. An-to-ni-us. Had some pretty crystals. Remember? Crystals." She lights the remaining lamps.

Jeremias sits up to inspect me. "Of course I remember you, lad. You had those beautiful pink beryls. Of course I remember. And what brings you here today? More of the same gems, I hope."

I open the bags. Strange. I haven't even looked at the ones I recovered from Drusus. I'd taken it for granted they were my crystals.

"You have them loose in those bags?"

I nod, taking out a handful. Their dusty surface shows they haven't been looked after over the last two years.

Jeremias notices, too. His eyesight must still be better than his hearing. He blows at the cluster I hand to him, then purses his lips and shakes his head. "Sad, sad. Look at this, here."

Corners are chipped and surfaces scratched. "They're lovely. But badly damaged, I'm afraid. Show me the others."

One by one he examines them, sighs, and arranges them in groups on the table. Drusus must have already sold the best ones and these here are the dregs.

After some minutes without speaking, Jeremias indicates one small set. "These here are all fine specimens. Wonderful. Wonderful." He nods. "Sadly, all the others are spoilt. All spoilt. I'll have a lot of work to save what I can and make them into something. Perhaps necklaces of small beads." He looks up. "You'll be wondering how much they're worth. Let me see, let me see. How much are they worth?"

Weighing each clump on a fine set of scales, he mumbles as he tots up their value in his head. "A bit more than ten *unciae*. But poor quality." His head shakes. "Can't offer more than sixty for poor quality. That would come to six hundred *folles*. Six hundred and ten. Let's say three *solidi*, since you're a friend of Antonius." He must notice my disappointment. "Three *solidi*. What do you say? I can't offer more, I'm afraid, because so many are flawed."

The whole tragic story runs through my mind. Why wasn't I more careful? Should I have fought back when Drusus stole them? I was nowhere near as big and strong then as I am now. He'd have thrashed me. He sold the best ones to Sartorius – including my Emperor with his attendants – and left me with the broken leftovers. Too late.

I accept his offer, mumble my thanks and leave, my head hanging.

Back with Laurus, I try to be my usual self. "My two years are over…"

"I'm well aware of that, Silvanus." He claps me on the shoulder. "You've mastered your trade. I'm proud of you." He picks up a parchment from his table. "Look, I've drafted a certificate. You're now a qualified boatwright. Congratulations."

As I read it, my mood improves. His praise for my diligence and skill is remarkable. "That's very generous. Maybe you've seen I've finished my boat? I've tried it out a couple of times and it seems very seaworthy. I've moored it just round the headland."

"Indeed, I've noticed. I spoke with Balbus, too. Said he helped you launch it and give it its first trials. He was impressed. Well done."

"Thank you." How to proceed? "Perhaps… perhaps you also heard I got married."

"Already? I knew something was brewing. Well, hearty congratulations!" He grasps my shoulders, then nods. "So, I suppose you'll be leaving us. I'm sorry to lose a competent man like you. If you ever change your mind, I'll be most happy to take you back – on full pay."

"Thank you very much. I'm most grateful for your kindness… and all the training and help I've received. You have a good team of workers here."

"*I* thank *you* for the compliment. It's important to me to treat my men well. And it pays when your workforce is happy and motivated."

"So… I ought to settle my debts." I bite my finger. "How much do I owe you?"

He pulls out a tablet from a shelf behind him. "I've kept track of all the costs for your boat and deducted your down-payment. You've done all the work yourself – with some voluntary help from Balbus, I understand – so I've only charged you for the materials." I see the total on his ledger: MDCXXVIII. "That comes to one thousand six hundred and twenty-eight *folles*."

A hasty mental calculation tells me that's almost eight *solidi*. With the three from Jeremias and what little is left in my purse, I don't have enough. My eyelids close and I utter a silent prayer.

"I also kept a record of your earnings, since you asked only to be given what you needed for your expenses. The two years' pay would come to almost two thousand. But you only claimed eight hundred and forty." I peer at his final figure: MCLX. "So you still have a balance of one thousand one hundred and sixty to your credit."

Again, I'm frantically calculating. I *can* pay my debts. And I'll be left with more than a hundred and fifty *folles*. Thank you, Jesus.

When the finances are settled, Laurus ushers me into the house to say goodbye to his wife and children.

I think I've found everything my sweet *Nitela* wanted. Even added a few treats. And some gardening tools and shoes for me. I take my leave of Anna, passing on warmest greetings from Priscilla. She tells me how very happy she was to be present at our baptism and wedding.

Antonius offers to help me carry my purchases down to the boatyard. Drusus, he understands, has indeed left the island. It seems the whole incident became the talk of town, so we have nothing to fear from him.

We stack the goods in the dormitory entrance – no one will steal from here – and then it's again farewell, to a very dear friend.

I toss and turn throughout my last night with Boatwright Laurus, and give up fighting wakefulness when the gulls start their plaintive crying. So, these two and a half years are over. I'm moving on to join the love of my life. Together we'll master the challenges ahead and find our way in this exciting world.

Balbus notices me rise and gives me a hand with my things. We lug them round the headland and stow them in the aft hold. I greet a fisherman who is preparing his nets; he offers to keep an eye on things as we go back for a second load.

I gape. Laurus and the entire team of workers are waiting for me. Balbus joins them. Between them, my master and a foreman hold the brass handles of a splendid oak chest. They indicate I should approach and read the inscription on its plaque: 'Silvanus. In recognition of your skill and camaraderie. With best wishes for your marriage with Virna. Boatwright Laurus and Crew.' They lower it to the ground so that I can open it.

Breathless, I bend down and fumble with the catches, then lift the lid. One by one I pick out saws, chisels, knives, planes, a mallet, an adze and a drawknife – all made of shiny steel and polished wood. Beautiful. I gaze up at Laurus, then round at my former colleagues. "Thank you. Thank you all so much. I don't know what to say. I didn't expect anything like this. But I'll treasure these as long as I live."

My eyes are wet as I embrace each man in turn, ending with Laurus himself. He also has trouble composing himself.

"*Valete*! And, again, thank you for all you've taught me. And for your friendship."

Balbus helps me carry the chest down to the boat, while two others bring the remaining goods. And I embark, for the first time braving the waves alone in my own little skiff.

CHAPTER TWENTY SEVEN

Two Tasks

RAUCOUS CRIES FROM circling gulls urge me on. I leave the shelter of the bay and sail out to the open sea. "*Heia!* At last!" Are any of the Gods listening? The world is opening its gates. Will my *Nitela* be happy to come sailing with me?

The boat handles well, especially with the added weight of the tool chest. Hampered by an onshore wind, I keep the anchor ready as I pass a conical peninsula and pull round into the next bay. Hugging close to shore, I recognise Virna's clearing – where it all started. Fond memories fill my heart. Next is the little fishing village where that girl gave me a fish. It's not long before I identify the harbour below the village where our house is.

Our house. What a wonderful feeling. I'm no longer alone. My dear, sweet wife is waiting for me.

As I approach the little pier, one of the locals comes over. "Fine little skiff, lad. Looks new."

"It is. I made it myself."

"What?" He gapes. "You made it yourself? But you're little more than a boy. Who are you?"

When I explain I'm Priscilla's husband, he clasps my hand, introducing himself as Fabricius, and shows where best to tie up.

"Malpus has a mule and wagon," he says. "He'll take your wares up the hill, I'm sure."

We transfer my purchases to the cart, including my precious tool chest. As we approach the house, I jump down and run ahead, shouting, "It's me, *Nitela*!"

A scream arises, and Priscilla rushes out, her hands covered with bread dough. "Oh, Silé, my *Ursus*, you're back."

Hugging her tight, we laugh and cry as I lift her off her feet and swing her round. "Yes, my dear. I'm back. I've missed you so."

"Not as much as I've missed you. I couldn't sleep without your muscular body snuggling up to warm me." Noticing the mule cart, she turns. "Malpus, how nice to see you."

"'Tis an honour for me, my lady. Are you now married to Aquila here? He's a lucky man."

She giggles and looks at me. "So, you bought a whole number of things, I see. Praise God."

We unload – every item instilling more joy in her than the last – and dismiss Malpus with a couple of *folles* for his help.

The weeks go by and on her days off, Priscilla enjoys sailing with me. To my amazement, she is quick to learn to handle the boat. Sometimes Fabricius joins us, teaching us the rudiments of fishing with a net and how to catch lobsters in wicker pots weighed down with stones. My childhood experience with crabs puts me off eating them, but we sell them. And I'm happy to eat fish.

One day the goatherd Catalus drops by. I slap him on the shoulder and ask how he is. He wants to talk, so we sit down to a goblet of wine.

He greets Priscilla and comments on the fine smell of herbs, then turns to me. "You remember the *Ludi Florae* last year."

"Of course I do. Was it only a year ago?" I screw up my eyes as I make a mental calculation. "You're right. So much has happened. I remember seeing you there, talking with Titus after Cerbonius's speech but I had to run off to rescue my wife." I frown at Priscilla who is listening from the hearth. "Only I failed."

Catalus wants no frivolity. "I was so moved by what the Bishop said that evening. I had been brought up to fear and pay homage to Flora. And all those other Gods. And I must admit I enjoyed watching Ceres's dancing girls. But…" His eyes bore into me. "I think Jesus was chasing me."

"Chasing you?"

"Yes. When Cerbonius challenged us to burn our idols and turn to his God – the God of mercy who offers to forgive us – it was as if Jesus was appealing to me personally."

"What do you mean?"

Priscilla leaves off crushing herbs for a stew. "I know precisely what you mean, Catalus." She sits on the end of the bench. "He loves you dearly and wants to make sure you are not trapped by those false Gods. He wants to set you truly free."

"That's what Titus said. How did you know?"

"Maybe Jesus put the thought in my head." It's she, now, who leads the conversation. I listen in astonishment. "Jesus wants to adopt us as sons and daughters of His Father, and offers us a new life."

The words ring a bell, and I think of a verse I learned, 'I have come that they may have life, and have it more abundantly.'

Catalus goes on. "I know that now. I was so afraid of those Gods. And then all the things I'd done wrong came to mind – mocking my little sister, stealing from our neighbours, lying about what I'd been up to with my friends, things like that. Jesus forgave me… and took away my fear."

"That's wonderful." Priscilla is radiant.

"He's made me so happy. Given me a whole new reason to live." He calms down. "Of course, Father got mad when I burned our family God, *Hectate*. That was in winter. But a few days ago something fantastic happened…"

"Go on."

"He said he'd noticed I was more respectful towards him and helpful in the house. I wasn't even aware of it. I told him about my new faith and after some discussion, he also turned to Jesus."

Priscilla jumps up and claps. "Praise the Lord!"

"So did Mother and Tibia."

I shake my head, not understanding their excitement.

With an earnest expression he now turns to me. "I heard you had been studying the Evangel, Silvanus."

I smile. "They call me Aquila now." I wave my hand casually. "I was only copying it."

"I thought…" Catalus's expression fades. "I wanted to ask if you would come round and explain it to us. There are so many things we haven't grasped yet. But…"

"We'll come." Priscilla says. "I'm not as familiar with the text as Aquila is. But we can read it together and ask God to show us exactly what it means. It will be so exciting. I can tell you what I've learned from Mother Martha. And what Jesus shows me day by day as I pray and listen to Him."

This has become a regular activity for us. Often Titus or someone else joins us. We read from one the Scripture scroll and ask God to help us understand it. Priscilla loves to sing a Psalm or one of her own songs – we're all learning them as the weeks go by – and Catalus's mother always offers us food. It feels like one big family.

One day after the heat of summer is over, Titus tells us Cerbonius would like to see us. How is it we haven't gone to see him yet?

On Priscilla's next free day – it's not always the same day of the week because the patients need care every day – we pack a loaf of bread and two freshly-caught fish. As we make our way up the hill, Priscilla picks some orange strawberry tree fruit, purple sweet myrtle and deep red mastic tree berries, forming them into a pretty spray.

Dela and Runel welcome us but Cerbonius doesn't appear. Strange. We find him reclining on a rough wooden *lectus* within the cave. He greets us with joy but I gasp when I see how weak he is.

"How kind of you to come to visit me." He stretches out both hands to grasp ours and pull us near. "And these autumn fruit – how charming. A pity my smell is failing. My dearest children, your presence revives my spirit."

"I'm sorry we haven't come around sooner," Priscilla pulls his hand to her heart. "We've been ever so busy…" Her face lights up as she smiles at me.

Cerbonius's eyes twinkle.

She blushes. "I had to get Mater Agathe's old house in order. And make presentable clothes. And I still care for Mother Martha's dear patients." She rolls up a cloak to make a cushion so Cerbonius can adopt a half-sitting position. "But enough of us. What's wrong with you, honourable Father?"

"Wrong?" He utters his characteristic chuckle. "Nothing is wrong with me, my dear. This old earthen vessel has almost fulfilled its task and is soon to set me free for the glorious life I long for." His face is radiant but his nod is feeble.

"But I don't want to belittle my time here on earth. By the grace of God I have enjoyed full and rich years." His eyes shine as he gazes into the distance, nodding as he reviews his life. "Although I rebelled against my father, my Friend – whom I didn't yet know – granted me a wise mentor." He nods. "When we were battered by a violent storm, He carried us safely to Tyrrhenia. Although I never deserved it, He gave me a wonderful wife." His lips mouth soundless words. "Even when the land was ravaged by war, He preserved my life. When I was summoned before the Pope, He cleared my name. Even when I was thrown to a wild beast, He delivered me…"

It sounds like some litany. He pauses, hardly acknowledging our presence. "Yes, and wherever I lived, parishioners and fellow-citizens showed me hospitality and friendship. Many books were provided for me and I had plenty of time to reflect and to pray. How wonderful it has been to fellowship with my Friend and to serve my flock."

Again he seems to have fallen asleep, but then continues with renewed vigour. "Perhaps my greatest joy was at the *Ludi Florae* some years ago, to witness many men turning from their idols to serve the true and living God. I'm so happy for you, my dear Priscilla. And for you, worthy Aquila." His attempt to squeeze my hand emphasises his frailty. "What a privilege it has been to have been chosen to help you in your walk of faith. What more could I have desired from this life? But, I ramble. Forgive me. How are you, Aquila?"

"I-I went back to Fabricia to wrap up my apprenticeship." My voice trembles. "And to bring my boat round…"

"What did you say? Your boat is finished?"

"It is."

"It's a real beauty," Priscilla adds.

"It is, even if I say it myself. Easy to handle and very stable."

"Hearty congratulations, son. That makes me very happy, as I may have need of it before long."

I blink and raise my eyebrows. "Did I hear you correctly, sir? You'll need my boat? Where do you want to go?"

"I'll tell you in a moment. But first I have certain requests to make, if the Lord still grants me strength."

"About the scrolls?"

"About the scrolls. And other things. Come, please sit down." He makes room on the couch for Priscilla; I pull up a stool. "I have been thinking about all I would wish to say to young people such as yourselves about the priorities and risks of life." He indicates a set of scrolls to the side. "And I have written down my thoughts for the benefit of future generations."

"First, let us remember that Almighty God created this earth for His pleasure and judged His work to be very good. All His handiwork, from the silk thread supporting this spider…"

Priscilla jumps, then with gentle care moves the creature to the side of the cave.

"…to our friend the sun and all the heavenly bodies. All things reveal His wisdom, His love and His power." He nods. "That is why it's profitable to observe nature… and to study the works of virtuous pagan philosophers.

"And we, His crowning creatures – man and woman, old and young – reflect His image. He wants us to enjoy our time on this wonderful earth, in fellowship with Him."

"Jesus said He came to earth to offer us an abundant life."

"That's right. Well said. I'm happy you mention that promise. It includes the bodily pleasures you now enjoy together." His distant eyes show how far away his thoughts are. "In my youth, when I might have enjoyed my dear Julia's intimacy, the Church considered the sexual act to be dirty, even sinful. How tragic. The Creator intended it as a noble and thrilling expression of marital love."

I grasp my darling's hand. Oh, how sweet her flushed cheeks are as we gaze at each other.

"Marriage is also an arena for learning to understand and serve one another. And to care for others whom the Good Lord may entrust to you, whether your own off-spring, or people in need."

She squeezes my hand.

He continues after a burst of coughing. "So God intended. But things are not as they might be – not by far. Much to His grief, certain followers of Jesus have misinterpreted His words about not loving the world, teaching that we should reject all beauty and all sensual pleasures." His stomach rumbles and a weak chuckle emerges from his mouth. "I do believe I've forgotten to eat."

While Priscilla cooks a fish soup, Cerbonius asks me about my days in Fabricia and in particular how Antonius and Anna are keeping. He's pleased Drusus has made no further appearance. My time with Laurus interests him – how he designs his boats; how he manages his employees, his raw materials, his tools and finances; what the mood was in his boatyard and how the other workers treated me; what I had learned, not only about boat-building and sailing but also about life.

"I'm delighted you have benefited from this apprenticeship, my son. Such skills will be of great value in your life." What is this leading up to? "But now, as Priscilla's husband, you are called to another, higher mission."

"And what is that?"

"You were busy copying the Evangel of John…"

"I know. I haven't finished. Perhaps I can take a few scrolls down to our house and continue copying there."

"That would indeed be a good idea. But I have another concern on my heart. Soon I will no longer be able to help people who are yearning for spiritual enlightenment. It now falls to you to assist such seekers to appreciate the life my Friend offers."

My hand flies to my chest. "Me?" I shake my head. "I don't think I can do that… yet." I look up. "But Priscilla could. In fact, she does already. We often go to Catalus's home. Do you remember the goatherd who told you about the squabbles between Ignatius and Romerius? His whole family has come to believe in Jesus." Cerbonius's beaming eyes encourage me to continue. "I read out a passage from the biblical texts and Priscilla explains how she understands it."

At that moment she returns with her steaming brew. Cerbonius nods his appreciation. He thanks God for His provision, dips a piece of bread in the fish potage and passes it to me, then one to Priscilla and lastly himself. He also blesses the goblet of wine and shares it with us.

I recall Jesus's last meal with His friends – though one was to betray Him – and especially His words, 'Dear children, I will be with you only a little longer… I am giving you a new commandment: Love each other. Just as I have loved you, you should love each other. Your love for one another will prove to the world that you are my disciples.'

As we eat, Cerbonius picks up where he left off, sometimes referring to a wax tablet on which he has made notes. "This world is no longer altogether as God intended it. We still may enjoy the glory of the heavens, the beauty of the flowers and trees, the wonderful diversity of birds and beasts, the joy of friendship." His whole body is again wracked by another bout of coughing. "But selfish, Godless men have in many ways corrupted the harmony and order which the Creator established."

"Like the *Langobardi*? And Drusus?"

"If we are honest, are not we also guilty? Have we always loved others as we love ourselves?" He gazes at me, then at my wife. "I have often failed, often done wrong. That's why I'm so appreciative of the forgiveness my Friend offers – at the cost of His own life."

"Are you saying Jesus's death somehow takes away your guilt?" I say. "I don't understand."

"Indeed, it's a mystery." He nods. "A wonderful mystery." After a moment, he looks up. "Great men of God have grappled with the question of sin and forgiveness."

"Is it so complicated, then?"

"No, on the contrary. I simply accept the facts. I know Jesus forgives my sin. How that is possible is of no real concern to me." His attempt to chuckle leaves him gasping for breath. "He came from the Father to usher in His Kingdom, and invited people to follow Him in building it."

"That was ages ago. He's dead now."

"Indeed, the political and religious leaders of the time resented Him challenging their institutions and had Him executed – without a valid reason."

I gape. "You mean, he didn't just die?"

"Indeed, his cruel death was that of a rebel on a Roman cross – carrying the weight of sin of all mankind." He nods. "But He knew it was necessary. It was the only way for Him to become truly one with us mortals, whom He came to save." His eyes light up as he continues. "The greatest wonder is, however, that His Father didn't leave Him in the tomb! On the third day, He rose again…"

"What?" I gape. "He came back to life after being dead for three days?"

"Indeed. He received a new kind of life. He is the firstborn of the New Creation. And He lives on – never to die – with those who put their trust in Him." Again that pensive look. "For many years now, His Spirit has comforted and guided me. And I enjoy the new life He gives – talking with Him and serving others."

I lower my gaze, considering his moving account, then face him again. "You said you had things you wanted to say to us, before… while we're here."

"I no longer have the strength to say all that is on my heart. It's in these scrolls. Take them."

I peer at him, hesitate, then unroll the first scroll. A numbered sequence of sections meets my eye, each with a clear heading. I scan the list in silence.

Priscilla raises her eyebrows and nods towards the reclining Bishop. He seems to have fallen asleep.

After some moments, he stirs. "Come here, Aquila, my true son…" Cerbonius places his arms on my shoulders as I bend over him, but then closes his eyes and his breath becomes laborious. "Ah, Raguel, Raguel, what has become of you?" He sighs, then again faces me. "Aquila, my faithful servant, I have two requests. Will you carry out my final wishes?"

My eyes blur. "Of course, Father. I'll do whatever you ask."

"It's good you have finished your boat and mastered the art of sailing." He forces a smile at my puzzled expression. "As you no doubt are aware, I will soon be leaving you…"

Priscilla gasps, wide-eyed; one hand covers her mouth, while with the other she tenderly strokes Cerbonius's feeble arm.

"But my Friend who cared for me so well on earth is inviting me to join Him in His new world. I go gladly." His smile spreads as he glances from one to the other of us.

"First, I ask that you, Aquila, together with Titus and whichever assistants he chooses, should carry my mortal remains to Populonium…" He tries to lift his arm to point to the north-east as he explains that's the town on the headland we can see on a clear day. "And lay them to rest in the tomb I prepared next to the Church I served for many years."

My heart is heavy. How will I cope without his encouragement, his wisdom, his great learning? "It will be an honour to do that for you, Father." I feel anything but glad at the thought.

"I'm afraid it will be a dangerous venture. The *Langobardi* are advancing southwards with devastating zeal. But my Friend will be with you and will save you from all peril."

A violent tremor shakes his whole body. When he recovers, he again regards us, his complexion radiating inner peace and joy.

Priscilla's face is wet, but her eyes shine bright. "I'm so happy you can go to be with your Friend Jesus. But we will miss you so much, dear Father."

He nods. "Such is the way of man." He struggles to control his breathing. "But I must tell you my second request. It may be equally difficult." He reaches for my hand. "Aquila, you are familiar with my library which Marcus looks after?"

"Yes, I was amazed when I saw how many scrolls you have there, both biblical and secular."

"I leave it all to you, my son… on one condition." He forces a weak smile onto his lips. "I ask you in all stealth to transport the biblical scripts – together with my commentary on the Evangel of John and these scrolls – to the care of the Abbot of the monastery on the Isle of Capraria."

Priscilla looks at me, wide-eyed. I gasp. "To Capraria?"

CHAPTER TWENTY EIGHT

Free!

"INDEED. FATHER PLACIDUS, one of Benedictus's closest disciples, is now Abbot of the community there." Cerbonius nods in reflection. "A worthy man of God."

My head jerks. "Are there really people living there?"

Priscilla looks alarmed. "You wanted to snatch me off to an uninhabited rock?"

"Don't you think that would be fun? We'd be free – just the two of us. I'm sure we'd find something to eat, fish and gulls eggs, for instance."

"Be serious, dear! Father was speaking."

"It might not be wise to take your charming young wife there. Too great a temptation for the celibate monks." Cerbonius's breath is too short for his usual chuckle. "As I was saying, you will take the scrolls to Father Placidus. His scribes will copy them."

I nod.

Cerbonius suffers a violent bout of coughing. "Do you give me your word you will carry out this task?"

The importance of this task to my mentor begins to dawn on me. I place my hand on his feeble shoulder. "I do. I promise."

"In that way we ensure our precious texts aren't lost." He shakes his head. "The *Langobardi* destroy all things holy and sublime."

For a moment Cerbonius is silent. Then his face contorts.

Priscilla notices, too. "Come, my dear, we mustn't over-tire the Father. We must let him rest." She turns to him. "Is there anything you need?"

He waves his hand in a gesture of dismissal, but then raises a finger. "Please summon Father Clemens from Fabricia to perform the last rites." Priscilla again covers her mouth and stares at him. "It's what the Church prescribes."

His eyes close and he seems to be sleeping, but then continues. "Titus and Marcus should also be present. And yourselves, of course."

Another lapse and another afterthought. "And, Aquila, please construct a simple casket to transport my remains to Populonium."

Heavy with sorrow and busy with arrangements, I welcome the moments alone making a coffin for the man who has taught me so much in the last years. I've learnt to share his wonder at the marvellous works of the Creator: trees and flowers, stars and beasts; his love for all he meets: young and old, weak and strong, rich and poor; his bold intervention for justice and reconciliation wherever there is discord; his passion to propagate the Holy Scriptures; his humble penitence, his faith and joy as he worships his Lord and Friend. Oh Jesus, I long for peace like that and a real purpose for my life!

Ominous dark clouds hang low and a stormy wind tosses the last brown leaves in wild flurries as we gather at the cave. Cerbonius forces a smile of welcome, a feeble hand grasping the arm of each one who bends over to kiss his leathery cheek. Priscilla is radiant, though her tears flow free, as she whispers, "Jesus is calling you. We'll join you later."

I am last. Only I can hear his whispered words. "Aquila – Eagle of the Lord – devote yourself to serving Him. He will grant you peace and purpose."

I freeze. My unspoken prayer! Does he read my thoughts?

We all marvel as he gazes heavenward with a rapturous expression. "I come… gladly."

Then, with his last breath, he chants that song of Julia's, which I had so often heard streaming from his holy rock before dawn:

> *I worship You, Father, Creator,*
> *I worship You, Spirit of power,*
> *I worship You, Christ, my Redeemer.*
> *I give You my heart at this hour.*

> *Your love knows no end and no measure,*
> *Your wisdom has given me worth.*
> *All glory to God, Who is mighty.*
> *Your Kingdom will fill all the earth.*

A resounding crash announces the fall of some tree nearby. Dela and Runel utter uncanny whines as they waddle around Cerbonius's couch. But he is gone. No one speaks.

With a tender touch, Titus closes the old man's eyes and Priscilla helps him wash his body, anointing it with myrtle oil, then clothing it in his Bishop's robe. She places a sprig of red berries next to his face on the white silk lining of the coffin. Father Clemens, sombre in his *toga pulla*, performs the prescribed rites, sprinkling consecrated water over the lifeless form while chanting strange incantations and prayers.

Strong gusts of wind buffet us as, with heavy steps of

silent grief, Titus, Marcus, Catalus and I carry the casket down to Titus's house. We stand the coffin cover with its prominent cross before the door. What seems like hundreds of people from far and wide pass through one by one to pay their last respects, accompanied by melancholy wailing from groups of older women outside.

Malpus arrives early next morning to transport the coffin down to my boat, which I have kept ready for some weeks. The three friends squeeze in with me. The wind is strong, so I keep the sail partially furled and, with some trepidation, we venture out into the turbulent waves. Catalus turns as pale as the silk shroud and holds his mouth closed. He leans over the side but can't prevent a violent retching; a mixture of salt spray and his last meal blows back into his face.

I've never been out in such rough weather before but Cerbonius's last promise is my assurance: "My Friend will be with you and will save you from all peril."

The westerly wind is favourable and though we can barely see them through the low cloud, we pass one promontory after another in quick succession. The only other ship we meet is a large merchant vessel limping towards the shelter of the bay of Fabricia, its mainsail torn and useless. After some hours peering between the gusts of spray and the menacing clouds, we catch glimpses of the red cliffs of Ilva's north-eastern headland.

Though tidal currents in the straits are renowned for their treachery, we press on at speed, driven by the storm. Black clouds, heavy with rain, surround us, hindering our orientation.

Titus leads in a loud prayer for God's guidance and protection and Marcus joins in singing a psalm.

Our combined weight means the boat is low in the

water and all I can do is clasp the steering oar with both hands and let the wind carry us onward. The others hold on tight, steady the coffin and check the sail ropes as my little skiff rolls and pitches in the huge waves. Lightning flashes and the almost instantaneous thunderclaps startle me, reminding me of my close encounters with Aquila.

Around us the rain is driving down in sheets, but somehow – by God's mercy – it passes us by.

Hours pass. Then the waves become smaller, more regular and a new sound reaches my ears: breakers pounding the shore. With no visibility, we brace ourselves for beaching or crashing onto a rock.

A loud 'Hallelujah!' resounds as our keel scrapes on pebbles and we come to a halt. Titus jumps into the shallow water and pulls on the painter, taking advantage of the rocking motion from the waves to tug the boat ashore. With the coffin removed, it's light enough to haul right onto the beach.

Where are we? The curtains of rain and the heavy clouds mean we neither see our surroundings nor know the time of day. But we've landed without mishap and to everyone's amazement, we're still dry.

Titus goes to investigate and returns after a short time with good news. By divine providence we've landed very near Populonium. A local man wept at the news the Bishop had passed away but showed Titus the Church and the tomb Cerbonius had prepared. He ran off, driven by a morbid fear of the advancing enemy.

With all haste, straining our ears for any sound of marching, the four of us lug the coffin to the graveyard, lower it into the tomb and replace the heavy stone cover. Titus recites an anthem of praise for the blessed life of the old Bishop, who meant so much to all of us.

The storm subsides as we return to the boat. Angled rays of sunlight peep beneath the clouds and glisten off the smooth sea – a sign of God's favour and an indication that the day is advanced. Just as we are setting off, our guide rushes up with bread and figs and wishes us God's speed.

We row out some way, filled with wonder as we now see the rocks between which we sailed without mishap. As we unfurl the sail – the wind is now from the east and not so strong – our attention is drawn back to shore. Flaming torches and a thunderous roar reveal hundreds of soldiers – many on horseback – advancing on the town. Our hearts weep as, before long, the evening sky is lit by a surging inferno. The *Langobardi* have arrived, as Cerbonius predicted.

Safely back on Ilva, we climb the hill as the eastern sky begins to brighten. Very aware of God's help and protection, we link arms on reaching the village and Titus leads us in a prayer of thanks.

Priscilla rushes up and hugs me, impatient to hear how everything went. She was unable to sleep but spent the hours praying and singing, confident our trip would succeed.

Everyday life – what does that mean now that my mentor has left us? Doubtless his answer would be: "My Friend is still with you. Follow Him!" Whatever *that* means.

I enjoy the evenings at Catalus's place. The atmosphere is warm and friendly. Priscilla's ability to lead the group amazes me, both explaining the biblical text and leading our times of worship. She has a beautiful voice and often teaches us new songs. I try to accompany her on my flute.

Catalus's father is a keen participant; he has been elected a local magistrate and invited some of the village elders to join our house church, as we call it. They are planning ways to support the poorer families in the region. We pray for wisdom and courage, that they would perform their duties worthily as upholders of truth and justice.

Titus says that's what the church is meant to be: a team of people Jesus calls together to represent Him on Earth, to reflect His character and continue His work; it's neither intended to be an institution nor a way of retreating from the hostile world.

I reflect on his challenging words, but something – a shadow from my past – is still holding me back from that wholehearted devotion to Jesus the others seem to enjoy.

"Follow Him!" Cerbonius would say. Whatever *that* means.

I'm happiest doing practical work – repairing things in the house or helping Priscilla with the more infirm patients. I've made a lightweight litter for moving frail people about, which helps Martha and Priscilla a lot.

"I've had plenty of time to think while waiting for the fish to bite." I drop my fresh catch next to the hearth. "I remembered the Bishop's second assignment – to take the scrolls to what's-his-name in Capraria."

Priscilla takes a look at the two large bluefish and several little *branzini* in my basket. "Father Placidus." Her memory is acute. "But it's far too stormy for you to go now in winter."

"I know. And, anyway, I really ought first to finish copying the Evangel of John."

"I had an idea." She starts gutting the fish. "It would be wonderful if we could have a copy for ourselves. Then we would be better able to teach Catalus and the others. Do you think that would be possible?"

"It would be a big task." I hang up my sodden cloak. "But wait! You could help. Your script is beautiful."

"I'd love to. I'm so thankful sweet Sabina taught me to read and write – at least one benefit I got from living in Elazar's home." She looks up from her messy work. "Why don't you make us a long table and bench, so we could work together?"

We spend hours copying texts and discussing what they mean. Cerbonius's words echo through my mind as we work on familiar passages. Priscilla often sees a different significance than what I had understood at the time.

"'The Word became human and made his home among us – full of grace and truth,'" Priscilla says. "That's Jesus. He's God's way of speaking to us.

"'To all who received him, who believed in his name, he gave the right to become children of God.' You see: you just have to believe."

"That promise is the first thing Cerbonius shared with me," I reply. "I've often thought about it. It sounds like joining a new family."

Priscilla comes to sit on my lap and squeezes me tight. "Exactly! I lost my family…" Sorrow fills her eyes and she can't speak for a moment. "But God has given me a new one – a new mother, new brothers and sisters, even a thick-skulled husband…"

"Hey! No need to mock." I knock my forehead against hers. "But I could do with a new father."

"You just have to believe…"

We enjoy a hot kiss. Then she gets up to fetch a goblet of wine. Drinking at the same time proves a bit messy. After a hearty laugh, we continue with our writing.

"What do you think Jesus meant with this?" I point to a place on my scroll. "The first bit is clear. 'Unless a grain of wheat falls to the ground and dies, it remains only a single seed. But if it dies, it produces many seeds.' He seems to be talking of people. 'Whoever loves his life will lose it, and whoever hates his life in this world will keep it for eternal life.' It sounds as if He thinks death is good."

"No. He certainly doesn't want us to die. Why would He have given us such a wonderful world to live in? And each other? How does it go on?"

I look back at the text. "'Whoever serves me must follow me; and where I am, my servant also will be. My Father will honour the one who serves me.'"

"Yes, you see. He wants us to follow Him, to serve Him."

"So, what does that mean – for us, today?"

"Trusting Him. Asking Him what He desires us to do. And sharing His love with people we meet, helping them to believe in Him." She seems to have it all worked out. "And, of course, thanking God for all He gives us." She looks heavenward. "You're so good to us, Father."

How I wish I could pray with such ease.

"I'm so grateful You gave me Aquila; he's so strong and clever. I love him with all my heart. Thank You for this little home. And for these inspiring Scriptures. You provide us with everything we need. I love you, Jesus."

Our eyes meet. "Am I supposed to say, 'Amen'?"

"Silly boy!" She throws her arms around me and we kiss, long and passionately.

"We'll have big, fat onions here, and lots of cabbages over there." Priscilla's arm sweeps over our vegetable patch to be. "And, of course, lentils and beans. And different kinds of tasty herbs. And perhaps juicy melons… Hey, you're not listening!"

I take my time carrying a large stone to a pile at the side of our little field. "I think I once told you about my family… It's been almost four years."

"Yes, I remember. I've been hoping you would tell me more about them. You have a dear little sister about my age, I believe. What's her name again?"

"I always called her Little Eli. But I wouldn't be surprised if she's married now. To my friend Rufus."

"That's lovely."

"They said they'd help Father with the fields and animals… and the terraces." I bury my face in my hands.

Priscilla drops her spade, comes up and puts an arm around my shoulders. "What's up? Something's troubling you."

"I tried to forget them…" My chest heaves. "Scrub them from my life. It was all my fault."

She turns me by the shoulders so I can't avoid looking into her warm dark eyes. "What do you mean?"

"It was my fault!" I'm screaming now.

Her gaze seems to penetrate my soul but she says nothing.

"I don't know what evil sprite got into me!" The words don't want to come. "To run off and leave that stone loose. I should have known he'd step on it and fall." I shudder, tears blurring my sight. "Deep down I loved him…"

She leads me to a boulder and we sit. Her arm pulls me close. "Tell me," she whispers.

"I just told you!" I shout. I wrench myself from her grasp and turn away. "I almost killed my father." My head drops into my hands. "Perhaps it would have been better if he'd died." I clench my fists and beat my forehead. "Then Mother and Little Eli wouldn't have had to suffer his cruelty all these years." I knit my brows and shake my head back and forth. "I destroyed my family."

She caresses my shoulders.

For a long time, my heaving chest prevents me from speaking.

"If I hadn't felt so guilty, I might not have escaped to the quarry that day. And I might still be friends with Pontus… and Lucilla. Now I have no one."

She leans on my back, throwing her arms around me.

"You have me, darling. Am I nothing to you?" Her tears drip on my neck.

Convulsive sobs wrack my whole body. A grunt is all I can manage.

"I thank You, Spirit of Jesus."

How can she even pray in a situation like this?

"You convict us… to help us repent. Have mercy on my beloved Aquila. Please release him from his sinister burden." Her head falls to my shoulder.

We stay until sunset. Then she stands, and with a gentle pull ushers me indoors. I offer no resistance. She makes a hot drink and sits next to me, her arm around my shoulders.

I sip the honey-sweetened beverage.

After many moments, Priscilla speaks. "He loves you all the same."

I look up, questions in my eyes.

"Jesus loves us just as we are. What hurts Him most is when we try to live without Him."

I see. For her it's always about Jesus. "How can He love me after what I did?"

"Jesus didn't come to call good people. He came to call unworthy sinners… to repent." The love in her eyes is irresistible. "He's longing to forgive you."

I drop my eyes again and continue to drink.

"Dear Silé, tell Him what's bothering you. He'll take away your guilt."

I sigh. "What good is it to tell him what happened? He must know already."

"Tell Him. Get it off your poor chest."

I turn aside. It's easier for me to imagine I'm talking to Jesus if I'm not facing her. Another deep sigh. "Jesus, I'm sure You know I loved Father… and Mother and Little Eli. Our home used to be a happy place…" I sigh. "But I was so fed up with the heavy work on the terraces. I wanted to have fun with the other lads. I don't know what

I was thinking. I knew that stone was dangerous. I'm so sorry."

Priscilla's warm hand grasps mine.

"So much went wrong after that." Again, my chest heaves. "I was miserable. I wanted to escape… to run away… to explore the beckoning world. Especially to get away from Father and my guilty conscience." My fists clench. "Everyone was unhappy. Father had constant pain and felt useless. He got in the way at home and kept shouting at Mother. He beat Little Eli with the hot poker." I bury my head in my hands, then shout, "But it was all my fault!"

I drop to my knees. "Forgive me. Please, Jesus, forgive me. Take away this guilt, I beg you. Give me a clean heart and let me love again. From now on, I want to live with You."

A warm tremor shakes my whole body and I fall on my side. Words ring through my mind: Sons of God… full of grace and truth… I have come that they may have a rich and satisfying life… children of the light… as we forgive those who sin against us. I've seen and heard them so many times.

"Thank You, Jesus." I find myself laughing.

Priscilla is kneeling next to me. She hugs me, then starts singing:

> *My Father in heaven, I honour your name!*
> *And long for your will to be done,*
> *That earth would be filled with your fame.*
>
> *I look up to You for all of my needs;*
> *And beg you forgive where I fail,*
> *As I forgive when my heart bleeds.*
>
> *I'm easily tempted and fall into sin.*
> *Please save me from evil and doubt.*
> *O Father, Your kingdom shall win!*

For the first time, I'm able to join in, praising God from the bottom of my heart.

"Oh, darling, it's wonderful. I have a new Father. In heaven. And He really has forgiven me." I kiss her on the lips. "But there's still something I need to talk to Him about."

"Go on then!"

Kneeling again, I turn from her. "Jesus. I wish You could do something to make my family happy." A sensation of calmness overwhelms me. "Thank You, Jesus. I hope things are working out with Rufus and Little Eli. Are they married? And helping with the practical work?" An idea pops into my head. "Perhaps you could give Father a different occupation... to restore his self-respect. You know how he always wished he could go fishing." Another inspiration hits me. Is it from Him? I push it aside. "And, Lord, it would be wonderful if you'd let me be friends again with Pontus and Lucilla."

"Amen!" Priscilla claps her hands. "You are so good, Jesus."

It's a new working day and we've come to a passage that I hadn't yet looked at with Cerbonius. It moves me deeply and I read it aloud:

"Love each other, just as I have loved you. No one has greater love than the one who gives his life for his friends. You are my friends if you do what I command. I do not call you servants anymore. Servants do not know their master's business. Instead, I have called you friends. I have told you everything I learned from my Father. You did not choose me. Instead, I chose you. I appointed you to go and bear fruit, fruit that will last."

"There's so much in these few sentences. I can't take it all in." I read it again.

"It's simple, really," Priscilla says. "Jesus wants us as His special friends."

"The Bishop always called him Friend. Now I see why."

"He chooses us and adopts us. And if we keep ever so close to Him, He promises our lives will be fruitful."

"What do you understand by that?"

"We will be able to do good. And to help others to believe in Jesus."

"I wish that would happen in my life. It's been such a struggle to try to do what's right and good for others. Most of the time I've only thought about what's good for me. I'm beginning to see that God's Kingdom exists wherever we care for the weak, and spread love and justice in Jesus's name."

"Yes. It was only after Mother Martha helped me to open my heart to Jesus that I was able to help her with the other patients. Now it delights me."

"But He speaks of giving his life for his friends. He says that's the greatest act of love possible. Is He talking about Himself? Or does it mean us?"

"He did give His life for us. But I think it can also apply to us." She peers into my eyes. "When I was caught at the fairground – you remember – I was ready to die. To go to be with Jesus." She nods. "And all the time Drusus held me prisoner, he could have molested me or murdered me. And if I had had to go back to Elazar, he would probably have had me killed. A slave has no rights." She nods. "I decided to stay faithful to Jesus. I prayed that He would be glorified, whatever happened. In the end, He saved me. And gave me a wonderful husband to top it all." She comes over and gives me a powerful hug.

"I'm not sure I'd be willing to die for Him." Gazing into those deep, dark eyes, I can't help but smile. "Especially if it meant losing my lovely wife."

"Oh – please God – I hope it won't come to that." She

grasps my hands. "But if He does take something away from us, I'm sure He gives us something better in return."

I glance back at the parchment. "In fact, He goes on to say, 'The Father will give you anything you ask for in my name.' That's amazing!"

"Let's try."

"What do you mean, let's try?"

"Let's pray for something in Jesus's name. Something that would really please Him." My dear wife is so down to earth. She places a hand on mine and raises her eyes heavenward. "Lord, let us help someone to put their trust in You."

That's it.

When she remains silent, I mutter, "Amen".

CHAPTER TWENTY NINE

Capraria

"IT'S TIME," I say, placing a last scroll in the box I've made.

"For what?" Priscilla looks up from mending a torn tunic.

"For me to take these to Capraria."

She starts. "Are you sure? The weather's still rather uncertain."

"I promised Cerbonius. And if I wait, who's to say it won't get worse?"

"I know, darling." She comes to me and puts her arms round my neck. "But…" Her warm kiss makes me tingle. "Somehow, I have a strange feeling about your journey."

"What do you mean?"

"Well, when I was praying this morning, it was as if a dark cloud closed in on me – so dark I couldn't see anything. And it made me shiver. I was so frightened. But then a ray of light broke through the cloud," she says, lifting her hand high, "and shone straight onto me." She brings it down to her breast. "And Jesus spoke to me, 'Don't be afraid!' he said. 'Even if you walk through the valley of the shadow of death, I will be with you.'"

"And is that a message about my trip?"

"I'm not sure." She gives me another kiss. "Look after

yourself, my dear *Ursus*! And come back soon!" She hugs me tight. "I'll be praying for you all the time. Jesus will be with you – and with me here."

I can't keep the journey altogether secret, since I need help to carry the scrolls down to the harbour. Titus again engages Malpus to pick us up in the middle of the night, then helps to load the box into the bottom of the boat. Priscilla hands me a bag of food and a skin of wine. I'd have forgotten again.

Fabricius turns up. When he hears I'm setting off alone, he's shocked. "You must at least take a sword. You never know what you might meet on the high sea."

I hadn't considered such dangers and glance at Titus and Priscilla. "No! I'm doing this for God and I trust Him to look after me. Jesus didn't want his followers to fight."

Titus says a prayer, then Priscilla gives me a big hug. "Don't be longer than necessary. I'll miss you very much, especially at night." She winks.

No one we know has ever been to Capraria but they say the harbour – for what it's worth – is at the north-eastern corner of the island. The first quarter moon has just set when I hoist the sail and put to sea. *Ursa Major* shows me the direction to take. The wind is gentle but blowing from the east, which is good, and it looks like it's going to be a fine day.

A song of joy bursts from my lips. "I praise You, God, for the wonder of Your creation – the stars, the wind, the sea – and for Your promise never to leave me."

I pick out Mars and Jupiter on the horizon astern, before a golden gleam appears and all the other heavenly bodies begin to disappear. Plaintive gulls accompany me, and now and then a splash and flash of silver remind me there's a great deal going on below the surface.

But I have an urgent mission – no time to think of fishing.

As I enjoy the food Priscilla gave me, I can almost feel her soft skin and silky black hair. I hear her merry laughter and her mellow voice thanking God for the scent of flowers, the beauty of a butterfly's wings, happy children's voices…

The sun is already high and the sail still full. I steer somewhat to starboard and judge my position to be about halfway.

What did Cerbonius mean when he urged me to devote myself to serving Jesus, adding 'He will grant you peace and purpose'? I turn my question into a prayer. "Lord Jesus, I'm happy to be making this journey for You – so that Your Word is preserved and made known – and I trust You will give me success. Whatever happens, I want to stay faithful to You."

A playful dolphin appears on my left, then reappears somewhere unexpected. For a long while I'm fascinated by its sleek form and agile movements – quite the king of the sea. With a flip of its tail it seems to say goodbye and disappears. I throw in a bit of my bread, hoping to lure it back, but a fish snatches it instead.

Soon white cliffs become visible on Capraria next to red rocks, topped by barren headlands. Valley after valley falls to tiny rocky coves, the breaking waves throwing up occasional bursts of white. There's no sign of habitation.

About a third of the way up the eastern coast, I lower the sail. The wind is unpredictable under the lee of the cliffs. I have to row. Progress is slow. I pass a rugged ridge sticking out into the sea and many little inlets. Rhythmic roaring and pounding puzzle me at first, until I discover they come from waves rushing in and out of a shoreline cave.

The northern tip of the island appears but still neither a harbour nor any settlement.

Behind me, the peak of Monte Capanne emerges from the distant haze, dominating the western end of Ilva. Somewhere there my dear wife is busy caring for Mother Martha's patients – doubtless singing – and now and then sending up a prayer for my success and safety.

I round another point and discover a deep inlet. As I approach, the first sign of human life is a path winding up the hill – too prominent to be caused by wild goats. At the foot of a cliff stands a low stone building and tucked behind a rocky outcrop, a boat, rather larger than mine, lies half hidden. There are no people in sight.

I drift in to the stony shore, jump out and tie up to a rock. What now? I can't unload the box of scrolls alone. And, anyway, to whom would I give them?

Lengthening shadows merge and envelop me as the sun sinks behind the hills. It's cooler and it looks as if a storm is brewing. "Thank you, Jesus, for bringing me here safely."

I examine the house. The door is open. It's empty, looks like storage space for something. Not very inviting, but I could sleep here if necessary. At least there would be some shelter when the rain breaks.

As I head back to the boat, two hooded men in dark robes appear from behind a boulder. I wave to them but they seem suspicious. I go nearer. "*Salvete*. I've come from Ilva."

The lanky one nods. He seems to be in charge. I interpret his questioning look to mean 'What do you want?' Is he dumb?

"I would like to speak to your Abbot – Father Placidus, I believe."

They glance at each other. Lanky points at me, then throws his arms out, palms upward.

"My name – my Christian name, that is – is Aquila. I

was sent here by Bishop Cerbonius. I have some things for Father Placidus."

His nod seems less than friendly.

The shorter one – I think of him as Dumpy – takes out a strange metal object and puts it to his lips. A loud, sequence of trills resounds. After a moment an answering strain comes from the hills. Back and forth the unmelodious phrases are exchanged. At last, the leader beckons me to follow him.

"Sorry to bother you, but do you think you could help me unload that box from my boat? I can't manage it alone."

More silent conferring, followed by a flick of Lanky's head. They come with me to the shore and together we carry the crate to land. Their reluctance to speak unnerves me.

"Is the holy Father far away? This is for him, but, as you see, it's rather heavy."

Ignoring my question, he points at the warehouse and we lug the box over to it. He indicates I'm to open it.

I hesitate, then comply. When they see the scrolls, Lanky holds up two fingers. I take out two of the precious documents and carefully close the lid again.

Another thought comes to mind. "Could we also take the loose items into the shelter of the warehouse? It looks as if there might be a storm coming." They glance at the sky, then without much enthusiasm, give me a hand to carry the sail, oars and other things to safety. "The anchor should be all right."

It's clear I'm to follow them up the steep, winding path. Lanky leads, I follow with the two scrolls, and Dumpy takes up the rear.

We trudge higher and higher. I turn up the collar of my cloak and rub my hands together. My stomach growls. Where are they taking me? Are the other scrolls safe back there in the shed? What about my boat? Maybe bandits live here in addition to the monks. Or pirates.

"How much farther is it?" Lanky makes a sign with his hands, which I can't interpret in the semi-darkness, and he presses on. Their language of gestures and whistles seems to fulfil their needs. But they're not much company for a stranger with many questions.

Buildings loom at last and singing resounds. I smell boiled fish. My stomach rumbles. I'm left in a waiting room with Dumpy, as Lanky goes off to announce my arrival. Silence, apart from the intermittent chanting of many voices emanating from another building.

At last I'm ushered into the presence of the elderly Abbot – tall, wide-shouldered, and with a strangely shaven head. To my surprise, he embraces me. "I bid you welcome." He indicates I am to sit. "To receive an emissary from Bishop Cerbonius on this remote isle is an honour indeed." So, somehow, Lanky managed to inform him who I am. "What may your name be?"

"They call me Aquila – Father Cerbonius gave me that name at my baptism."

"Aquila – a pioneer of the Church." He nods. "And you have sailed alone from Ilva? When did you leave?"

"Before dawn this morning."

"No doubt you are hungry." He turns and calls out. "Severus, bring some victuals for my guest."

He busies himself with some scrolls, allowing me to eat. "And how is the good Father?"

I lower my eyes. "I'm afraid he passed away some months ago."

"Praise God!" He raises both hands high. "Then he's free to enjoy life to the full. But tell me about him."

Taken aback by his reaction, I recount what I remember of his last moments. But Father Placidus wants to hear how he lived, what he undertook. We speak at length. They had met at Benedictus's monastery in Monte Cassino many years ago.

"And what brings you here?"

I tell of the two tasks Cerbonius made me promise to undertake as he lay dying, and show him the scrolls I brought up with me. One is in my script, from the Evangel of John, the other a part of Cerbonius's treatise.

He glances at them. "Excellent. I shall examine them when I have time. And you brought more such?"

"Yes. A box full. We left them down at the warehouse near the landing place."

"They will indeed be very precious to us. I'll send for them in the morning."

Heavy rain drums on the roof of the small, sparsely-furnished room I'm offered for the night. Though tired from the long journey, thoughts of my sweet Priscilla fill my mind. How is she coping without me? In my drowsiness, I keep reaching out in vain for her warm softness. It's long before I sleep.

Morning comes. Was it thunder or the sound of chanting that woke me? It's still stormy and wet.

Unfamiliar with the monastic routine, I wander out to the beautiful flower garden with its central fountain, and take a seat under a covered walkway that extends along three sides. Behind me is the chapel, opposite me the refectory, and to my left a hall of some sort from where the voices emerge. The rain continues to beat on roofs and paving stones.

Father Placidus comes out to me when the monks are at work – some in the kitchen, some tending the garden or feeding the hens and goats, others copying documents, I'm told. "I have read through those two scrolls. Cerbonius's exhortations are pearls of wise counsel. I wanted to have the others fetched but I'm told the rain has caused a landslide and the path is impassable. Anyway, we wouldn't want to risk them getting wet in a downpour like this. I understand they are under cover in the warehouse."

I nod.

"I hope you're not in too much of a hurry to get back."

"Well, I do miss my dear wife but, other than that, I have time."

"As a married man of the world, you would find it difficult to observe our Rule. It is rather severe but helps us concentrate on our Lord and what's important in life. Feel free to wander around the monastery. You are welcome to attend the *Collatio* after Vespers."

"I don't know these customs, I'm afraid. What happens then?"

"Of course you don't. We all come together as a group to pray and read from Scripture. Then each monk shares how it speaks to him. It's the only time of day when everyone is allowed to speak."

"That would be wonderful. I don't know much of the Scriptures yet, but I'd love to hear how your monks understand it."

"But first our midday repast will be served in the refectory there; it will be a meagre spread of poached fish and boiled oats, but adequate for our needs. Please come to my cell afterwards so that we can talk in more comfort. It's dismal out here in the rain."

Intricate colourful pictures on his walls captivate me. A woman, her clothes hanging loose, stands before a crouching Jesus, who is writing something with his finger in the dust. Many small figures around the edge suggest a watching crowd, while some well-robed men are slipping from the scene.

"That must be the woman who was caught with the wrong man." I look more carefully. A gentle firmness emanates from Jesus's face as He gazes at the woman. "Jesus didn't condemn her."

"That's correct. We all sin but He forgives us."

Another picture depicts Jesus sitting on a hillside addressing a crowd. A third shows frightened men in a sailing boat battling against towering waves. Jesus is standing in the bows, shouting at the wind. Was He with me in my little skiff?

I move to the last one. Three men on crosses against a black sky. Women and soldiers cower in the foreground. Jesus, in the centre, His contorted face gazing heavenwards, is bleeding from a gash in His side. One of the other victims wears a pleading expression, the other sticks out his tongue.

Father Placidus lets me contemplate the picture in silence for a while. "It's moving, isn't it? Icons like these help us in our contemplation and prayer."

"Do you make them?"

He laughs. "Not I personally. One of the brothers. He is a gifted artist and also illustrates the codices we produce."

My eyes open wide. "Could you show me a codex? I've never had a chance to hold one or look inside. Cerbonius only had scrolls."

"I have one here. It's the Evangel of Marcus." He lifts the elaborate cover and shows me how to turn the pages, then hands it to me.

I examine the fine parchment and meticulous script with initial letters and tiny images illuminated in gold, red, blue and green. "Marvellous!"

I start reading. '*Initium Evangelii Jesu Christi, Filii Dei.*' Like the other, it speaks of the messenger John who baptised people in the river Jordan. Then, Jesus's first words raise a shiver in me. 'The time is fulfilled. The kingdom of God is at hand; repent and believe the good news.'

I look up at the Abbot. "It's wonderful. So well-made

and the illustrations are superb." I smell the page, stroke it, then close the codex and give it back to Father Placidus. "But the best part is the Good News that Jesus brought God's kingdom down to us." I shake my head. "Why doesn't everyone believe in Him?"

He takes the codex from me. "You are not long a follower of His, I understand."

"No. I was brought up to fear the ancient Gods. Aquila the Avenger in particular." I pull out my amulet. "I was introduced to Jesus by Father Cerbonius. And by my wife… She helped me to get to know and love Him as my Friend. That was only some months ago."

"And you still wear that talisman?"

"My aunt Ceres gave it to me when I was little. She's the priestess of Jupiter. I suppose I should take it off now I'm over eighteen, but I never had a coming-of-age ceremony."

"But now you follow Jesus. You don't need that bond to the old God. In fact, it may hold you back in your faith."

"Do you think so?"

"We need to be careful not to compromise with the powers of darkness. Jesus has conquered them, but if we still show them our allegiance, they can be a stumbling block to us. Many Christians wear a cross instead."

"Now you mention it, my wife has a dove brooch from her mother. It's the only thing she could keep."

"That would be a symbol of the Holy Spirit. Was she originally from Africa?"

"Yes, Carthago. How do you know?"

"The Coptic believers often wear doves."

With some hesitation I grasp my pendant. Bitter memories of Ceres's hateful indoctrination invade my mind, but also the release I felt at discovering the mighty Aquila was only a pile of boulders. How odd that I have been given exactly that baptismal name. I'm sure it was no coincidence. I raise my eyes to face Father Placidus. "I belong to Jesus now." Then I lift the necklace over my head and gaze at the little eagle. "You no longer have any power over me, Aquila." I'm not sure what to do with it.

Father Placidus responds. "I could ask my sculptor to make a Christian symbol for you, if you like."

"I would like to wear a cross. Jesus chose the path of suffering – even dying on a cross – instead of trying to overcome his enemies by force."

"'No one has greater love than the one who gives his life for his friends.'" He says, quoting the last passage I read with Priscilla! "A cross also reminds us to be willing to die for Him." His earnest gaze makes me take note. "Don't throw the talisman away. I think you should make a point of showing your wife, and your parents and aunt, that you now have a new life and have rejected that symbol of fear and oppression."

My parents? Aunt Ceres? "I… haven't seen my family for years. I'm not sure how they would take it if I tell them I've abandoned their religion."

"Is not Jesus with you? Come, let me pray that He will give you courage."

He does just that.

CHAPTER THIRTY

Journey home

IT'S A NEW day, bright and sunny. I seek out the Abbot.

"I was very pleased to be able to attend the *Collatio* last night. The brothers' love for God really impressed me. But today I had another idea. Could I help with clearing the path? I'd like to be useful."

"That's great. You may accompany Flavius and Petrus and see what can be done."

It turns out Flavius and Petrus are none other than Lanky and Dumpy. They are carrying pickaxes and shovels and find some tools for me too. I understand now that an assignment like this does not absolve the monks from their onus of silence.

An overhanging cliff collapsed in the heavy rain during the night after I arrived and caused a major landslide, completely blocking the way. New rivulets have formed and continue to spread reddish mud across a wide area of the hillside, covering it with a slippery layer.

I suggest we first dig a channel to divert this flow before attacking the piles of rocks and loose rubble. They show their agreement with signs. It's heavy work, but we make good progress. I'm relieved when they take a break. Petrus brings out a flagon of wine and a loaf of bread, which are much appreciated. Then we return to our labour.

By mid-afternoon we've shored up the mudslide and carved a new route around it, digging out steps in the steeper places. When Flavius and Petrus return to the monastery, I go off to explore the headlands.

Strangely shaped boulders – conjuring up images of fabulous monsters – remind me of the hills above Submonte; the flowers are similar, and greenish-brown lizards abound. As I round a ridge, I freeze. Before me is a herd of large, shaggy-haired goats, grazing on the sunny slope. They see me but are not alarmed. In fact, one dappled youngster approaches, sniffing the air and gazing at me. Its mother raises her head and watches from a distance. I hold out my hand and the kid comes near, then licks my fingers.

Soon the king billy decides enough is enough. His call – more like a bark than a bleat – is unambiguous. My inquisitive visitor leaps into the air and scampers back to its mother. I burst out laughing.

Not wanting to disturb them, I wander higher and soon find myself on the top of a sheer cliff. An unfamiliar perspective of my home island presents itself, a ring of cloud surrounding the peak of Monte Capanne. If my eyes were sharper, I'd be able to pick out the harbour where I moor my boat; perhaps even our house with my sweet *Nitela* weeding the vegetable patch. I rub away my tears.

Plaintive cries from halfway down the cliff draw my attention. A colony of gulls is nesting on tiny ledges. They are different from the yellow-legged ones that are so common around Ilva. These have conspicuous red beaks. I watch, fascinated, as one takes off and glides in smooth loops over the choppy sea far below, then swings back and lands with precision on the narrow sill next to its nest.

I lift my arms high and gaze heavenwards, the rising breeze ruffling my hair. "I praise you, God, for the wonder of Your creation – so varied, so elaborate, so perfect. You

314

have placed us over all the beauty and marvel of these flowers and beasts, and entrusted us with the care of Your world." My head drops. "I'm ashamed of how we have failed You. We've neglected our responsibilities and caused so much strife. And yet You love us. Thank you so much for sending Jesus – full of grace and truth – so that we can know You in all Your glory."

I wake early to discover a fine day. Father Placidus sends me together with four monks to fetch the chest of scrolls. While at the warehouse, they help me carry the sail, oars and other things back to my skiff. Both boats were tossed about in the storm and are covered with seaweed and full of water, but it doesn't take us long to deal with that and I'm glad to see they are not damaged.

As we take turns carrying the heavy box up the hill, our newly made path passes its test of serviceability.

Father Placidus takes all day to examine the documents. He is delighted with Cerbonius's admonitions and loses no time in assigning one of the brothers to transcribe and illustrate them on folios, so that they can be bound into a codex. The complete copy of the Evangel of John is also prized, as they only possessed portions of it. Two scribes are given the task of copying it right away, their other work being considered of secondary importance.

Although I love the monks – especially Father Placidus – and enjoy the peaceful atmosphere of joy and faith, it's time to head back to my *Nitela*.

The sun hasn't yet risen as I take my leave of each brother in turn, receiving wishes for health and Godspeed from several of them. The kitchener hands me a sack of oat cakes, dried figs and wine for the journey. I would have forgotten again.

Flavius and Petrus, whose responsibility is to keep a

lookout for passing ships and meet anyone who lands, escort me down to the harbour. I'm touched that Father Placidus makes the effort to come with us.

As I'm about to say farewell, he points at my new pendant. "I see Quintus did a good job."

I finger the simple cross hanging on a silver chain round my neck. "Yes, it's lovely. He carved it from a seashell." My thoughts fill with Jesus, letting men nail Him to such a cross, out of love for us. "Look how the colour changes as you view it from different angles. It seems to be alive."

"May it ever remind you of your living Lord and Friend's love for you."

I nod. Yes, He rose from the grave and is alive for evermore. My friend now, not only Cerbonius's.

The Abbot takes a parcel out of his bag. "I have another gift for you and your dear wife, though I haven't yet had the chance to meet her."

My mouth drops open. It's the codex of the Evangel of Marcus, which I saw in his cell. "You're giving it to us?" I clutch it to my chest. "Thank you ever so much. We will treasure it. And learn from it. And teach others."

"We can always make further copies here, but you seem not to have much of the Scriptures at your disposal. I'll be honoured if you put it to good use."

We embrace each other – even Flavius and Petrus are now dear to me – and I push my boat into the water. "God be with you and bless you."

"May the Lord protect you on the way and grant you a speedy crossing. Farewell!"

I row out of the sheltered bay, catching a last glimpse of three waving monks as I round the point.

It's now clear to me that the monastery is nestled on that high plateau between hills – invisible from the sea – as a precaution against invaders. This meant, of course, that – apart from that one evening on the top of the cliff

– I hadn't been able to observe the sea while I was there. So I'm surprised by the sight of a large merchant vessel in the distance, sailing towards me along the coast of the island. I guess she's heading for Porto Pisano. What is she carrying? Mundane items like grain, oil and pottery? Or more exotic things – Arabian horses, oriental spices, silks and gold?

They have the advantage of a south-westerly *libeccio*, which means that my progress in the opposite direction is slow. I drift too far east whenever my sail catches even a touch of wind, so I lower it and keep rowing close to shore, around one little headland after another. Perhaps once I'm south of the island, the wind will be more favourable.

A sailor on the huge ship waves, as our paths are about to cross. We are passing a large promontory, when a slight movement near the shore catches my eye.

No!

Shooting out right in front of me from one of the natural caves is a narrow *lembos*, driven by a dozen oarsmen.

Pirates!

A figure standing in the bow beats the air with his arm, urging the rowers to increase their speed, to ram the towering trader.

Panic breaks out on the deck as the sailors call all hands to the railing and unsheath their scimitars. They won't be able to avoid the collision.

Is this to be a close-up repetition of that event in my childhood, which so traumatised me? I can't bear it. "Jesus, help!"

What can I do? With every stroke the rear-facing oarsmen struggle for air, their bare torsos gleaming with sweat, but they are so engrossed in their effort they haven't noticed me, though I'm so near. Nor has the leader, who is already swinging a grappling hook in preparation for boarding.

An idea springs to mind. Without further thought, I grab my anchor and hurl it toward the pirate's galley. The rope twangs as it unfurls. Will it reach? With bated breath I follow its flight. The anchor grazes the leg of one of the rowers, then drops and snags firmly over the gunwale. As the rope tightens, it causes a slight check to their momentum and jerks my skiff forward.

Propelled by an unfamiliar inner drive, I mount the thwart, amazed that I am able to maintain my balance, raise one arm high and shout, "In the name of Jesus, stop this barbarity!"

Then I gasp as the leader totters from the jolt and swings round to face me.

Drusus!

His eyes grow wide and his jaw drops. For a moment he seems paralysed. Then he throws a hand in the air and shouts to his sweat-drenched rowers, "Avast heavin'!"

The men have learned to obey without question. All twelve oars pause in the air. Eleven faces swing round and glare at me; the injured one man bends over, groaning, and clutches his bleeding thigh.

No crash.

Dragged by my anchor rope, the pirate boat circles, bringing the bows – and Drusus – closer to me.

"Silvanus! Am I seein' a ghost?" Is it anger in his voice? Hatred? It sounds more like terror. He drops the boarding hook and clutches his head with his good hand. The boats drift nearer. Drusus seems too shocked to notice his oarsmen drawing their cutlasses.

One slashes my anchor rope.

Another leaps across into my dinghy. "Ha! Jesus! Do you think he can help you now?" His guffaw is mocking. "Rather beg mercy of Neptunus!"

Defenceless, I mutter another arrow prayer, then reply, "My life is in God's hands. I'm ready to die if need be."

He swings his weapon.

At the same moment Drusus also jumps onto my deck, causing my boat to rock and theirs to swing away. My assailant loses his balance. The blow that would have slashed off my head instead crashes onto my shoulder.

Agony. I collapse. Blood spurts from the wound.

Swooning from pain and shock, I barely register Drusus pushing my attacker into the sea.

Angry shouts.

Violent shivers.

Everything is spinning.

Blackness.

The doleful cry of a seagull wakes me. It circles overhead. A second one. Watching me. My lips are dry but it's too much effort to moisten them. My back aches. My right arm refuses to move. Bright red strips of cloth cover my shoulder. Pain racks my upper body and I screw up my face. The only relief is to faint again.

I blink. Blue and white nothingness. Is this heaven? Where are you, Jesus?

My surroundings come into focus. I'm lying on the floorboards of a boat – my boat – too weak to sit. The sail is up. How can that be? Searing pangs throb in my shoulder.

My companion notices me stir. He bends and puts a wineskin to my lips. "I'm so sorry, Silvanus. 'Ow are you?"

Am I dreaming? Drusus? – Jesus, help me! – I gasp. "My shoulder."

"'Tis a bad wound. I've done wha' I could to bind it up but you've lost a lot o' blood."

"I'm so cold. The pain…" I screw up my face. "I can't bear it."

"'Ow can I say 'ow sorry I am?" He breaks down. "I would'n' listen. Virna plead with me any number o' times to repent but I only laughed at 'er. Since then, Jesus…"

"Jesus?" I murmur the wonderful name. "What do you know about Jesus?"

"Not much. But He's been houndin' me. Even last night He come… shinin' white… would'n' let me sleep. 'He begged me to stop me villainy."

"He… spoke to you?" My astonishment gives me unexpected strength.

"Many's a time. An' I takes no notice. 'Til this 'appened."

"What?"

"You turns up where you had no right to be. Jus' in time to stop me attack. 'Twas a miracle, I reckon." He breaks down. For some moments he can't speak. "Why did it have to come to this afore I'd heed Him?"

I'm shivering and feel frail. "Water!"

"'Fraid there's no water. Only a few drops o' wine." He puts the skin to my lips.

The sky is swaying. Seagulls. Why doesn't Virna help me? I'm so hot – freezing – sick. Agony. What's Drusus doing here, that filthy crook? I'll get my revenge.

As I forgive when my heart bleeds.

I can't move. My arm. My arm! Where has it gone? I clutch my pendant. Not Aquila, a cross. Did Drusus say something about Jesus?

I'm yours, Jesus. Help me! Take me home!

My head is swimming. "Ghhh!"

Someone leans over me. "Wha' you say? Can I do somethin' fer you?"

He offers me a drop of the winc. "We're nearly there. But yer so weak. And delirious." He glances heavenwards. "Oh, God, why didn' You stop me earlier?"

Tormenting thoughts fill my mind: the baskets; the crystals; kidnapping Virna; the fight... Again I hear my *Nitela* singing that lovely prayer: *As I forgive when my heart bleeds.*

Does he deserve to be forgiven? Of course not; he deserves to be crucified. But what about me? Jesus showed me mercy, in spite of all I had done. I screw up my face and Drusus again brings the skin to my lips.

"I..." My moistened palate lets me whisper a few words. "I... forgive... you."

The sky disappears and soft lips touch my forehead. Tears drip onto my cheek.

A voice speaks. "Oh, thank you, Silvanus." He sobs. "An' thank You, Jesus."

I drift off into that upper room where Jesus is washing His friends' feet. And I am among them.

CHAPTER THIRTY ONE

Priscilla's Epilogue

I WAS CHECKING the first sprouts in the garden and waiting for my bread dough to rise, when a red sail in the distance caught my eye. I recognised Aquila's little boat. Ignoring the heat, I rushed down the winding path and arrived at the port, drenched with sweat, my legs trembling and my chest heaving.

But someone else – a big man – was sailing it! As it got nearer, the tousled hair looked familiar. Sergius. Or Drusus! What on earth was he doing there – in our boat?

He shouted. At first I didn't understand. Then, "'E's 'urt. Badly 'urt."

I pleaded with Jesus. Had that crook somehow tracked my Aquila down again and taken revenge on him after all these years? I couldn't bear the thought.

He brought the boat in. As I caught the painter, my darling lay still on the deck, dry blood everywhere. With trembling fingers, I tied the rope to a post. Drusus gently picked him up and carried him ashore.

I called his name and grabbed his limp hand, but Aquila didn't respond. My breath came in gasps as I stared at his torpid form.

Fabricius appeared. Sizing up the situation with one glance, he showed us a hut where Drusus could lay my sweetheart down.

Oh, how I wept. He was breathing but unable to speak. I kissed him, my tears dripping on his face, then kept stroking his pale cheek.

"I can't tell you 'ow sorry I am, Virna." Drusus hung his head and sobbed. "'Twasn' me who injured him… But I'm to blame." He struggled for words. "I did wha' I could to help him – believe me – but he's lost so much blood." He broke down.

Fabricius came back with water. I wetted Aquila's lips. A slight movement. I lifted his head and he swallowed a few drops, then almost choked. His chest heaved with every breath.

Drusus spoke. "I can't do no more fer 'im, I'm afraid. It's you he needs now. But I mus' tell you this. He said he forgive me." He turned his face heavenward. "Jesus! Oh Jesus, can you forgive me?"

I didn't see him leave.

Fabricius must have summoned Malpus. We brought Aquila home and laid him on the bed. I gave him a few drops of Mother Martha's buckthorn and rosemary elixir. It revived him for a moment.

All through the long night I sat next to him, holding his hand, singing his favourite songs and praying for God's will to be done. Every so often I gave him a dose of medicine.

At dawn, a thrush began to sing for joy. He opened his eyes and smiled at me.

I bent to touch my lips to his clammy forehead. "Aquila, can you hear me?"

He mouthed a, "Yes, my dear." He seemed content, although the way he screwed up his face showed that every movement caused him agony.

"I have something important to say to you, darling." I pulled his good hand to my lips. "I'm expecting a baby."

He squeezed my hand and tears came to his eyes.

I kissed him, being careful not to touch his wounded shoulder, then lifted his hand to my belly and said, "In here. Your child." A slight caress. "I was so happy when I knew." I turned my eyes heavenward. "Oh, Jesus, please let him recover, so that our dear baby can have a father."

Into my mind came the promise He gave me before Aquila left: 'Even if you walk through the valley of the shadow of death, I will be with you.'

My darling's lips began to move. I bent close. In short bursts, with long gaps between them, he whispered what was on his heart. "I love you so much, my dear… so happy… about the baby…"

His strength was spent. After a long, agonising moment, he continued. "The monks… gave me a cross…" I had noticed the beautiful mother-of-pearl emblem glittering in the light. "And an Evangel… codex… in the boat."

He again fell into unconsciousness – far deeper than normal sleep. His body was so drained, his skin pale, cold and clammy.

When he stirred, I gave him more of the elixir. That brought him around again for a while.

He told me about the pirates, and Drusus.

Another relapse. I snatched a bite to eat.

He spoke again. "A bright light! He's smiling." His eyes shone. "My *Nitela*, I love you… Look after my child… fulfilled my tasks."

I broke down, sobbing, kissing him again and again. "Oh, I love you, too, my *Ursus*. I'll miss you so very much. Go to Jesus now. We'll join you later – your baby and I."

With his last strength he continued. "Take my boat.., to Father."

"Me? But I don't know your people." I gasped. "I… I'll do it… for you."

"Tell them I love them… Give my eagle amulet to Ceres… I have a new Father…"

I was singing his favourite song when I sensed his spirit depart, leaving an empty shell.

"Oh, Aquila, my darling *Ursus*, you always said a new world was beckoning. Enjoy it. Forever. With your wonderful new Father."

THE END

CHARACTER NAMES

Primary Characters

Silvanus
  A country lad who is seeking a better life; also called
  Silé, Ursus, and later Aquila

Cerbonius
  An old exiled Bishop, who befriends Silvanus

Cornelius
  Silvanus's father

Drusus
  An ex-pirate and crook; also known as Sergius

Lucilla
  A friend of Silvanus and Eliana, sister of Pontus

Pontus
  A friend of Silvanus and Rufus, brother of Lucilla

Rufus
  An older friend of Silvanus and Pontus

Eliana
  Silvanus's young sister

Virna
  An escaped slave, originally from Carthago; also
  called Nitela, and later Priscilla

Secondary Characters

Aelius
Silvanus's uncle, the village smith

Albanus
Keeper of the Fabricia caupona, Cornelius's friend

Alessandro
A guest in Albanus's caupona

Anna
Antonius wife

Antonius
A market stall trader, husband of Anna

Benedictus
(Benedict of Nursia) A founder of several monasteries governed according to his famous "Rule"

Brutus
Father of Pontus and Lucilla, the village carpenter

Catalus
A goatherd in Marciana

Elazar
A rich patrician, who bought Virna as a slave

Franciscus
A friend of Antonius

Gaius
A stablehand in Albanus's caupona

Gallus
A servant from Marciana caught by pirates

Ignatius
A contentious landlord in Podium

Jeremias
A jeweller

Julia
Cerbonius's deceased wife

Laurus
: The master boatwright

Marcus
: Cerbonius's friend and neighbour

Mater Agathe
: An elderly, crippled patient in the House of Healing

Maxillus
: The Duumvir of Fabricia (one of two magistrates)

Mother Martha
: The matron of the House of Healing

Placidus
: One of Benedictus's closest disciples

Procius
: The magistrate of Marciana

Raguel
: Cerbonius's son

Romerius
: A landlord in Marciana, owner of Gallus

Sabina
: The daughter of Elazar, a friend to Virna

Salome
: Virna's friend in Carthago

Sartorius
: A jeweller

Septima
: Titus's wife

Titus
: Cerbonius's friend and confidant

Totila
: The penultimate King of the Ostrogoths

Vigilius
: The Pope who summoned Cerbonius to Rome

Bold names indicate historic characters.

GLOSSARY OF TERMS

Adonay roei lo echsar. Binot desheh yarbitzaini, al mei me-nuchot yenahaleini
The Lord is my shepherd, I lack nothing. He makes me lie down in green pastures
(start of Psalm 23 in Hebrew)

Africanus
(or Scipio Africanus) A Roman general during the Second Punic War and later consul

Alamanni
A Germanic tribe, which invaded Gaul and later northern Italy

Amphora
(plural: amphorae) A large, elongated clay pot or jar for storing and transporting wine, oil, etc.

Amulet
A small object worn around the neck as a protection against evil, bad luck, disease, etc.

Aquila
(eagle) An alternative name for the Roman God Jupiter; also, an eagle-shaped rock in the north-west of Elba

Atrium
enclosed courtyard in many Roman houses

Auster
  The Roman God of the sirocco wind, who brought
  heavy cloud cover and fog or humidity

Avast!
  Stop!

Balneum
  bathroom

Barbarian
  Various pagan or uncivilised tribes from northern
  Europe, which invaded the Roman Empire

Belisarius
  A general of the Byzantine Empire under Emper-
  or Justinian, who attempted to reconquer much of
  the Mediterranean territory of the former Western
  Roman Empire

Benedictus
  (or Benedict of Nursia; c. 480–543 or 547). A Christian saint, who founded several monasteries in Italy
  and formulated the "Rule of Saint Benedict", containing precepts for his monks

Braccae
  Shapeless trousers of wool or skin tied at the waist
  and ankles by cords

Branzini
  A fish; the European sea bass

Byzantine
  Relating to the ancient Greek city Byzantium, which
  Emperor Constantine I made into the new capital
  of the Roman Empire in 330 AD; later renamed
  Constantinople

Capraria
  The ancient name of the rocky islet of Capraia,
  north-west of Elba

Carbatinae

A sort of of rustic leather shoes or sandals

Cauda

penis

Caupona

A Roman inn, where travellers obtained food and lodging

Centuria

A unit of approximately 100 Roman soldiers

Cerbonius

A Bishop of Populonium during the Barbarian invasions, renowned for miraculous incidents in connection with the Pope, angels, and the Ostrogothic king Totila; he fled to the island of Elba when the Lombards attacked, and was later made a saint

Cervisia

Beer

Challah

A special Jewish plaited bread eaten on Sabbath and holidays

Chione

The nymph or Goddess of snow

Cicero

A very influential Roman philosopher, politician, lawyer, orator, political theorist, consul, and constitutionalist

Circus

A large open-air venue used for public events such as chariot races, horse races, and other forms of entertainment

Cithara

A stringed instrument similar to a lute, often used to accompany a singer or someone reciting poetry

Codex
> (pl. codices) An early form of book, made of sheets of handwritten paper or parchment, and bound with thick covers; codices gradually replaced wooden writing tablets and scrolls

Constantinople
> The new name given to Byzantium in honour of Emperor Constantine I; modern Istanbul

Corsa
> The ancient name of the Island of Corsica

dies Veneris
> Friday

Domine
> Sir (as a respectful form of address)

Dominula
> Miss (a respectful form of address)

Dominus Italiae
> Lord of all Italy

Duumvir
> (Latin "one of the two men") The official Roman title for two joint magistrates

Ecce!
> See! Look!

Emmer
> One of the earliest cultivated forms of wheat

Evangel
> Good news; the Gospel of Jesus

Fabricia
> The main town of Ilva (Elba), originally on the hill above the port now known as Portoferraio

Fasces
> A bundle of wooden rods, sometimes including an axe with its blade emerging, and symbolising a magistrate's power and jurisdiction

Favonius
> The Roman God of the west wind, who held dominion over plants and flowers

Feria
> (plural feriae) A "free day", on which people, especially slaves, were not obliged to work; one of the primary features of the Roman calendar

festina lente
> (hasten slowly) Equivalent to more haste, less speed

Fibula
> A brooch or pin for fastening garments

Focaccia
> flat oven-baked bread, which may be topped with herbs or other ingredients

Follis
> (plural: folles) A large bronze coin; approximate value 210 to a solidus

Fortuna
> The Goddess of fortune

Franks
> A Germanic tribe, which conquered most of the Western Roman Empire

Gladius
> sword

Goths
> An East Germanic people, which played an important role in the fall of the Roman Empire

Goyim
> A Hebrew word meaning 'nations'; by implication 'non-Jews' or 'gentiles'; used pejoratively to refer to Barbarians or Vandals

Hectate
> A Goddess associated with crossroads, entrance-ways, witchcraft and sorcery

Heia!
> Yippee!

Hercle!
> By Hercules! An interjection used (by men only) to express strong feeling

Hercules
> A son of Zeus or Jupiter, a divine hero; the name of Silvanus's dog

Hobble
> To prevent an animal from moving by tying their legs together

Ilva
> The ancient name of the Island of Elba

Ides
> the 13th or 15th of the Roman month

in situ
> in its original position or place

in spiritu et veritate
> in spirit and truth

Io!
> An exclamation of joy or triumph

Jupiter
> The Roman God of sky and thunder, often represented as an eagle (aquila)

Justinian I
> Justinian the Great; the Byzantine emperor from 527 to 565

Labdanum
> A sticky brown resin obtained from rockrose shrubs, used in herbal medicine and as a perfume ingredient

Langobardi
> Lombards; a Germanic tribe, which invaded Italy and founded a kingdom in the northern part of the country in 567 AD

Lectus
> couch

Lembos
> A light naval vessel, chiefly used for piracy

Libeccio
> A south-westerly wind off northern Corsica

Liberta
> freedwoman

Libra
> A Roman measure of weight, equal to twelve unciae; a pound

Lictor
> An officer, attendant on a magistrate, who bore the fasces and was responsible for punishing criminals

Liquamen
> (or garum) A very popular fermented fish sauce, used as a condiment

Longinus
> A military governor of the Byzantine Empire, based in Ravenna

Ludi

Public games, such as horse and chariot races, held
in the circus for the entertainment of the people, and
often the major feature of religious festivals

Ludi Florae

A licentious, pleasure-seeking festival in honour
of the Goddess Flora, held at the end of April and
lasting six days

Macchia

dense fragrant Mediterranean shrubland, consisting
of evergreen shrubs such as holm oak, Kermes Oak,
tree heath, strawberry tree, sage, juniper, buckthorn,
spurge olive and myrtle

Mane bonum!

Good morning!

Marciana

A hillside town in the north-west of Ilva, near Podium

Mastic

resin obtained from the mastic tree, used as a medicine

Mauri

Fierce raiding tribes of north-west Africa

Meditrinalia

A Roman festival celebrated on October 11 in
honour of the new vintage, which was offered as a
libation to the Gods for the first time each year

Menafa

Carthaginian word for 'napkin'

Mercurius

The Roman God of commerce and financial gain

Mons Jovis

A mountainous island south of Elba; current name:
Montecristo

Neptunus
> The Roman God of the sea

Nitela
> Dormouse (an affectionate name)

Novum vetus vinum bibo, novo veteri morbo medeor
> I drink new and old wine, to be healed of new and
> old sicknesses
> (a maxim recited at the Meditrinalia festival)

Oecus
> The formal dining room of a Roman house. The
> menfolk recline on couches around a low table

Ostrogoths
> A branch of the later Goths (the other major branch
> being the Visigoths), who, under Theoderic the
> Great, established a kingdom in Italy in the late 5th
> and 6th centuries

Pes
> foot (unit of length)

Pelagius
> The Pope's representative during the Gothic block-
> ade of Rome (542 to 546 AD), when he made great
> efforts to spare the lives of the people. Pope from
> 556 to 561 AD

Physic
> A medicine or drug, especially a cathartic or purge

Planasia
> A low-lying island off the south-west corner of Elba;
> current name: Pianosa

Podium
> balcony or stage

Podium
> The ancient name for Poggio, a hillside town in the
> north-west of Ilva, near Marciana

Pol!

By Pollux! Truly! Really!

Populonium

An ancient coastal city about five miles north of the modern city of Piombino

Pugio

dagger

Salve

medical ointment used to soothe the head or treat various skin problems

Salve!

(Plural Salvete!) Hail! Hello!

Scrippum

knapsack

Semimodius

A unit of measure; approx. 1 gallon. As an affectionate name: a young lad; a 'half-pint'

Solidus

(Plural solidi) A gold coin weighing about 4.5 grams, at this period worth 210 folles

Somnium Scipionis

Scipio's Dream, the sixth book of Cicero's De re publica, describing a fictional vision of the Roman general Scipio Aemilianus

Spelt

An ancient species of wheat which was an important staple food in Late Antiquity

Stoa

covered walkway or portico around a town square

Strigil

brass or wooden body scraper, used to remove oil, sweat and dirt after bathing

Submonte
> A fictional village on the western slopes of Monte Capanne, Ilva

Sui generis
> in a class by itself; unique

Taberna
> (plural: tabernae) A Roman shop, consisting of a stall or booth in the market place

Tabula
> board game similar to backgammon

Talisman
> An object believed to have magical properties, such as bringing good luck or protecting from evil or harm

Toga
> A distinctive wollen garment of Ancient Rome which was wrapped around the body

toga pulla
> A dark grey or brown toga reserved for periods of mourning

Totila
> King of the Ostrogoths from 541 to 552 AD; a skilled military and political leader. By 543 he recaptured most of the territories in Italy that the Byzantine forces had recovered from the Goths

Trivia
> The Roman Goddess of sorcery and witchcraft

Tyrrhenia
> A region of Central Italy, covering present-day Tuscany, Lazio, and Umbria

Uncia
> (Plural unciae) A Roman measure of weight; an ounce

Ursa Major
> The Great Bear or Plough, a constellation in the northern sky

Ursa Minor
> The Little Bear, a constellation in the northern sky

Ursus
> Bear (an affectionate name)

Vale!
> (Plural Valete!) Goodbye! Farewell!

Vergelius
> Virgil, an ancient Roman poet of the Augustan period

Vigiles
> The firefighters and police of Ancient Rome

Vigilius
> Pope from 537 to 555; he summoned Cerbonius to explain his custom of celebrating mass before dawn, to which his parishioners had objected

Vilicus
> A servant who had the superintendence of a villa, including all slaves

TIMELINE

AD	Story Events
535	
536	
540	
541	
542	Cerbonius visits Benedict of Nursia
544	Cerbonius made Bishop of Populonia
546	Pope Vigilius summons Cerbonius
547	[or 573] Cerbonius released by Totila after the bear licks his feet
561	
567	
568	Silvanus's first trade trip with father
570	Cerbonius flees to Elba from Lombards [Legend says 547 or 573]
572	Silvanus alone in Fabricia. Silvanus meets V. and Cerbonius family conflicts
573	Cerbonius mediates civil dispute
574	Silvanus's apprenticeship
575	V. kidnapped and freed
576	Death of Cerbonius Miraculous journey to Populonium
577	Trip to Capraia

Historic Events
Gothic War phase 1
Sun dark for nearly a year; Pope Vigilius appointed
Ravenna reconquered by the Byzantines Ostrogothic King Totila wages Gothic War phase 2
Plague of Justinian afflicts much of Roman Empire
Pelagius (later Pope) aids famine-stricken people of Rome with own fortune; Totila visits Benedict of Nursia
Justinian sends Belisarius to free Italy
Totila captures Rome from Belisarius Pelagius induces Totila to spare the people
[or 543] Benedict of Nursia dies
Byzantines control all of war-ravaged Italy
Lombards invade Italy, absorbing remaining Ostrogoths
Lombards conquer Milan
570-572: three year siege of Pavia. Byzantines can defend only coastal cities
Pavia falls, made capital of the Lombard kingdom of Italy. Lombard King Alboin murdered
Lombards conquer Tuscany and establish duchies of Spoleto and Benevento under Zotto
Justin II sends Baduarius to Italy to fight the Lombards
Baduarius killed in battle

ACKNOWLEDGEMENTS

Grateful thanks to the following sources:

Trustees for Harvard University for the use of data from Philip Grierson's Byzantine Coinage © 1999, Dumbarton Oaks Research Library and Collection. Used by permission of Dumbarton Oaks, Washington, DC

Biblica Inc.™ for various scripture verses taken from the Holy Bible, New International Version®, NIV® Copyright © 1973, 1978, 1984, 2011

The following experts have given me invaluable information about the Isle of Elba and life in Italy in Late Antiquity:

Prof. Paolo Ferruzzi, dramatist, restorer of historic buildings and author of books on the history of Elba

Silvestre Ferruzzi, architect, painter, founder of the *Museo civico archeologico di Marciana* and author of books on the history of Elba

Angelo Mazzei, host at *B&B Poggio*, musician, polyglot authority on the history of Elba

Tamara Tännler, scientific research associate, *Augusta Raurica*, Switzerland.

The splendid antique maps were created for me by Russian cartographer Polina Vorontsova.

I have benefitted immensely from the wisdom of countless bloggers and online authorities on fiction writing; special mention must go to K.M. Weiland of *Helping Writers Become Authors* for her refreshingly pertinent tips and to the late intrepid John Yeoman of *Writers' Village*, who even deigned to meet me at his local pub for a lively lunch and chat.

I received a great deal of valuable feedback on my very weak first chapters from François and Julie Rochat and Brijesh Luthra, as well as from Jill marsh, Kelly Jarosz, Libby O'Loghlin and others of *The Woolf* and the *Zurich Writers Workshop*; also from Rebecca Carter, Monica Mynk, Patrick Null, Jordan Phillips, Paylor Paylor and further members of that exciting online critique platform *Scribophile*. But my most long-suffering and relentless critiquers were undoubtedly Gabrielle Matthieu, Brad Towers, Sabrina Haslimeier and Caroline Summers of the *Otherworlds Writing Group* in Zürich, who struggled through the entire first draft. To all these folk I express my most grateful thanks. Without your perceptive observations this book would never have got here. Fay Sampson of the *Association of Christian Authors* gave an early version of the book a harsh but realistic review, which prompted me to make major revisions. A later version was critically reviewed by Margaret May Nelson, Claire O'Sullivan, Lily C Fen and Lois Arbie, whose feedback was also most appreciated.

For several years my faithful wife has tolerated my frequent reclusion to my halfway-up-the-stairs workspace, and even volunteered to listen to an early reading. I hope she wasn't too shocked.

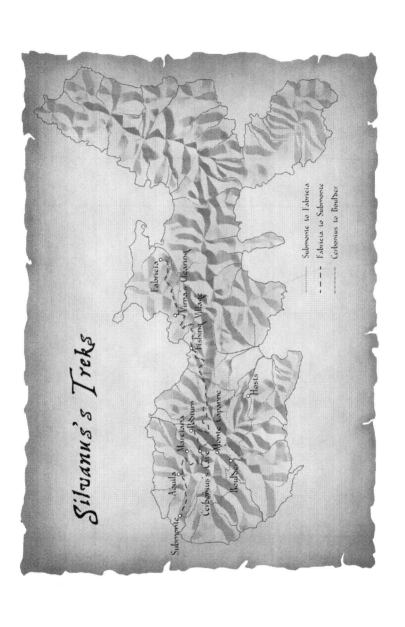

Printed in Great Britain
by Amazon